The

Memory

Chasers

By: Sandy Beech

Sandy@TheMemoryChasers.com

Editor: Lindsey Nelson
Illustrator: Miles Lewis

Table of Contents

Part One – The Ham Shack

Preamble

"The Poem"

why was I that person
what was there to be so angry about
why did you leave home
what were you looking for
your mom paid
for all your dad's discipline
and you just kept indulging
just to show you could
I've reread your letters
the never-ending disappointment
the desperate pleas to change
and you never wrote back
but Mom always loved, unconditionally
as Dad dug in his heels
it's a miracle it would ever change
but it did
I'm trying to avoid that now
I can't wait years to give in
to accept who you are
I love who you are right now
when we hug goodbye
do you feel what I feel
does your heart sink
fearing the last visit
words never revealed

Of all the things I've cherished while going through Sally's belongings, this poem is at the top of the list. The funny thing is, it wasn't even written by her. I wrote it to her years ago during a particularly hard time in our relationship. Sally was smack-dab in the middle of being a young adult and a teenager. She was a young adult trapped in a teenager's mind. The poem was the result of once again leaving my daughter in uncertain circumstances. I had to be a dad and tell her what to do, and she had to be a teenager and disagree with all of it. She couldn't help but be the antagonist. I couldn't help but be a dad. The circumstances are immaterial. That it was the last time we'd look at each other cloaked in these roles wasn't.

The tears still well up when I think back on that day, when I pulled away, stiff necking to not look back. Down that mountain road I rolled, smearing tears across the landscape. It was obvious that we were both exhausted of our positions in the relationship. She was tired of being told, and I was tired of telling. We needed to just be friends. Often I wished my own parents could have figured that out. For parents, it's inevitable that you'll one day be looking straight at yourself from your own parents' perspective while trying to make sense of your child. It was this generational connectedness I felt that day as I drove away. As I headed off into that brand-new day, I felt the warmth of her presence. As I drove along, I revisited the hollowness I felt with my own parents at a similar moment. For my parents and me, it came way too late. I knew then I didn't want to wait another second to enter that next step as a dad. This next step seemed to be occurring as our distance grew, and I felt she knew this too.

I love this poem because it apparently had the effect that was intended. I know this because she had it framed, on display prominently in her home. It reflects what I felt when I left her that day so long ago. It was one of those cherished moments as a parent when you do something very deliberate, and it works. Yeah, I did something right, but for me it was declaring that a moment meant something, it meant something for both of us, and I got to glorify it in writing. I documented a sweet microcosm of changing relations.

As I drove the rest of the way home that day, I slowly composed myself and began to understand what all this meant. Our similarities were so obvious, but did she see this? I know I didn't understand shit when I was her age. At her age, I was mad at something I couldn't begin to explain. I didn't even know it was about something. I was just mad. I examined the circumstances of our upbringings to assess their similarities. Though there were plenty of differences in our lives, the similarity of growing up overruled all other influences. Did I tell her that? Did I tell her I get it, that you feel alone in an overwhelmingly frightening world? Did I tell her that it will all work out, that it will be okay?

Within days of getting home from that trip, I sat down and composed this poem. It was typical of things I've written that I liked. It didn't take long to write and required no editing. It just flowed from my mind to the paper. My mind knew what to say and when to be done. It seems weird, but I was used to this kind of thing. I'd been writing since I was young. I was pleased. I immediately mailed it to her.

While going through her belongings, I felt all the other stuff she left behind seemed somewhat hollow. That is, except for her writings. She had been squirreling away any and all things she had written through her shortened life. Much of it was her own writings, mostly poems scratched out on a variety of small notebooks, each representing a different time in her life, like tree rings. There were boxes of letters from various friends and relatives that were neatly organized by sender and ordered by date. I was drawn to these documents; they seemed to be her true story, written by her and those very close to her.

Scene of the Crime

By the time I had reacted to the news of her passing and made my way to her mountain home, much of the scene and been cleaned up by the authorities. She lived in a modest cabin tucked up at the base of the glorious fourteen-thousand-foot Mount Princeton overlooking the Arkansas River Valley. Her cabin was fully intact and had the feel that it was well lived. It seemed as though she would be walking back into her home at any minute. Perhaps she was out back gathering firewood to stoke her woodstove for the morning. The cabin was not where she was found, however. The property had several old outbuildings, one of which she had converted into an art studio. It was in this outbuilding that she had breathed her final breath.

I was waiting for the sheriff to take down the police tape that cordoned off the art studio as they were wrapping up their investigation. As I struggled to finish my coffee, the sheriff came in through the back door and introduced himself. His name was Sheriff Bill Broadless. He appeared to be what you'd want in a rural county sheriff. He was larger than life and spoke in a slow and deliberate tone that reeked with sincerity. He was a longtime resident of Chaffee County and had worked his way up through the force to his current role. I had the distinct feeling I knew him but couldn't place it. I asked him if we had ever met, and he explained that Sally spent two summers working for his rafting company. Apparently, Sally was one of his favorite guides. Broadless offered his condolences and suggested we had probably met while she worked for him. I could see tears well up in the big man's eyes as he struggled to compose himself. I suddenly felt strangely alone, realizing this stranger knew Sally that well.

Sheriff Broadless told me I could take a look at the studio but wanted to fill me in on the sketchy details that were emerging regarding Sally's death. At this point I had no clear idea of what had happened to her. There was some vague discussion that she'd been electrocuted.

Sheriff Broadless started in, "I'm not sure if you're aware of what your daughter was working on, but it doesn't appear to be art. She was found alone on the floor of her art studio. She was lying in a spaghetti tangle of electrical wire. These wires were connected to a bizarre helmet she was wearing. Though we'll rely on the autopsy's findings, it appears she was electrocuted through this helmet device. I've got to warn you that the studio has a strong odor of burnt human tissue and hair. Other than that, we're not sure what happened. There seems to be no foul play involved. It appears that whatever she was up to went horribly wrong and resulted in a high-voltage electrocution. I'm really sorry you have to go through this, but if you're ready, we can go have a look."

I could smell the thick acrid stench of burnt flesh and hair before we even entered the studio. At that moment I wasn't sure I wanted to proceed. What horror show lay waiting? As I hesitated, Broadless put his arm around my shoulders and asked if I was okay. I assured him that I wasn't but was ready to proceed. As we ducked to enter the small door, a large, long-haired cat bolted out through the door, squeezing between my legs to get outside. It startled me and imparted a strange feeling of more than a cat leaving the studio. It felt like a metaphor for something unimaginable. For now, I couldn't provide any meaning to this other than it was more than I could process. We entered the studio, and I gazed upon the strange scene before me. I wasn't looking at an art studio at all. It appeared to be a low-tech science experiment.

In the middle of the room was what appeared to be a treadmill that was draped in a heap of rainbow-colored wires. The wires terminated on one end into a vintage sixties orange motorcycle helmet. On the other end, the wires snaked off to the back of the room and appeared to be connected to a computer. Directly in front of the treadmill were what looked like two large projection screens. They extended from the floor to the low ceiling. The screens were slightly curved around the front of the treadmill. The studio was tidy, which led to the conclusion that a struggle was not involved. The few windows the studio had were completely covered with black insulating material. The only natural light came in through a glass skylight. Looking up and out of the skylight, I could see Mount Princeton rising to the heavens. There was what appeared to be a twenty to thirty-foot TV antenna centered in the skylight, towering above the studio. Coiled around the antenna were more of the rainbow-colored wires. What in the world was she up to? What was she trying to accomplish? Something was definitely wrong with this picture. The sick feeling of imagining her dying in this remote shack completely alone suddenly overtook me. My head began to pound, and my gut clenched as my mouth began to water. I ran for the door and barely made it out before I heaved my coffee across the melting snow.

Funeral Pyre

I had met McIntyre a couple times when Sally first moved to the Arkansas Valley. They were river rats together, living in a van down by the river. They met while working for Bill Broadless before he got involved in politics and policing. He was the original river rat of the Arkansas Valley. Apparently he had the first official permit to take commercial trips down the Arkansas River through Browns Canyon. When Sally and McIntyre were raft guides for his company, it was near the end of his tenure as chief river rat. As often happens, this shared early adulthood experience bonded them for life. While McIntyre didn't hang out with Sally as much as she used to, she was Sally's closest confidant prior to her death. McIntyre, or Mac, as she preferred to be called, was my connection to Sally's last days and hopefully her final wishes.

As we sat in Salida's Brown Dog Coffee shop, our conversation slowly evolved from reminiscing of special times with Sally to the more sobering discussion of her final wishes. Other than wanting to be cremated, I had no idea what type of internment Sally would have wanted.

Before I could ask Mac if she had any idea what Sally's final wishes were, she blurted out, "You know Sally wanted to be cremated?" I replied that I knew that. "You don't understand; she wanted to be cremated via a pyre, a funeral pyre!" she exclaimed. As I attempted to stop the coffee shooting out of my nose, Mac finished her declaration with fingers wriggling skyward in the universal sign of fire and smoke. She culminated this gesture with a respectful namaste.

Apparently, the two of them had discussed this at some length. I was aware of Sally's interest in Eastern religion but never knew how serious she was about it. I was never really sure what she was serious about—she had a variety of disparate interests. None of her interests seemed to be trivial however. The last I knew, she was perusing her earliest interest, which was art, painting to be precise. That was why her art studio looking more like a science experiment was a big surprise.

Mac went on to explain how this came to be and how it was going to be fulfilled. "One thing Sally was for sure was an environmentalist. She was aware of the environmental impacts modern burials have. Embalming fluids are the primary concern," Mac explained. "Most embalming fluids are formaldehyde based. While it readily biodegrades in the soil, it's recognized as a carcinogen by the EPA. Did you know that over eight hundred thousand gallons of embalming fluid are introduced to the soil every year in this country? Of course there's also a shitload of varnished wood and metals associated with the caskets that get buried each year as well. These are materials that could be better used building things that improve our lives, not degrade the world we live in.

"Sally originally was thinking a standard cremation would do the trick, but you know Sally; she had a flare for the dramatic. One day we went over to the San Luis Valley to explore a couple of hot springs we'd heard about. After a wonderful soak at Valley View Hot Springs, we decided to head into Crestone for a bite to eat. We knew a little bit of the history of Crestone. It was a total hippie town that had legitimatized itself with the introduction of numerous spiritual sites. There are centers for Tibetan Buddhism, Zen Buddhism, Hinduism, as well as a Carmelite monastery, and let's not forget New Agers. There is even a ziggurat on a hill overlooking the San Luis Valley.

"While having lunch, we noticed there was a fire of sorts not too far off. Its smoke was rising above the trees and a building that blocked our view of the actual fire. We asked our waiter where the smoke was coming from.

" 'That would be our porta-pyre over by the cemetery.'

" 'What on earth is a porta-pyre?' Sally asked.

" 'That's the town's funeral pyre, you know, where you cremate the dead in an outdoor funeral service. It's not really portable anymore, but we just like the joke so much we still call it that.'

"That's all Sally needed to hear," Mac said pointedly. "She spent considerable time learning about Crestone's funeral-pyre process immediately following that trip. You know it's almost impossible to be cremated on a pyre in Crestone these days, that is unless you're a local. Did you know it's the only place in the country that funeral pyres are allowed? Apparently, the surge in nontraditional burials overwhelmed Crestone, and they had to severely limit outsiders from participating. Sally used her considerable charm to convince them to let her into the inner circle, so to speak. I think she may have taken advantage of a loophole the city council created for special circumstances. They will sell a teeny tiny plot of land to a select few by which the new landowner can claim residence and reserve a pyre cremation service. Who knew?"

Since Sally was to be cremated, there would be no preserving the body. We only had a few days to make all the arrangements; her body wouldn't keep. It wasn't lost on us that conventional orthodox Jewish tradition requires the dead to be buried within twenty-four hours. We did the best we could to contact relatives and friends. There were no grandparents and only a couple of aunts and uncles from my parents' generation. In short time, it became obvious that this was going to be an impromptu ceremony. Those who could rally and make it would have to do.

So there we were, strangers in a strange land, the land of Crestone. The couple dozen who made the trek to Crestone for her funeral service were not too freaked out by this human barbeque that was about to take place. A number of relatives who expressed their outrage and disgust, needless to say, didn't show up. I'll say that I was unsure how this was going to play out. Was I going to be able to handle this? I kept an open mind, as I like to think is my practice, but setting your daughter on fire, yikes! I was told that the actual cremation would take four to five hours. Upon completion, we'd have several pounds of ashes, which would be a mix of the combustibles and her remains.

It's considered an honor to be the ones who light the pyre. This task was to be performed by my estranged wife, Rachel, my son, Benjamin, and myself. Neither Rachel nor Ben were shocked by Sally's request. They, of course, knew her well enough. The pyre had been constructed by a local Zen Buddhist monk. This included the placement of the body. The pyre itself was a rectangular structure made of pine tree trunks with a platform six feet in the air that Sally's body rested on. At its base was an imposing pile of cut firewood atop a masonry firepit.

After the Buddhist monk offered his prayer for the dead, the three of us provided a few words to the small gathering, and each of us laid a symbolic juniper bough on the pyre. We then lit the pyre with a wooden torch that we held in unison. The flames very quickly erupted into a massive fire that enveloped Sally's body. The simultaneous feeling of horror and amazement overtook all of us. No one could speak for what seemed like an eternity. Slowly, starting with the three of us, the crowd began to sob. The sobs relented into wails of uncontrolled weeping. The weeping, like some magnetic force, started pulling everyone together in the sincerest embrace imaginable. First it was the three of us. We hugged so close that our faces were pressing against each other. Our tears intermingled as we wailed in some unknown language. This quickly spread to the rest of the group. In a strange, organic way, we all created a circle around the pyre and slowly started rotating around its center. I started howling in primal, guttural fits. Soon the entire gathering was wailing and howling; only now it wasn't sorrow that was being expelled—it was pure anger. Though it wasn't words we were bellowing out, we all knew what the sounds were saying. Why did you take her from us? Why? What possible good did her demise bring to anybody? Eventually the rotating about the pyre began to slow, and the wails began to soften. In near unison, the circle of pain collapsed to the ground in a heap. The wailing rapidly diminished, and it grew ominously silent. And then something unexplainable happened.

Without a cue, the bluebird sky immediately above us erupted in a swirling torrent of azure-and-orange light. It swelled and retracted as it throbbed with varying intensity. Curtains of light rose from the ground to thousands of feet in the air in an instant and then back down again. All the while, the two colors swirled around each other without mixing. The swirling light paused in place for a second a few hundred feet above us before rapidly ascending high into the sky. We were now all enveloped in an ethereal glow of spinning light. A humming crackle of static electricity tickled our skin and propped our hair on end. The spinning maelstrom of light then enveloped each of us in individual cocoons of orbiting light.

My mind suddenly was overcome with a sense of well-being and contentment. Warmth emanated from my core outward in repeating pulses of gratitude. It left a tingling path of knowledge and understanding. What-on-earth-is-happening thoughts tried to break through the scene. I saw the others staring boundlessly into the sky with astonished looks on their faces. What was happening prevailed. I felt voices or thoughts from outside myself. I felt a strange sense of community from the others. I heard the thoughts of those around me. I felt their emotions. Somehow we were telepathically communicating. Suddenly, a static, harmonic gray wave vibrated in my skull. It rapidly built and blurred everything; sight, sound, and feeling were rubbed out. As the crackling subsided, a low-frequency disturbance built and vibrated me to the bone. Then—*bang!*—an eardrum-pounding explosion of sound. The earth let loose a shaking jolt. As we lay there on the ground stunned, the planet seemed to be losing it, shaking and rumbling. Off to the side, I saw the funeral pyre wobbling; I thought it was going to come crashing down. Then pure, absolute darkness and deafening silence prevailed.

Slowly, the group began to stir from what can only be described as a fugue state. Though the ceremony started in the early evening, somehow it was sundown. Inexplicably, we had lost several hours. No one could speak; there was nothing to say that would explain this. To the east, rising up out of the San Luis Valley, were the mighty, snowcapped Sangre de Cristo Mountains. The entire range was cloaked in an ethereal glow of radiating bloodred light. No one spoke; we just stared in amazement from the ground. As I gazed at its glory, I realized what we were looking at: Sangre de Cristo, the blood of Christ. Good lord, it was beautiful. Then it struck me like a plank across the head. God has a strange sense of humor. Our family was Jewish. That we were now staring at a phenomenal sunset named after Christ's crucifixion

9

was disturbing, to say the least. In my best gallows humor, I yelled out, "It's the blood of Christ, and Christ was a Jew." In unison, the gathered heap broke into laughter. The laughter built and built until it was a combination of belly laughing and crying.

The ceremony had now completed the circle from grief to anger to joyous celebration. As we collectively climbed back to our feet and gazed upon the pyre, something was amiss. Sally's body was gone. It got very quiet as a chill came wafting down from the bloodred mountains. No one could speak. The fire, though still burning strong, had lost its initial intensity. No one was going to say it, but everyone was thinking it. What just happened? What time is it? Why is it now sundown? Where is her body? Did it burn up during our time lapse? What happened to us? The lights and telepathic communication, the boom, and then the shaking followed by total silence? Were we really telepathically communicating? Was it possible that her body just rose into the heavens? Did she have anything to do with the light show, the communal empathy and loss of time, the bloody glow? All were speechless.

The gathering gradually turned into a wake. The booze started flowing as the sky gave way to night. It would be one of the few times I wouldn't drink a drop. I guess I wanted to savor the spiritual feelings that were still tingling in my nerve endings. I felt strangely light afoot and warm from the inside out. The bottles were passed around, and conversation restored a sense of normalcy.

I took Rachel aside and held her face in my palms as I looked deep in her eyes. "I've always loved you deeper than I can explain. So much of my life would have been impossible without you. I want to make it all up to you."

Rachel replied, "I know, Sandy. I know."

After the Pyre

The next morning, Rachel, Ben, Mac, and I were huddled in a booth, sipping coffee, awaiting our breakfast at the Patio Pancake Place in Salida. The talk was sparse; we were all waiting for someone to break the ice and start the discussion on what happened the night before. The elephant in the room needed to speak up. Did it really even happen? If it did, what did it mean? Was there an explanation?

I decided to take the lead. "Did you guys see the news this morning? According to the USGS, we experienced an earthquake last night. They recorded it on their seismogram thing. It was centered near Crestone, they said. Plenty of people in the valley reported feeling it. So that seems to explain that part. I don't know what to think about the lights and boom that followed."

Ben started in with stammering uncertainty, "You know...I've read that...sometimes...earthquakes can generate noise. From what I remember, it's usually a boom or something, and it happens just before you feel the actual shaking."

"Is that so?" I encouraged. "I'd love to read up on that. Perhaps there *is* an explanation."

At this, Rachel blurted, "What do you mean, explanation? It wasn't just an earthquake and noises and lights. We just torched our daughter, and somehow this peeled open some cosmic connection. I don't know about you guys, but even now, I don't feel grounded at all. I still feel the overwhelming sense that there's more around us than we can see or touch. I don't know what it is, but I'm sure feeling it. Didn't you guys feel it? Didn't you hear the others' thoughts? What happened to her body? Why did five o'clock turn into eight o'clock? What happened to that chunk of time? Did we all pass out? I'm scared, Sandy. What happened? Where did her body go?"

"It's okay, Rachel. You're right, honey; some really weird shit's going on. I feel what you're saying. I just thought we'd try to make sense of what we can make sense of, and maybe this would help us understand what seems unexplainable. The bloodred glow over the mountains, well, that was just the sun setting. We've all seen the Sangre de Cristo phenomenon before. It's just the light of the setting sun—"

"Stop it, Sandy." Rachel sobbed. "It's way more than that. You can't just break this down into digestible bites of reason. Something happened up there that's beyond us; why can't you just accept that?"

11

"Mom, Dad's just trying to figure some of this out," Ben tried to assure her. "If we break this thing down into discrete events, perhaps it'll make more sense. We were all very raw at the pyre, and I, for one, had enough alcohol once things got going; it does seem a bit foggy—"

"No, no, no!" Rachel pleaded. "Explaining any of this is an excuse to ignore that there was something going on that we can never explain. We should try to accept that this was the work of God or something way bigger than us. Why don't you want to see that?"

Just then Mac broke her silence. "There's way more going on than we know how to explain. What we witnessed was more than coincidental natural phenomena. Ben's right; earthquakes can generate noises, sometimes very loud noises. The swirling lights we saw prior to the earthquake have also been witnessed before. They've actually been seen in the San Luis Valley many times. I'm really freaked out about the missing time and Sally's body. Where did it go?! Sure, we can say that her body incinerated in those three missing hours, but what the hell happened? How can we just be missing three hours? Sure, some of it can be rationalized, but that doesn't explain the timing of the events. Why did all this happen during her cremation? I heard what everyone was thinking and feeling. I know Sally had something to do with this. I know it. I'm scared. This wasn't the first time."

Upon that declaration, Mac broke down sobbing hysterically. As she held her face in the palms of her hands, the three of us looked at one another, mouthing the words *not the first time*. We anxiously gave Mac time to compose herself. What did she mean, not the first time?

"Are you okay, Mac?" I pried. "It's going to be all right. We've all been through a lot, perhaps more than any of us can ever explain. Do you want to tell us what you mean by not the first time? How could Sally have had anything to do with this? She's dead."

"I know she's dead, damn it! I was there. I saw the whole thing!"

The table became completely silent at this admission. Up until this point, everyone believed that Sally had died alone. What did happen that night? Was Mac involved somehow? I, for one, was really confused, confused to the point that my head began to pound. I put my arm around Rachel and brought her in close. This only brought more tears from Rachel, and it seemed obvious we all needed to take a break. I suggested we head back to the cabin and gather our wits.

Once back at the cabin, we spent some alone time collecting our thoughts. Our cabin was one of a half dozen laid out in a semicircle around a huge, flat lawn. On the opposite side of the lawn churned the South Arkansas River. The entire complex was cradled under a grove of enormous cottonwood trees. I sat myself down in one of the Adirondack chairs that surrounded a firepit just ten feet from the river. I loved this spot. The River Orchard Place was a well-lived, old-school Colorado mountain retreat. It was originally a hunting retreat for the muckety-mucks of a bygone era. Much of the grounds were neglected and run down. The owners had great hopes for the property that were stymied by their lack of cash and motivation. It had everything I wanted in a getaway: silence, shade, river, wildlife, and a curious past. We stayed there many times over the years, so I always found immediate comfort. My favorite spot was always right there by the river. The rushing water has a way of soothing one's soul. My mind tried wandering but kept jumping to attention when it circled back on what we went through. What in the name of God was going on?

Within a half hour, the four of us had regrouped around the firepit. Everyone was somewhat calmer. It seemed to me we had better backtrack to the beginning of this evolving story. Since this seemed to be centered on Mac, I leaned toward her and asked her if she could tell us everything she knew about the events leading up to Sally's demise. I assured her it was okay, that we just wanted to know what happened.

Mac started slowly to keep her emotions in check. "I'm so sorry I didn't say something sooner. I really didn't know what to do. I guess I panicked. What's going to happen to me? I'll tell you everything, but I don't want to go to jail. Please don't tell anyone, please."

I calmly told her that things were going to be okay, and no one was going to put her in jail. At least that was what I thought at the time. "Mac, we have a right to know what happened, and I'm sure the authorities are going to want to know as well. Let's just start here with what you can tell us, and we'll deal with the rest later."

She started back in. "I'm sooo sorry. I'm just completely freaked out by all this. I don't even know what's going on, especially after last night. Okay, I'll do my best to tell you what happened."

As we awaited her story, something didn't feel right. Mac's behavior didn't instill a sense of confidence. I'm sure I wasn't the only one with these thoughts. Rachel's death grip on my hand was evidence. Ben seemed completely agitated and was beginning to clam up.

13

"I really hadn't seen much of Sally in a long while," Mac restarted. "She called me a couple months ago all excited about a project she was working on. She was almost manic about this project. I really didn't have any idea what she was talking about. She was rambling on about memory chasing or some such thing. She said it's centered on a new form of meditation. It's not meditation where you just sit there, quietly trying to let go of your thoughts; it's active meditation, she told me. Sally said she figured out that she could achieve a meditative state while jogging. She called this active meditation. She claimed this was the link for us Westerners to embrace meditation where traditional meditation had eluded us.

"But this was just the jumping-off point for her," Mac continued. "Sally said she'd set up a lab in her art studio. She installed a treadmill for her active meditation and was experimenting with a variety of external-stimulus devices to aid in the meditative process. She had strobe lights, a true mirror, a huge projection screen, virtual reality goggles, and something she called a God Helmet. Somehow all this shit together was going to enable her to achieve not just a meditative state but one that involved an out-of-body experience. While in this state, somehow she was going to revisit her past. She thought she could revisit her past by recalling her memories in detail via a transcendental state. I don't know; it all seemed so crazy. That fucking helmet scared the shit out of me. It was so menacing with all those frigging wires coming out of it…but it was the light—it was the light that killed her."

Mac was starting to break down. I suggested she take a few breaths and try to calm down. She looked me in the eyes with a hollow, helpless look, all the while mumbling about the lights. "It's gonna be okay, Mac. Let it pass," I encouraged her.

While wiping away tears, Mac gathered herself and proceeded. "I didn't know what to think after her call. I really didn't want any part of whatever it was she was working on. It was way out there. She wanted me to come over and help her out with some new procedure she was working on. I kept putting her off until *the night*. She said she needed help on just one part of the process. It was a safety issue. I reluctantly agreed to come over.

"I pulled up to her cabin, it was early evening, and it was a gorgeous night," Mac went on. "No one answered my knocks on the door, so I went around to the studio. Spacey jam-band music was rattling the little studio. I ducked as I entered the low doorway. What lay before me is burned into my memory. She was jogging on the treadmill with a huge tangle of rainbow-colored wires streaming from an old-fashioned motorcycle helmet she was wearing to a row of computers in the back of the room. She had no idea I was there yet. In front of the treadmill was a curved projection screen that bent around the front of the treadmill. Images of what appeared to be home videos and still pictures of her childhood where rapidly flashing on the screen in time with the music. A strobe light pulsed in sync with the music and images. As I was about to announce my presence, an ethereal glow of blue-and-orange light began to fill the room from the skylight. I looked up through the skylight and couldn't comprehend what I was looking at. An enormous swirl of blue-and-orange light was spiraling around the huge antenna that was anchored inside the studio. It was exactly like last night but way more intense. The swirling light suddenly grew much brighter, and without warning, a huge boom rattled the room, and the ground began to shake violently. Simultaneously, the room flashed with a bright-white light, and all the power went out. I was instantly immersed in total darkness and silence.

"It was so overwhelming I didn't even realize I had been knocked to the ground," Mac continued. "My ears were ringing as my eyes slowly adjusted to the darkness. What the fuck just happened? What the fuck just happened to Sally? I started calling out her name but got no response. I fumbled for my phone and turned on the flashlight. I shined it toward the treadmill and saw Sally crumpled on top of it, draped in a labyrinth of wires. I crawled over to her. The studio was filled with a light cloud of smoke. As I got close to her, I could see wisps of smoke coming from her helmet. I reached for her while calling her name. She wasn't responding. As I turned her over, I could see that the smoke was coming from her hair. The smell was putrid. I put my cheek down to her mouth to feel for breath. There was none. I pulled her in tight as I tried not to totally lose it. Then out of nowhere, a soft voice filled the room. The voice wasn't coming from Sally, but it was her voice. The voice was coming from the sound system. It said in a calm and comforting voice, 'It's so beautiful; it's so beautiful, Mac.' It scared the livin' shit out of me. I jumped to my feet and ran to my car, and off I went."

Mac's confession didn't turn out the way any of us could have predicted. The combination of the events at the funeral pyre and learning of the circumstances of Sally's death didn't spur an overwhelming desire to understand either event. No one had the energy to sit down and work through the issues that were occupying our every thought. None of us raced back to Sally's cabin to explore the details of what she was up to. None of us dove into research regarding earthquake-related phenomena. In fact, it would be months before anyone would even go back to Sally's cabin to deal with her effects. While the entire scene was nothing short of fantastic, it didn't instigate a search for discovery. What it did do was send all of us into a horrible depression. Losing someone very close will certainly do that, but knowing that her death was entirely preventable was a massive gut punch. I've known people who have lost a child to suicide, and the pain I saw in their eyes was so deep that it's hard to imagine how they'd ever recover. Our pain was certainly approaching this level.

In the days that followed, the four of us went our separate ways. Rachel went back to San Francisco, and Ben went back to New York. No one knew where Mac ended up. She left shortly after her revelation, without a single goodbye. None of us had the strength to sit down with the authorities and update them on what we'd learned. There seemed no point. I went back home to Denver and augured in to what would be my final drunken stupor.

Awakening

"Dad, it's Ben *again*. Why won't you answer your phone? You're really starting to freak me out. Are you all right? I need you to call me back; we've got to talk."

Delete.

"Mr. Beachcomber, it's Willy, my friend. How are things? I've been needing to talk to you. I'm really sorry I couldn't make it to Sally's service. I've been thinking of you *a lot*. I really hope you're dealing with all this. Know that there are lots of people who care for you, no one more than me. Please call me back. I'd love to hear your voice. I love you, brother. A hui hou!"

Delete.

After I deleted every message from the previous night, I lay staring up at the ceiling from my bed, still fully clothed. It was the crack of noon, and I was wondering if I'd ever get up and feed myself. Probably no time soon. The one call I needed to hear was once again absent. Why won't she call me back? Likewise, last night's memory was once again absent. I fumbled with my phone to piece together what I'd been up to. Perhaps the ten calls I made to Rachel had something to do with her not calling. I knew I couldn't lay there much longer, as I'd start thinking about how my life had become so wretched. I tried to clear my head, only to feel the horror of yet another massive hangover—my reoccurring reality. Each and every day was a prison of repetitive hangovers and drunkenness. I couldn't bear to face my reality. I couldn't stand listening to my conscience wrestle with my decrepit state. I couldn't begin to face up to the facts. I had a million things I could blame this on. Just leave me alone, I thought. As I struggled to figure out how to deal with myself, the phone rang. It was my dear friend Buddy.

"Where the fuck are you, Sandy? We're about to tee off. Please don't tell me you forgot," begged Buddy.

"Uhhh, I guess so," I stammered. "Golf? We're golfing today?"

"Ahh come on, man; don't do this to me," implored Buddy. "You don't remember anything, do you? We talked for over an hour last night. What's up with that? Jesus!"

"God damn it, I'm sorry," I said pathetically. "I'm so sorry, but I can't. I'm still in bed."

"Ahh come on, man. Get your sorry ass out of bed, and get over here. You can meet us on the course."

"Not now, don't do this to me now."

"Who's your Buddy, Sandy; who's your Buddy?"

"Ah geez, Buddy, you know I can't turn you down when you talk to me like that."

"You better not turn me down. I'll see you on the third hole; get your ass over here."

I didn't bother to change my clothes or even brush my teeth. I hustled downstairs, guzzled some orange juice, and off I went. I'd really blacked out last night. I couldn't even remember talking to Buddy, let alone that we had golf plans. What a mess. Thank God for people like Buddy. I wondered what I'd even said to him. It must have been a lot if we talked for over an hour. Oh God, what did I tell him?

I caught up with Buddy just after they finished the third hole. Buddy came running over to me and gave me a huge embrace. He expressed his deepest sympathies for my loss and assured me he was there for me. Buddy and I went way back. We met at Arapahoe Basin years ago. Our friendship started as ski buddies, and though we still skied together, it was golf that our friendship evolved around now, as it was our favorite warm-weather pastime.

As we pulled up to the fourth hole, Buddy introduced me to our partners. As he liked to put it, they were our designated pigeons—strangers they paired us with. I introduced myself to Monte and Tim. As it turned out, they lived near me. We exchanged pleasantries, and then Buddy started in on the betting scenarios and how I didn't deserve any strokes. "We're playin' straight up, like it or not!"

"You gotta be kidding me, Buddy. You always start with that bullshit. You're a single handicap, and you know it. I'm a measly twelve handicap; you gotta give me a couple a side!"

"One stroke a side—that's it," Buddy said coarsely.

"Okay, one stroke a side, but we're playing two down auto-pop on our usual nine-hole match play with eighteen being the tiebreaker. None of your penny-stock bullshit."

"Jesus, Sandy, easy does it; one stroke a side it is."

The game was on. We'd turn the course into a microcosm of life, replete with struggles and successes, mourning and rejoicing. We'd go from cheering each other on to silently hoping the other would fail. Other than the comradery, I treasured golf as a meditative function. To play well can take immense concentration. That concentration blocks everything else out. There's no room to think of anything outside the golf bubble. You're no longer being annoyed by passing thoughts, brain chatter. Of course one ultimately loses concentration, and a bad shot shocks you back to reality, and the zone evaporates. The better golfer knows how to get back to that meditative state and get there fast. And that's how a round with Buddy would go, back a forth for eighteen holes. Rarely would the winner be determined before the eighteenth hole.

As the four of us were waiting on the tee box, Monte and Tim were talking about something that caught my attention. I listened until I was sure they were talking about Dr. Bear, our family dentist.

"Wait a minute there, Monte; are you talking about Dr. Bear the dentist?"

"Yes, we are. Do you know him?" replied Monte.

"I do; he's our family dentist. Did you say he got arrested?"

"He's my dentist too," Monte went on to explain. "Yeah, he got arrested for a pill scam. He was writing bogus scripts to two guys like every other day. You know they watch that shit like hawks. His addiction obviously got the best of him."

"Holy shit, that's awful," I offered. "I really like that guy. He was always real interesting and personable, certainly for a dentist."

"Yeah, I like him too," responded Monte. "It's really sad; he'll probably lose his practice. Lord knows how his family will handle this. He has several young kids."

"Oh, wow, you're right. His kids would frequently be in the office, like it was their home away from home. That's just tragic."

We teed off and headed down the long, plush par five. I couldn't believe what I'd just heard. How can that happen to someone who seems to have everything going for himself? He must have just lost total control to addiction. My mind wandered off, thinking about Dr. Bear, imagining what that would be like, to be addicted, to be controlled by an outside force, to have no free will. Then it struck me hard and certain. I did know what he was going through—I'm addicted to alcohol! How am I any different than Dr. Bear? If that's the case, then what's to prevent something equally destructive from happening to me? For one of the few times in my life, fear overtook me. It felt quite possible that something horrible was going to happen to me. I felt tears welling up and was overcome with self-pity. I began to feel weak in the knees, so I knelt down to compose myself. As I was hoping this feeling would pass, I realized how hungover I was and began to feel sick. Off in the distance, I thought I heard someone call my name.

"Sandy, Sandy, are you okay, man?" inquired Buddy.

"Oh shit, oh shit, Buddy," I stammered. "I don't think so; no, I don't think so."

"Hey, it's gonna be okay. I know what's going on. You told me everything last night. Did the Dr. Bear thing set you off?"

"Oh Jesus, Buddy, it sure did. I gotta be honest with you. I don't recall a damn thing about last night. Did I spill my guts? Was I a complete mess? I'm so sorry, man. I don't want to be dumping on you."

"It's okay, Sandy; it's all going to be okay. I know what you're going through, what you're dealing with. It's okay, man, you told me enough last night—I get it. It's not as bad as you think; you can change; you just gotta have a big plan. Take some deep breaths, and let it pass. Let's walk this hole in; it'll give you some time to collect yourself."

I picked up my bag, and we started walking to the green. Buddy began reminiscing about our past. How we met at A-Basin and how I had an immediate impact on his life. He relayed a story about how I pulled him aside one night and confronted him about his partying. I apparently told him that he needed to respect and even be fearful of booze and drugs. We all like to party, but it should never define who we are. It can take over if you're not careful. I didn't remember any of it. Holy shit, how could I have had such an impact on someone and not remember it? Jesus. He told me he never forgot that night, that no one had ever coached him like that. He was very grateful. As we walked up to the side of the green, I thought what a clever thing that was to say to someone in my position; he really understood how to communicate in a dire situation. I walked up to Buddy and pulled him in for a much-needed hug. As I held him, I thanked him for being my friend and told him what a wise, wise man he was.

As we walked over to the tee box, I wasn't sure how this was going to play out. Before I had time to consider my options, Buddy picked up right where we left off. Looking off into the distance, he proclaimed, "All right, Sandy, it's your box; fire away. We'll restart here. I'm comin' after your ass; all square with five to play on this nine, game on, you hack."

"Good luck with that. You're going down this time, my friend."

We finished our round with all kinds of golf drama. I won the front nine, but Buddy fought his way back to win the back nine. It came down to the final hole, as it always seemed to. Buddy beat me on the back nine and won the match with the eighteenth-hole tie-breaker. It was a fitting end.

In the parking lot after we loaded our clubs, Buddy walked over to me; he had a tattered, dog-eared paperback book in his hand.

"Hey, Sandy, I have something that might help you with your drinking. It's a self-help book that really bailed me out when I was struggling with booze. It's nothing like anything I've come across, and believe me, I've looked long and hard for help. It was written by a guy named Trimpey, Jack Trimpey. He's the real deal. It is nothing like AA. Give it a try; it certainly can't hurt."

The book was titled *Rational Recovery*. I wanted to resist taking it as I despised self-help books. The book's worn condition clearly showed how much it meant to him. I clutched the book with two hands and patted my heart with it.

"Thanks, Buddy, are you sure you want me to have it?"

"Of course, I wouldn't offer it if I didn't think it could help."

"Thanks, man, I'll let you know what happens. I really appreciate you being there for me. I totally respect your opinion and will pursue this. I'll call you later, and you can tell me what we talked about last night."

"That would probably be a good idea. I'll await your call. I'm always available for you. It's much easier when you have someone you can relate to on these matters. You're definitely gonna be all right, Sandy. Let's do this again real soon. I miss playing with you, brother."

"We'll do it again real soon. I love you, my friend."

21

Over the next few days, I spent considerable time contemplating my condition. I took stock of my life from as many angles as I could. It was becoming shockingly clear how far I'd drifted from myself. I thought about how I used to be successful at resolving problems via deep introspection and contemplation. I recalled that I used to let serious problems ferment in my brain for a period of time, and by doing this, my subconscious mind would always return insightful ideas of resolution. I recalled that jogging was a way I used to jump-start conflict resolution. To me, jogging was more than a way to stay in shape. It used to be a form of meditation for me. It dawned on me that jogging as a form of meditation was what Sally was talking about, active meditation. How could I have not gotten that connection until just now? Active meditation, yes, active meditation was exactly what I needed.

I worked my way through Jack Trimpey's book and was dumfounded by his approach to combating addiction. It was so simple; it seemed impossible that his methodology wasn't mainstream. Trimpey claimed that one has to merely quit drinking. That's right, just quit drinking. Of course it's an entire book, and there's much more to it, but in a nutshell, that's it—just stop it. Apparently 40–70 percent of people quit drinking all on their own without rehab, therapy, AA, or support groups.

As I was lacing up my running shoes, I contemplated what music I'd listen to on the restart of my active meditation. I chose an obscure group that always filled me with energy and excitement. I selected the album *Lanzafame* by the band Tap Tap. There was no way to describe this band; its sound was so unique. Their beautiful, driving rhythms were contrasted by heavy, dissonant, and frenetic acoustic-guitar bashing overlaid with simple, distorted, twanging electric-guitar leads. Tap Tap was a favorite of Sally's as well. It was our theme music on the drive to A-Basin for a day on the slopes. As I headed out on my run, the very first track sent me tumbling back to those precious drives with Sally, speeding up I-70 with the both of us head banging and screaming the lyrics together. It was glorious, a true father-daughter-bonding experience, precious and private. As I plodded along, I started connecting to that running feeling I hadn't felt in years, detachment. The rhythm of running is in tune with all that is human. Most certainly, it is in step with the heartbeat.

For me, the physical part of running was just a setup for the mental part. Runners need encouragement while running, and for most, the best encouragement is music. The best music matched the pace of your footfalls and, at times, your breathing. *Just follow the beat, and let your mind wander* was the mantra. Once your body connects in this manner, there's enough going on that your mind is occupied. From there, one could focus singularly on nagging conflicts and let the subconscious float remedy ideas, or zone out and wave at passing thoughts. Running is a jumping off point for meditation; it puts one closer to that quiet place that can then be guided to problem-solving or pure, regenerative meditation. It was a perfect symbiotic relationship between body and soul.

Jack Trimpey's model was simple and homegrown; it was nothing new. Booze makes you feel good, and some folks want to feel good more often than they should. The drive behind this desire lies in a small, primitive portion of the brain called the midbrain. This part of the brain controls all involuntary functions responsible for survival. The midbrain was the caveman brain. We give little thought to this part of our brain. The part of the brain most of us think of is the neocortex, or new brain, as it was the last part of the brain to evolve. This is the massive, crenulated gray matter where higher functions take place. The neocortex comprises 76 percent of the brain. It controls sensory perception, motor commands, and reasoning. The perplexing part of addiction is that all addicts know what they're doing is harmful to themselves and probably others, yet they keep abusing. There was a battle going on between the conscious rational brain, the neocortex, and the primitive midbrain. Most people don't have a battle to fight; they simply control their behavior through good old-fashioned reasoning. For the addict, the midbrain voice overpowers the reasoning of the neocortex. Jack's methodology called for the separation and isolation of the midbrain's voice from the rational reasoning of the neocortex voice. By identifying the midbrain's voice and recognizing it, one could shut it down by ignoring it.

As the days passed, my mind started to clear. While this was a welcome relief from how I was feeling and thinking, it also came with significant reckoning. One thing all addicts have in common is immense guilt. The drinking covers all this up, but when you stop, you meet your behavior straight on. It can be overwhelming and, at times, embarrassing to look at yourself from a removed perspective, viewing one's selfish behavior.

One particular run, I stumbled across the most welcoming realization. All the heavy guilt was not easing up much, and while I was focusing on this, I was visualizing myself from above. Out of nowhere, I was struck with self-pity. As I saw myself down below, I thought, Wow, you've been through a lot, and now you're doing what you need to do—you're fixing yourself. Why are you so hard on yourself? You're just a human like everyone else.

I realized where this was going, and I braced myself for the coming wave of emotion. I have to love myself, accept that I've got warts, just like everybody else. Forgive yourself, I thought, just forgive yourself. With this thought, the warmth of love started to spread from my inner core outward in a tingling wave of self-recognition. When the wave reached my heart, tears of joy came to my eyes. I was experiencing love in its purest form—the love of self. I now understood what's meant by "you've got to love yourself before you can love others." This was to be the second satori of my lifetime. It was going to lead me out of this mess.

"Hi, Ben."

"Dad?"

"Yes, how have you been?"

"Oh my God, you're such a dick."

"I'm sorry I've been ignoring you. I've been dealing with some heavy shit here. I want you to know everything is good, and I've broken through to the other side. How have you been?"

"Ah, Jesus, Dad, you're killing me. You have no idea what's been going through my mind. It's not just me either. Mom's worried sick. Your calls really freaked her out. Buddy called me the other night and filled me in a bit. He seemed really worried. Ah, Dad, are you all right? What do you mean you broke through to the other side? Other side of what?"

"I know, Ben. I had to clean myself up. I was a mess. I'm soooo sorry I've treated you like this. It's gonna be all right though. I've been doing some serious soul-searching, and well, I think I'm done with booze. No, I am done with booze. It's a long story, but know that things are going to be different, way different. I'm sorry I haven't been there for you. I'm so sorry."

After talking through the heavy stuff, we eventually brought it back to Earth. We talked about Sally for a long time. We reminisced about our fond memories of her and how much we missed her. We eventually got to the topic of the strange events at her funeral pyre and at her passing. We talked about the device she'd been working on that took her life. Ben informed me he'd been obsessed with the bizarre phenomena that occurred both at her death and at the funeral pyre. He couldn't stop thinking about the Memory Chaser device and had been researching what components he could. He was particularly interested in the God Helmet.

"Dad, you won't believe this, but the God Helmet is a real thing. You can buy one online! I got one recently and have been experimenting with it. I've only had it a few days, so it's not clear to me how it works yet."

"You what? I don't know if I like this idea. No, I don't think I like this at all."

"It's okay, Dad. It's really not a big deal, at least not yet. I gotta figure this out—it's important to me. I need to know what happened to her, and I need to know what she was up to. We need to go back to her cabin and try to figure things out."

"Oh, I don't know about that, Ben. I don't think I'm ready for that."

"Dad, we gotta go back, even if it's just to clean up her stuff."

"Well, we do have to do that, but I still don't like you messing with that monstrous device. That thing killed your sister."

I started reading again; a couple of books really hit home. One was *Unbroken* by Laura Hillenbrand. *Unbroken* is a World War II story about an American GI's experience in Japanese prisoner-of-war camps. The protagonist was Louis Zamperini who, prior to the war, was an Olympic runner. Louis was terrorized by Mutsuhiro Watanabe, "the Bird." He was savagely beaten to within inches of his life numerous times by the Bird while in the POW camps. No one escaped the brutal treatment of the prison guards, particularly from the Bird. Their conditions were beyond deplorable, from starvation and exposure to total sensory deprivation. To survive, many of the prisoners resorted to recoiling into their memories as a way to escape their harsh reality. One high-ranking American officer was able to retreat so far into his memories that he was capable of recalling books he had previously read in their entirety. He took to entertaining his fellow prisoners by "reading" books from memory word for word. I had no idea the human mind was capable of such a thing. How was that possible? I couldn't get this out of my head. Maybe it was possible to revisit memories. Maybe Sally was onto something. Apparently the human mind was capable of such feats. Maybe Ben was right—we needed to reconstruct what she was up to.

I found myself becoming addicted to running. My goal on any given run was to completely disengage. This would be manifested in increasingly longer stretches where I would totally lose track of time and space. This was starting to happen to me frequently. When I'd come out of my meditative state, I'd realize I had just run a quarter mile or so without any recollection of it.

One of the most dramatic examples of this was a run I was on just after a pristine snowfall. It had snowed four or five inches the night before, and it was a perfect bluebird Colorado morning. I was so in tune to my run that I

25

entered a transcendental state. The fresh snow made my footfalls feel like I was running weightless on pillows. The snow dampened any sounds that tried to penetrate my headphone solitude. I was way out there. Out of nowhere, something was pushing me from behind, just below my waist. I didn't come out of my trance until I started to fall forward. I thought I was being hit by a car and prepared to be run over. As I fell forward, I stretched out and dove into the freshly fallen snow. I landed with a great puff of powder. As I reeled around in the whiteness, a dog bounded on top of me and went for my face. Rather than tear into me, it started licking my face with abandon. This totally blew me away—so zoned out and into my run, I had no idea where I was or what was going on around me. It could have been a car, and I wouldn't have noticed until it was too late. This was powerful stuff.

"Hello."

"Sandy, how're you doing? It's Rachel."

Long pause…

"Um, I'm doing well. How are you?"

"I'm fine, honey. I got a call from Ben the other night. I guess you finally called him back. You know you really made his life a living hell. Why do you think you can do that and then just sweep in and declare everything's okay, that you've changed?"

"Well, this isn't starting the way I envisioned."

Longer pause…

"Hey, listen," I restarted. "I know I've been selfish and blind to others. I know I've been that way to you. I don't know if I can ever make that up to you, but I do know this. I'm not making excuses. I'm owning up to my bad behavior, my selfishness. I don't know if being sorry carries any weight with you, but I am deeply sorry. I'm moving on with my life, baggage and all. I'd love to explain where I am with all this, but only if you're ready."

"Sandy, you know I love you; you know that, don't you? What you probably don't know is that I'm still hearing drunken echoes from your relentless, pathetic, badgering messages. Do you remember calling me over and over? Jesus, Sandy, how do you expect me to flip a switch and believe that you've now broken through to the other side. What does that even mean?"

"It means just that, Rachel. It means I found a way out of my drinking. I'm done. I'm finally done. You're gonna have to take my word on that for now. I was a mess after the funeral pyre. I was desperately depressed and didn't deal with it. God, I wish I didn't make all those calls, but I did, but that was then…"

"Sandy, I don't know what to tell you. Don't you think I've been through hell too? What do you think it's been like for me? We lost our daughter, for God's sake, we lost our daughter…" Rachel trailed off, crying. "I can't talk about this now. I just can't. I'm sorry. Sandy, please go with Ben."

Click.

Ah, Jesus Christ. This is a real fucking mess. I lay back on the couch in blinding bewilderment. This's going to be a lot harder than I thought. God damn it, why did I make all those pathetic calls. I'm such an idiot. I continued to lay there for what seemed like an eternity, pondering my predicament, staring at the ceiling. I've been so self-obsessed with getting sober and figuring myself out that I've once again ignored the needs of others. I slowly began to feel as though it wasn't so helpless. That this, too, would be part of my mission. I had to start including how I treat others as part of my new self. Why wasn't this self-evident? What was wrong with me? Was there something wrong with me? I struggled for a minute with self-doubt and then stared it down. I was not gonna let this bring me down. It was all part of the process—just add this to the mission. It was gonna take some time, but I could get her back. I had to get her back. I licked my wounds one last time and headed out for a run.

"Hey, Willy, it's Sandy!"

"Sandy, oh, Sandy,"

"I'm sorry I haven't called you back. It's been quite the slog. I really have been through the wringer and needed to sort myself out."

"I get that, Sandy. This is your journey, it's yours alone, but you're not exactly alone. Tell me what's going on. I'm here for you, brother."

I filled Willy in on everything I'd been enduring, from Sally's passing to my recent sobriety. I spilled my guts to him, and it was so relieving. He was so patient; he just listened. I told him about my call with Rachel earlier in the day, that it was very painful. I told him about my conversations with Ben and how he wanted to go to Sally's cabin, a mission of discovery and truth. We ended up focusing on what had happened at Sally's the night of her death and at the funeral pyre. Willy was a geologist, and I thought he might know a little something about earthquake-related phenomena. This really got him going; he was a very existential person. I asked him if he could verify if there were any earthquakes in the area on either night. He told me it would be easy to verify that. He said that he was vaguely familiar with earthquake lights and sounds and that he'd do some research and get back to me.

"Ah, Willy, you're the best. I really appreciate you letting me bend your ear, for being there for me. Why don't you think about coming out to Colorado? I'm starting to think Ben is right; we gotta go to Sally's. Maybe you could come visit Ben and me in Chaffee County?"

"I'd love to, Sandy. I'll let you know. I'll smell you later, okay, Sandy?"

I spoke with Ben and told him that I thought he was right—we needed to go to Sally's cabin. He was so excited he could barely contain himself. He said he'd make some quick plans and be on my doorstep lickety-split. I was now feeling as big as a house. I was ready to find out what exactly happened to my daughter. Out of nowhere a poem my brother wrote years ago surfaced.

"Problem Solved"

if you wait
put it off
long enough
you're dead
and it's over
problem solved

Return to the Cabin

When Ben's arrival date came, I could hardly contain myself. There was so much positivity running around my brain that it almost made me feel guilty. Within a few months, I'd transformed from a broken shell of a man who saw little in the future to a man who couldn't wait to find what it held. This transformation was so self-centered that I felt I'd ignored the loss of Sally. All that pain was there, but I had pushed it deep and out of the way. Perhaps that was one of the reasons Ben was coming here. Perhaps the journey ahead included resolving the loss, to feel the pain, and also to let it go.

My thoughts turned to Ben and his crazed talk the other night about the God Helmet. I was definitely not sure what the hell the God Helmet was all about. I could tell you this: I had no desire to zap my brain with that neodraconian device. Who knows, maybe this thing was integral, or possibly indispensable, to Sally's memory-chasing efforts.

As I approached Denver International Airport, I closed in on the infamous devil horse affectionately known as Blucifer. Blucifer greets travelers at the entrance to DIA's main terminal turnoff. It's a thirty-two-foot-tall, nine-thousand-pound bright-metallic-blue mustang with glowing-fire-red eyes. Blucifer stood reared on his hind legs, at the ready. It was an unsettling statue, to be sure. As I stared in wonderment, as most people do, I was thunderstruck by a memory that was suddenly dislodged. The artist, Luis Jiménez, was unceremoniously killed while constructing the beast. While attempting to attach Blucifer's head, the supporting structure gave way, and Blucifer's head came crashing down on top of Luis. Luis suffered a severed artery in his leg and bled out. Realizing the similarity in circumstances between Sally's demise and Luis's sent a bolt of electricity coursing through my body. They'd both died from a freak accident while in direct pursuit of their craft. Blucifer was completed by family and friends and survives as a testament beyond the mere artistic creation. Now Ben and I were about to attempt the same thing, to complete Sally's work.

Since being sober, I had regained access to memories I had thought were long gone. I was remembering things I didn't know I'd lost. In conjunction with this or because of this, I frequently had feelings of connectedness. A newly recalled memory of a tender or empathetic event could fill me with a rush of emotions so strong it would make me weep. While recalling tender moments can be emotional for anyone, for me they commonly evoked a connection to something external to the memory. In this case it was Luis. I would never look at Blucifer the same way again. Most travelers couldn't understand Blucifer. They would stare in discontent at this possessed, devil-eyed sentry whizzing by their window. From now on, Blucifer would represent an artist suffering under his work, whose legacy was lifted up by his surviving clan. I felt the blood surge as I realized we were about to lift the mantel of Sally's dream. What that would ultimately look like, I couldn't even imagine. I could only hope the end result was not a devil-eyed metallic-blue mustang.

As I was coming out of Blucifer's grip, I rounded the final turn to the passenger pickup at DIA's infamous tented terminal. Ben was there with a massive backpack and what looked like a bowling-ball bag. As I pulled to a stop, all the while staring at Ben, I had a flash of Ben as my father. He looked exactly like him. And then, just as abruptly, he was Ben again. Now *there* was a connection. I hopped out of the car, and we embraced, neither wanting it to end. What seemed like an eternity since we last saw each other melted away in an instant. Through hugging, we communicated all the emotions we experienced during the funeral and since. We felt each other's pain, loneliness, and longing. We felt the love for one another more than anything. Strange how simple human contact can evoke so much feeling, power. Ben tossed his pack and bowling-ball bag in the back seat, and off we went.

As Denver shrank away in our rearview mirror, we started up Turkey Creek Canyon on State Highway 285. Highway 285 takes you through some of the most beautiful country the state has to offer. Despite all the places Highway 285 takes you, Turkey Creek Canyon is by far the most dangerous section of this long and winding road. I recalled a bumper sticker that commuters from Evergreen to Denver used to proudly display that read "Pray for me; I drive Highway 285." They weren't kidding. It was a four-lane highway with curves so sharp that you had to slow down to forty miles an hour just to stay in your lane. Most of the praying took place in the winter when Turkey Creek Canyon could be snow and ice covered. Whenever I was on this road, I couldn't help but think of Kerouac's Dean Moriarty, aka Neal Cassidy, cruising madly, barely in control of a stolen Coupé de ville.

"So, Dad, you won't believe what I've learned about Sally's experimentation," Ben chattered with contagious excitement. "I really think she was onto something. I believe she was using imagery and what she called active meditation to dislodge herself from reality into some sort of transcendental state. I really think we can recreate her experiment. It gives me chills just thinking about it. Did you round up all the photos and home movies like we talked about?"

The drive to Sally's cabin outside of Nathrop, Colorado, took a little over two hours from Denver. It's a gorgeously soothing ride. The road changes character roughly every twenty miles or so. Turkey Creek Canyon rises up into the foothills of the Rockies from the vast expanse of the high plains. As we passed through Conifer, the road stretched out into an elongated two-lane roller-coaster thrill ride that passed through the north end of Pikes Peak country. Pikes Peak granite forms rounded pink hilltops that breach the cover of picture-perfect ponderosa pines. This stretch ended abruptly as we reached the crest of Crow Hill, where we were treated to a spectacular view of the Platte River Valley as we dropped steeply down into the town of Bailey. From Bailey, the highway follows the North Fork of the South Platte River to Kenosha Pass. The character here is defined by the valley that contains the impeccable South Platte River. Its waters beg you to stop and drop a fishing line for an angle at a rainbow trout. We passed little towns with names from a bygone era, like Shawnee and Grant. The hills then gave way to much-larger mountains on either side. Occasionally, massive snowcapped and treeless behemoths were visible beyond the bounding lesser-valley hills.

"You know the experience has to be tailored to the user; that's why we need as much historic personal imagery as possible," Ben continued at a manic pace. "What about music, Dad; did you remember to grab all your archived shit? The music is so critical, but I think it'll be different for everyone. It's all about distractions and letting go. The strobe is brilliant, Dad…"

As we crested Kenosha Pass, the scenery changed yet again. When we rounded a sharp right-hand turn, the most exquisite view unfolded directly in front of us. The vast expanse of South Park spread out below the road and stretched well beyond the horizon. South Park is an intermontane basin whose gentle grassy hills and expansive flats defy a grasp of scale. This high chaparral is over a thousand square miles of grassland, which used to be the summer hunting grounds of the Ute Indian Nation. Its western boundary is guarded by the towering Mosquito and Park mountain ranges. Seemingly endless peaks that exceed fourteen thousand feet stand sentry with their year-round snowcapped peaks. Driving through South Park, we're dwarfed by the scale of the surroundings. At times, no matter our speed, we seemed to be standing still. Norman Rockwell homesteader ranches from the 1800s accented the natural beauty. We couldn't help but imagine what homesteading in this foreboding landscape was like back then.

"Did you know a strobe light can induce seizures in some people? In fact, some music can have the same effect," Ben continued at a pace now equal to our speeding vehicle. "Apparently a precise visual-harmonic pattern can affect the same part of the brain as an equally precise musical rhythm. What does that say about how our brains work, how the senses are interconnected?!"

31

After summiting Red Hill Pass, the road descends into Fairplay, and the landscape subtly changed again. Now in the middle of South Park, the feel was one of being held captive. The surroundings had us in their rapture. We began to feel sleepy as the terrain became hypnotic. Though our speedometer kept creeping up, it was never fast enough—the rolling, grass-covered hills oh so slowly passed by. Again the scale confused, and we felt tiny and motionless.

"I've been really getting into running too, Dad. I don't feel like I'm getting the whole meditative thing though," Ben rattled on. "Maybe I just have the wrong music. I sure hope you have your cross over music with you—that's gotta work. Remember Tap Tap? I love that group. Sally did too. She used to go crazy when I'd play them."

The turnoff for Hartsel at Antero Junction signaled that a new 285 personality was approaching. This next phase of the drive drops into Trout Creek Canyon. Trout Creek Canyon is the gateway to the upper Arkansas River Valley. As we descended, the canyon tightened, and the landscape became dominated by steep, barren granite walls and rises. The gentler slopes were covered in piñon pine, and its valley floor was devoid of water. This harsh country demanded attention, as there were no straight portions to the road. Midway down the canyon, one of the greatest spectacles of the trip suddenly dominated the horizon. Rising up behind the foothills' foreground was grandiose Mount Princeton. In one turn and seemingly out of nowhere, the entirety of this imposing fourteen-thousand-foot snowcapped beauty filled the horizon. Mount Princeton and its sister mountains of the Collegiate Peaks rose from the relatively flat-lying Arkansas River Valley, which enabled us to see seven thousand feet of sheer mountain-front relief. Nothing was blocking the view from base to peak. The scale of this vista was mind boggling. Its effect caused me to howl like a crazy man every time I encountered it. Ben and I let out our best coyote-moon howl as we dropped into the headwaters of the Arkansas River Valley. Sally's cabin was at the base of this behemoth mountain. We were now entering Sally's stomping ground.

"Dad, do you know what's in my bowling-ball bag? I found out where to buy a God Helmet online. You won't believe this thing…"

"Hold it right there, Ben. I can't wait to explore and understand all of this, but I told you that thing scares the shit out of me. Let's just hold off on that for now. We're almost to the cabin, and I think we need to be prepared for this."

The Arkansas River Valley is right out of a Hollywood Western. Its entire western edge is framed in by the Sawatch Range, which includes the Collegiate Peaks. This impressive range is home to fifteen peaks that exceed fourteen thousand feet. These mountains define the Continental Divide, where water on the east side, including the Arkansas River, drains to the Atlantic Ocean, and water on the west side drains to the Pacific Ocean. The east side of the valley is guarded by dry, rugged foothills that are bounded by the Mosquito Range to the north and the Sangre de Cristo Mountains to the south. The valley floor is home to large, picturesque homestead-era cattle ranches. Expansive fields of hay are broken up by piñon pines, and where water permitted, aspen and cottonwood flourish. The key element in this valley is no doubt the Arkansas River. For the most part, it is confined to the eastern side of the valley and is only visible from 285 were the river swings to the west. It's a seasonal river that rages in the spring and early summer from ample snowmelt. The rest of the year, it's underwhelming in terms of water flow. Its waters are pure and extremely clear during low flow. It's a blue-ribbon trout fishery that's home to some of the best white water rafting in the country. The rafting was what brought Sally here, and the valley's stunning beauty was what kept her here.

As we made the turnoff for Sally's cabin, I pulled the car over. I took hold of Ben's hands and looked him in the eye. "Are you ready for this, Ben? This is going to get very, very intense." Ben's face turned solemn, and for the first time on this trip, he was speechless. I didn't need to say any more. I put the car in gear, and we headed up the slope to Sally's cabin.

Cabin Fever

As we pulled into the parking area in front of Sally's cabin, the reality of what we were about to face pulled hard on my heart. I could feel cracks in my certainty forming as my gut tightened. This lonely, little cabin seemed inconsequential compared to the grand landscape that it pretended to belong in. Mount Princeton loomed in the background and seemed to be making a statement to this humble abode. The grand mountain appeared to be both protector and destroyer. My wandering gaze focused in on the massive antenna rising from behind the cabin. I was thrust back into the moment as I recalled the antenna's significance.

"Dad, are you there. Dad?"

"Oh wow, sorry, I was out there somewhere."

"Welcome home, homey."

"This place has some power to it, doesn't it? I don't think I'd want to live here by myself. Sally had some balls to live here all alone. I can't imagine. Hey, what do you think the deal is with the antenna? It's way too big for a TV antenna, and why is it anchored in the middle of her studio?"

"I have no idea, but it looks more like something a ham-radio operator would use. Perhaps the studio used to be a ham-radio office."

We hauled our luggage into the cabin. The place was definitely in need of a serious cleaning after sitting empty for months. I took the only bedroom and left Ben with the living room couch. The cabin was no more than five hundred square feet. I would guess it was built in the early 1900s as a hunting or summer cabin. It wasn't meant for winter living this high up in the mountains. The exterior was classic mountain style. It consisted of longitudinally halved logs aligned vertically, with the bark side facing outward. The roof was corrugated tin with a hundred years of rusted patina. The interior walls and ceiling were classic old-school Colorado knotty pine. The tiny kitchen was open to the living area, and a small wood-burning stove was the centerpiece. The windows were original panels of single-pane glass that leaked horribly. Her main piece of art was a tapestry of the Grateful Dead's Steal Your Face, or Stealie, as the Deadheads call it. It's a classic Grateful Dead art piece that's the cover of one of their albums of the same name. The center is a skull viewed from above with its skullcap removed, revealing a lightning bolt that fills the middle of the cranial cavity. It signifies enlightenment via LSD. The apple did not fall from this tree. I would have killed to have this setup when I was her age.

34

I put on a pot of coffee and took a seat across from Ben. It was late afternoon, and the sun's angle signaled evening was approaching. I figured we'd have a cup of coffee and discuss our plan. We'd had phone conversations as to what Sally was up to, but now we were here, and the anticipation took on a more sinister feel. I didn't learn much on my aborted visit. I wasn't ready for any of this then. That glimpse of her final world seemed like a still photo now, seared into my brain. It all seemed so sci-fi. Were we to go into her studio and just turn something on and—*wiz, bang*—we'd be looking at a time machine?

We decided that it would be smart to take inventory of the entire studio—document each piece of equipment and determine if each was working and possibly what their functions were. Ben had brought some equipment for troubleshooting. He had his laptop, some electrical tools, and a plethora of software. If we could understand the parts first, perhaps this would help us better understand how everything worked together. We finished our coffee and headed for the studio.

The studio was similar to the cabin. It was of lesser-grade construction, as it seemed to be leaning in multiple directions. The only reason either of these structures were still standing was that the climate was so dry. The valley only gets eight inches of moisture a year. It's so dry that it literally crunches when you walk over its brittle ground cover of bone-dry twigs and pine needles. One errant match would set the countryside ablaze.

As I bent over to enter through the low-hanging door, Ben let out a screech. I sprang to attention and slammed my head on the doorframe. "What the fuck!"

"Oh shit!" Ben exclaimed. "Did you see that frigging cat! It came lunging out of the shadows right at me. What's that all about?"

Out of the corner of my eye, I could see the tail of a cat running off into the woods. It was the same cat that spooked me when I was here last. "That's the same cat as before, Ben. The long-haired menace! I guess we'd better be on our toes."

We entered the studio and paused to take it all in. In the middle of the room was the treadmill, still draped in those rainbow-colored wires and that damn God Helmet. It was exactly as I remembered. The sun angled through the skylight in distinct rays. Minute dust particles sparkled in the beams of light. We gulped in unison.

"So this…is where they…found her?" Ben stammered. "I'm so sorry, Dad. I didn't know. This is real shit. I'm sorry. We gotta do this, don't we?"

"Thank you for that; it is some real shit. Let's do this."

Ben took out his phone and started taking pictures—the untainted scene, if you will. I'm glad he got right to it, as it was going to get real heavy if we didn't get down to business. Standing back, we scanned the room with intense criticism. The treadmill lay more or less in the middle of the room. Directly in front of it was a curved two-panel projection screen. Directly behind the projection screen was the massive antenna that extended up through a skylight and climbed over twenty feet into the air. It was constructed of three two-inch rods connected in a triangle by geometrically positioned reinforcing studs. Rainbow-colored wires were tied to one of the main supporting rods and continued skyward, out of sight. Behind that was a storage area that abutted the back wall. There were a variety of boxes and filing cabinets and a full-length mirror. At the back of the treadmill lay what appeared to be the brains of the operation. Hanging directly behind the treadmill was a ceiling-mounted camera and a projector of sorts. Below this, a mass of wires led to two card tables against the front wall. The tables were home to a variety of computing equipment. There were two oversized desktop computers and a laptop, monitors, and various peripherals connected to them. Wires from all over the room converged at the back of the computers. Most of what we were looking at seemed rather pedestrian and underwhelming. From the floor, a bizarre, mechanical armature rose to waist height just off to the side of the treadmill. At the end of the arm was a pine bough. Now this would need some explaining.

We began looking a bit closer at each component. Starting with the treadmill, we noticed something was missing. The raised control panel and handholds were removed. It was just a flat treadmill with no obvious controls. In addition to the wires leading out of the God Helmet, there were wires coming out of the bottom of the treadmill that also led to the computer bank. We assumed this meant the treadmill was controlled through the computer system. Then we noticed something really odd. Directly in front of the treadmill at about knee height was a pedestal. On top of the pedestal was a large crystal. It was a perfectly formed cube, and it was as clear as pure glass. This, too, had wires leading over to the computer bank. Lord knows what this thing was about.

We then began to trace the multitude of wires that emanated from the back of the computers. Most of them went back to the components we identified. We followed a bundle of wires to the massive antenna that was anchored behind the projection screens in the storage area. Finally, we followed the last of the wires off to the far side of the room. These wires connected to a nondescript cubic box about the size of a footstool. It had no external character other than a few colored lights and slotted air vents at its base. It was plugged into an uninterruptible power supply. We had no idea what this could be. Perhaps it was a mass-storage device.

The skylight above was now limited to the faint twilight lingering over the mountains off to the west. I was getting tired and felt we had done enough for now. "Ben, I think this is going to do it for me," I said with a slight yawn.

"Really, Dad? This is just starting to get interesting. Don't you want to turn some of this shit on and see what happens?"

"No, I think I want to save that for when I'm fresh. I'm headed to bed. Knock yourself out if you like." I headed to the door.

"All right. I'm going to stay up for a while and dig a little deeper. I'll see you in the morning."

"Okay, Ben, but please don't touch the God Helmet without me. Good night." And off to bed I went.

I awoke to the clanging of pots and pans and dishes. The sun was just coming up. What's Ben doing out there? I ground my eyes with the heels of my hands and further messed my hair in an attempt to wake up. I liked getting up early, but it was usually on my own terms. Sitting up, I pulled on my sweats and stumbled to the kitchen. There was Ben working on multiple breakfast items at once. His Jewfro was now looking like a mad scientist's. Something was definitely up. "What's going on, Ben?"

"Jesus, Dad, you scared the shit out of me. Sup?"

"What's up with me? You're the one who's up! What's for breakfast? I can only imagine what you've been up to. Have you been up all night? Did you do any time traveling?"

"Oh God, Dad, you can't even imagine. Yes, I've been up all night. The shit works, Dad! There's lots to do, but I'm starting to understand what she was doing and how. I had no idea how adept she was with computers. She made it so simple to use. Her use of the third-person perspective is crazy."

"Hold on there, tiger. I just woke up; give me a chance to sort myself out. I need some coffee, and we'll discuss this over breakfast. You planning on sleeping today?"

The morning mountain air was delightful but chilly, so I started a fire in the woodstove and sat down with my coffee. I can't wait to see where this is going. Ben's been up all night getting this thing working, God. I knew he could figure stuff out, especially techy stuff—but, Jesus, one night? I can't believe it; is this really going to happen?

We sat down in the breakfast nook and had Ben's famous bacon and eggs. The key is to cook everything in bacon fat. Good Jewish breakfast. My brain was now starting to function, and looking straight at Ben, I inquired in my best *Caddy Shack*, "Well, we're waiting?"

Ben did not hesitate; he started right in. "She's got it set up to run various programs. A program runs the whole thing in unison. Everything is integrated. You start a program, and it keys up music and projects a scene on the screen. The program I was playing with starts with a natural setting in the woods, like around here. In its simplest form, you get on the treadmill, and as you start moving, the scenery moves past you as it matches your pace. It's realistic but two dimensional and flat. This part of it is really nothing new, but this is just the beginning.

"The strobe lights are real interesting. When activated, they pulse to the music, like right out of the sixties or something. Again, nothing new, right? What's really cool is they also affect the lighting in the projected scene. In this program, you're running through a grove of aspen trees. The light from the sun is flickering randomly as it breaks through the partially covered canopy. The flickering isn't quite random, however; there's an undecipherable pattern to it. This is because you're moving through beams of light at a particular pace. The strobe light picks up on this pattern and intensifies it. So now the whole room is pulsing to the cadence of moving light beams. It's a weird sensation.

"Remember what I was saying about light and music and how it can cause seizures? It's kind of like that, but you don't have a seizure. If you kind of defocus and let the pulsing light take hold, it pushes you into a hypnotic state. You know what's going on around you, but it almost seems secondary or third person, like you're separated from your surroundings. It's hard to describe, but it's real; you don't really have to try too hard; you just gotta let go. It's funny because, since I started running, I've been searching for something to help me achieve Sally's active meditation. I've noticed a mild version of this effect when running through broken light. It could be tree leaves or even something like a cyclone fence. The light just has to be broken up. It's all about the light, Dad."

"That's crazy. I've read about light-source modulation and its effect on brain wave patterns, so that makes sense. So hang on—back up a minute. Everything was working? You just turned it on and—*bam*—it works?"

"Of course not, Dad. I *was* up all night."

"Okay, brainiac, I'll take your word for it. Please continue."

"Yeah, so that was the strobe light. Of course it gets even better. The trippy part is her use of the virtual reality goggles. I did a little research on this at home. They've discovered that you can use virtual reality to dislodge yourself from your body. You can create an out-of-body experience with virtual reality, seemingly at will. The concept is this: the content feed in the virtual reality isn't a computer-generated scene but your current scene, only you're viewing yourself from behind and slightly above, in real time. Your eyes are essentially spatially repositioned behind and slightly above your actual position. In this case, you're witnessing yourself from behind progressing through the scene on the screen in front of you. You can solidify the out-of-body experience with what's called tactile congruity. This means as you're running through the forest and you brush up against a tree branch, you're touched in real life by a stick or branch in the exact same spot on your body. This enforces the concept that the removed perspective of your body is really you. Believe me, 'cause I tried it; this really fools the senses."

"Are you telling me you had an out-of-body experience last night? Are you shitting me? I always thought that was some rare, unexplainable phenomenon. Isn't it related to near-death experiences with the tunnel and the light or hovering over yourself while nearly dying on the operating table?"

"That's all true, but this is apparently true too. They have documented it as being reliably repeatable. Imagine that—*poof*—you're out of your body. I don't know, but, yes, I did try it last night, and I did have an out-of-body experience. What's becoming apparent to me is that Sally's use of multiple-sensory inputs done simultaneously jogs your mind to who knows where. I'm not sure where I went, but I don't know when I'll sleep again. I'm so wired, and honestly, I'm afraid of where my sleeping mind will go. It's that weird, Dad."

"Holy Jesus, Ben, that's some crazy stuff. So the weird armature with the pine bough, that's the tactile input? That thing slaps your side in time with the projected scene? That's diabolical—I love it. So did it work as it did in the publications? Were you scared? What does it mean to be out of your body exactly?"

39

"First of all, there's sooo much going on that there's no time to be scared. I think part of it is just pure sensory overload. Your mind recoils a bit and attempts to filter some of it out. This filtering kind of fogs the experience and swirls it all together to the point you're not sure what's sound and what's light, and as a result, you're not sure where you are in the scene. Underlying all this, you're frigging running on a treadmill. Without the virtual goggles, it's very mesmerizing, and you kind of get pulled into the scene projected on the screen. That alone is quite compelling, but when you use the virtual reality goggles, it enters a whole other realm. At first it's completely disorienting and dizzying. Honestly, I don't know how I didn't fall flat on my face. Very quickly, however, you get used to viewing yourself from behind, progressing through the wooded scene. At this point you're not really having an out-of-body experience. It's when you brush up against a tree branch in the scene and it's simultaneously replicated by the armature whacking you on the same spot that your mind freaks. *Bam*—you're more than watching from behind and above: you are behind and above. You know it's you out in front, but your entire being is spatially removed and is hovering and following yourself as you jog through the woods."

"Wow, that's completely crazy. So if you're viewing yourself from behind, how does the projected scene get into the virtual goggles?"

"Well, that part is a bit kludgy, but I have some ideas how to improve it. It's currently set up so the rear camera is also recording the projected screen. The screen can be viewed head-on when not using the virtual reality goggles. When using the virtual reality goggles, there's a second position setting for the screens. They both rotate ninety degrees so that the curved part is vertically oriented, and they slide down and toward the treadmill so that they align with the rear-mounted camera. This enables the projected scene to fill the camera frame. It's really quite an elegant solution, but like I said, I think I can improve on it."

I took the last sip of my coffee and sopped up the remaining egg yolk with my bagel. Ben started collecting our dishes and moved into the kitchen for cleanup. We were both suddenly silent, taking in and contemplating what Ben had learned about Sally's device. We had not even been here for twenty-four hours, and we'd learned so much. As my mind wandered further off, it eventually settled on a single question. Mac said Sally was working on a device that enabled her to recover or revisit memories. I think she called it memory chasing. How does that fit into what we've learned so far? What does active meditation and an out-of-body experience have to do with memory chasing?

"Ben, what about the memory-recovery aspect? I thought that's what this contraption was all about? That's what Mac said anyway. You haven't said anything about that yet. Are you saving that for last?"

"Yes, that's true, but I'm not saving it. I haven't seen anything of the sort yet. I was really only focused on one of her programs. The run through the woods appeared to be an older program and seemed to me to be a primer or introduction to the apparatus. Oh, and it was labeled *program number one*. There's still a lot to learn here. I have a feeling there's much more to figure out. Why don't you get cleaned up and dressed, and I'll walk you through what I've learned so far."

Ben set the apparatus up in its basic mode, just a treadmill with the wooded scene progressing on the screens. I stepped up on the treadmill and began jogging at a slow pace. The scenery progression matched my pace precisely. I sped up my pace, and the scenery passed by at exactly my increased speed. This alone was impressive but not really anything new or groundbreaking. Then he turned on the music. I had selected some Sly and Robbie classic-seventies dub, as it was a great example of the style of music that helped me reach a meditative state while on a normal run. I adjusted my tempo to match the music, and the rolling scenery immediately matched my pace. I jogged along and, by the middle of the second song, was completely mesmerized. I felt totally relaxed and in harmony with the music and the passing scenery.

As I progressed, the pine forest gave way to majestic aspens. I entered the aspen grove, and the sunlight was breaking through in scattered beams of light. At this point, Ben activated the strobe light. This greatly intensified the hypnotic effect of the broken-light patterns, as it was somehow syncopated to the strobe. At first it was a bit disorienting, but soon it meshed with the scene and the music. I squinted my eyes, as I commonly do when jogging, to help disengage with my surroundings. This made it all seem very real. The blurring of the scenery enabled me to withdraw into my mind and concentrate on the music and connect my footsteps with the beat more precisely. My mind started wandering further and further away. I was not thinking about anything specific. My thoughts were not being consciously guided. It was like I was daydreaming, observing the unguided musings of my mind. I almost forgot I was jogging on a treadmill. I was actively meditating. Then I heard a voice. It sounded familiar. Who was that? I calmly noted. The voice got louder, and it was then I realized it was Ben.

"Dad! Dad! *Dad!* Are you all right?

"Holy shit, Ben, you startled me." I slowed my pace down and then came to a stop and hopped off the treadmill.

41

"Where do you keep going? You must've been enjoying your run," Ben continued. "Sorry, I had to take a call, so I went to the cabin. It went way longer than I anticipated. Have you been running this whole time?"

"Well, yes, I have," I replied. "Why? I was just getting into it."

"Just getting into it—that's funny, Dad. You've been out here running for at least thirty minutes."

"What're you talking about? I just got going, and you interrupted a very soothing run. I think I was actively meditating. Wait—did you say thirty minutes? There's no way that's possible."

"Oh it's not only possible—it *has* been thirty minutes since you got on that thing."

I was completely dumbfounded. How was that possible? It felt like just a few minutes. What just happened? I immediately thought of an axiom I had about running. I figured you'd know you were in a meditative state when you lost track of time and space while running. I recalled my run not long ago in the fresh morning snow. I was totally zoned out and was tackled by a dog from behind. What I had just experienced on the treadmill was very similar, but the fact that I was in rapture for thirty minutes set it way apart.

"Wow, Ben, that was crazy. That was truly amazing. I'm afraid of what else this thing does."

"Are you all right? That's crazy—you had no idea you were going for half an hour? You really took to that experience. Why don't you sit down for a minute, and I'll set up the virtual reality program. This is really gonna blow your mind."

I took a seat while Ben fiddled with the equipment. He rearranged the screens and set the computers to cue the next adventure. As I sat there gathering my thoughts, I imagined Sally's effort to get this whole thing going. How did she do all this? There was clearly more to my daughter than I ever imagined. How could I have not known she had these talents. I felt a warmth spread over my body. It was more than warmth—I was feeling her memory, her presence. The warmth turned to joy. I was feeling her soul by being around something she held so dear. The joy then poured down my cheeks. I started to sob. The sobbing started to mix with joyous laughter. Was I losing it? This is so powerful, I thought.

"Dad! *Dad!* What's going on—are you okay?"

"Oh Jesus, Ben, wow, I really was out there," I said, gaining my composure. "I'm okay. I just started thinking of Sally and all she had done here and how I didn't really know her and the next thing I know I'm bawling like a baby."

Ben came over and hugged me deeply, and then he started crying. As before, the sobbing eventually evolved into hysterical laughter. We hugged some more, and Ben said, "You know it's okay to miss her, Dad."

I was suddenly choked up again and barely got the words out. "I know, son. I know now."

We took a break and went for a short hike. The property Sally's cabin was on covered forty-some acres. We headed uphill toward Mount Princeton to find the western edge of the property. The thin air made us look like unfit city folks. We had to stop and catch our breaths every hundred yards or so. Granted, it was all uphill, but it was humbling for a couple of runners. Soon we came across a barbed wire fence and figured this was it. Though we were only a third of a mile from the cabin, the unobstructed view of the Arkansas River Valley from the higher vantage point was exceptional. Mount Princeton and the Collegiate Peaks guarded our backs to an elevation of fourteen thousand feet plus. Out in front of us spread the Arkansas River Valley. The sloped terraces of rocks and gravel that used to be part of Mount Princeton reached nearly continuously to the Arkansas River on the east side of the valley. Sharp tributary valleys that cut into the sloped plain gave refuge to a variety of trees and brush. In the distance, dark dots of cattle mowed away in the prairie grass. Taking it all in gave us pause and soothed our souls.

Gazing off in the distance, I asked Ben, "Do you ever wonder why she did this? It's one thing to have the know-how, but what was driving her? What was she trying to figure out? What was she looking for?"

Ben cleared his throat. "Sort of…but I don't know." He paused to collect his thoughts. "Don't take this the wrong way, because I believe she could have done all this, but did you ever think someone was helping her?"

"Wow, that's a big one. I guess I haven't. If there was someone else, that would kinda explain why this seems so unexpected. Maybe I do know Sally, and it's someone else that I don't know. Of course Mac didn't say there was anybody else. Either way, I still gotta wonder about the *why*."

43

With that we headed back to the cabin and had some lunch. Ben told me a little more of what to expect when I strapped on the virtual reality goggles. I was ready but also a bit nervous. We finished our lunch and headed for the studio. Ben put the finishing touches on the settings as I readied myself for another adventurous run. I've always wondered what an out-of-body experience was about. Many people relate it to the soul leaving the body. That seemed to make sense to me but really only in a deathbed setting. Something definitely happens at death. I've seen it more than once. Right at the moment of death, you can feel a presence escaping their body. Your own body tingles as it senses this essence, like unexpectedly bumping into someone in the dark. It's not spooky though; it's a primal, ethereal understanding without knowing. You feel the person's soul escape, seemingly skyward. At that instant you understand there is way more going on than you ever imagined. A feeling rushes and overcomes your consciousness, a feeling of absolute joy because you realize they are not done but going somewhere else. It doesn't sound like that's where I'm going, thank God. Just a little hover through the woods—not a big deal.

"Okay, are you ready for this, old man? I hope you went to the bathroom 'cause this'll work it right out of you!"

"Jesus, Ben, give an old man a chance," I retorted. "Just promise me you won't go off and forget about me again. Please hang out next to the treadmill while I try this out."

"Yeah, yeah, yeah, I promise I'll be right here. Just fall to the left if you're going down, Dad."

With that Ben fired up the program. The scene started just as before. I was on the edge of a pine forest. I started walking toward the forest, and the scene progressed toward me at a slow pace. I pulled the goggles over my eyes. I had selected a playlist that started with an old favorite. *My Life in the Bush of Ghosts* by Brian Eno and David Byrne was one of the most transcendental albums I'd ever heard. The music alone can send you to strange places. The lead vocals are samples from disparate sources. Samples include a radio–talk show host, an evangelical preacher, Muslim prayer chants, and my favorite, a sample of an actual exorcism. It is rhythm driven with tons of spacey overlays, perfect for active meditation.

The goggles were a bit confusing at first because the imagery was somewhat jumbled. Something snapped in the signal, and—*boom*—everything became clear and vivid. I saw someone running just below and in front of me, and it was very confusing. A sensation started to overtake my body. I was struck with a wave of vertigo. I felt like I needed to stop, so I slowed down. The running person slowed down at exactly the same time and at the same pace. This was very discomforting, and I involuntarily threw my arms out as if to catch myself. The runner threw his arms out simultaneously, and it was then I realized that the runner was me. Oh yeah, out of the body, how could this not have been immediately apparent.

The shock of the removed perspective initially disrupted all other thought as my brain tried to resolve what it was witnessing. I settled down and picked up my pace to time it to the music. It started to feel enjoyable. I saw my body thumping away down there, but I was feeling it up here. It was like there were two of us. Yes, two of us, just like I learned from *Rational Recovery*. There was the conscious, thinking brain and the primal, subconscious brain. It felt like I was riding an invisible horse, chasing myself down. I started to play with primal, running Sandy by twirling my arms. I saw primal Sandy's arms twirl, but conscious, thinking Sandy felt it. This was very freaky but also seemed to solidify the disconnection. I was disembodied. But who was guiding who? I focused on the run and tried to relax. Deep breaths, I thought, deep breaths.

Deeper into the forest I went. I could see it was lit up ahead, it was the aspen grove. The broken beams of light started breaking across running Sandy. The strobe came on slowly as the flickering beams intensified. I squinted my eyes in an attempt to fade into the scene. It was getting really weird. I realized the disembodiment was more than just computer trickery. I was up here, but I was also down there. I felt like I should be able to talk to running Sandy. The trees narrowed, and a low-hanging branch whacked my thigh. I felt a strike precisely where I saw running Sandy get struck. This was it— *bam*. The armature had mimicked the scene with a whack on my actual thigh. The tactile congruity sent me into full-blown out-of-body reality. I was truly seeing myself, not just as an observer but as an empathetic, silent participant. It was like seeing yourself in the mirror for the first time. Oh, so that's what I look like—that's me. I was reminded of classic Hollywood plots where the main character is in heaven, watching their bad behavior.

By seeing myself in this manner, I was feeling a closeness, a connectedness to myself. I was overwhelmed by a sense of empathy. I felt like I should be cheering myself on. I started to notice details about myself. I was beginning to understand simple things that I never before recognized. My left foot flings out to the left on my back stride. I'm not quite symmetrical, and why am I looking down. Look up; look up, I encouraged, and I did. I saw my hair for the first time from behind. I have a cowlick I've worried about my whole life, but now I saw it was just hair being hair, like anybody else's. I saw what I looked like, warts and all, and it was sooo moving. It's-okay-to-be-me thoughts flooded my brain. I was overwhelmed with a sense of recognition.

So that's what I look like, and it's okay—it's all okay, Sandy. I was seeing myself for the first time.

I settled into the run and let the music guide me. I squinted and defocused in an effort to meld into the scene. I brushed up against more low-hanging branches and was struck by the armature again. Each time this happened, it dislocated me even further. It felt like my hovering position was moving farther away and then back again. Each time, I felt like my connection to running Sandy was getting more tenuous. Where would I go if I got too far away? I couldn't leave running Sandy alone—what would happen? Warmth began to spread from my feet up through my body. I didn't like where this was going and began to panic. Was this the near-death experience? Was I witnessing my own soul leaving my body? For some reason I wanted to see disembodied Sandy, so I turned my head around to look up at myself. This sent me fading to the left, and the next thing I knew, I was feeling discomfort and pain. My arm struck something hard, and I saw myself lying on the ground. I was very confused, as I wasn't lying on the ground in the scene, but off the side of the treadmill. Then everything went black. I heard a voice from afar, and then it seemed to get closer. I knew that voice—who was it? Something was tugging at my shoulders.

"Dad, Dad, *Dad!* Are you all right? Holy shit."

I pulled the goggles off and was staring up through the skylight. I saw the antenna reaching skyward in the blazing afternoon sun. As I was about to respond to Ben, I realized something was staring at me through the skylight. I raised my arm to point at it, but it pulled away from the opening. "Ben, it's that darn cat again. What's the deal with that thing? That cat is starting to spook me."

Ben helped me to my feet and led me over to the couch. I realized I was exhausted and needed to regroup. That was some trip. It only lasted a few minutes, I think, but was so very powerful. The disembodiment really stressed my mind and, I assumed, caused my fatigue. I really didn't expect it to be so emotional. I certainly didn't expect to be flooded with empathy for myself. It felt hauntingly similar to the satori I had when I was examining my behavior with alcohol, when I realized I needed to forgive myself, that I was no different than anyone else, when I learned to truly love myself, warts and all. Somehow observing myself as a disinterested party, to observe myself live from a distance, generated a powerful sense of empathy and connectedness. Strange that being out of my body would induce a feeling of connectedness.

"Earth to Dad. Earth to Dad; come in, Dad. Where do you keep going, man? You fell right off that thing. Are you all right? How does your arm feel? You landed right on it. I guess we shouldn't be turning around while on the treadmill. You know you won't see anyone back there?"

"Yeah, yeah, yeah, I'm sure this shit is just another run in the park for you. I guess I freaked a bit there. It was crazy, Ben, I was really getting into it, and then the tactile-congruity thing started whacking me, and that sent me to another level of disembodiment. I felt myself getting farther and farther away. That's when I panicked because I wasn't sure if I was going to come back. I don't know why I thought I'd see myself back there. What was that all about?"

"That is weird. It's almost like your body took control and wanted to see where its consciousness was. How about that for evidence of two beings in one? That's powerful shit for sure. I gotta get on this thing again."

We spent the rest of the day taking turns on the disembodiment treadmill. After a few runs, we became more comfortable with the device. Having the goggles on seemed normal and less of a distraction. As it turned out, the end of the run took you right back to the beginning of the scene, at the entrance to the forest. It was an infinite loop. It was brilliant yet so obvious. It never felt repetitive. I suppose the brain had enough to deal with to not become bored with the repeating scenery. It was beginning to feel like a marvelous toy, only it wasn't an object—it was a game for the mind and, perhaps, soul.

That night over dinner, I told Ben I had a lunch date with a good friend, Willy. I explained to Ben he was an old college buddy that I had reconnected with. I told him I related to Willy what happened at the funeral pyre, that there seemed to be an earthquake and a bizarre corresponding light show, and about the experience Mac witnessed at Sally's. Willy was a geologist. I asked him if he could explain the phenomena. I guess he'd done his research and wanted to get back to me about his findings. "He's gonna be coming through town tomorrow, so we're gonna have lunch. You want to go with me, Ben?"

"Hell yes, I wanna go. I remember Willy. He's one irreverent scientist. I always wanted to be like him, especially the geologist part. I'll never forget when he crushed my dreams: He told me to not even think of being a geologist. It will surely feed your mind, but it will never feed your family, he said. Can you believe that? Where has he been? It's been forever."

"He said that to you? That's certainly irreverent. Willy's kind of been all over the place. He did his best to hang on to a career in the oil-and-gas industry with its wild boom-and-bust cycles. He did some time overseas in the business, Jakarta I think he said. He told me he got fed up being laid-off every few years. I think he also got tired of the conservative nature, the good-old-boy network of oil and gas. He's piddling around, part-time consulting for the geothermal-energy business now. Well, good, I'm sure he'll be pleased to see you. He was hoping you'd come along."

Geologist Fault

We awoke to yet another bluebird Colorado day—cool, crisp air and a cloudless sky of the deepest blue imaginable. I always thought on days like that, this is why I live here. In Colorado, you are constantly reminded of this, as these types of days are a regular occurrence. We had our coffee outside to take it all in. After a short walk around the property, we showered, dressed, and headed into town.

Salida is about a half hour from Sally's. It's a quaint Western town that was originally a major railroad hub for the Rockies. Its downtown has many of the original brick buildings beautifully restored to their late-1800s Victorian/Edwardian charm. The railroads are long gone, but the town still supports a thriving ranching community. It has nothing in common with towns along the I-70 corridor, which have been overrun by the ski industry and the masses that support it. Salida retains much of its original feel and look. While it has become somewhat of a retirement community for Front Rangers, it looks the same to me today as it did thirty years ago, the first time I came here. Its populous is not just retirees and ranchers; there is a thriving white water rafting community as well. The Arkansas River flows right through the east side of town. Because of this, it is home to FIBArk, the world's first white water competition. The river rats provide a youthful vibrance and a decidedly hippie feel to the town. This is what brought Sally here, white water rafting and a decent party scene. I've always loved Salida—she seems so welcoming and kicked back.

As we entered town, we headed down F Street and made our way to the Boathouse Cantina. The Boathouse has the best location in town; it sits directly on the Arkansas River. You haven't been to Salida until you've spent a leisurely afternoon at the Cantina drinking beer and admiring the view out the open-air windows on a lazy summer day with good friends. Perfect, now where was that wily Willy?

As we entered the Boathouse, we rounded the corner to the main dining/drinking area. I was looking for Willy when I was grabbed from behind in an enormous bear hug. "Mister Beachcomber, my Beachcomber, so good to smell you my friend." It was Willy, and his presence was bigger than ever. Willy let me go and turned to Ben. "Holy Jesus, it's little Ben turned big Ben." He bear-hugged Ben and lifted him off the ground. "Last time I saw you, you were just a little kid; now look at you." We finished the greeting off with a three-way bear hug that culminated in a group belly laugh.

Willy was a big man with an even-bigger heart. He wore his emotions on his sleeve and read other's emotions instantly. Somehow life always seemed concentrated in this man, and just being around him brought the glow of life out of you. Our original connection was somewhat spiritual. When I was in high school, my dad took me to visit the college that I would eventually graduate from. We toured the campus, visiting all the pertinent buildings of this small liberal arts college. It seemed all right to me, but being eighteen, I needed to know I'd make friends. Buildings don't provide much comfort in that category. It didn't occur to me that I needed a sign to say it would be all right, but that's exactly what I got. As we were about to leave the geology floor of the science building, I noticed one of the student offices had a poster proudly displayed. It was Stealie, the Grateful Dead's Steal Your Face artwork. I was a big Deadhead then, and I knew in an instant that I'd have at least one friend. That was all it took. I applied and was accepted. Within the first few weeks at my new school, I was invited to a party. As I was parking my car in front of the party house, I unceremoniously banged into the car in front of me. Several of the partygoers came out to see what the bang was all about. As I got out of my car, they approached with red Solo cups in hand. As I looked over the group, I noticed the obvious ringleader was wearing the iconic Stealie shirt. I knew instantly this guy would be a great friend. It was Willy, wily Willy. The rest was history.

We made our way to a table overlooking the river. Willy ordered beers for him and Ben, and I made do with my usual soda water and lime. I'd never not drank with Willy, and this was weird. In his impeccable way, he sensed the weirdness and dissolved it like an alchemist. "Don't worry, Beachcomber. I'll still love you when I'm drunk and you're not." It was a beautiful gesture that came out just right, humor and understanding. Thank God some things just never change.

"So, Dad, what's with Beachcomber?" Ben inquired. "I assume it's your nickname that I've never heard of."

"Well, Ben, you gotta say his full name, and you'll get it," Willy jumped in. "Sandy Beachcomber. Get it?"

"Oh God, Dad, really, Sandy Beachcomber? That's like a bad dad joke, but I kind of like it."

"Come on, Ben," Willy jumped in again. "It's perfect! In fact, it was perfectly delivered to me via a lightning bolt of LSD one beautiful spring day, the day your father and I got started on our quest to decipher the universe."

This jolt of understanding of our relationship caused Ben to spit his beer all over Willy. Then the laugher began, and it wouldn't stop. We laughed until we realized it wasn't really that funny, then we laughed at that. We were embarking on a fairly trippy endeavor, and here we were with Captain Trips reminding me of my roots. Within just a few minutes of being around Willy, everything felt as it had so many years ago. Having Ben there felt so right. Everyone needed a little Willy. We settled in, got caught up, and told a few stories. We eventually came to the crux of the biscuit: what was going on at the pyre and at Sally's cabin with the lights and earthquakes. Willy had something to tell, and I was ready to hear it.

"So, Willy, I'm anxious to hear what you found out," I said. "We've been into some weird science ourselves, and I want to tell you about it, but first, what did you learn?"

"All righty then, is it that time?" Willy extolled. "I did uncover some things. I gotta tell you though, some of it is way out there. Let's make sure I understand the timeline of events. You said at Sally's death there was an event that included a cosmic light show that culminated in an earthquake. Then a few days later at her funeral pyre, there was a similar event. In each case, the swirling blue-and-orange lights preceded a loud boom then an earthquake. Didn't you say there was a report of an earthquake in the news or something the next day after the funeral?"

"Yeah, that's it in a nutshell. Oh, and we did seem to lose track of a couple hours, woke up tripping, and Sally's body disappeared," I added sarcastically. "Yeah, that's it. I'm sorry; that was outta hand. Yes, first the swirling lights, then the boom, and it culminated with an earthquake. Apparently the same thing happened at Sally's cabin. We obviously weren't there, but one of Sally's best friends witnessed it."

"Hey, it's okay, Sandy. I can't imagine what you've been through. Losing Sally is bad enough, but then God jumps in the middle of it, I get it—that's a lot."

"We did read the next day that there was a minor earthquake outside of Crestone," Ben added.

"Well, good then, we're on the same page—just wanted to make sure I wasn't barking up the wrong tree. This is the deal, boys: I checked with the USGS, and they definitely have record of earthquakes in that exact time frame. One on the day of Sally's death that corresponds to the reported time of death. This one was a 3.1 quake and was centered underneath Mount Princeton. The other one occurred at the time of the funeral and was centered south of Crestone under the Sangre de Cristo Mountains. This one was a 3.7-magnitude quake. You know earthquakes can and do generate sound that can be quite loud. So that's really the easy part and maybe nothing more than confirming what you already knew. You'll be surprised to know, however, the remaining phenomenon has been discussed in the literature. Mostly it's been pooh-poohed, but it's recognized."

"All right then," I replied. "We got earthquakes nearby, and they make booming sounds. Please go on. What about the remaining phenomenon? What do you mean pooh-poohed?"

"It's not well understood, but there have been a number of scientists that have investigated lights that are clearly associated with earthquakes. Oddly, very few of them are geologist. Of course I'm thinking maybe I should change this. So you guys know a little geology, don't you? You've heard of plate tectonics, mountain building, and the like? Well, associated with these things is what physically happens to the rocks. They get crumpled, folded, and faulted. Along mountain fronts, you always have lots of faults, and some of them can be quite large. These large faults are directly associated with the mountain-building process, which is typically driven by tectonic forces. The Arkansas Valley and its southern counterpart, the San Luis Valley, used to be connected along a structural feature called a rift system. This rift system went for hundreds of miles and was an attempt at breaking the continent apart. Thankfully it failed. Did you know the Arkansas River used to flow through this valley and continued southward through the San Luis Valley? Anyway, these large, regional faults can build up huge amounts of stress. When the stress exceeds the rock strength, the rock ruptures, and we get an earthquake. So that's the basics—oh, then you feel the shock wave traveling outward from the epicenter. These are huge forces at work here; it's not hard to imagine it's gonna make some noise."

"That's very interesting," injected Ben. "Is there a lot of faulting going on around here?"

"There is a lot of faulting, but it's not an active-plate boundary like California, and it's certainly not the damaging, high-magnitude style of faulting. This is where it starts getting really interesting, you guys. The lights, what about the lights? There are plenty of documented accounts, even photos and videos of lights that coincide with earthquakes. The lights can be varied in their presentation. Commonly, they're multiple single-point lights of varying color and intensity. Sometimes they are very similar to ball lightning, which typically moves around, sometimes quite fast. Other times these lights can be sheetlike and multicolored. These sheets of light have been reported to move around like a curtain being pulled up and down, similar to the aurora borealis.

"There is one researcher who stands out amongst all the rest regarding light phenomena associated with geophysical forces. His name is Dr. Michael Persinger. He taught psychology at Laurentian University in Ontario, Canada. I guess he held a geology degree as well, so there's one for the good guys. I don't pretend to understand exactly how the light gets generated from the stress of a fault, but suffice it to say, it happens. Apparently, the stress builds up weak magnetic and corresponding electric fields around the fault zone. At the surface, this can concentrate in the form of high-energy plasma and the resultant lights, which he called anomalous luminous phenomena, or ALPs. The ALPs leave behind a residue on the surface composed of various minerals, including sulfur compounds. He has a whole theory, as you might expect; it's called the Tectonic Strain Theory. Using a variety of UFO-sighting databases, he correlated lights reported as UFOs over the last fifty years to major fault boundaries and found that 40 percent of the time there was a strong correlation. Of course he's not saying there are UFOs, just that strange lights correlate to earthquakes and are probably ALPs generated by the earthquakes, not UFOs."

I looked over at Ben, and his mouth was hanging open. "Ben, are you getting all this? Well that's some crazy shit there, Willy, great balls of fire. So you think that's what happened? The lights were generated by an earthquake?"

Ben chirped up, "That's crazy, Willy. Did you know that the San Luis Valley has some of the highest-reported UFO sightings anywhere on the planet? It's become a thing there. There's an actual UFO sighting area in the valley just north of the sand dunes near Crestone. This guy charges like twenty-five bucks to lie in the middle of the desert in the hope of spotting a UFO. He's even built an elevated viewing platform and has a gift shop that sells snacks."

"What?" Willy said with astonishment. "Someone is always trying to make a buck. To continue—'cause that ain't all, folks—Dr. Persinger was a psychologist, and his focus was on neuroscience. In particular, he was searching for a connection between brain function and spiritual experiences. In a clinical setting, he used pulsating weak magnetic fields to stimulate the brain. I believe this magnetic field is focused on the temporal lobes. His subjects reported a wide variety of emotional responses, from calming and clarity of thinking to feeling the presence of others, including the Almighty. This is crazy stuff, I'm telling you. His wildest-reaching claim is that magnetic fields in the brain are connected to Earth's magnetic field. Ultimately, he was looking for a link between individuality and a collective

53

brain of all humans that is supported by Earth's magnetic field. Somehow, he showed empirically that the sum of all living, human brain energy is equal to the energy in Earth's magnetic field. He also believed that people can and do communicate over vast distances through Earth's magnetic field. He demonstrated, in a clinical setting, that two people can communicate rudimentary thoughts when spatially separated. In this experiment, one of the subjects was asleep, and the other was an artist contemplating a still life painting. They were separated by hundreds of feet in different rooms. The artist wrote down what he was thinking about while contemplating the still life, and the sleeper wrote down what he was dreaming about. When comparing their recollections, there were way too many similarities to be a coincident. Apparently it was repeatable."

"That's astounding, but what does it have to do with our issue?" I inquired.

"Well, I'm getting to that, Sandy; hang on—back to the ALPs. The lights generated by the stress field of a fault system are more than just lights, according to Persinger. They have or are electromagnetic energy. They are integrated with Earth's magnetic field. When you were surrounded by the swirling lights, you were also surrounded by a weak electromagnetic field. This electromagnetic field can do some weird shit. ALPs have been documented to cause seizures, blackouts, feelings of otherworldliness, connection to others, and the presence of the Almighty. Persinger postulates that ALPs are connected to Earth's magnetic field, which, as I said, could contain connections to all human brains."

"So are you saying that the fugue state we were in at the funeral pyre was the result of being bombarded by an electromagnetic field?" I inquired.

"Look, Sandy, I don't know what happened, but this guy's work would suggest that it's a strong possibility," Willy replied. "Besides, we don't have a better explanation, or any explanation other than this, for that matter. If this is true, I'm gonna hunt Dr. Persinger down and worship him! His theories seem completely crazy, but I swear, if he's right, it could be the first step in really understanding what we as humans really are. Perhaps we are one enormous collective organism—wouldn't that be wild? His God Helmet is friggin' crazy. You know you can order one online."

"Whoa, whoa, whoa, did you just say God Helmet?" I said in astonishment. "How do you know about the God Helmet?"

"Yes, I did; that's what I was telling you," Willy responded. "It's the device that elicits good vibes all the way up to meeting God. I guess I didn't mention it by name, but yeah, that's what it's called, the *God Helmet*."

"Holy shit, Willy," Ben chimed in. "The God Helmet is one of the devices Sally was screwing around with. You know when they found her she was wearing one. I got one recently to try to figure out what she was up to. It seems instrumental in her quest."

"You have one? Sally had one? Are you kidding me?" Willy retorted. "Now there's a cosmic connection, eh?"

"Oh my God, Willy," I cried out. "This is connected in so many ways. How is it that the same guy who developed the God Helmet is the same one that has a theory that ties into the earthquake lights and our fugue state? This is getting very weird indeed. Wait a minute—Sally must've known this. It can't be a coincidence, can it?"

"Well, Sandy, now you'd better tell me about your weird science. I'm a little bit lost here."

I told Willy about Sally's studio and the Memory Chaser. I walked him through what Ben and I had been working on. The treadmill, the projection screen, the strobe light effect of light patterns, the virtual reality goggles, and the out-of-body experience, the whole thing. I told Willy where we were in deciphering Sally's device. I explained how we seemed to be only scratching the surface of what her Memory Chaser could do. I expressed my fear of the God Helmet—a well-founded fear. I expressed my reluctance to trying out the helmet. Now, however, my curiosity was getting the better of me. I knew we'd eventually have to try the God Helmet, but I was quite anxious. Now, not only could I not keep putting it off but I was thinking we'd better get on it. Thinking about the connection to Dr. Persinger's research sent chills up my spine. I needed to know more about this guy and his work. I wanted to immerse myself in it. Who is this guy?

We finished our lunch and wrapped up our discussion. As we headed to the door to go our separate ways, Willy put his arms over both our shoulders and pulled us in close. He said, "Well, boys, I used to say I was only in it for the entropy, but it looks like there is perhaps a way out after all. Maybe there is more structure to our world than we ever imagined. I wish I could come back with you and see the Memory Chaser, but I gotta get to Cheyenne by sundown. I'll be smellin' you later."

"Willy, you gotta promise us you'll come by and check this thing out when you get some free time," I said.

"Time, my friend, is always free; it's the space part that's costly. I truly hope you guys and Rachel can get to the other side of Sally's death. She was a beautiful person and apparently an exceptionally wise one as well. Godspeed, my friends."

We hopped in the car and headed back to Sally's. "I gotta make a stop on the way back," I told Ben. "I need to drop by the county building and pick up Sally's death certificate. It'll just take a minute."

"Okey dokey, Dad, it sounds kind of gruesome and final though."

"I know, but it's just another piece in settling her estate. I gotta do it."

We pulled up to the county building, and I headed to the coroner's office. I'd never met a coroner, let alone been in one's office. It was a small office in the back of the building. I rang the bell on the reception desk, and a clerk came from out of nowhere, asking how she could help. I told her what I needed, and she asked me to have a seat while she rounded up the records. I took a seat thinking how weird this was, how sterile, how practical, how impersonal it all was. I heard a conversation emanating from the back office. It was the clerk and an unidentified gentleman. It sounded like there was something wrong. After a few more minutes, a man in a lab coat came out from the back office with an envelope in his hand. He walked over to me.

"You must be Mr. Stern. I'm Doctor Daver. I performed the autopsy on Sally. How are you today, Mr. Stern?"

"I'm well, thank you. Is everything in order?"

"Well, yes," Daver said. "First off, I want to extend my condolence for your loss. I hate to see a young life taken; it's very sad. I have to say that I've never seen a case like this before. I assume you know what the preliminary cause of death was?"

Uh oh, I thought, what is he about to tell me? I get that he probably hadn't seen a case like this, but what did he find out? What does he mean? "Yes, it was electrocution."

"Yes, well—" Daver coughed, as if to give himself time to sort out his words. "The thing is, Mr. Stern, I'm not sure what the cause of death was."

"What do you mean?"

"Well, you see, when she was brought in, it seemed like it was going to be a cut-and-dry case. She had mild burn marks on the sides of her head, and her hair was slightly singed. Sheriff Broadless stated in his report that she was wearing a helmet that had a multitude of electrical wires connected to it at the time of death. I guess assumptions were made, but the facts are the facts, sir."

"And what are those facts?"

"Well, the facts are the cause of death was not electrocution. I can't tell you how she died. I don't have an explanation. There was nothing even close to definitive. There was one odd thing I did notice. Burnt hair has an overwhelming scent. It can drown out other scents, so I didn't notice it at first."

"Notice what?"

"There was a distinct smell of sulfur in her oral cavity. I have no idea why that would be; do you, Mr. Stern?"

"M-m-me?" I stuttered. "Sulfur? No, I have no idea."

It Is You

After hearing what Willy had to say about the God Helmet, we knew we had to try the thing out. We decided to do this on its own, separate from the Memory Chaser. Ben explained that we should use the God Helmet he purchased; it would be safer, and he'd already experimented with it. We both figured that messing with Sally's helmet might not be the best idea. Neither of us wanted to touch her God Helmet after the results she'd had. Ben pointed out that the device he had was a newer, improved version of the helmet. It was not really even a helmet but a set of straps that helped support what looked like a sweatband loaded with electronics. Sally's helmet was an actual motorcycle helmet fitted with similar electronics. This newer version would be less bulky when we eventually integrated it into the Memory Chaser, Ben said. This all seemed good to me. I suddenly realized how glad I was that Ben was familiar with it. I had gone from fearing for him using it to collaborating with him on how to use it ourselves.

I did some basic research and found out the God Helmet was invented by a man named Stanley Koren. It was originally called the Koren Helmet. At some point, Dr. Persinger got involved and helped develop it into what it is today. Dr. Persinger's intent was to use the God Helmet to test one of his hypotheses regarding how the brain works. Persinger believed the sense of self had two components, one originating in the left temporal lobe and the other from the right temporal lobe. The left side, he believed, was the dominant hemisphere regarding sense of self. He felt that both sides contributed to the sense of self, but they contributed in different ways. Normally, the two sides worked in conjunction to create the whole.

Throughout history, human consciousness has been described as two separate selves: the conscious and the subconscious, the id and the ego, the voluntary and involuntary, the heart and the soul. The God Helmet could be used to disrupt the connection between the two. Early results of the God Helmet indicated that the normally subordinate right hemisphere intruded on the awareness of the left hemisphere. This resulted in a strong feeling of two coexisting selves. This was what was responsible for feeling the presence of others, including spirits, while under its influence. Ultimately, Persinger was trying to show that paranormal experiences, such as the detection of spirits, ghosts, past lives, and perhaps even God, were the result of hemispheric disruptions. Persinger was trying to explain religious and mystical experiences as symptoms of an out-of-balance brain, in this case, hemispheric disturbances. I could only imagine the fuss this would cause in religious and mystic circles. If all this were true, could it mean God truly was dead? Oddly, laypersons who have sought out the God Helmet experience are mostly doing it for its mystical powers. They aren't trying to explain anything. They're trying to experience something they're totally out of touch with, God, or at least a connectedness to something beyond their life experience. I guess one man's junk is another man's treasure.

It was an unusual Colorado summer morning; it was cool, and low-hanging, water-laden clouds obscured Mount Princeton. It was perfectly calm, with the exception of the occasional breeze brought in by the misty spray of clouds barely able to hold their moisture. The humid air held with it a sense of foreboding. We weren't sure if we should shrug it off or embrace it. As we walked to the studio, I looked at Ben and asked him what he was thinking. Ben looked me straight in the eye and said simply, "Under the water, carry the water, Dad." So many things flashed through my mind when he said that. It meant many things, but I think he probably meant something specific this Talking Heads song refers to beyond the water reference. I took it to mean that we now found ourselves living in a shotgun shack, wondering how we got here. How indeed?

I took a seat on the ragged, old couch and let Ben fit the God Helmet to my skull. It was a rather underwhelming piece of equipment. It was essentially two crisscrossing straps that helped support an elastic band that went around my head like a sweatband. Attached to the elastic band were eight pairs of magnetic coils that had wire leads coming off of them. The wire leads connected to Ben's laptop. The God Helmet functions were controlled via software. It seemed simple enough. I had no idea to what degree the software settings altered the effects of the God Helmet. Apparently Ben did, and that was good enough for me.

"All right, are you ready, Dad?"

"Yes, I'm ready; zap away."

Ben hadn't explained much about what to expect. I had been hearing about the God Helmet for a while now, so it wasn't like I was unfamiliar with it. He just told me he'd be putting it through its paces and wanted me to narrate what was going on in my mind. Well, all righty then, I thought, put me through my paces.

"I'm going to start nice and slow. Let me know when you start feeling anything, anything at all. Are you going to be all right?"

"Okay, will do. I'm definitely a little nervous about this whole thing, but I'll be fine."

With that, Ben activated the God Helmet. The device made no noise whatsoever, and there were no vibrations from the magnetic coils. As I sat there, I tried to relax as best I could. I tried to think of anything besides what was going on. Just relax; just relax. Don't follow your thoughts; just let them flow past you; don't engage. Ben asked me if I felt anything yet, and I told him I didn't. I looked over at him, and he seemed to be concentrating intensely. He brushed me off and said I shouldn't be looking at him, that I should just gaze off into empty space about six feet away from my face. I took several big breaths and exhaled slowly—just relax.

My mind wandered, and I found myself thinking of the movie *Man on the Moon*. This was a movie about Andy Kaufman. Kaufman, a famous comedian, was notorious for elaborate and dramatic ruses. He would create situations where the observer was never sure if they were completely made up and staged or absolutely real. In the end of the movie and in real life, Andy was dying of cancer. Running out of options, he seeks out help from mystics to cure his cancer, in this case Filipino psychic surgeons. The psychic surgeons began to work on Andy's abdomen. As they pushed and pulled on his stomach, they appeared to be pulling out slimy chunks of his guts. At first, Andy can't believe what he's seeing, but then he realizes it's all a big scam. Of course, Andy is well versed in scamming, and the irony laid out before him is cruel, as he sees it as payback for all his huckstering. The joke was on him this time.

This is all a big scam, I thought. How silly of me to think magnetic coils were gonna take me to the promised land. Maybe this whole thing was an elaborate scam put on by Sally. Maybe she wanted to leave us a huge, unsolvable puzzle? And then I felt it. It started as a barely detectable low rumble emanating from inside my head. The rumble was soon accompanied by an intense feeling of anxiety and then foreboding. I was feeling very uncomfortable.

The rumble now sounded more like muffled voices. Off in the distance, I could hear another sound, more of a crackling sound. Both sounds started to feel closer and clearer, one from the left side and one from the right. The mumbled voices were high pitched and sounded modulated and staccato. It reminded me of alien speak from countless sci-fi movies, clicking and popping but muted, and though undecipherable, it clearly sounded like language. The crackling was similar in that it, too, sounded like language, but it was more of a low frequency with less contrast. It was becoming more fuzzy and staticky. I recognized both sounds but could not place either.

I was feeling ill and closed my eyes. With eyes closed, I couldn't believe what I was looking at. It was the visualization of these sounds. The left side was vague, slender stick figures constructed of a multitude of thin, subparallel, jerky lines moving frenetically. The right side was nondescript, squat, cloudlike figures morphing with rhythmic bass-heavy static that was disturbingly calm as compared to the stick figures. The two seemed to be in conflict, with both trying to push the other out of view to dominate the scene. I audibly gasped with recognition. I knew what I was experiencing was not new to me. I'd witnessed this before. I was beginning to feel nauseous. It was from a recurring dream I had as a small child. It was usually brought on by a high fever. It was more of a nightmare, as the two entities seemed to be alive and in mortal conflict. It was so scary that I'd inevitably end up in my parents' bed, praying for it to end while hiding between my parents' warm bodies. I was always fearful of what would happen if the conflict escalated or if one side won.

I tried to focus and observe the primal conflict objectively. A sense of sheer terror overtook any hope of understanding the vision. The nausea became overwhelming. I started convulsing, and my mouth began to water. Ben must've noticed; I could hear his voice from a faraway place.

"Dad, Dad, *Dad*! Are you all right?"

"No, I'm not all right." With that, I jumped off the couch, which ripped the God Helmet off my head, and I vomited all over the studio floor.

"Jesus, Dad, are you okay? What's going on?"

I crumpled to the floor while trying to stay out of my vomit. Holy shit, I thought, holy shit. I was stunned by the experience. Not those guys again, not twitchy and static. I recalled I had names for them. As I was gaining my composure, Ben came over and knelt next to me.

"It's okay, Dad. Take deep breaths, and let it go; just let it go. Did I fail to mention some people get sick from this thing the first time?"

I weakly got to my feet with Ben's help and flopped back down on the couch. Ben went next door to get a mop to clean up my mess. I sat there staring up and out of the skylight. The view was obscured by moisture built up on the glass. It was gray beyond the fogged glass, and as I recalled the weather, I was suddenly grounded again, like nothing happened. I was just sitting on the couch stunned. That was some primal stuff.

As Ben was cleaning up my mess, I started to describe to him what I experienced. "It was not what I was expecting, that's for sure. It was very tense, not relaxing at all. It was a nightmare from my past, when I was very

61

young. It seemed like it was never going to end, just like it felt way back when. How long was I going?"

"You weren't going more than a couple of minutes. Don't tell me it was hours for you, Dad."

"No, but it was way longer than that. Jesus, Ben, here we go again. Time is no longer constant—is that it? This is giving me the chills. The dream, or nightmare, was about conflict between two primal sides. The two sides were opposites of sorts. They weren't people or even beings; they were vague figures, one linear, twitchy, and scratchy, and the other was stout, muffled, and of a low frequency but just as disturbing. They were trying to push each other away and take over, I guess. I didn't wait that long."

"Oh, Dad, I'm sorry. I had it on the nightmare setting."

"What? Why would you do that?"

"Come on, Dad, I'm just joking. It doesn't work like that."

"Ah geez, come on, man."

"Come on, Dad; that was priceless, nightmare setting." Ben laughed. "Why don't you go wash your stinky face off, and we'll try something different. The controls are squirrely. There are no presets or anything like that. I gotta tweak the output. I think I know what to do to improve your experience."

While in the bathroom staring into the mirror, I spoke to myself. "What are you doing, Sandy? I don't like where this is going. What are you doing? Have you lost your mind?" I was answered in the form of a flashback. I recalled an actual satori I had years ago while staring in a bathroom mirror at myself. My sudden enlightenment back then had more than a little help from LSD.

My most impactful experience in college had nothing to do with what I was studying or the people I got to know. It had to do with the effects of LSD. I had managed to get a hold of some extremely pure LSD. The acid was called windowpane, as it was infused on tiny, clear gelatin pyramids that looked like glass. My satori was just a few minutes out of that night's adventure, but it has stayed with me all these years. I was hanging out at my house with my buddies. We were all completely tripping our brains out. Everything, of course, was extremely funny. Nothing and everything seemed to make perfect sense simultaneously.

We had Toots and the Maytals blaring "Pressure Drop." I got up to use the bathroom. While washing my hands and staring into the mirror, I was singing along with Toots: "It is you (oh, yeah), it is you, you (oh, yeah)." Like a thunderbolt from the heavens, an immediate recognition of self struck me. *It is you* suddenly had massive spiritual significance. More precisely, my reflection was telling me that it was all up to me, that perception was everything. The way I perceived myself was entirely up to me. If I saw myself as a strong, confident person, then that's who I was. If I had low self-esteem and thought little of myself, then that's who I'd be. It was all up to me; it was you who set the stage.

If I viewed the world as a positive, wonder-filled place, it would be so. View the world as a constipated mess, and that will be so. You make it whatever you want it to be, so why not take control and make it your own? Accept that you play a big role in everything. Perhaps this positivity is infectious and others will catch it.

The recognition of this sent a chill through my body. That my reflection was telling me this seemed normal. The chill began to tingle and ultimately turned into warmth that radiated outward from my groin. "It is you (oh, yeah), it is you, you (oh, yeah)." When the warmth reached my brain, I recognized what it was. It was pure crystalline love, the love of self. At that moment, I was truly feeling unadulterated love. It wasn't love for someone else but of myself. I was going to be okay because I now understood that so much of the confusion I was experiencing as a young adult was, in a moment, lifted away. I was going to be okay because it truly was up to me. How simple, how beautiful, how Zen, I thought.

When I came back to the studio, Ben had put on some music and had adjusted the lighting. There was a much-cooler vibe in the room, and this relaxed me. I made my way to the couch and let loose a huge sigh. "What's next?"

"Let's try this again. Go ahead and put on the helmet. I think you're gonna like this a whole lot more," Ben said reassuringly. "Each time can be completely different. This time we've got some happy music playing, and the lights are low; it's all good. Focus on the music if it starts getting weird."

"I like how you think, and I'm into it, but I got an idea."

"What's that?"

"Well, while in the bathroom, I had a flashback of a satori I had in my college days, and I have an idea."

"You had a flashback of one of your college trips?"

"I'm serious. For some reason I was just recalling a very enlightening moment that had a profound impact on my life. It involved *seeing* myself for the first time. I want to try something out." I explained my experience to Ben. I told him the whole story, LSD and all.

"So you were tripping, eh? I knew it."

"It is you, oh yeah, yeah, yeah," I sang.

"Come on, Dad, really?"

"Come help me with something."

I led Ben to the far side of the studio, back behind the screens and next to the filing cabinets. "Do you see this?" I said, pointing at a free-standing full-length mirror. "This is a magic mirror. Do you know what it is?"

"It looks like a mirror," Ben said sarcastically.

"It's not just a mirror; it's a true mirror. Help me drag this over by the couch."

"What's a true mirror? Does it tell the truth about the viewer? Is it like mirror, mirror, on the wall? What, Dad, what?"

"Well it kind of tells the truth but not what you're thinking."

We carried the mirror over by the couch in a position where I could wear the God Helmet while gazing into the mirror. I had Ben stand in front of it and asked him what looked different.

"I'm not sure, but something is very weird. My movement in the mirror is all wrong. Oh, wait a minute. The lettering on my shirt isn't reversed; I can read it. Wait, what's going on here? This is too weird."

"It's what's called a true mirror. In a normal mirror, everything is flipped or mirrored, right? In a true mirror, you see things as everybody else sees you, straight on. It's a perplexing phenomenon. Did you know mirrors don't actually flip anything? They just present the light back at you. As it turns out, the viewer is the one who is flipped. Think of it like this: If you wrote a word down on a piece of transparent paper and viewed it from the backside, what would you see? You'd see the word mirrored. The reason is obvious; you're looking at it from the wrong side of the light. That's what happens in a mirror. Now reach out as if you're trying to shake your hand in the mirror. In this mirror the proper arm reaches out to greet you. If you did that in a regular mirror, you'd be reaching toward your left arm. You can't shake your hand in a regular mirror."

"I had no idea; that's crazy. It's really wild. When I lean left, the image leans right. That is very disturbing. Oh look; my hair is parted on the proper side—what?"

"Yes, the part!" I exclaimed. "The folks who sell these things make a big deal out of the fact that the only person whose true face you never see in real time is your own. They point out that while everyone else sees us correctly, no one sees themselves correctly in a mirror. They claim the true mirror has all kinds of therapeutic benefits. It's all about self-identification. Apparently people really connect with their reflection when it is presented without mirroring. I've always wanted to have one of these."

"Well who knew? I kinda like this."

"This is what I want to do. I want to try the God Helmet while staring at myself in this mirror. I'd like you to cue up Toots and the Maytals, "Pressure Drop," and make it loop when it finishes, just in case I want to go longer. I'm going to try to recreate my satori. Who knows—maybe the true mirror will enhance the dislodging of the self."

I adjusted the helmet, relaxed into a positive stance, and stared into the true mirror. Ben fired up the God Helmet while ushering words of encouragement as if he were coaching me. It felt reassuring. The music seemed just right. Toots was singing the sacred words: "It is you (oh, yeah), it is you, you (oh, yeah)." Breathe. Just breathe. I stared into my eyes and concentrated. I slowly realized that my face was very different. It was as though I was watching a movie of my face up close, only it was in real time. Every little move I made was duplicated, but the true mirror made it feel very surreal, as if it were someone else, yet it was me.

As before, I felt something barely detectable from far off. This time it was more of a humming. The kind of humming that tickles your ears when you plug your nose and hum at just the exact ear-tickling frequency. How funny, I thought, that thing is trying to tickle me. Then the hum went from sound to pure feeling. The feeling was one of pure joy. It started in my groin and leaked outward, like warm water slowly heating me from within. Was I pissing my pants? It felt so orgasmically good. I knew this feeling. It was the onset of drugs, the initial surge of euphoria from LSD perhaps.

Though my eyes were open and I was gazing at myself, it seemed like they were shut, and someone was flooding my face with bright-colored lights. Each orgasmic surge corresponded with a pulse of warm, welcoming light. Suddenly Toots broke through with the chorus again: "It is you (oh, yeah), it is you, you (oh, yeah)." It is me, I thought. How curious, because it is me. I'm feeling me. Overlaid through the light was my face, but I was seeing it from afar. I was flooded with empathy for myself. What is the matter with him, or me? It's okay; you're going to be okay, I told my far-off self. The words were echoing in my mind, and then the echo turned into a real voice, my voice talking to me. I was telling myself, it is you; it is you.

I felt a weird connection to my body. I felt every limb, each foot and hand, every joint, every muscle all at once, yet individually, as if all the parts were sentient and reporting back to me. I could focus on a specific spot on my body and feel what was going on at that spot. "It is you (oh, yeah), it is you, you (oh, yeah)," Toots implored. I wasn't remembering my satori; I was living my satori. I closed my eyes and contemplated these words. If it's me, why is a separate voice, which is me, telling me this? Is it my subordinate right brain intruding? It's assuring me in the second person that it is me as well. Just like before, I was telling myself that it is all about how you see yourself, how you see the world. This sent another huge pulse of euphoria surging through my body. As the surge dissipated, I knew what was going on, and I was overcome with joy, with pure love.

I began to laugh, not because it was humorous but because the secret was so obvious, just like before. The secret wasn't a secret, you dumbass; it was more than right in front of you—it is you. So Zen, so simple. Accept yourself, and embrace it kept ringing in my head. It is *you-u-u*. The feeling of love was overwhelming. Now I was belly laughing at this simple satori. I stumbled backward and flopped onto the couch and stared up at the skylight. Almost instantly, like the crack of a whip, I rocketed back to Earth. I heard a familiar voice, and I turned my focus to the voice.

It was Ben, and he was staring at me, mouth agape. "That'll do, donkey, that'll do," he said, impassioned.

Godspeed

Over the course of the next month, Ben and I worked tirelessly on understanding the intricate workings of Sally's Memory Chaser. We had integrated the God Helmet, a key component. We ran the beginner program over and over until we were convinced we'd learned all we could. Through the course of repeated runs with the virtual reality–generated out-of-body-experience—VROBE—setting and the God Helmet, we began to realize subtle changes in our state of being. We became more and more relaxed and at peace with ourselves. Our clarity of thought became more and more crisp. We seemed more in tune with our surroundings. Colors seemed more vivid and sunlight more intense and warming. We were able to concentrate in ways I've never experienced.

To some extent, it felt like the two of us could communicate without speaking. We first noticed this when we started finishing each other's sentences at a frequency that seemed unnatural. There were times when we'd be working silently on a problem and eventually one of us would speak. What we were saying would always start off midsentence, but we somehow knew what came before the actual spoken words. At first we didn't think anything of it. We just figured we were so immersed in our work that we just weren't listening closely enough. Then we started paying attention to these events and realized that this wasn't the case. Our sentences really did start in the middle or somewhere well past the beginning. Despite this, we always knew what preceded the spoken word the other was saying. We were actually communicating telepathically on some level.

Two people that are very close to one another, both physically and emotionally, will commonly finish each other's sentences, as well as know what the other is about to say. Married couples do this all the time. This was way more than that. This would be spooky for most people. I believe that our enhanced clarity and cognitive acuity accepted this strange behavior as normal. It was like we were ascending to a higher level of consciousness. Our communication skills were ascending as well. It just seemed logical at the time. I'm sure our isolation must've played a role in this as well.

Ben started calling me Broccoli. Broccoli was a nickname given to Lieutenant Reginald Barclay of the Starship *Enterprise* (*The Next Generation*). He was a very bright man but behaved as someone stricken with Asperger's syndrome. He had no social skills, and his lack of self-confidence made him come across as dimwitted, despite his obvious genius. Ben and I loved *Star Trek*. I made him watch all the originals as well as *The Next Generation* as a kid. One of our favorites was the "Broccoli" episode. In it, Broccoli goes from what I just described to perhaps the smartest man

67

ever. Unbeknownst to him, he had been contacted by an alien probe. The probe slowly alters Reg's brain structure. His newfound genius changes his behavior, and he starts treating his shipmates with arrogance. He decides his brain isn't powerful enough, so he creates a device in the holodeck that links his superbrain into the ship's computer. He is now one with the ship's computer. There's a scene where he's in the holodeck sitting in a captain's chair that's wired to the hilt. Above him is a device that is sending pulsing beams of multicolored light directly at his brain. The scene is powerfully believable. In the end, it turns out it was the aliens' probe that changed him into überman. The aliens did this so Broccoli could prepare the ship to travel halfway across the galaxy to go meet them. They meet the Cytherians, learn a bunch of stuff, and Barclay returns to being just Broccoli again.

It never occurred to us that we'd turn back into regular Reginald Broccoli. It also never occurred to us that we weren't responsible for our newfound enlightenment. We went along with it and didn't question it. This seemed preposterous given that Broccoli did not retain his genius, that his genius wasn't his own making. This was a pattern—at least with me, not recognizing the obvious. There we went, blindly about to stumble onto something so much bigger than us.

We decided it was time to take it up a notch. Ben had been playing with Sally's other programs. He liked to stay up late and explore what was next. The morning after a particularly long night for Ben, I was up, fumbling around for some coffee, and I realized he wasn't in the cabin or outside taking in the morning beauty. I fired up the espresso maker and headed next door to the studio to check on Ben. As I entered the studio, I sensed something wasn't right. The screens were skipping and repeating a short clip of Sally running through a crowd of people. At the end of the clip, she turns her head around toward the camera and says, "Hurry up, Chase; you're going to miss it." It was then I noticed Ben crumpled on the couch. I walked over and shook him awake. He looked up at me, and I could tell he'd been crying. "Are you all right? What happened? Who's Chase?" He slowly raised his head, rubbed his eyes, and stopped midthought.

"Oh my God, Dad, that was intense. It was too much, seeing Sally was just too much. There is someone else. I think she was trying to reach him. I think she was trying to visit or recreate him somehow."

"It's okay, Ben. Let's go next door. I have coffee brewing."

We headed next door, and I served up my famous Venezuelan espresso. It was clear Ben was very moved by what he'd witnessed. I kept him off subject to help him gain his composure. Ben very quickly collected himself and began piecing together the night's adventure.

"So I started working my way through some of Sally's more advanced programs," Ben started. "I can't believe how organized she was. It's almost as if she was setting this whole experiment up for someone else. The programs are neatly categorized with detailed explanations of what each one does. Most of the events, as she apparently liked to call them, were designed for her use. Each event is a run through a specific place and involves select people. Usually the places are from her past. For instance, one labeled "You *Can* Go Back Home" is a jog through our neighborhood in Evergreen. It seems to be a compilation of home movies, footage that she must have shot, and Google Earth 3D images. None of it is very crisp and seems to be intentionally out of focus. Then it gets really weird. We're all in it. You and Mom and me are in it."

"Wait, wait, wait. What do you mean, we're all in it? How is that possible?"

"It's true. She's edited and spliced various video sources together to create a path for her run. Sometimes they're short and loop back to the beginning, and other times they're longer and linear. The home movies have lots of people we know in them, including our family. Then it gets really weird. Overlaid on the scene are people she's inserted. The people are all quite crude graphically. Sometimes they're just standing there, and other times they're walking or running alongside her. She turns these people into friends and family by pasting images of their heads on the bodies. There are even friends from high school in it. It sounds crazy, because if you viewed one of these videos by itself, it looks rather comical as it's so crudely produced. Still shots of heads riding on moving bodies in a scene, that's barely believable. When you defocus the scene and add in syncopated music, light, and then remove yourself from your body and add in some God Helmet mojo, it's quite believable. I think that your brain is so desperate to make sense of it that it converts it into something more real than it is. It pulls out the corresponding memory."

"Wow, now that's genius. It's a well-known phenomenon that the brain will try to fit what doesn't make sense into something that's familiar when confronted with conflicting or confusing stimulus. How in the world did she figure all this out?"

"I don't know, but she did. Maybe she did have some help."

"I assume that would be Chase. Who is he, a boyfriend?"

69

"Well, yes, how'd you know?"

"You don't remember? When I woke you, the Memory Chaser was stuck in a short loop, like a skipping record. It was Sally running, and while looking back at the camera, she tells Chase to hurry up or he'll miss it."

"Oh yeah, you're right. Last night seems like one big blur. There's more. I think Chase was probably her boyfriend—I'm not sure. There are several programs that seem to be about him. These programs are composed almost entirely of recent video footage of the two of them running together. It appears to be shot up here in the mountains. There's even one scene or event that's shot running rapids. I assume it's on the Arkansas. It's really wild because the camera is set up behind Sally at the back of the raft. She's guiding it. You see everything from behind and just above. It's set up to run in the VROBE mode. It's weird though because it's Chase, whoever he is, and a third person sitting in the front of the raft. I'm not sure who that third person is, but I swear it's Mac. You're gonna wanna see these events, Dad. I think they're leading us to the memory-chasing function.

"I've run all these events with the VROBE function and the God Helmet, and it's really intriguing. It's definitely emotional but something's missing. I believe the event needs to be tailored to your own experience. The people in it and the setting are meant to help you recall your memories. By emulating the event, maybe this triggers or reactivates those memories. I say this because when I ran the You *Can* Go Back Home event, it had a profound effect on me. The other program events didn't have near the same effect. I assume it's because in one I'm seeing people and places I'm familiar with, and in the others, it's Sally's memories, not mine.

"Seeing you and Mom in a scene I'm intimately familiar with is very powerful. It reminds me of the slideshow you put together of Gran and Granddad for their funerals. Just seeing still photos of them in that emotional state was very powerful. I felt like the pictures were more than pictures; they took me back to those times and, as a result, emulated the emotion of that time. My point is that pictures can be very powerful, as they connect you with an emotion that's tied to the people in the photos. What if her plan was to amplify this feeling by using more than just photos? Starting with active meditation, she then introduces video and a variety of stimuli, all while being dislodged via the VROBE with enhanced emotions brought on by the God Helmet. I'm not positive, but it seems to me she was trying to recreate memories of this Chase dude."

"Yikes, that's something. That all makes perfect sense. Now I'm really anxious to see these programs. Let's get some breakfast, and then you can walk me through them. Do you want to get some rest first?"

"Yeah, I'm whooped. I think I need to lie down for a bit. Why don't you check out what I keyed up on the Memory Chaser, and I'll be out in a while."

"I think I'll wait for you on that one. I've been wanting to take a look at Sally's paper files in the back of the studio. Maybe I'll do that first, and when you get up, we'll have a go at the Memory Chaser events."

More Poems

I headed to the studio while Ben got some sleep. I had been curious about Sally's writings. She was a prolific writer, mostly poetry and short stories, but she also wrote actual letters to her friends and family. I loved that she wrote letters; it's such a lost art, as well as a way to truly connect.

Sally was very organized, as revealed by how she had filed everything away in old-fashioned filing cabinets. Much of it was typical stuff, taxes, warranties, receipts, photos, and the like. She had one cabinet dedicated to her personal writings. It was mostly poems but also short stories and musings. She had stories she had written as far back as middle school, neatly categorized by date. She even filed her letters from others. One folder was labeled "Chase." I couldn't bear to look at that one.

As I weeded my way through her files, I was struck by a feeling of her presence. The structure of her past was so neat and cared for. She was like that. As a small child, Sally was very particular about how she cared for her belongings. Everything, especially gifts, were special and needed taken care of. She hated it if you attempted to organize her stuff. It was her way or the highway. She was definitely a type-A personality.

I recalled her at two or three years old. She was swaddling her baby doll just like we had done with her. The swaddling never seemed quite right. Over and over, she'd fold the tiny blanket around her baby doll until it was perfect. What was going on in her mind that she was dissatisfied repeatedly by her swaddling effort? She was searching for perfection at such an early age. That's a lot to live up to—when your mind demands perfection. I was suddenly overcome by a feeling of empathy for her. "Oh, Sally, what you've done is perfect; don't you see?" Her whole life she had struggled with the pressure to be perfect. That we couldn't help her with this was painful. I felt the pain of parenthood while also feeling her anxiety to make things perfect. "Oh, Sally, it's fine just the way it is" never seemed to work for her—she was driven.

As I read through her poems, with each one, I felt closer and closer to her. I really loved her political/social commentary. I kept digging and reading. What a legacy, I thought. It may not all be great writing, but much of it was so precise, so pertinent. It seemed to me to be a great representation of a person. Way more than a memoir or a life story told. It was pure emotion caught on paper. In a way it was timeless.

I had lost track of time. I'd been in the studio for several hours, but it only seemed like an hour at most. I figured I'd better have a look at the Chase files. I really didn't want to, but the fact that Chase was somehow tied into the whole memory-chasing thing, I figured I'd better, no matter what I'd find and wished I hadn't. Most of the file folder consisted of letters and poems he had written to her. Most of this was very personal and, at times, very heartfelt and mushy. He certainly wasn't the writer that Sally was. It was often clumsy and awkward but extremely sincere and revealing. One poem really struck me; it reminded me of my early efforts to capture the feelings I had for a past love. I recalled an entry I made years ago. It was short and to the point and started with "I was in love once, but I'm better now." Funny yet so tragic. Like Chase, even an amateur writer of poetry can capture the deep emotions of love that they are enduring. This poem was definitely one of those.

"The Kiss"

these eyes are mine in the night
reaching out I meet them
agreeing passionately with a stare
upon contact muscles relax
arms drape over around and under
with every contoured grace
eyes too close to focus
warm breath on neck
tracing upward leaving
cool wet trail
now lips in contact
body heat rising
saliva blends
minds meld
ahhh

Their relationship was now clear. They were more than an item—they were deeply in love. How come no one else knew? Sally was no different than the rest of us; she wanted companionship. Who could blame her? But why was this secret? Why didn't she want to share this? It seemed so sad. Perhaps she had found what she was looking for, and then for some reason, it was gone. What happened? Where did he go? Was she really spending her time trying to recreate him? Was it just lost love or did something happen?

I figured I'd had enough and started to file the entries I'd been reading. As I was putting them away, I saw that one had fallen to the floor. I picked it up and noticed the title seemed oddly familiar, "Not This Spud." It was in Sally's handwriting. This seemed almost too familiar. As I read the poem, I was dumbfounded.

"Not This Spud"

it's time to get down to business
this business of writing
to spill the beans
get it out for all to see
it's time to stop tying knots
to stop folding coconuts
let's point at the man
let's run him into a corner
and film it for his TV
I'm sick of this hideous guilt
I've done nothing but to bare
all this mental strife
I want to be rid of this righteous guilt
this hopeless despair
it's time to get out of Dodge
to cleanse this yellow panic
from our tense selves
no more wandering in anxiety
I won't let them take
this dove to the streets
I'll flush the land first
I'll damn the man
and his righteous propaganda
I'm sick of your opinions
I can't digest another bite
your botched civilization
won't suck me under
I'll never fold my coconut
I need these thoughts

I'm no monkey man
I'm no hollow man
you've been sneaking
up on us now for too long

I don't need big brother
I will not be fooled
by this forced guilt
by this mind fuck of yours
my God dances
he is not grace
my God rolls in laughter
and pisses in the river
I'm no monkey man
I'm no stuffed man

you're not accusing me
not this time
I don't need protection
I've turned in my paranoias
I will not be fooled
by this circular reasoning
by this political blackmail
my God walks with me
he is not selfish
my God wears no clothes
he barks at the moon
I'm no monkey man
I'm no bald head.

This wasn't just any poem. It was way too familiar. What was it that seemed so close? The words could have come from my mouth forty years ago. Was it possible that we thought that much alike? The words all rang with decisiveness and clarity, a young person's rage for sure, but who was that young person? It felt like I was reading my own words, and then it hit like a lightning bolt. Those are my words. How was that even possible? Time-traveling words from Sally's mouth! Jesus Christ, was this really happening? Now, I couldn't say I could recite anything I've ever written, but this was weird—I knew these words. They were mine for sure. What was going on? I could've believed identical themes from two generations—but not exact wording. This was becoming scary. Cross-generational communications? How about brains connected via the electromagnetic-communication highway? I paused for a moment and then folded up the poem along its original seams and tucked it into my shirt pocket. How was I going to explain this to Ben? Was this really happening? Sally wrote something forty years removed from when I wrote the exact same thing? I folded up Sally's literary tent and headed for the cabin to digest another bite of strangeness.

You *Can* Go Back Home

Ben was in a determined mood like I'd never seen before. He kept mumbling as he tweaked the controls on the Memory Chaser interface. It all seemed right though. We needed to get after it. The shit was piling up and needed to break through. This thing was primed, and we were ready to go.

"Ben, there's something I need to tell you."

"Please tell me you have answers and not more clues. I don't think I can bear more weirdness."

"Oh it's weird, weird as hell, Broccoli!"

"Good one, Dad. Well, what is it then?"

"Yesterday morning I was looking through Sally's files, her paper files in the cabinets. I spent quite some time going through them. It was really revealing and emotional. She was such a good writer. I discovered that this Chase guy was her boyfriend. They were in love. I'm not sure what happened to him, but it makes more sense now, that Sally was trying to reconnect with him."

"I kind of figured that. So what's the big deal?"

"Well, that's not the big deal. You're not going to believe this, Ben. One of the poems she wrote is…is not right. Something's going on."

"What isn't going on, Dad? Please tell me."

"Sally wrote a poem that I believe is word for word the same poem I wrote over forty years ago—that's what's weird. I can't explain it, but I'm certain they're the same."

"What? How is that even possible? Are you sure she didn't just copy your poem? That would make sense."

"No, I'm sure. I've never shared any of my writings. I'm not even sure if they're still around."

"Oh Jesus, that's very spooky. How's that possible?"

"I have no idea, and I'm having a hard time accepting it. Let's just let this sink in for a bit, and maybe something will come to us."

"Well, we'll just add that to the magical mystery pile then."

"I'll share the poem with you later. For now, I'd like to try your new event out."

"Okay, are you sure you want to do this? It's time to time travel—are you ready for this?"

"Reporting for duty, Captain. Make it so, Number One!"

"Step right up; step right up, son; take the trip; see the show!" Ben cajoled in his best carnival barker voice.

"All right but take it easy on me; you're starting to freak me out. I'm a virgin after all."

"You're such a pussy; strap in and hold on. This is the trip to Evergreen, only I messed with it a bit. Get ready for your family reunion. Just remember you *can* go back home."

I strapped on the God Helmet, adjusted the virtual reality goggles, and started trotting on the treadmill. I turned and looked back at Ben and gave him a nod of approval. With that, Ben fired up the You *Can* Go Back Home event he had described to me. He had it set to play with the Talking Heads' "This Must Be the Place"—a classic song about home. What a perfect fit. In an instant, I was propelled to Evergreen, Colorado, to the home we raised our kids in. I was just down the driveway from our old home. I scanned the horizon and took in the glorious property we spent so many years at. The God Helmet sent surges of longing and belonging through my nervous system.

I heard people cheering, and some of the voices sounded familiar. I was still in first-person viewpoint, moving at a trot. As I gazed around, I instantly recalled the scene. It was the Evergreen Lake run. We did it every Fourth of July. We usually filmed as much as we could. As I stared into the scene, I realized there were people I recognize just ahead. I ran toward them and saw it was my old neighbors and Evergreen friends cheering me on. I ran toward them at an increasingly faster pace. As I closed in, one of them slapped me on the butt, telling me, "You go, boy." This activated the articulated armature, and I was simultaneously whacked across my hind quarters in exact sync with the imagery. *Wham!* I started to pull away from my body.

It was no longer a video; it became a disembodied dreamland. I felt a need to stop it, so I reached out to grab myself as I drifted away from my body, but it was no use. I was in the captain's chair, hovering just above and behind, observing myself at a specific time in my past. I was seeing myself do something as part memory and part trippy VROBE-induced reality. The God Helmet was sending surges of awe and astonishment that made my hair stand on end. I strained to focus, but I felt disoriented and uncomfortable. It all felt so real. It was way more than a memory of the Evergreen Lake run. I was reliving it exactly as it had happened.

I remembered what Ben was saying about accepting it and defocusing. I tried to relax and let it parade past me—do not engage. It hit me that I knew what was coming up next: a long stretch through the woods up and over the hills that surround Evergreen Lake, then the smooth path along the golf course that bordered the lake. The broken light in the woods set off the strobe light, and I became mesmerized. It was so very peaceful. I wasn't thinking about a past event—I was *in* this past event. Was I ready for the next phase of this run? I knew who was going to be there. Could I handle it? As I crossed over Bear Creek and headed for the Keys on the Green clubhouse, I could hear her voice. A deep, emotional warmth suddenly overtook me; was it the God Helmet?

The voice was Rachel's, of course, just like I remembered it. She was waiting for me at the halfway point of the run. That year she had injured her knee, so running was reduced to cheering for others. Her voice became clearer and clearer. I was staring at her intently, and then it happened. It wasn't long, but it was real: I was somehow there, not watching a video, not forcing myself to believe something, no slideshow at my parents' funerals. I focused on Rachel's face as I approached and could see the detail in her expression. The pure joy she was emanating tingled my spine and made me instantly feel stronger. I felt the intense bond we shared; the love was so fierce and as real as it was that day so long ago. I ran up to her and gave her a huge hug, but there was nothing there. I started to stumble but caught myself.

The fake hug felt so real, like I was actually holding her. The hugging sent more warm surges through my body. Was it love or the God Helmet? The love we shared was evident in that moment; it was so strong tears came to my eyes. I could swear I was actually there; it was too intense. As I started off again, she blew me a kiss just as she had that day. As I ran back along the north side of the lake, history came pulsating back at me—just relax and let it come to you. I passed more people that I knew, and they were calling my name out, cheering me on and slapping me on the back. Each strike drove me further away from my body. One by one, their long-lost names came to me. Their faces and voices were so real, so vivid; I felt a closeness, a bond. I was recalling details about these people and this scene I had long forgotten.

How I missed them, how beautiful Evergreen was. Then, suddenly, I snapped back to first-person viewpoint, staring at the screen, only now it was just a movie. I let out a huge sigh in disappointment and slowed down to a stop.

"What happened? Why did you stop? It was all working so beautifully," I said.

"I'm not sure; the VR goggles just cut out."

"Ben, it was so real. Rachel was so beautiful and the look in her eyes. Oh, how I miss her. All the people, Ben, people I had long forgotten. How did you do that? Did you try out this event too?"

It was then I had a peculiar thought come out of nowhere. Was Ben trying to get me back together with Rachel? What a good kid. I appreciated it, but at the same time, I knew I had to have a talk with him. It wasn't me that was preventing this from happening.

"Yes, I did try this event out. It's a good one. As you'll recall, I ran in this run too, as did Sally. I was way ahead of you of course, but it still works for me too because of the perspective the footage was taken in. I think Sally had the camera mounted on her hat. It's very powerful, don't you think? You almost ran off the treadmill—what was that all about?"

"When I came up to Mom, I tried to hug her, but there was nothing there. That was really strange, but it didn't seem to interrupt the experience. I did stumble a bit. I can see how things could get outta hand real quick. Wasn't it weird seeing all those familiar faces from the past?"

"It's incredible. So many people I had forgotten about. Running right past Mom was really eerie but also very comforting at the same time; it was very emotional. It was weird seeing old Evergreen friends; one by one, their names came to me out of nowhere. Since I ran this event a few days ago, the memory of that day is still quiet vivid and continuous, like it happened yesterday. It feels strange. It feels like a chunk of time got reordered. That day now occupies a temporal part of my brain that makes it feel recent. It keeps rerunning it in my mind. I'll recall a face, a person I haven't seen in years, from the event and it activates a little narrative about that person. It's like the event activates other memories associated with that day."

"Wow, that's curious. This thing really works, Ben. It's reactivated our memories! What do you mean it reordered time?"

"It's hard to explain. You know when you see a movie and for the next couple of days you keep thinking of it, rerunning it in your mind? It's kind of like that. You're still actively processing the movie, examining subtle plot nuances and character traits. The difference is how real it seems. The memory is a continuous one. I can fast-forward or rewind to any part of the event and look around and examine my surroundings. I can examine and ponder way more content than what's in the actual event. I'm not reliving the event; I'm having total recall of that day, that memory. It's not a group of snapshots; it's continuous like a movie, only it's my memory. Does that make sense?"

"Yes, it does. I don't have the benefit of looking back on the experience yet, but I can see how that could happen. So the event has set your memory of that day solidly in the present? That could be troubling."

"Maybe so, but that it opens up memories that aren't even in the event is really interesting. It's like the experience activates memories beyond what're in the event. It's activating memories that are associated with it as well."

As Ben tinkered with the Memory Chaser's VR goggles, my mind started to wander. It appeared Sally was onto something big. What was she looking for?

"Hey, Dad, I think I got this thing figured out," Ben said as he jogged on the treadmill. "Yeah, that did it. Everything seems to be in order."

"What was wrong with it?"

"I'm not totally sure, but there was a lead on the VR battery that didn't seem secure."

"All right, I'm ready to give it another try."

"I got something special for you I put together. You made it almost to the end of the 'Home' event, so I want you to try this out."

"What is it?"

"Remember all the old photos and videos I had you round up?"

"Yes, of course."

"Well, I composed a new run with the content. It's totally tailored to you, only it's a little different."

"How do you mean different? This is all pretty different, Ben."

"Well a lot of the footage doesn't lend itself to a running scenario. I used a lot of still photos and ran into the same problem. I did my best to merge a running scene with the footage and photos. It's kinda hard to explain. I wired the virtual reality goggles a little differently. In parts of the event, your left eye will be viewing the archival images, and your right eye will be viewing the passing scenery. It takes a little getting used to, but if you try not to concentrate on any one thing, the left and right eye will merge the images with the scenery. Like I said, it takes getting used to and is a little unsettling at first. Believe me though, it works."

"Okay, if you say so—you're the man. I'll give it a try."

"All righty then, there may be some pulling on your heartstrings."

Oh great, I thought. What next? Where is he sending me? I climbed on the treadmill and put on the God Helmet and goggles. I began at a slow pace, and when the music started, I increased my speed to match the beat. This time it was UB40's first album, *Signing Off*, a great meditative set of dubby ska. It has always been one of my favorites; my brother turned me on to it when it was new.

The scene starts off at the same place as the first event we experimented with, at the edge of a pine forest. I was viewing myself from above and behind, just like before. It felt weird as ever. I was between first person and being removed from my body. I entered the forest, and I started to feel the effects of the God Helmet. A warmth emanated from my core. I sensed that there were others with me, perhaps just far enough back in the woods as to not be seen. I tried to relax and let it come to me. Meditative footfalls, defocus, and let it come to you.

I could see light off in the distance. It was the aspen grove as before. I brushed up against a pine bough and was struck by the armature. *Wham!* I was instantly residing out of my body. *Whack!* Another limb slapped me, and again the tactile congruity sent me even further away.

I was then viewing a slideshow of my family. It was Rachel, Sally, and Ben. The images were flying by too fast to fully comprehend. Then, as if they were listening to my thoughts, the images slowed down and matched the beat, my footfalls. In between images, I saw the aspen grove, and the strobe was dancing with the beams of broken leaf light, keeping time with the music. There was a pattern to the changing images' cadence. It started with

Rachel and me, then Sally, then Ben, and finally all four of us. Each image stream was of a different time frame, starting with our recent past and progressing back to our young family. It culminated with a tiny, far-off image that quickly zoomed in to take up the whole scene. It went through each of us individually in age order again. They were far off and accelerated toward me, expanding and filling more and more of the scene until the image took up the entire frame. It continued to Ben and started at the beginning again.

The God Helmet provided a sense of their presences. First vague but then the feeling intensified as they got closer. I felt they were with me. I recalled specific traits each had. The images were projected on the aspens; the leaves and white tree trunks were the projection screen. It was very trippy. At one point, I could swear I smelled Rachel's perfume, delicate lilacs. I was completely relaxed, and the images felt more like a presence, a separate feeling for each family member. I almost forgot I was running, so I focused on the beat and fine-tuned my pace. There was a lot going on, but I let it flow over me like a summer rain. Run into it, I thought. I realized I was not looking down on myself anymore; I was everywhere at once; I was a presence mingling with my family's presence. Then the images stopped coming. I was back to jogging in the forest at what I thought was the end of the run, where it looped back to the beginning. I caught my breath and focused. It looked like I was going around again.

Back in the forest I went. Merged into the forest scene was film footage of my wedding. We were married outside at the base of Arapahoe Basin. I was back to hovering above and behind. I got whacked a few more times and faded further away each time. I saw myself from behind, running up the aisle toward the huppah that framed the ceremony. I wasn't making any progress; I was stuck in one spot, running in place. It was a bit comical, so I focused on Rachel to avoid ruining the moment.

It started to turn into a memory, not a projection, a very real and vivid memory. She was beautiful; everything about her was perfect. My emotions skyrocketed, and I was tingling all over. I was feeling everything I felt at the huppah that day—including nervousness. Mostly I felt a hugely powerful draw between me and Rachel. I was remembering detail that I couldn't even see: The delicate lace around her nape. The fabric buttons on her wedding gown. The baby's breath flowers in her hair. The vibrant color of her face. Her beautiful smile that couldn't stop. I looked at myself and was stunned. Look how happy I was. Where did that guy go? That guy was so proud and ecstatic.

A tingling sensation was running back and forth across my scalp. I scanned the wedding party and saw my brother, best friend, and Rachel's closest mates. Oddly, they didn't seem young, even though this was twenty-five years ago. It was me that wasn't old. It's how memory works; I am part of it as it occurred. I was reliving it from that time frame. This sent a wave of recognition surging through my body. I contemplated that perhaps time was a farce. I was transported back to this memory, and it felt live. I was in it as if it were then, not just a recall.

Though the perspective was straight ahead at the wedding party, I was able to look around at the attendees. Our parents and aunts and uncles and cousins and close friends were all here. I could see beyond the camera's view frame, and it felt totally normal. All these people I cherished. They all looked so vibrant and alive. The rush of love was almost too much to take, so many details I had long forgotten. My father had a mustache that he apparently grew for the event. My mother's facial expressions were so authentic and heartwarming. Rachel's parents looked so proud and engaged. I heard the breaking of glass and turned toward Rachel as the crowd cheered, "Mazel tov!" I missed the best part, damn it. Rachel and I held up our clasped hands and let out a screech. We then ran from the huppah up the aisle straight at and through me. Wow, that was freaky. The wedding scene faded away, and I was running alone in the forest again, nearing the loop back.

I was exhausted and couldn't believe I was going to do another lap. The music encouraged me onward, and back into the woods I went. Slowly, a single image appeared way off in the distance, too small to make out. It got closer and closer and eventually filled the frame. It was my mother, and she was very young and, oh, so beautiful and stylish. Her image seemed to be projected on the pine boughs and tree trunks like before. I felt the love in her smile and blew her a kiss. The God Helmet weakened my knees with parent-child-bond emotions. I was whacked by low-hanging branches several times, and it was replicated by the armature. I drifted further off with each strike.

Another image was emerging from far off; it was my dad. He looked so cool and at ease with himself like he normally did. His presence filled me full of confidence, as if he were guiding me forward. Next up were my siblings. Similarly, one by one, they emerged from far off and ultimately filled the screen. Their presence was so welcoming and warm. They were young, and I felt as though I was young as well. I could see, off in the distance, the aspen grove was approaching. As I neared the grove, the light started to break up. The flashing beams of light were pulsing with the music. It was just the aspen grove, no images. I began to feel intense anticipation. It must be the God Helmet. What was going to happen? Something better happen—this feeling was making me anxious.

I could hear voices, but I couldn't make out what they were saying. They sounded familiar. I began to make out figures mingling and talking. The image and voices slowly became clearer. It was my extended family. I heard my grandfather's voice. He asked everyone to gather round for a family photo. It was very clear now. I was at my grandparents' farm, in the backyard of the farmhouse. I saw my parents and siblings. I saw my aunt and uncle and cousins. The broken, strobe-enhanced light was pulsing to the rhythm of the music. Again I appeared to be running in place, directly in front of the gathering. There were other relatives there as well, people I hadn't thought of in years. The God Helmet sent surges of belonging, of their presences. Heaving emotions pulsed through my body. I began to be more of a presence and less of an observer. It was so long ago, I thought. Tears of longing welled up in my eyes. It was so powerful.

I was at the farm—a place we all loved so much. It was where my great-grandparents, my grandparents, and father grew up. There was lots of chatter. The voices were so comforting, so soothing. I heard my grandfather call out my name, "Sandy, get over here; we need a family photo."

Then I heard my two cousins in unison, "Yeah, get over here, zit face." I couldn't believe what I'd just heard. Did they just call me zit face? Then from the right, I came bounding in.

"All right, zit face, you made it," cheered one of my cousins. I joined the group and faced the camera. I was upset.

I suddenly realized what came next. I was not ready for it, not now. I didn't want to remember this. Staring into the camera, I yelled out, half choked up, "D-d-d-don't c-c-call me z-z-zit face; that's mean." I was stuttering. Oh my God, I used to stutter. I hadn't thought about that for forever. I had blocked that out of my mind years ago. I stared into my childhood face, closer and closer. My entire face was covered in acne, and I stuttered. Oh my God, you poor thing.

Though my face was covered in acne, it was not what I saw. I saw a sweet young boy. I saw a beautiful boy who just happened to have acne. Just like millions of young kids who deal with acne, it was a huge deal to me. It had a major impact on how I felt about myself. Now I was observing myself deal with it. Though it was hard to watch, I realized little Sandy shined right through the acne. It was just acne, an outer crust of no making of my own. I saw who I really was, and it dawned on me that others probably did as well. The stuttering was a massive shock, however. I was praying I didn't have to hear it again. I was lost in the scene until I heard a loud *smack*. I pulled my view out and saw my cousin being whacked on the back of the head by his dad. "Don't let me hear you say that again, *ever!*" Wow, others did care about my little problem. Why didn't I know that at the time? The whole scene was too much to take in. That it felt live and real was profound. I was face-to-face with a critical element of my upbringing. I couldn't handle it. I stopped running, ripped the goggles and God Helmet off, threw them to the floor, and jumped off the treadmill.

"Jesus, Ben, why would you do that to me? Why would you put me through that? That was way too much," I yelled.

"T-t-t-toooo s-s-soon?" Ben stuttered.

"Fuck you, Ben," I yelled. "Fuck you—that was mean!"

With that, I stormed out of the studio and wandered up the hill to collect myself.

Halfway to Nirvana

Over the next couple of days, Ben did his best to explain his choice of family footage in the event he created. This of course led to a much broader discussion. We had both experienced the Memory Chaser in all its glory. I was experiencing what Ben was talking about—the events I took part in were solidly in the present. They were available via random access and were filled with detail not in the imagery. The memories were out of place and having undue impact on day-to-day life, especially troubling given many of the memories were long forgotten. Ben explained that he thought the Memory Chaser could be used to help resolve internal conflict. This is why, when he discovered the footage of me zit faced and stuttering, he thought it could have therapeutic value. By forcing me to witness my troubled teenage self, I'd see it for what it was and let it go, warts and all. Never mind he had no idea I ever stuttered, had chronic acne, or had a problem with either one.

The more we discussed what it all meant, the more we began to realize the potential of the Memory Chaser. The more I analyzed what Ben put me through, the more I began to realize he was right. Seeing myself as a zit-faced stutterer made me realize that there was more to me than that. I was the one who'd let it define me. "It is you (oh, yeah)." I was a cool little kid that was loved. It sure didn't feel like that at the time, but now I knew it was okay—it was always okay. Moving forward, maybe I won't think that people's first impressions were a bad one. I'll stop casting my insecurity onto how I think others perceive me. I apologized to Ben for cursing him out, and he apologized for putting me through it and then making fun of me. I told him it was a very powerful gift, and I was grateful.

We continued to experiment with the Memory Chaser, tweaking events that we had run and developing new ones. We figured out that the most effective events were centered around a connection with one person; while groups were impactful, a memory of one person was more focused and powerful. We realized that film footage that included motion was extremely effective, but it was a rarity in all the stock footage we had access to. Apparently Sally knew this and had created her own events that were captured this way.

We spent considerable time viewing and running as her in the events she had created. We were hoping to find clues as to what she was searching for. We spent hours discussing the implications of the Memory Chaser as a therapeutic tool. At this point, we both had plenty of experience witnessing the power of revisiting our pasts. The combination of various input stimulus and active meditation was real and, at times, overwhelming. We now knew it not only worked—but worked beyond any preconceived notion. That the memories would persist as a current event that you could replay on demand was troubling. At first it seemed delightful; you could reexperience the Memory Chaser–revived memory whenever you wanted to. It was a two-for-one deal, we thought.

As we ran more and more events, it became apparent that we were disrupting the linear structure of memory. Chunks of the past were occupying the time/space of real time. I couldn't help but think of what Nietzsche had said so long ago. It is vital that we forget. Not just because the mind would be overly cluttered but that simple enjoyment of the same or similar experiences would not be new again. New experiences that were similar to previous experiences would be redundant and devoid of originality as the memory would still be fresh.

There were plenty of unanswered questions, however, some obvious but also some subtle and perhaps more intriguing. That we might never understand Sally's motives seemed inevitable. That there was hardware that we had no clue of the function was unacceptable. The crystal cube positioned in front of the treadmill and the mysterious mass-storage device were central to our gap in fully understanding Sally's mission. We now knew that the two probably functioned together, as we discovered they were directly wired together via fiber-optic cables that were tucked into the floorboards. What their purpose was and how to activate them was a complete mystery.

It was early one evening as I sat in the cabin absorbing the woodstove's welcoming heat while reading Sally's writings that Ben approached me with a strange look on his face. He told me he found something that I'd better have a look at. I asked him what it was. He hung his head and shook me off, telling me I'd just have to see it.

I got up and followed him to the studio. Ben's silence punctuated the serious nature of his discovery. Once in the studio, Ben turned toward me and put his hands on my shoulders and looked me straight in the eyes.

"Dad, I ran across some footage of Sally. There were a number of files in a hidden directory on her desktop. I don't know why I didn't think of looking for hidden files, but I found something that's really important. Several of the files are footage of her documenting her quest. I haven't viewed all of them yet because, well because…Oh God, Dad, I found footage of her final minutes!"

Ben pulled me in for an extended hug, and he began to weep uncontrollably. I held him close and assured him it was going to be okay. I guided him to the couch, and we sat down together. As he slowly composed himself, he attempted to explain, but the words were interrupted by halting gasps. I told him again that it was okay and that he should take some deep breaths. After a few minutes of silence, Ben began to explain what he'd discovered.

"The footage is Sally running in an event on the Memory Chaser. I believe it's when she died. It's all really too much. It's what Mac described to us, more or less. She left out one thing—the crystal…" Ben trailed off. "You'll just have to watch it."

"Okay, Ben, that's what we should do then."

Ben took a couple more deep breaths and made his way to the workstation. He cued up the footage and told me as sincerely as possible, "This is it, Dad."

The footage began, and we were viewing Sally from behind and above, from the same position as the VR camera. A spacy jam was wailing as she ran at a steady pace in time with the music. She was wearing the VR goggles and had the original God Helmet on. There was a multitude of rainbow-colored wires streaming off of the God Helmet. The camera's view was a wider angle than the VR camera. We could see beyond the projection screens, including a portion of the skylight.

The scene was set in an old-growth aspen grove. It was not the same aspen grove—the trees were enormous. There was broken light breaking through the canopy, as in the original event. The beams were distinct, solid columns of light separated by near darkness. The columns were pulsating to the music. We could barely hear her panting to the beat. Slowly, a small silhouette appeared off in the distance. We could hear Sally speaking but couldn't make out the words. The silhouette morphed into a man as Sally was closing in. As Sally approached, the man turned toward Sally—it was Chase. It was hard to make out, but it sounded like she was saying, "Catch me if you can." Sally ran by Chase, and off she went into the forest.

She continued running through the aspen grove alone. Another image appeared off in the distance. As Sally approached, the image started to fill the screen. It was Rachel, only now it was not a still image—it was close-up video of her face. She was talking, but there was no sound, just her beautiful face offering silent words of what appeared to be praise. Rachel's face faded into the scenery, and off in the distance another image was forming. This time it was me, and like Rachel, I converted from an image to close-up footage of myself talking to the camera with no sound. I didn't recognize where the footage was from, but we were somewhat younger, and it seemed to be staged. As I dissolved into the scenery, the footage flickered and went

89

black for a second. The footage resumed, and the beams of broken light were colored. Some of the beams were a deep azure, and some were orange.

The footage flickered again, and when it steadied, the studio was illuminated with a subtle glow. The glow began to pulse in alternating azure and orange light. The pulsing colors were entering through the skylight. Crackling could be heard breaking through the space jam. Sally's God Helmet was slowly being surrounded in a halo of pulsating light. The colored halo was composed of rotating bands of alternating azure and orange. The bands were spinning at an extremely rapid pace around the helmet.

The lights were slowly making their way down each individual wire leading from the God Helmet. The wires appeared to be coated in a thin layer of pulsating light. Some of the wires were coated in azure, some in orange. The light emanating from the skylight became more intense and rotated around the antenna. We could no longer see any of the scenery on the screen—it was too bright. The footage began to shake.

Suddenly, something in front of Sally began to glow with an intense white-and-indigo light. It was emanating from the cube. We got fleeting glimpses of the glowing crystal as Sally's body moved about from her running. From inside the crystal, radiating electrical charges began reaching outward. The charges looked like tiny indigo lightning bolts. They were pulsating and orbiting in a circular pattern about the crystal like a Van de Graaff generator at full charge. It was getting more intense with each second. It was hard to believe Sally was still running with all that was happening—it was like she was expecting it. In an instant, the radiating electrical charges from the crystal cube started bending toward Sally. Simultaneously, the halo of light on the God Helmet was reaching down toward the crystal cube. The two light sources were being drawn toward one another—they were intermixing.

The swirling lights from the God Helmet pulsed down to the crystal cube as the arcing electrical charges from the cube were tickling the God Helmet. The light sources were now completely intermingled and continuous. With a great rush, the swarm of indigo lightning bolts enveloped the God Helmet and, within a split second, reversed course and retracted back into cube. It pulled with it the azure-and-orange God Helmet light. The stream of light from the God Helmet was now a continuous flow of high energy light or plasma and quickly built in intensity. The energy stream was raging from the helmet to the crystal cube at an extremely high rate of speed. It became clear that this was not just an electrical phenomenon, current running from one place to another. It was Sally herself, leaping from her body through the helmet and into the crystal cube. Were we witnessing her soul leaving her body?

The footage began rattling so violently that it was hard to make out what was going on. The light became so bright that barely anything was discernible. Then a massive boom struck, and the footage went completely dark. I couldn't believe what we just saw. It was totally silent and dark. Just as we were thinking it was over, a rustling could be heard—something was moving. A weak light began to illuminate the scene. Its source was off to the right, beyond the frame of the camera. A soft, shaky voice was barely audible. As it got louder, we heard what it was saying. It was a girl's voice, and she was calling Sally's name. It was Mac. The light and the voice were getting closer. The room was smoky, and dust particles were hanging heavily in the air. I was afraid to look. Mac's silhouette was now barely visible at the bottom of the frame. She was crawling across floor. He phone's flashlight was bouncing about as she made her way to the treadmill. We got glimpses of Sally's body crumpled on the treadmill. Mac called out Sally's name again as she began to weep. She was now directly to the side of Sally's body. Then a clear and perfectly enunciated voice spoke. It was Sally's voice, and she said in a calm but exulted tone, "It's so beautiful. It's so beautiful, Mac."

Part Two – One Year Later

Version Two – The Egg

In the past year the Memory Chaser has seen remarkable enhancements. Ben and I believe that it is approaching what Sally envisioned the device should do. Nearly all of the components have been redesigned in version two. The net result is a reliably consistent and more vibrant experience. None of this would have been possible without the assistance of Astral Computational, a biotech company we partnered with. They provide the technology muscle behind new developments and in return own fifty percent of the commercial applications we are developing together.

The projected video that used to be presented on two curved screens is now an immersive miniature 360-degree theater. This was accomplished by the introduction of a large, elongated sphere that encloses the treadmill. The elongated sphere, or Egg, as Ben likes to call it, is lined with a 360-degree LCD screen. The view forward from the treadmill is very similar to the original Memory Chaser, only now it extends all the way around and behind the participant. The scene moves from the front along the sides and trails away in the back. The perspective provides a near three-dimensional feel for the runner.

The virtual reality goggles, which provided the participant with a perspective from above and just behind the user, are no longer necessary. While the user's live image is still captured from the same perspective, behind and above, it is now digitally integrated into the LCD scene. This is not only more realistic but also frees the user from the cumbersome distraction of the VR goggles.

The spatial-congruity armature has been replaced with a bodysuit. The bodysuit looks like something a downhill skier would wear. It's jet black and has a mesh of wiring woven through the entire suit. The wiring can produce tactile sensations anywhere on the user's body. A variety of sensations can be mimicked, from a whack, to a pinch, to the sensation of someone gently touching the user. It can even simulate the sensation of hot or cold at a specific location or over the entire body. These tactile sensations are programmed into the progressive scene and timed to specific events, just like the tree branch. Now, however, the tactile control is way more significant in the overall experience. It's no longer just running into a tree branch. A hug causes the suit to grip the user as if they were actually being hugged. If the sun comes out during a run, the suit heats up, simulating the beaming sunlight's warmth. It's really quite amazing.

The God Helmet has also been enhanced. It's now encased in what resembles an Apollo astronaut's inner head garment. The early astronauts nicknamed it the Snoopy Cap, after the cartoon dog, for its black-and-white panels. Ben likes to call it God's bathing cap. Ben has doubled the number of magnetic coils to sixteen. The additional magnetic coils provide the ability to focus the God Helmet's magnetic energy to exponentially more targets in the brain by altering which coils are active. This, in addition to more robust software controls, provides a more predictable sensation in the user. Ben and the folks at Astral designed presets for a variety of emotional states. Feelings like happiness, sadness, fear, anxiety, or joy can be elicited with the flip of a switch. The crème de la crème is the fine-tuning of the God experience. There is now a preset that emulates a feeling that the user is in the presence of otherworldly beings, or God, if you will. While we experienced this sensation with the original God Helmet, it was never predictable when or if it would occur. It can now be induced on demand with specific software settings. It's truly crazy.

A key component that Astral Computational developed was the animation of a single still photo. They wrote software that can turn a single image into a moving, talking, animated, three-dimensional version of the subject. Astral Computational also helped us expand some of the concepts Sally had developed. They enhanced the functionality of the insertion of animated characters into stock video. With minimal participant-provided images and video, animated video can be easily constructed and inserted into user-provided video.

An intriguing effect Astral Computational developed is the aging of a participant from images the user provides. A single image of a participant as a child and as an adult can be animated into a seamless aging video. Though this is nothing new, when integrated into a Memory Chaser event, the results are quite compelling.

Ben and I have been exploring the beneficial applications the Memory Chaser could be used for beyond purely recreational endeavors. This led us to two population groups. The first group is people with severe memory issues. The idea is to help people with dementia, particularly those with Alzheimer's, recover lost memories. The second group is criminals who have committed serious crimes, particularly violent crimes. We believe having violent criminals revisit their criminal acts could force them to confront their hideous behavior. By witnessing their actions, it could force them to become empathetic and have remorse. This could be their first step to correcting their behavior, hopefully forever.

93

Astral Computational helped me set up version two of Memory Chaser in a mall kiosk in Denver. The goal was to get as many people to try it out and build a database of their experiences. This will help us fine tune any issues with the Memory Chaser as identified by the participants.

While all of these improvements are a great accomplishment, the biggest joy for Ben and me has been how close we feel to Sally. Through the whole process we have felt her presence as if she were guiding us. My only wish is that Rachel could be with us and experience what Ben and I have. I miss her so much.

Reunion at the Cabin

Heading up the gentle incline to Sally's cabin, I'm overwhelmed by the massive expanse of Mount Princeton. The mountain fills the horizon and half the skyline. I wonder if this behemoth of a mountain is a creator or a destroyer. Its time scale from creation to destruction seems impossible to imagine. As I get closer to the cabin, I realize I can see the top of the studio's antenna peaking over the sharp rise in front of me. The skyward-reaching antenna is perfectly aligned with the upper peak of Mount Princeton. Why have I never noticed this before?

As I get out of the truck and stretch, I hear the screen door on the cabin creak and slam shut. Before I can turn toward the cabin, I hear Ben's excited greeting. "Dad, Dad, oh my God, it's so, so good to see you!" We run toward each other and simultaneously stumble short of the ground before rising and engaging in an extended bear hug. As we hug, we realize how funny the synchronized near fall was and begin to laugh uncontrollably mid bear hug. It's one of those belly laughs that makes you cry.

While trying to catch my breath, I barely get out, "Ah, Ben, my sweet Ben, how ya been?"

As we separate, Ben starts a rapid-fire diatribe. "Oh, you can't believe how pumped up I am! Willy is out of his mind with excitement. He really thinks he's onto something, something big. I don't quite understand it all, but I'm sure he'll get us up to speed. The lights, Dad, the lights!"

"Jesus, I thought we were onto something big. Let's go inside, and you can fill me in."

I take my bag to the small bedroom and go to the kitchen to prepare some espresso. As Ben starts back in at a manic pace, I wonder if he really needs espresso.

"Why don't you slow it down a touch, and start at the beginning. How did Willy happen to come here?"

"So I got a call early yesterday morning, and it's Willy. He said he was in Poncha Springs and wanted to see us. I told him you weren't here, but I'd love to see him. He said he'd be right over."

"That's so Willy—he just pops up out of nowhere."

"I'll say. It was only eight in the morning. I almost didn't answer the phone. He shows up about half an hour later all hopped up and kind of manic. He told me he was following up on some fieldwork. He said he had met with Dr. Persinger's people. Willy told me that, after meeting with Persinger's people, he was convinced that the Tectonic Strain Theory was real. Not only were the lights a result of geologic strain but the lights clearly caused strange mental states in people who were exposed to them. He was saying that the people exposed to these lights suddenly became telepathic. I don't know, Dad—it all sounds crazy."

"That is crazy. Did he say when he was coming back?"

"He was headed to Valley View Hot Springs in the San Luis Valley to check out some sort of trench that exposed a fault. He said he was also going to look up some Buddhist monk in Crestone. This guy knew something about ALPs, and he was going to meet with him. I don't know, but now it all seems like a dream or something."

"When is he coming back?"

"Oh yeah, sorry, he said he'd be back in a day or two."

"Well, that'll be perfect; it'll give us some time to get caught up on each other's work."

"Yeah, you won't believe how version two is coming along. The final improvements are working flawlessly. There're just a few glitches I have to work out, and then I think it'll be ready for prime time. Let's finish our coffee, and I'll take you out to the yurt and show you where I am with it. The consultants have been a real godsend."

"That sounds great. I can't believe how quickly this has all come together. So Astral Computational really delivered? I knew they'd come through for us after I spent some time in their shop and they walked me through a mock-up. Did they solve the dyed-air problem? Does it project in three dimensions yet?"

"Did they ever, it works like a charm. So what do you think, Dad? It's really happening! All our ideas are nearly in place. It's really quite remarkable. Don't you think Sally would be so pleased?"

"I can't tell you how happy I am. Sally would be so very proud. I just wish she were here with us. I gotta see the final version action. So you've been working in the yurt? How's that space working out?"

"The yurt's been an excellent work space. I really want to move the Egg to the studio. Though I'm not sure why, I think having it integrated with the antenna is going to be important. Let's head out there after you tell me about your work in Denver. Have you contacted the doctors and the prison folks?"

"I have indeed, Ben. I've had several meetings with the doctors and professionals at the Alzheimer's Association chapter in Denver. I even got them out to the kiosk at the mall, and they got to experience the Memory Chaser for themselves. They were impressed with the experience but weren't convinced of its application.

"I had a rather interesting couple meetings with the folks at the Criminal Rehabilitation Clinic. There's a psychiatrist there, Dr. Charles—he loves the Memory Chaser. Originally, I got a lot of weird stares from most of the staff. From the beginning, however, Dr. Charles seemed genuinely intrigued. I think he convinced the others to keep an open mind about the concept because my follow-up meeting had a much better reception from his staff.

"Though I've been frustrated with the kiosk setup, I think it's accomplishing what we set out to do," I explain. "I had nearly one hundred people participate, and they all provided feedback. The automated survey was really helpful; thanks for putting that together."

I explain to Ben that my initial meeting with the folks at the Denver chapter of the Alzheimer's Association was somewhat awkward. "My presentation went well regarding the functionality of the Memory Chaser. I gave them my usual spiel explaining how the device works. I told them how our target group would be middle-aged people who were afflicted with early onset Alzheimer's. I explained how anyone with severe memory issues who is somewhat agile and moderately fit would be a target candidate. I told them I was looking to them to help sort out candidate selection for the initial clinical trials.

"One of the young doctors in the group was very excited about the concept. Her name is Dr. Lisa Souvenir. She asked if they could experience the Memory Chaser. I told them they could, but we should start with Dr. Souvenir. The others would be welcome, but I'd only have time to customize it for one participant. I instructed Dr. Souvenir to email me a variety of pictures of her and her parents and siblings, preferably from special events in her life. The images should span from when she and her family were young to present day.

97

"The next week the group showed up right on time. They all had their running clothes on. Each one of them got a short run in the Egg. The imagery was the event that had our family members zooming into view from deep in the forest. The group was very excited; I heard them chattering manically about their experience while I was rigging up Dr. Souvenir to the Memory Chaser.

"As she was nearing the end of the event. I heard Dr. Souvenir cry out as the image of her elderly parents filled the frame. The God Helmet monitor was maxed out on the God setting. I wondered if she was all right, and then she screamed out, 'Good Lord, have mercy!' I asked her if she was okay, and she nodded her head in the affirmative. I told her in a calm voice that she was nearing the end. I told her that when she exits the forest, she should slow her pace down and be prepared to stop running.

"Dr. Souvenir slowed to a stop and ripped the God Helmet off, tossed it to the floor, and ran out of the dome to the portico. I think she was crying. I ran after her and saw she was being comforted by her colleagues. I stopped and asked from a slight distance if she was okay. Dr. Souvenir pulled herself together, turned, and looked me in the eye. She said, 'I'm quite all right, Mr. Stern, quite all right. I think that'll do for today.' One of Dr. Souvenir's associates came over to me and said it would be best if we continue this at another time. They gathered their belongings and off they went.

"A week later I got a call from Dr. Souvenir. She was very apologetic regarding her reaction to the Memory Chaser. I assured her that it was not only okay but was a common first reaction from many of the participants. She told me that her experience was traumatic and somewhat of an overload on her senses. She went on to explain how the images pulled related memories seemingly out of nowhere. She really took to the out-of-body experience, claiming she was seeing herself from a totally new perspective. She was overwhelmed by a sense of empathy and compassion for herself. She got all choked up when recalling the final image of her elderly parents. Dr. Souvenir claimed the image of them was accompanied by an overwhelming sense of an otherworldly presence. It was like a warm, welcoming, tingling sensation that was beckoning her and her parents upward. She said she knew immediately what it was. Both her parents passed away in the last year. It was the same experience she had at their dying bedsides. She thanked me profusely and asked how she could help me promote the Memory Chaser."

"Jesus Christ, Dad, you must've freaked—that's intense!"

"Yeah, I was so glad to get her call. I was thinking I scared her off for good. I will say this, seeing others experience what we have experienced is quite moving and fulfilling. It's a sort of validation that we're not crazy. This thing works!"

"So what happened with the jailers?"

"First off, they aren't jailers; quit calling them that. They are professional psychiatrists who work in the criminal-justice system helping rehabilitate serious criminals. They're trying to help these people overcome whatever drove them to commit their crimes."

I tell Ben about my meetings with Dr. Charles and his staff at the Criminal Rehabilitation Center in Denver. "I explained to the group how the Memory Chaser works, that the various components together sets the stage to revisit lost memories. I told him that, for your clients, reliving their crime from a removed perspective would be a powerful experience."

"When I finished my presentation I took a long pause and paced the front of the room while examining my audience. It was quiet for a long time. I guessed I had made my point.

"Then Dr. Charles finally spoke up. He said, 'Tell me, Mr. Stern, this is all fairly incredible stuff, but I have to ask you—what is your motivation?' "

What is my motivation indeed…

The Laurentians

I awake from a deep sleep. I'm not sure where I am at first. I know I'm not in Denver. The late-evening sun blazing on my face causes me to hide under a pillow. I smell fresh pine in the air, and it all comes rushing back. I'm lying on the couch in Sally's cabin. I try to rub the sleep from my mind with the heels of my hands. It's a slow process. I sit up and smack my dry mouth in an attempt to generate some saliva. Where's Ben? I get up and shuffle my way to the bedroom. No Ben. I go to the bathroom and splash cold water on my face. I cup water in my hands and slurp up its vitality. I put my shoes on and head out to the yurt.

I hear a spacy jam emanating from the structure. After I enter, I'm standing in front of the Egg. Multicolored light is strobing out of the elongated sphere. The Egg seems to be filled with deep-blue smoke. As I get closer, I see that Ben's in the Egg, running away on the treadmill to an event. It's a very space-age-looking sight. I take a seat and wait for Ben to finish.

As the music falls silent, the lights in the Memory Chaser go dark, and Ben emerges from the Egg. "How was your run?" I ask Ben.

"I was just trying out some tweaks I did to the Mem Chaser. How was your nap?"

"Wow, I was out hard. What are you working on? Are you gonna let me take it for a test drive?"

"Of course. Come check it out. It's really humming now."

As I approach the Egg, I notice the smoke is gone. "What happened to the smoke or dyed air or whatever it is? What the heck is dyed air anyway?"

"Isn't that a cool name for it? I'm not sure how it works, but it's not smoke at all. The people at Astral Computational are crazy. I don't know how they come up with some of their concepts, let alone follow through and make their ideas reality. The dyed air is created by exciting the nitrogen in the air inside the Egg. There're several pad-mounted ultraviolet emitters inside the Egg. Somehow they modulate the ultraviolet emitter's frequency, and it excites the nitrogen in the air. The excited nitrogen fluoresces with a deep indigo color. The cool thing is that the indigo light disrupts visible light traveling through it. It very slightly slows the visible light down but not evenly. The video, which of course is light, arrives at the viewer's eyes at slightly delayed times depending on its color. They're kind of secretive about the specifics, but believe me, it works. They like to say it's a very sophisticated version of the 3D glasses you wear in 3D movies. I'm sure it's more complicated than that, but like I said, some of their technology is highly proprietary, and we're on a need-to-know basis. The delayed arrival of the light spectrum creates a three-dimensional effect."

As I'm about to climb into the Memory Chaser, we hear rapid-fire horn honks coming from the driveway. Ben and I look at each other and say simultaneously, "That's gotta be Willy." We run out of the yurt to greet Willy.

We run toward each other and collide in a group hug. Midhug, Willy starts jumping up and down, and we join in as if we just scored a walk-off home run. As we pull away from each other, no one says a word—we just stare at one another. I can see Willy is tearing up. I ask him if he's okay.

"Ohana, man, ohana," Willy says with a Hawaiian accent. "It's been a long, strange trip, I'm fine, but I'm so glad to be here, so glad, ohana."

"Let us help you with your stuff," I offer. "Been doing some dirt work? I love your rock hammer; you look like you're right out of a Western. Don't draw that thing on me."

Willy makes like he's ready to draw his rock hammer out of its holster. "Draw, pardner," he says with a cowboy drawl.

We gather up Willy's bags and head into the cabin. Ben and Willy crack beers, and we take a seat. I can tell Willy is a bit disheveled and not really himself. He clearly has a lot going on in his mind. I suggest that we get a fire going in the firepit outside. Willy seems to like that idea. I ask Ben if he'll get it started and we'll be out in a minute.

As Ben gets the fire going, I walk over to Willy and put my hands on his shoulders. "It seems like you've got a lot on your mind, my friend. Are you okay? You know we're here for you, don't you?"

"I know you are. It's been crazy since I saw you last, especially the last two days. I'm not sure where to start. Let me chill for a minute. There's a lot to tell, believe me."

We hang out and chitchat, then make our way out to the firepit. The fire is raging, and the darkening sky is filled with gorgeous pastels of orange and blue from the setting sun. Willy and Ben quickly proceed with follow-up beers. It's starting to look like it might be a long night.

101

"So, Willy, what the hell's going on? Ben tells me you're onto something big—what's it all about? I have an idea based on what Ben's told me, but why don't you start from the beginning?"

"Well, right after we met last year, I really got thinking about what happened at the funeral pyre and at Sally's cabin here. You know I'd been thinking I was kinda done with the whole working thing and felt like I needed something new to do. After meeting with you and Ben in Salida, I couldn't stop thinking about the strange phenomena, the ALPs. That it was possibly related to faulting and earthquakes seemed like a perfect fit for me to investigate further. I read as much of Persinger's work as I could get my hands on. He was quite widely published. Whether you believe his theories or not, you can't deny his approach was solid. You know, the scientific method and all. His papers are all backed up by controlled experiments, observations, and measurements. Anyway, after I felt I was fully versed on his work, I tried to contact him. He was still at Laurentian University in Ontario. When I called the university, I was told that he had passed away a little over a year ago. I couldn't believe it. I'd missed an opportunity of a lifetime. I was stunned.

"I immediately did some research regarding his death and found several tributes to him as well as a couple obituaries," Willy continued. "He was really highly thought of in certain circles. It was tragic for many people. For some reason his departure date rang a bell. It was then I realized it was around the time as Sally's death. I looked through my notes and found Sally's date of departure. Sally and Persinger died on the same exact date! I couldn't believe it. How was this possible? Is this one of those there-are-no-coincidences things?"

"Whoa, whoa, whoa," Ben exclaims. "Are you kidding me? That can't be possible."

"Oh my God, Willy," I cry out. "Holy Jesus, that's spooky. Are you positive?"

"It really happened; I assure you. That's just the beginning, my friends."

"What happened to him?" I recoil. "How did he die?"

"I don't know; it wasn't in his obituary. Everyone assumes it was a heart attack, as it was so sudden and he was apparently in good health. There are rumors that they couldn't determine the cause of death. That would only be fitting for such an enigmatic man."

I look over at Ben and see that he's staring at me, mouth agape. I know precisely what he's thinking. "Willy, you know Sally's death was originally thought to be from electrocution. When I met with the coroner to get her death certificate, he told me that the cause of death was undeterminable. Surely this is just a coincidence?"

"Is that so? I'm beginning to believe that there truly are no coincidences. There is more though, much more."

"Yeah?" Ben interjects. "Please, do tell."

Willy then drains slowly off his fireside seat and pours to the ground just far enough away from the fire as to not be burned. As he lies there, spread eagle on the ground, he begins to wave his arms and legs as if creating a snow angel in the dirt. His flailing arms and legs slowly come to rest. As Willy lies there on his back in the pine-needled dirt, he starts back in on his encounters as he stares up through the clearing in the massive ponderosa pines at the emerging stars.

"I eventually connected with some of Persinger's colleagues at Laurentian University. One gentleman was especially helpful; his name was Dr. Strange. I told him what my interests were, that I was researching ALPs, and wanted to pick their brains on some of Persinger's theories. I related the experience you all had at Sally's funeral pyre and the odd circumstances surrounding Sally's passing. He was very receptive to my inquiries and suggested I come to Laurentian for a sit-down meeting.

"A couple weeks after our conversation, I made my way up north to Laurentian in Sudbury, Ontario. Sudbury is just north of Lake Huron. It's an old nickel mining town. I read somewhere that the nickel deposit is related to a comet impact billions of years ago. Anyway, I met Dr. Strange and a couple of his colleagues. We gathered in a conference room on campus for several hours. I got to air all my questions regarding Persinger's Tectonic Strain Theory. I had a hard time connecting anomalous luminous phenomena, or ALPs, to tectonic strain. What are the mechanisms that connect subsurface strain to electromagnetic phenomena on the surface miles above the strain source? I was especially interested in hearing their thoughts on the strange phenomena experienced by folks who were in and around ALPs activity. The most powerful phenomenon was telepathic communication between those enveloped in the ALPs light. I told them that this was experienced by the attendees at Sally's funeral. I related to them that the telepathic communication at the funeral culminated with a fugue state that lasted for several hours.

"Dr. Strange and his colleagues were very patient with me. Many of their explanations regarding Tectonic Strain Theory were calculus based. There was a time I probably could have followed their detailed formulas, but that was a long time ago. The more geologic-oriented discussion was like candy to my hungry mind, however. One seemingly sound theory they described was that the electromagnetic energy traveled up fault planes to the surface. Fault planes, especially open fault planes, are commonly lined with mineral precipitates. Some of these minerals are highly conductive and can provide a low-resistivity pathway for electromagnetic energy from the deep-seated strain to the surface. As I was interested in mapping likely locations for ALPs activity, they gave me some of their research that described in detail what minerals would most likely be present in ALPs-correlated fault zones. This information could be very helpful in identifying these areas.

"These mineral deposits cover a broader area beyond a narrow fault zone and perhaps would make it easier to locate the actual fault zones. While I'd read that this was the case, it never occurred to me to use these occurrences as a mapping technique to locate faults. Dr. Strange told me that some of the minerals deposited by ALPs had magnetic properties and, as such, could be located with magnetic sensors they'd developed. I was now getting really excited that I might be able to locate future ALPs-activity locations."

"That's incredible, Willy," I said excitedly. "Is that your plan? To go find where the best spots are to witness ALPs activity?"

"Precisely, Sandy—that's my plan, and I'm sticking to it!"

"Is that what you were doing in Crestone?" Ben inquires.

"Yeah, sort of. The USGS did some work there recently. They call it trenching. They took a backhoe and dug a ten-foot-deep trench forty feet long to intersect a fault in cross section. I visited it yesterday and collected some samples."

"That's really cool, Willy," Ben responds. "Did you find any of the minerals they were talking about?"

"Possibly, the precipitates are tiny crystals, too small to identify without a microscope or more sophisticated instrumentation. That's my next step. I collected a couple dozen samples from the trench. I have my microscope in the truck; we'll see if my mineralogy is still any good."

"So did they know much about the effects ALPs events have had on people?" I ask.

104

"Yes and no. They aren't much closer to understanding why people experience things like telepathy or encounters with 'others.' They showed me a database that they had compiled over the years of interviews with those that have had these types of experiences. They said there was a remarkable similarity in what these people were describing. The database covers over twenty years of events from around the globe. The most common experience was the ability to read each other's thoughts, to telepathically communicate with those around them. Some folks described a sudden closeness to lost relatives and friends. For some, it was way more than a memory but was described as a presence of dead people. Some reported having similar thoughts or feelings of living people who were thousands of miles removed. Apparently, it wasn't uncommon for subjects to enter a fugue state after having a particularly intense ALPs encounter, just like what happened at Sally's funeral. They said people described it as becoming exhausted after the experience, like it drained them of all their energy and they just passed out.

"Near the end of our meeting, Dr. Strange got real serious and looked me straight in the eye and asked me if I was ready for this. I didn't know what to say, so I asked what that could be. He asked me if I was familiar with Dr. Persinger's work on telepathic communication. This had nothing to do with tectonic strain and related ALPs events. This was straight-up telepathic communication. I told him that I was familiar to the point that I'd read his papers. Dr. Strange then told me that Dr. Persinger believed, and had some proof, that the intensity of telepathic communication was directly related to Earth's magnetic field. He described how Earth's magnetic field fluctuates in intensity over time. For some reason, there's a strong correlation between low-magnetic intensity and telepathic communication. Dr. Persinger had demonstrated this in clinical settings numerous times.

"Dr. Strange then asked me if I was familiar with magnetic polar reversals. I told him that I was and reminded him I was a geologist, after all."

"Well, I don't know what a polar reversal is—what is it?" I ask.

"Oh, sorry, Sandy, sometimes I forget who my audience is, no offense."

"None taken. I think I'm following you so far, but you got me there."

"Isn't that when the north and south poles switch polarities?" Ben asks.

"Precisely, Ben. In a magnetic polar reversal, the poles switch polarity so that a compass would indicate that magnetic north is geographically south.

Geologists have known about this for over fifty years. There's direct evidence of this in the rock record. In fact, reversals have happened hundreds of times in Earth's history. Magnetic reversals happen every two hundred thousand to three hundred thousand years. As it turns out, we're about three hundred thousand years overdue for the next reversal.

"Dr. Strange then told me why this is important. Magnetic polar reversals are not instantaneous; they can take thousands of years to fully flip. The time between reversals is full of flux in Earth's magnetic field intensity. The magnetic intensity can go from zero to full strength very quickly. Most interesting is what happens when there is no magnetic field. Dr. Strange then got to the exciting point. He told me that there's a lot of rumbling in the geophysical community that a polar reversal has already begun. Apparently there's enough evidence that various researchers are about to publish this finding. He told me that he and his colleagues' work supports this.

"Now, recall," Willy said excitedly as he hopped back up on his log seat while taking a long pull on his beer, "that Dr. Persinger believed that telepathic communication was more likely to take place when Earth's magnetic energy was low or quiet? Well guess what? We are about to enter the mother of all telepathic potential, the complete silencing of Earth's magnetic field! I shudder to think what this may mean!"

"You mean we're going to be able to read each other's thoughts or something?" Ben asks skeptically.

"I don't know about reading thoughts. I'm not sure what that even means. I'm saying that, according to Dr. Persinger, telepathic communication could possibly become a common thing."

"That's the craziest thing I've ever heard, Willy," I say, struggling to understand the implications.

"It's real crazy shit," responds Willy. "It's so crazy that I gotta take a piss and collect my thoughts."

As Willy takes care of business in the woods, Ben and I sit there staring through the fire at each other while shaking our heads. It's a lot to take in. What did this have to do with the Memory Chaser? For the first time I questioned if we were pursuing the right path. For some reason I knew that Ben was thinking the same. Out of nowhere, in my head, I hear Dr. Charles's fateful words: *What is your motivation?* What indeed. Before I can say anything, Ben gets real still, and while looking straight into my eyes, asks, "Dad, what's our motivation here?"

Willy comes bounding toward the fire from the darkness of the surrounding woods. He's talking to himself, or so we think. As he gets closer, we can see he is cradling something in his arms. "Who's a good little kitty? Who's a good little kitty? You are; you are. Look what I found, you guys!"

"Oh my God, Willy, it's that creepy cat," Ben says excitedly. "Where did you find her? I haven't seen her in a couple months. How'd you pick her up? She won't get near us. Are you a cat person or something?"

"Oh I love cats, and they love me for some reason. Ever since I was young, cats can't get enough of me. She practically jumped into my arms. Is she yours, Ben?"

"No, not really, she lives here I guess; she kinda comes a goes as she pleases."

"Willy, that's spooky," I say. "That cat has been lurking about, observing us from afar. She was here when I did the walk-through with Sheriff Broadless after Sally died."

As Willy sits down with his new found friend, all the while stroking her long fur, he looks up at us and asks, "Are you ready for the rest of the story?"

"There's more?" I ask, somewhat stunned.

"Yeah, my trip to Crestone, you gotta hear this."

"I don't know if I'm ready for more," I reply. "But let's hear it."

"So after we wrapped up our meeting, Dr. Strange and I went out for some lunch before I headed back. Dr. Strange explained that the San Luis Valley was an area he and his team have been interested in for a long time. Dr. Strange told me that the San Luis Valley has some of the highest-reported UFO sightings in the world. A large number of these sightings were correlated to earthquake activity by Dr. Persinger. Persinger believed these lights were, in fact, ALPs activity, not UFOs."

"Didn't you tell us something about this on your last visit, Willy?" I ask.

"I did indeed, but now I know so much more about it. Dr. Strange told me that he had a connection there that he communicates with periodically regarding ALPs activity in the area. He suggested I pay him a visit. His name is Sid R. Thor. He's an eclectic man who was born into the Kiowa Indian

Tribe. He's a mathematician that converted to Buddhism. It took me a while, but I finally took Dr. Strange up on his suggestion and contacted Mr. Thor. We set up a meeting, and that was one of the reasons I went to Crestone yesterday. I spent this morning with him."

"What?" Ben questions. "A mathematician turned Buddhist monk? Now I've heard it all!"

"No, Ben," Willy snaps. "You haven't heard it all; listen to this."

"Sid spent the morning telling me about the recent goings-on in Crestone. He was very welcoming and excited to talk ALPs activity around Crestone. He was eager to hear how the folks at Laurentian University were doing. He then told me about the recent lights in Crestone.

"Sid told me that, over the past couple years, the frequency of ALPs occurrences had really picked up in and around Crestone. It has really caused a stir there. Many people have reported that they've experienced strange things, like telepathic communication and the presence of spirits, when exposed to the ALPs. He told me that he had experience with ALPs himself. Get this—he said he had an experience when he was younger that was the driving force behind him converting to Buddhism and becoming a monk. It wasn't at Crestone, however. It was right here where we're sitting!"

"What do you mean, right here, Willy?" I demand.

"Yes, right here. He said he used to live in Sally's place some twenty years ago. He had an office in the studio where he did his numerical analysis for NOAA."

"How did you figure that out?" Ben inquires.

"When I told him the story about Sally, one thing led to the next. We discovered the little cabin he lived in twenty years ago was this very place. He called it the ham shack because it used to be a ham-radio station in the early sixties before he lived there. He said one day, when he was working in the studio, he had an incredible experience. What he described was exactly what happened at Sally's funeral pyre and presumably here as well. He said, out of nowhere, a strange light was beaming through the skylight in the studio. When he looked up out of the skylight, he couldn't believe what he was looking at. A massive swirl of orange-and-blue light was twisting and pulsating up and down the antenna. Within seconds, the spinning intensified and the light rapidly dropped down the antenna and filled the room with dancing orange-and-blue light. He said he felt his mind lift up and away

108

from his body. He had an out-of-body experience that was accompanied by overwhelming emotions that rapidly alternated from ecstatic joy to complete empathy. He said he suddenly felt connected to life itself. From his removed perspective, he saw himself for the first time, as he described it. He saw who he was and felt almost sorry for himself as his body looked so tiny in the grand scheme of things. Suddenly, a massive boom rattled the studio. This was followed by shaking from what he later assumed was an earthquake. The last thing he remembered was watching his body, which was cocooned in swirling light, fall to the ground, and then he passed out."

"Holy Jesus, Willy," I say, astounded. "Holy Jesus!"

"Holy Jesus is right! After that experience, he gave up mathematics and moved to Crestone to study Buddhism under a Rinpoche there. He's lived there ever since with his wife and son. I met his son, Chase; he's a real interesting character."

"Did you say Chase?" Ben and I say in unison.

"Yes, Chase, what's wrong? You guys look like you've seen a ghost or something."

Confirming Chase

I awake to the sound of someone singing off in the distance. It's Willy, and he's singing the Grateful Dead's "Ripple." He seems awfully chipper for seven in the morning, especially after all the beer last night. I look out the window to see what he's up to. Willy is sitting at a card table, looking through a microscope. He must be examining samples he collected from the fault in Crestone. I put on a pair of sweats and a hoodie as the morning air is chilly and crisp. As the creaky screen door slams behind me, Willy looks up from his scope and greets me. "Ohana, my dear friend, how are you on this glorious morning?"

"I'm not sure, to be honest; my head still hurts from your revelations last night. It was like taking a sip from the fire hydrant."

"Sandy, you know you can't sip from the fire hydrant. You gotta open wide and take it in, brother!"

"Thanks for that wisdom, but I was just trying to convey—"

"Come on, man. I was just trying to lighten it up."

"I'm trying to wake up here. I'm a little slow. Do you want some coffee?"

"That would be dandy, Sandy. You got any of that Venezuelan espresso?"

"I sure do; let me get right on it."

I head inside and brew up my best espresso. The smell of strong espresso always makes me think of an old college buddy. Gonzo is a common friend of ours. He's Venezuelan. His mom used to send care packages of Venezuelan espresso and superrich chocolates from Caracas when we were in college together. Willy and I always kept tabs on when Gonzo was going be getting the next care package. We'd be sure to be there to help celebrate the gifts with him. I cherish those days, and the smell of strong espresso takes me back there. I'm still using the stove-top espresso maker Gonzo gave me. Recalling a memory like this now seems to be more meaningful than ever. Could I revisit this memory with the Memory Chaser? Wouldn't that be wonderful? For now, I'm content to experience it the old-fashioned way, via the trigger of a smell. I put our coffee and bagels on a tray and head out to rejoin Willy.

"Here you go, my friend. Sorry, I don't have any Venezuelan sweets to go with it."

110

"Ah, Sandy, do you remember that shit? It was the best, so friggin' sweet. Talkin' 'bout sweet, I miss that Gonzo—he was the real deal for sure."

"I was just reminiscing about Gonzo too; have you spoken to him recently?"

"Wasn't he the best? I haven't spoken to him in a couple years. The last I heard, he was done with environmental work and was chilling out in Florida with his family. I guess he has several rental properties he's bird-doggin'."

"I need to give him a call; it's been too long."

Willy and I sit around his card table and indulge in our coffee and bagels. It's oddly silent as we break our fast. So many thoughts are swirling in my head. I don't know where to begin. I have so many questions. My mind wanderings are suddenly interrupted when I realize that Willy and I are staring directly at each other. As I register how odd this is, Willy, so very slowly, starts leaning my way without breaking the stare. As he gets too close for comfort, our stare is broken by the smacking of his lips. "Oh, I do love you, Sandy," Willy says in a sultry voice. "Kiss me, you fool!"

"Ah, Jesus, Willy," I complain as I pull away as fast as humanly possible.

Willy's contagious laughter bellows, and we immediately become captive in the hilarity of the moment. We laugh until tears are rolling down our cheeks. Suddenly, all I can think of is how much I love this man. Things always go better with Willy.

As we compose ourselves and finish our coffee and bagels, my mind goes right back to where it was minutes ago. I need a plan. I need Willy to set up a meeting with Chase as soon as possible. Before I can offer my first question, Willy starts in.

"So Chase was Sally's boyfriend? From what you told me last night, there doesn't seem to be much room for coincidence. Hell, I guess we've come to the conclusion that there are no coincidences now, haven't we?"

"Given that he's in the hood here and lived in this very place as a child, I'd say it's slim to none that he's not Sally's Chase."

"Oh, I'm sure you're right on."

"So how are you going to set up a meeting with me and Chase and Ben?"

"Oh, that should be easy enough. I'm headed back to Crestone tomorrow to dig into my geologic work. I'll meet up with Sid and explain the whole thing. I'm sure he'll help us get a meeting set up. Don't worry about that, Sandy. I'll take care of it ASAP."

We're suddenly interrupted by the creak and slam of the screen door. We turn toward the cabin and are shocked by what we see and hear. It's Ben running toward us in his boxer shorts screaming, "Oh my God, we're idiots, total idiots!"

As Ben closes in on us with his Jewfro in full bloom, he is screaming, "I can't believe we didn't think of this last night; we are such idiots!"

As usual, I suddenly know exactly what he is talking about. As Ben turns his bugging eyes toward me, we both scream out, "The Memory Chaser!"

With a look of being left out of a joke, Willy begs, "What are you talking about?"

Ben, in a manic pace, struggles to get the words out of his racing brain, "We have video of Chase and Sally. We can settle this right now. You said you've met him, right? All you gotta do is verify it's him in the video."

"Well why wouldn't we do that?"

We all get up and immediately head for the yurt. Ben hurries to the computer and frantically looks up one of the events of Sally and Chase. I help Willy get in the Egg and Ben starts the event. This is going to be one of the shortest mysteries of all time. Ben comes over to the side of the Memory Chaser with me, and we both peer through the side port of the Egg.

It's a familiar event where Sally challenges Chase to catch her. Ben fast-forwards the event, and slowly a small silhouette appears off in the distance. The silhouette is morphing into a man and Sally is closing in. As Sally approaches, the man turns toward Sally; it's Chase.

With that Willy slowly turns his head toward us revealing a shit-eating grin. "Oh it's him, Jerry; it's him."

Ben runs over to the computer and shuts down the Memory Chaser. I help Willy climb out of the Egg, and the three of us huddle up. We're staring at each other with looks of astonishment, not knowing what to say. Out of nowhere, I'm floored by emotions of relief. For once we have uncovered an answer instead of more questions. I have a feeling we have a clue to uncovering Sally's mysterious passing. I remember what our motivation is. Now all we have to do is sit down with Chase and hear his story. As I try to compose myself, Willy puts his arms around me and Ben and whispers, "You idiots, Sally's device is called the Memory Chaser—chaser, you idiots, Chase her!"

Ben and I turn toward each other and simultaneously utter, "Huh, who knew?"

"Well I can think of two who didn't," Willy harasses.

"Holly shit, Dad, it's really him. What are we gonna do now?"

"Well, Ben, it's him for sure, but I don't think that changes what we talked about last night," I explain. "We've got to confront him and get his story. I was just talking with Willy when you came running out of the cabin half naked. Willy said he'd set something up. He's headed to Crestone tomorrow to continue his geo work. He said he'd discuss it with Sid and have him be the intermediary. Isn't that right, Willy?"

"That's right. I'll take care of the meeting; don't you worry, Ben. I'm sure Sid will do the right thing. It's got to be done."

"It makes sense to wait for you to set up a meeting with Chase before I head back to Denver," I say. "Why don't you give us a call when you get that set up, and we'll head to Crestone then?"

"Of course, Sandy, I'll take care of it as soon as I can."

"So what's your plan for mapping faults in Crestone?" I inquire. "I'm very curious how that's going to work out."

"Well for now, I want to finish examining the samples I took at the fault trench," Willy explains. "It's been a while since I've done microscopic mineral identification. It will take me some time to get the mineralogy right."

"What are you seeing?" Ben questions. "Are you seeing the minerals that the Persinger folks said would be there?"

"I'm not sure, Ben," Willy replies. "One thing for sure is that there are some metallic minerals in the samples. You can tell this with a simple magnet test. Whatever a magnet attracts is at least metallic and, therefore, conductive to electricity. Whether they're magnetic is another question. That would be best answered by knowing exactly what the mineralogy is."

"I love simple tests like that," Ben says. "Sometimes we make things way too complicated."

"Yeah, isn't that the truth?" Willy answers. "I love simple techniques that help narrow down the answer.

"So, I think, by tomorrow, I'll be ready to head back to Crestone. My plan is to use Dr. Strange's micro-magnetometer device to locate areas that have been exposed to ALPs energy. I want to sample fault exposures for magnetic minerals. It's big country out there, so I'll need to be selective. I think the existing maps will help me do that."

"You have a beautiful way of explaining complicated subjects, Willy," I compliment. "It all seems so logical and doable when you describe it."

"Well thanks, Sandy, I accept the compliment."

"What are your thoughts on the whole polar reversal thing?" inquires Ben. "Do you think it's gonna happen? How will we know?"

"Well, apparently it's already started. I'm not sure what it all means. I guess we'll find out, hopefully sooner rather than later. For now, I'm focused on this whole ALPs thing. I think I have my hands full."

We spend the rest of the morning discussing all that Willy had uncovered regarding ALPs and the effects on people exposed to them. We discuss the curious similarities between ALPs and the Memory Chaser. Both bring on strong feelings of empathy and awareness. We tell Willy how Ben and I seemed to be communicating in what could only be described as telepathy after prolonged experimenting with the Memory Chaser. We discuss how the Memory Chaser often brings on feelings that there are others nearby, something that ALPs exposure seems to cause as well. Sometimes it felt as though the others were more spirit-like than actual people. Why are such profound feelings brought on by two totally separate experiences? What is the tie between the two? Coincidence is no longer an acceptable answer.

Willy is very interested in our advancements with the Memory Chaser and encourages us to follow it to its logical conclusion. He suggests that our separate pursuits might take us to the same place. Though I can't explain that, it's hard to argue with.

The next morning, Willy is packed up and ready to head off to Crestone. He tells us to expect a call in the next couple of days regarding our meeting. He assures us he won't say anything to Chase. He'd leave that up to us. We thank him profusely and wish him luck on his mapping efforts.

Chase Encounter

"Hello, Sandy, is it you?" Willy questions. "The connection's really bad."

"Yeah, this is Sandy. I can barely hear you; is this Willy?"

"Yes, it's me. I got it all set up; you two gotta get down here."

"You got a meeting set up?"

"Yes, Sandy, tomorrow you and Ben are gonna have dinner with Chase at the Shambhala Mountain Center here in Crestone. It's all taken care of."

"Oh Jesus, Willy, you aren't screwin' around. This means so much to us. We thank you from the bottoms of our hearts."

"Of course, Sandy, it's at six tomorrow. Call me when you get here. If you can't find it, just ask. Everyone here knows where the Shambhala Center is. We should meet beforehand and discuss…"

With that, the line goes dead. I stand there for a minute, staring at my phone. Discuss what? I hope there aren't any complications. Maybe it's to facilitate our introductions. I guess it'll have to wait until tomorrow.

Tomorrow takes forever to arrive. It's midafternoon when Ben and I head out for Crestone. It's only a ninety minute drive, but we want to take a look around Crestone and visit Sally's funeral-pyre location. From Mount Princeton, it's a straight shot south on State Highway 285 through Poncha Springs and up and over Poncha Pass. After we crest Poncha Pass, the vast expanse of the San Luis Valley reveals itself. The massive valley narrows at its northern end and is over seventy miles wide at its southern end. The eastern side of the valley is guarded by the perfectly linear and towering Sangre de Cristo Mountains. These nearly continuous, majestic snowcapped peaks extend as far as the eye can see. The western boundary is defined by the foothills of the San Juan Mountains. What lies between is an incomprehensibly flat valley floor. It's desert brown and covered in nothing but sagebrush. The valley is mostly devoid of any surface water. On a clear day, you can see Great Sand Dunes National Park far off in the distance.

This was once all Ute Indian country. In the 1500s, the first Spanish explorers passed through here. The San Luis Valley was part of the Spanish Land Grant. Ultimately, the valley was taken by the United States as part of the spoils of the Mexican-American War. To this day, there's a strong

Hispanic presence in the valley. Sadly, the Utes were moved to a reservation farther south.

As we drop to the valley floor, the scale of the place overwhelms us. It seems endless. We have a distinct feeling the valley sediment fills a space that is as deep as the Sangre de Cristos are high. It's truly captivating.

The town of Crestone sits slightly above the valley floor on the eastern side. Twenty miles down valley, the turn to Crestone commences a nearly imperceptible rise to the eastern edge of the valley. It seems like years ago that we were here for Sally's funeral. As we pull into town, we head straight for the funeral-pyre grounds. I look over at Ben, and I can see what I'm feeling in his facial expression—pure horror. I ask him if he's going to be okay. Ben tries to gulp out an affirmative but settles for a nod.

As we approach the pyre grounds, we see there are many cars parked around the ceremonial site, and smoke is rising above the wooden privacy fence. Apparently there's a service going on, and we'll have to wait for another time to visit. I stop the car, and we both stare silently at the wafting smoke as it makes its way to the heavens. I look at Ben and tell him it's going to be okay. We'll be back to pay our respects at a later date.

I turn the car around, and we head back to town. We park the car and take a leisurely walk around Crestone. There isn't much to the downtown. It's only a few blocks of one-story commercial buildings, half of which are pueblo-style architecture. We eventually take a seat in the small city park next to a babbling brook.

I sense that Ben is troubled so take his hand and ask what he's thinking. Ben looks me in the eyes with his lower lip trembling. "I don't know, Dad. Yesterday I was excited about what we were going to learn, but now I'm kinda mad. What's wrong with Chase? What's he hiding? Why didn't he come forward and tell us what he knew? They were in love, and then he just abandoned Sally. I don't get it."

"I don't either, Ben. Look, we're going to meet him shortly; let's try to keep an open mind and hear what he has to say. Maybe there's an explanation. I don't know. It's totally understandable that you're mad. If I weren't so overwhelmed right now, I would be too. Let's get through this together; maybe we'll feel different after we hear him out."

"I guess so, but right now I just want to clock the fucker."

"I get it. Please wait to clock him until we hear him out. Oh, and one other thing, don't lead him on with what we know—let him do the talking."

We sit for a bit, trying to prepare ourselves for what awaits. I call Willy to announce our arrival. "Hey, Willy, it's Sandy; we're in Crestone at the city park. What's the plan, man?" Willy directs us to the Tibetan Buddhist stupa on an overlook south of town. He says that Sid reserved the site for half an hour for our introductions. Willy says that this is a very unusual arrangement, that Sid put it together for us, and that we need to be highly respectful, as the stupa is an extremely sacred place. I assure him we'll be on our best behavior and that I am deeply thankful.

As we pull up to the stupa, we stare in amazement at what is laid out before us. We feel as if we are in Tibet. The stupa is a bright-white double-tiered platform with golden accent inlays. Atop the platform is a flared cylindrical pedestal topped with a blazing-gold ornament that resembles a chess rook. Strung from the top of the golden ornament are Tibetan prayer flags hung radially outward and around the stupa. The stupa is on an overlook that offers a panoramic view of the San Luis Valley. It's very impressive, to say the least.

As we park and get out of the car, we see Willy and who we assume is Sid exit the stupa. I look at Ben and ask him if he's ready. He assures me he is, and we head toward our current destiny.

As we approach, we feel the seriousness of the moment build. "Sandy, Ben, so glad to see you," Willy begins. "This is Sid R. Thor. Sid is one of the sitting Buddhist monks here at the Crestone Mountain Zen Center. As you know, he is Chase's father. Sid, this is Sandy and Ben Stern."

With that, Sid bows with hands together in a prayer gesture. His bright saffron robe is comforting and auspicious at the same time. He then steps forward with arms stretched out wide. As he hugs me, he offers his condolences for Sally's passing. He tells me that he wants to help with our healing and promises he will do what he can to make this happen. He then turns toward Ben and hugs him tightly, offering a similar condolence. As he pulls away, he takes Ben's face in his hands and pleads with him to have compassion for his son. "He's a wonderful young man and deeply regrets how things made their way to this point."

Sid then motions us toward the stupa. He has us stop at the entrance. Inside is a larger-than-life golden statue of the Buddha. In front of the Buddha, with his back to us, is a man sitting in the lotus position praying. Sid softly calls to the man, "Chase, it's time; come meet our guests."

Chase slowly rises to his feet and turns toward us. As he wipes tears from his face, he looks up at us and struggles to smile. Chase is a tall, slender, gorgeous man. His long, dark hair is accented by sparkling blue eyes. He's wearing cargo shorts, sandals, and a beat-up tee-shirt that reads "Crazy Wisdom." I have a strange feeling come over me—I've seen that phrase before but have no idea where.

Chase greets us with a bow and then offers his condolences. "I really don't know where to even begin. As you know, your daughter, your sister and I were very close. I really have no excuse for handling her passing the way I did. Please let me try to make it up to you, if that's possible. I'll tell you everything I know. I am so, so deeply sorry for what I've failed to do for you and your family; you deserve so much more. She was a beautiful person, so special in every way."

With that, Chase collapses in Ben's and my open arms and begins to sob uncontrollably. We lead him away from the stupa to the overlook of the majestic valley. The three of us stand wobbly kneed as we gaze off into the endless distance. Ben and I are at a loss for words. It simultaneously occurs to both of us that Chase shoulders as much pain as we do. Instantly, he's no longer the mysterious outsider that we harbored contempt for. He's someone that has more in common with us than differences. He's going to help us see this through, and we're going to help him remove his enormous weight of guilt. He is immediately family. Chase breaks the silence with another plea, "Please tell Rachel how sorry I am for her loss. Tell her how horrible I feel about what I have failed to do. Tell her that Sally was an incredible person that I loved so very much."

"Gentlemen," Sid offers. "If you are ready, we can head to the Shambhala dining room and relax a bit, and perhaps you'll be ready for some dinner soon."

"Of course, Sid. Thank you, sir. Thank you for getting us together, especially at this beautiful site," I reply.

As we settle in at the dining room, it's clear that we need to get the conversation going as we all are very nervous and awkward. Sid jumps right in and suggests that we learn a little bit about each other, as that will ease us into our discovery quest. That's smooth of Sid; he certainly seems to understand people. Sid tells us that they will let us have some privacy, and he and Willy leave the room.

119

With that, Chase offers his story. "I grew up in Chaffee and Saguache Counties. I've really only been away from here when I went to college. I completed a physics degree at the Massachusetts Institute of Technology. I'm not sure what I'm going to do with it, but for the last couple years, I've been kind of chilling here in Crestone, teaching yoga. I used to teach yoga at Mount Princeton Hot Springs Resort as well. That's where I met Sally. I'm also on the city council here in Crestone. It's been really nice to be with my folks while I sort my next move out."

Ben and I both give our background stories. We tell him about our immediate histories, but we get the feeling he knew all about us. I jump right to the aftermath of Sally's passing and explain that Ben and I both dropped everything to try to figure out what happened to her. I tell him how we went to her cabin and dove into understanding the Memory Chaser. I explain that Ben was able to figure the thing out in fairly short order. I ask Chase what his involvement was in the genesis of the Memory Chaser. I ask him to tell us the details of his involvement and what happened to Sally. I ask him what Sally's motivation was.

"Like I was saying, I met Sally while teaching yoga at Mount Princeton. She was a student of mine. We struck it off immediately. Since her cabin was just down the road, I started visiting her frequently. It all happened so fast. We took a liking to each other right away and began spending more and more time together. Sally was such a beautiful person, Mr. Stern. I'm sure you know that. She didn't take me out to her studio for quite some time. She slowly brought me into what she was working on. When she eventually took me into the studio, I couldn't believe what I was looking at. I really wasn't sure if her stories of active meditation and memory visitation were bullshit or if it was for real. Once she took me in the studio, it became apparent that it was very real. I had no idea how smart she was. She was a programming wizard and understood hardware way better than me."

"So the Memory Chaser was all her making?" I ask.

"Oh, most certainly it was. The Memory Chaser was all her doing. Her motivation was never very clear. I think, like a lot of us, she wanted to revisit her childhood. I think she was troubled by how she left home at an early age. She really missed you guys and Rachel. She talked a lot about growing up in Evergreen; she really missed that place. She wanted that time back, I guess. There was another side too though. She thought the Memory Chaser could help people. Like many things she took an interest in, she pushed it as far as she could."

"Well obviously things went too far, but what do you mean specifically by that, Chase?" I question.

"There definitely seemed to be a mystical side to the whole thing. She definitely felt, in some way, it was her destiny to build this thing, and then I came along, which seemed to strengthen this feeling. The fact that I lived in her cabin as a small child blew her mind. She was always looking for connections in things that most people blew right by. What happened to my dad in the studio really solidified for her that something was out there that she needed to be part of. You've heard what happened to Dad, haven't you?"

"Yes," Ben says. "Willy told us the whole story. It kinda blew our minds as well. It certainly had an impact on Sid."

"That's for sure; it was a nexus in Dad's life course. I've heard the story many times. I can't deny that I wish I could have the same experience. After I told Sally what happened to him, she became obsessed with integrating the antennae into the Memory Chaser. It seemed logical at the time but also dangerous. I was convinced she was asking to be electrocuted during a lightning storm. She was persistent though. I helped her rig wiring to the top of the antennae. We put sensors at the top that could receive magnetic energy. This was wired indirectly to the God Helmet. She wanted to replicate what my dad experienced. This gave me grave concern. Like I said, I was very worried she'd get electrocuted."

I'm getting annoyed. The longer Chase goes on, the more apparent it is that he was more involved with Sally's Memory Chasing efforts than he initially indicated. I decide it's time to get to the point. "Chase, I'm gonna be straight with you: were you with her the night she died?"

This seems to catch Chase off guard; he instantly freezes up, and his lower lip begins to tremble. We can tell he's trying with great difficulty to compose his words. "Mr. Stern, Ben, I was not there. I relive those last couple days continuously. Why was I so stubborn? Why didn't I just swallow my pride and go there? Oh my God, I'm so sorry. I could have stopped her."

"What do you mean, you could have stopped her?" I ask sternly.

"She wasn't supposed to run the Memory Chaser events by herself while connected to the antennae. We agreed on that. I made her promise. Sally became more and more anxious about experiencing an ALPs event. She was getting reckless with it. She thought that ALPs might be related to atmospheric disturbances. She wanted to run the Memory Chaser events during thunderstorms. She knew how dangerous that was, and like I said, we had a pact that we'd never do that. She became belligerent about it. When I insisted that she shouldn't pursue it, she called me a pussy. We had a huge fight that escalated to the point where I had to leave. That was a few days before…before it happened. I should have been there; oh God, I should have been there."

Chase hangs his head in his palms and begins to sob uncontrollably, repeating over and over that he should have been there. Ben and I each put a hand on his back and pat him softly. It's then that Ben and I realize that Chase didn't know the exact circumstances of her death. According to Dr. Daver, Sally wasn't electrocuted. What killed Sally was not determined.

"Oh Jesus, Chase," I utter. "You don't know, do you?"

"Know what? What don't I know?"

"I'm so sorry. For some reason, we thought you knew. Sally wasn't electrocuted. The sheriff thought that was the case when they did the investigation, but the coroner determined otherwise."

"She wasn't electrocuted?" Chase asks, trying to hold back tears. "What was it then?"

"The fact is, Chase, the autopsy was inconclusive. The coroner said that she definitely wasn't electrocuted. That's really all we know."

"I still should have been there. I could have done something."

"It's not your fault, Chase," Ben confirms. "We don't know what killed her. You can't blame yourself. Sally may have made a bad choice; either way, it was her own doing."

"Chase," I inquire, "you know she videoed some of her Memory Chaser events she ran in?"

"You have footage of it, don't you?"

"Yes, we do."

That's too much for Chase, and he gets up and leaves the room. Shortly after Chase's departure, Sid and Willy come back into the dining room. Sid asks us how it went. We explain to Sid that it was very hard on Chase. We tell him what happened and that we'd like to offer Chase a chance to view the video of Sally's last minutes. It really isn't something that can be explained with words, we tell him. "I know this sounds really gruesome and painful," I explain. "Something happened in her final moments that we don't understand. We're hoping that Chase might have some insight." Sid says he'll discuss it with Chase. He suggests that we stay and have something to eat. We're both totally spent and thank him for the offer, but we think it would be best for us to head home. We thank Sid profusely for all that he'd done for us and tell him we'd be in touch. We thank Willy as well and tell him to give us a call and let us know how the mapping is going.

As we drive back toward Crestone from the Shambhala Center, we're both completely silent and somewhat in shock. Something doesn't seem quite right. As my head slowly rotates toward Ben, I can see he's turning toward me as well. We both say in unison, "What just happened?"

"I'm not sure," I offer. "I think we learned a few things, but I don't know. I'm not comfortable with Chase's story—something's missing."

"I'll say, Dad. I don't trust him; he's definitely hiding something."

"I'd have to agree with that. It's what he's not saying that's troubling. Hopefully he'll come have a look at the video of Sally. He didn't say anything about the crystal cube."

"I know. I'm convinced he had something to do with that thing."

"Let's try to keep a positive outlook. It may take a few more steps to learn all there is. Let's see if we can visit the funeral-pyre site on the way out of here. Oh, thanks for not clocking him, Ben."

We pull up and get out of the truck. There are no cars or people, and it's eerily silent and still. The sun has just set, and the sky is a deep blue with a few brightly colored orange clouds riding the mountain front. Off to the east, bathed in golden-hour light, is the endless barrier of the Sangre de Cristo Mountains. The pyre grounds are surrounded by a circular wooden fence. It resembles an old Western fort perimeter with its vertically placed, narrow pine trunks. We enter the grounds as a waft of cool mountain air brushes by us. We immediately feel the power of the place as memories of Sally's funeral service rush through our troubled minds. We take a seat on one of the wooden benches that encircle the pyre.

As we stare out at the emerging twilight, we both take deep breaths and sigh in unison. The beauty of the place seems to be wrestling with our burgeoning sorrow. It occurs to me that this is one of the functions of the place, to provide comfort with its beauty and calm the broken heart. I'm about to say something to Ben when a muffled crackling interrupts the silence. It sounds like fireworks from a distance, but it feels very close. A second waft of cool air momentarily chills our goose bumped skin further. The crackling is now accompanied by a barely perceptible low-frequency hum. Our attention is directed skyward to faint wisps of meandering orange-and-blue light. It slowly descends upon us. Mesmerized by its movement, we brace for what we fear is to come.

Our thoughts are suddenly switched, like a changing TV channel. We're both simultaneously viewing the pyre from a distance, from just outside the privacy fence. The pyre is ablaze, and there's a gathering of people around it. We are having an out-of-body experience. We both feel strong sorrow come over us, but somehow it isn't our emotions we're feeling—it's someone else's. It feels like we're standing too close to someone who's witnessing the funeral pyre burn, and their emotions are rubbing off on us. As we strain to see the faces of the attendees from this alien perspective, we confirm what we're looking at. It's Sally's funeral service, and we can see ourselves and the others that were there that night. Rather than being frightened, we're intrigued and curious. Our gazes suddenly and forcefully refocus on the back of a woman. As she turns around, we can see that it's Mac; we zero in on Mac's shirt—it says Crazy Wisdom!

Crystal Light

I wake early with many a troubling thought. I keep telling myself that this is all part of our journey. Every time we seem to be making progress, something bizarre interrupts. I try to stay positive about Chase's entry into the scene, but last night's experience at the pyre was very disturbing. Ben's words are still echoing in my mind, "Oh Jesus, Dad, Mac is in on it too!" I know it's time. I pick up my phone and call Rachel.

"Hello, Sandy?" Rachel says in a sleepy voice.

"How are you dear?" I offer weakly.

"Why are you calling me this early? Do you know what time it is?"

"Yes, I know, but we have to talk."

Since I took the Memory Chaser on the road to Denver, Rachel and I have been having meaningful phone conversations. While it's clear that she isn't ready to see me, she has taken a real interest in what Ben and I uncovered regarding Sally's Memory Chaser. Ben's visit to San Francisco really had an impact on her. Ben has a very sincere and convincing way about him, and I'm sure he piqued her interest in the Memory Chaser. It's obvious to me that she wants to witness Sally's creation but is torn—she'd have to be with me.

"It couldn't wait until a reasonable hour?"

"Well, apparently not, Rachel. Some really weird things happened yesterday. We met with Chase Thor for starters. You remember who Chase is, don't you?"

"Of course I do. Since you told me about him, I haven't stopped thinking about what his role is in this whole thing. Ben certainly doesn't like him. How did you find him? His last name is Thor, really?"

"Well the last few days have been a whirlwind, to say the least. Willy was here and shared some amazing discoveries. His work took him to Crestone where he met up with Chase's dad, Sid. Willy didn't know anything about Chase; it was pure happenstance. I know I'm kinda glossing over this because I'm trying to get to the point. The point is we met with Chase. His dad is a Buddhist monk at one of the retreats in Crestone. Prior to becoming a monk, he lived in Sally's place. He lived here with his wife and Chase nearly twenty years ago. Chase is a local. He met Sally at a yoga class he was teaching at Mount Princeton."

"Well, what did you learn from him?"

"Yes, of course. I'm a little scatterbrained from the whole experience. To be honest with you, he didn't tell us enough. As we figured, he was very much in love with Sally and was working with her on the Memory Chaser. Prior to the accident, Sally was really pushing the envelope on what the Memory Chaser could do. He tried to stop her, but they had some kind of nasty fight. He wasn't there when she died. He's been carrying a huge amount of guilt because he feels responsible for the whole incident. He feels he could have prevented the whole thing."

"I'm sorry, Sandy, but you woke me up at seven in the morning to tell me this? What are you trying to get at?"

"My point is that we need to get to the bottom of what Chase knows. He's hiding something. I think I know how to get him to fess up. I want to get him over here to the studio to view the video of Sally's last moments. He needs to see what happened with the raging lights and the crystal cube, how it seemed to pull Sally's soul into it. I'm almost certain he knows what that was all about. I want you to come out here and help with this. It's eerie how he seems to know all about us, and we know nothing about him. He spoke about you like he knew you; it's all very weird. I think if you were here, it might push him over the edge."

"I don't know, Sandy. How am I gonna make a difference?"

"You have to trust me on this, Rachel. It's more than a hunch. I think you being Sally's mom will just be too much for him—he won't be able to hide the truth from you. There's more though."

"There's more, more what?"

"Last night Ben and I visited the cremation pyre in Crestone after meeting with Chase. Something very strange happened to us. It was very similar to what happened at Sally's funeral. We were visited by the same lights, just like that night. It wasn't quite the same though; it only lasted a couple of minutes. The lights where swirling and all that, but it wasn't nearly as intense. As the lights descended upon us, we were suddenly viewing someone else's memory of the funeral. We could see ourselves, all of us mingling around the burning pyre, only the perspective was from just outside the perimeter of the pyre grounds. It was bizarre; it was like watching a movie or something. Suddenly, our view of the scene focused on a woman. It was Mac, and she was wearing Chase's shirt. In an instant, the whole thing was over. The lights were gone, and we were back to normal, just sitting there on a bench next to the pyre."

"Now you're starting to scare me. How can you see someone else's memories? That's crazy talk. What do you mean you saw Mac wearing Chase's shirt? You're not making any sense."

"I know it all sounds crazy; hell, it *is* crazy. It all has to do with what Willy's been investigating. He believes what happened last night and at Sally's funeral are a natural phenomenon that's induced by geomagnetic forces deep in the Earth. These forces generate magnetic lights at the surface that have strange effects on those enveloped in them. He calls them ALPs. It's a long story, and I'm not doing a good job explaining it, but it's happening in increasing frequency in and around Crestone. We revisited Sally's cremation last night—I swear. Mac was wearing Chase's shirt. I know this because Chase was wearing the same shirt when we met with him. The shirt had the words *Crazy Wisdom* printed on it. Maybe the real question is, why would Mac be wearing Chase's shirt?"

"Okay, okay, Sandy. I think I've heard enough for now. Let me think about this. I'm not sure if I'm ready for all this, but let me give it some thought."

"Look, I'm sorry to get all weird and heavy on you, especially at such an early hour, but please give this some serious thought. Ben and I are getting close to figuring some big stuff out, with the Memory Chaser and now with ALPs. I'm sure it all ties in with Sally's death. I need to get Chase to open up, and you can help make this happen."

"Well, we'll see. Goodbye, Sandy."

"Thanks, Rachel, I love you."

Frustrated, I get up and go outside. As I wander around the property, my mind is racing faster than I can keep up with. After circling the cabin and outbuildings several times, I take a seat at the firepit and stir the ashes with a stick. My mind is settling down as I draw therapeutic symbols in the ashes. Out of nowhere, a brilliant thought lands in my head. Sally's ashes, yes, Sally's ashes. We never spread her ashes, and it's been over a year. I'll convince Rachel she needs to come out and spread Sally's ashes with us...

127

My baby epiphany is interrupted by the creak and slam of the screen door. I look up to see Ben walking slowly toward me. "How's it going, bud? Did you get any sleep after last night? I sure didn't."

"Not really, my mind wouldn't settle down. It just kept racing all night."

"It was a heck of a day. Did you figure anything out staring at your ceiling?"

"I don't know. The ALPs thing has me really puzzled. How does someone else's memory worm into our brains? Whose memory was it? I keep coming to the conclusion that it had to be someone who had an interest in Mac. Why else was the focus on her? That person can only be Chase. Maybe he was there at Sally's cremation pyre. Maybe he was too freaked to join us and was watching from outside the fence. Maybe there was something going on between Chase and Mac? It makes sense to me."

"That's some flawless logic, Broccoli, flawless. I just got off the phone with your mom. I'm trying to get her out here. Maybe you can help convince her to come?"

"What's going on? Why now?"

"Like we talked about last night, I think Chase has more to tell us. I think if we can get him over here to witness Sally's last moments, it'll have a big impact on him, and maybe he'll open up. I think Mom being here will ensure he'll open up. He seemed to have feelings for her. If Mom is hesitant to come here, I have a secret weapon."

"Secret weapon, what does that mean?"

"You know, we never spread Sally's ashes. I'm gonna tell Mom that we're way overdue on fulfilling this obligation. We can't do it without her."

"Good one, Broccoli!"

Over the next few days, Ben walks me through the completed version two of the Memory Chaser. Though I've been working with the new version for some time, the completed version is remarkable. It's scary how real it feels. Nearly every aspect of it is improved. Not having to wear the VR goggles is very freeing. The meshed imagery of my running body against the progressing scenery is nearly seamless. Ben is getting really adept at image manipulation and the insertion function that Astral Computational provided. The dyed air provides an ethereal effect that feels three dimensional. I really love the spatial-congruity suit. It really solidifies the connection to the event.

128

The God Helmet is nearly flawless. Ben fine-tuned the presets to a couple dozen common emotional states and a few not so common.

I can't help but feel so very proud of Ben's mastery of the Memory Chaser. There's no way I could have figured any of this out. I'm excited about our upcoming clinical trials in Denver. We have some work to do, but I'm ready to start setting up meetings and get the actual trials on the calendar. I also want to spend some time studying the database of reviews from the participants who ran in events at the mall. This would be beneficial information for the upcoming clinical trials.

"Hello, this is Sandy."

"Ah, hello, Sandy, this is Chase."

"Chase, how are you?"

"I'm okay. I want to talk to you about something."

"What's that?"

"Well, I think I want to take you up on your offer. You know, the video of Sally's last moments. I think I need to see it."

"Well, of course, Chase, I think it would be good for you. You know it may not be an easy thing to view."

"I'm sure it won't be, but I think I need to do it."

"Let me have a look at my calendar, and I'll get back to you."

"That would be great. I really appreciate it."

It now appears that the die has been cast; we're about to cross the Rubicon. What lies on the other side will hopefully be worth the journey. I talk it over with Ben, and we devise a strategy. He had already talked to Rachel and made some progress, but she wasn't there yet. I tell Ben that it's time to use the ashes card. Hopefully this will put her over the edge, and I can set a date for Chase and Rachel to come to the cabin.

"Hello, Rachel, it's me."

"I know it's you, Sandy. Are you calling to get me to come out there?"

"Now why would you think that?"

"Don't be silly. Ben won't leave me alone. Did you put him up to this?"

"Of course not, that's Ben just being Ben. You know he's a little matchmaker."

"Don't flatter yourself. I know what's going on. Where are we going to spread the ashes?"

"Ummm, yes, the ashes. I thought that was going to be my line."

"You think you're so clever, don't you?"

"Of course I do, Rach; clever is my middle name. Can you come next week?"

"I'll be there next Tuesday. Oh, and, Sandy, I love you too!"

"Oh, Rach, I love you more than you'll ever know."

"I know, Sandy."

I'm so ecstatic, I think I might piss myself. I run outside, and before the creaky screen door can slam shut, I'm screaming at the top of my lungs. As I run in circles babbling uncontrollably, Ben comes running out to see if I'm okay. I run over and grab him and lift him into the air. "Oh you sweet, sweet boy! I don't know what you told her, but you did it—you did it. I love you so, so much. Thank you, thank you, thank you! *Yeehaw!*"

"I guess this means she's coming?"

Tuesday morning is here, and Ben and I are pacing back and forth in the cramped cabin quarters like caged beasts. We'd had enough coffee for an army. I'm not sure who's more excited. In anticipation of Rachel's arrival, we forgot the whole Chase part of the equation. Ben still has a huge head, since he's taking full credit for getting Rachel to come here. As he relishes his accomplishment, he grabs me by the cheeks and questions, "Who's your buddy, Dad? Who's your buddy?"

He won't stop until I answer his question. "You are, Ben; you're my buddy." I think I hear something, so I lower the volume on our celebratory music. "Is that? Could it be? Yes, I believe it is! I hear a car coming up the driveway!"

We both run for the door and round the house as Rachel pulls into the parking area. I open the door to her car and practically drag her out. She's so gorgeous my eyes begin to water. The three of us group hug, and as our heads touch, the tears start raining down; no one speaks. As the sobs retreat, we all kiss and hug even harder. It has been far too long. What a glorious moment!

We head into the cabin as Ben starts in on one of his famous diatribes. He's going a mile a minute. Rachel's trying to take it all in without losing it. She's always a champion at controlling it when it matters. It's been a long time since she was at Sally's cabin.

"Mom," Ben says excitedly, "I got a surprise for you! I'm gonna make your favorite!"

"No you aren't—are you gonna make us some matzo brei?"

"Hell yeah, I am. Matzo brei coming up!"

As we sit in the living room enjoying Ben's matzo brei, we begin to settle into each other's company. "Hey, Dad, remember how you used to call it matzo wad? I love how you still put syrup on it; you're such a goyim!" That really gets Rachel going; she nearly chokes on her food from laughter. We finish our treat and hang out in the cabin telling stories of old. It all seems so normal and natural—it's effortless. Before we know, it's nearing twelve o'clock. I interrupt the storytelling and announce that we better focus a bit on Chase's arrival. He's going to be here soon.

"I know this is all happening very fast, but this is the schedule we have to deal with," I explain. "Chase will be here shortly. Are you two ready for this? Rachel, are you sure you want to watch the video?"

"Of course I'm not ready, Sandy. I'm scared shitless, but I'd rather be thrown into this than have time to think about it."

"Dad, everything's ready in the studio—let's do this!"

As we step outside, we hear gravel pop under the weight of Chase's car. We approach his car as Chase slowly climbs out and stands motionless, staring at Rachel. Before I can say a word, Chase begins.

"Rachel, oh my, what a pleasant surprise. I'm so glad to finally meet you!"

The three of us look at each other shocked. That's certainly creepy.

"Well, thank you, Chase. I guess you know who I am?"

I guide everyone around to the back, and we have a seat at the firepit. We exchange some pleasantries and try to loosen up. We share some stories as we all relax a bit. I'm still quite anxious, however, and want to get on with it. I stand up and pace a few steps. My palms start to sweat as I gather my thoughts.

"I don't want to rush this, but I think we'd better get down to business. I'm sure there will be lots to discuss after the viewing. Sorry, that was a bad choice of words, but you know what I mean. Why don't we head to the studio. Ben has everything ready to go."

As we make our way to the studio, I put my arm around Rachel, and she reciprocates. I look at her and tell her it's all going to be okay. She knows what's coming, as I had described it to her, but a little comfort can go a long way.

We gather around the curved screens of the original Memory Chaser. I ask if everyone is ready. I tell Ben he can take over from here. Ben takes a couple deep breaths and makes his way to the workstation. He cues up the footage and tells us as sincerely as possible, "This is it, you guys; this is it."

We are viewing the same footage that Ben discovered. It is Sally running in her final event. I hold Rachel's hand as the scene progresses. As Rachel's face fills the screen and morphs into a silent movie, I can tell Rachel is getting upset. I hug her from behind and can feel her begin to tremble. The event continues and we are watching the studio fill with colored light. As the light intensifies, the footage begins to shake. I hear Chase gasp as the scene becomes surreal.

An energy stream is racing from Sally into the crystal cube at an extremely high rate. It is clear that the energy stream is Sally's soul moving into the crystal cube. We all gasp as Rachel lets out a bloodcurdling scream. The studio is rattled by a loud boom, and the scene goes completely dark.

There's complete silence in the room. I feel like I'm gonna get sick to my stomach. Rachel turns toward me; she's cupping her hands over her gaping mouth. She starts screaming in horror, "Oh, my sweet child, my sweet child!" Before I can react, Chase pulls Rachel in close with both arms and assures her it's okay. I look over at Ben, and he's staring at me, mouth agape. We hold our positions for what feels like an eternity.

Chase breaks his reassuring words with and unexpected announcement, "It worked! I think it worked!"

Rachel pushes Chase away and, while pounding on his chest, screams at him, "What do you mean, it worked? Are you fucking crazy; you killed my daughter; you killed her!"

I quickly separate them and hold Rachel tightly. "It's okay, Rach; it's okay. I don't think that's what he meant. It's okay, honey." I take Rachel outside, and we have a seat at the firepit as I continue to comfort her.

We can hear Ben's voice escalate as he curses Chase out. "You bastard, you fucking bastard, why would you say that to my mother?" We can barely hear Chase's voice, and then we hear a resounding thump, and it goes silent. Jesus, did Ben just clock him? I race back to the studio and find Ben pacing back and forth as he rubs his clinched fist. Chase is prostrate on the floor of the studio, holding his face and moaning.

"Oh Jesus, Ben, that was a bit much, don't you think? Are you okay, Chase?"

Chase begins to sputter, "Holly shit, you fucking punched me—what the fuck?"

"You had it coming, you shit," Ben accuses. "Why would you say something like that? What on earth are you talking about, it worked? If it worked, Sally would still be here."

"No, you don't understand; that's not what I'm talking about. The crystal, I think it worked."

"What do you mean, Chase?" I demand. "What about the crystal? What do you mean, it worked?"

"Let me explain."

Chase slowly gets up on his feet while shaking the sting from his now-swelling face. Ben's still pacing about the studio, muttering to himself. I'm not sure what to do. I walk over to Chase and put my hands on his shoulders. I look him straight in the eyes and tell him, "You better have a damn good explanation." Chase isn't responding so I ask him again, "Well, what is it then?"

"The crystal, it's a very specific kind of image-capturing device. It feeds the magnetic charge from the crystal into the light-freezing chamber. It's a device I worked on when I was at MIT. It captured Sally's image, only it's more than that. The chamber should have captured the light exactly as it appeared at the time of maximum flux. It's not an image though; it's a replica of the light exactly as it happened. It froze the light in time. It stops light and holds it exactly as it happened. That's what I meant by it worked."

"What are you talking about?" Ben insists. "That's crazy talk."

"It's not crazy; it's my thesis work from MIT. Let me play it back for you. You'll understand when I show it to you."

"Well let's have it then," Ben insists. "Show us what you're talking about."

Chase walks over to the computer bank and starts fiddling with the controls. He suggests I go get Rachel. As I walk out the door, Rachel is making her way back to the studio. I explain to her what's going on the best I can, and she insists to see this through. We both head into the studio and are greeted with a blinding light emanating from the crystal cube.

"What's going on?" I demand.

"Bear with me," Chase pleads. "I need to do some fine-tuning."

Rapidly, the light blazing outward from the cube retracts to its interior. The cube begins to glow a vibrant golden yellow. Very slowly, the golden-yellow light begins to expand beyond the outer surface of the crystal while maintaining its exact dimensions. The light cube is perfectly centered on the crystal. The edges of the light cube are precisely defined and crisp. The light cube continues to expand until it's roughly six feet on all sides. In an instant the light cube interior becomes lined with a series of precisely spaced parallel indigo planes that resemble crystal facets. The indigo planes are atomically thin and are vibrating at an extremely high rate. In a series of pulses, the number of indigo planes multiplies exponentially until they fill the light cube. The activity inside the light cube subsides, and it becomes perfectly still. Very slowly, an image starts to emerge inside the light cube. As the image acquires more and more definition, we see that it's an image of a person. The resolution refines itself with precise mathematical iterations. It becomes clear that it is a three-dimensional image of Sally from the viewpoint of the crystal cube. It appears to be a hologram of unimaginable resolution. Sally is frozen in a runner's pose. The look on her face is a combination of astonishment and ecstasy. The details of her face, her clothing, and the Memory Chaser equipment are captivatingly realistic. She looks more real than life itself.

The light cube flickers off momentarily, and when it reappears, the indigo planes are gone and Sally is enveloped in arcing streams of orange-and-azure light that are pointed directly at us. The narrow streams of light are cored by extremely thin, arcing indigo veinlets. It becomes evident that this image was captured moments before her death. The light cube flickers off a second time, and when it reappears, the four of us gasp in unison. Emanating from each of Sally's eyes are opaque beams of white light. She looks like she's shooting laser beams from her eyes. The beams terminate on the outer edge of the light cube. We can see in cross section the inside of the beams. The beams' interiors are filled with infinitesimally small squiggles that appear to be characters or code. The characters are rapidly and continuously morphing in a vaguely detectable pattern. The morphing patterns of characters inside the light beams are the only motion in the entire image.

Frozen Light

As we sit around the firepit staring into space like undead zombies, no one can speak for what seems to be an eternity. What on earth did we just witness? I try to speak, but my throat is parched and seemingly stuck together. I clear my throat and offer to fetch something cool for us to drink. I hand everyone a tall glass of iced soda water with lime. I take a long pull on what feels like life-giving nectar. As my throat clears, I look at Chase. "Well, do you mind explaining what that was, Chase?"

"Um, well, yes, it's a projection of light contained in the light-freezing chamber."

"What the hell does that mean?" Ben says.

"The box you guys call a mass-storage device is something I worked on while at MIT. The chamber contains sodium. It's not just sodium though; it's gaseous sodium that's been atomically altered so that its atoms are perfectly aligned and completely still. The motionless cloud of sodium atoms is extremely cold. It's referred to as a Bose-Einstein condensate. It's so cold that when you direct a beam of light into it, the light completely stops. The light is captured exactly as it was when it entered the gaseous sodium. It captured the light reflecting off of Sally. We call it frozen light. What you saw was a hologram of the frozen light."

"Okay, Chase," I say. "I'm not sure I understand anything you just said. What do you mean, you froze the light? Isn't the speed of light a universal constant?"

"Sort of. Light travels at a constant speed in a vacuum. Light traveling through any medium slows down, albeit by an imperceptible amount. I studied under Dr. Lena How at MIT. She basically took this concept to the atomic level and created a medium that could not only slow light down but actually stop it completely. Trapped in the light-freezing chamber is the actual light that was reflecting off of Sally. It isn't an image at all. We just viewed Sally as if we were there when it happened. Of course, the hologram was a duplication of the light in the chamber. I created the hologram for presentation purposes."

"All right," starts Ben. "You're way out of my league, so I'll assume what you're talking about is true. Why did you do this? Why not just take a picture of Sally?"

"Well for one, the light-freezing chamber has been a hobby of mine since I graduated. It's actually a small portable version of the chamber that Dr. How built. For the portable version to work, the input light first has to pass through highly energized sodium. The cube is a pure crystal of halite, which is a type of sodium. I have a theory that the energy associated with ALPs can energize a halite crystal to a point where it preps the light sufficiently for the chamber to accept it. Apparently it worked. It's not a picture at all. The light in the chamber can be viewed in infinite magnification. It's no different in that respect than peering through a microscope. With the proper viewing equipment, I can zoom into Sally's skin, for instance, to the molecular level. The other reason is, Sally and I wanted to study ALPs energy. By capturing the light emanating from the ALPs cloud, we'd have a specimen to study. In some respect, the device has essentially captured time."

"What is wrong with you guys?" demands Rachel. "Did you not see the beams of light coming out of Sally's eyes? Jesus Christ, that's what we should be talking about. Did you see inside the beams? It looked alive. What was it, and where was it going? I shudder to think!"

"Well, Chase," I say, "what were the beams of light?"

"Honestly, I have no earthly idea."

"Earthly idea," I respond. "Do you have any nonearthly idea?"

With that, I stand up and take Rachel by the hand and ask her to go for a walk with me. We leave Ben and Chase and head up the hill in back of the cabin to the overlook. We hold hands the entire hike up the hill without saying a word. The view from the top is spectacular as usual. It's another bluebird Colorado day; the sky is a deep blue and completely cloudless. The air is crisp and exceptionally clear. From the overlook, we can see the entire Arkansas River Valley spread out before us. It's stunning, and we're both overcome by its beauty. We take a seat on the rock ledge and put our arms around each other. Suddenly, I feel whole again as a gathering warmth begins to emanate from my core outward. I turn to Rachel, and we embrace in a life-affirming kiss. As our lips separate, we announce in unison, "I've missed you so much!"

Is this possible? All my heartache and longing lifts away in an instant, in one glorious kiss. Am I dreaming this? Is it really happening? Do I deserve this? I look deep into Rachel's eyes and ask her, "Is this really happening?"

"Don't be silly, dear. I thought I just told you with that kiss!"

"Rach, I've dreamed of this day forever. I love you so much, and I want you to know—"

"Let's just enjoy this moment. I'm here for you; let's just leave it at that."

And just like that my life accelerates to a whole new plane. There are so many questions in my mind, but I guess I know when to leave well enough alone, and that's exactly what I do.

As we sit there arm in arm, staring off into the immense distance, Rachel asks me, "So where should we spread her ashes? This spot seems to be perfect. She'll be able to keep an eye on her valley. What do you think?"

"It's perfect; maybe we can spread them in two places. I think we gotta spread some in the Arkansas River. She spent so much time rafting there. She can be one with the water she loved so much as well. The water will take her where she wants to go."

"Oh, you're so right. Why didn't I think of that?"

"I have just the spot. Do you see that prominent hill on the other side of the valley? That's Ruby Mountain; it's the start of Browns Canyon. Down valley halfway to Salida, there's an abrupt end to the closer hills; that's the end of the canyon. Just upstream from that is Seidel's Suckhole. That was one of her favorite rapids. It's an easy hike from Hecla Junction to Seidel's Suckhole. What do you say we spread some ashes here and at Seidel's?"

"Sounds like a plan, Sandman. Let's make it so."

With that we collect ourselves and make our way back down to the cabin. As we approach the cabin, we see that Ben and Chase are deep in conversation. They're animated and fully engaged.

"What's up, you guys?" I question. "Seems like you've made up?"

"Oh my God, Dad," Ben blurts out. "You won't believe what Chase and I discovered. I was explaining to Chase what happened at the funeral pyre after we first met him. I told him how we experienced a mini-ALPs occurrence. You know—how our consciousness was overtaken by someone else's memory of Sally's cremation. I described the whole thing, how we were suddenly viewing the cremation service from outside the pyre grounds, that we could see ourselves and others mingling about the pyre like it was a movie. I told him how it ended abruptly as we were looking at Mac and that Mac was wearing his Crazy Wisdom shirt."

138

"Exactly," Chase jumps in, "I was dumbfounded when Ben told me what happened. After I ended our meeting abruptly that night at the Shambhala Center, I went back to the stupa. I went there to collect my thoughts and meditate. While I was meditating, I also had an encounter with ALPs. It was identical to what you guys experienced. I was meditating on Sally's cremation at the pyre site. You know, I was at Sally's cremation, but I was too guilty to enter the pyre grounds, especially after I'd been avoiding you all. I was watching the ceremony from the exact perspective that you two experienced. Ben and I believe my memory of the event was cast into your minds, apparently via the ALPs."

"Well that makes perfect sense," I say sarcastically. "So that's it? Chase went zap and transported his memory to us. Well I guess you guys figured that one out, thank God. What's next? We're all going to be swimming in each other's thoughts? I, for one, am not ready for that, no, sir, not ready."

"Dad," Ben speaks up. "Remember what Willy was telling us about Dr. Persinger and all? I think we experienced exactly what he was talking about. I think it's real, and it happened to us."

"Yeah," Chase says, "Crestone has a history of unexplained phenomena; usually these phenomena involve strange lights and their effects on those enveloped in them—even the natives have accounts of these types of events in their oral history."

"All I have to say is that what happened happened. I can't deny that," I retort. "It's all too much. I'm gonna need some time to sort this out."

"Come on, Sandy," Rachel chimes in. "This is starting to get crazy. Maybe what we need is a little crazy wisdom?"

"Oh Jesus, Rach, not you too?" I say, exasperated.

"Hey, Dad," Ben offers. "Not to change the subject, but Chase and I were talking about having a look at the antenna in the studio. He thinks that the wiring needs to be checked out. He thinks that we should check all the wiring to make sure it's all working. If we're going to do this, it would be a good time to move the new Memory Chaser into the studio and wire it to the antenna."

"Well now you're talking about something I can relate too. Hell yes, let's get gen two into the studio and hook it up. It'll be a good test run before our clinical trials in Denver. When did you want to do that?"

"We thought we'd get on it first thing tomorrow. Chase has asked if he could run in some events in the original Memory Chaser before we dismantle it. I think it would be good for him and maybe provide some closure too. Oh, and one other thing, he has asked if he can hook up his light-freezing chamber to gen two when we move it into the studio."

"Well aren't you two getting along swimmingly? Of course, knock yourself out. It would be wise to replicate the original setup as best we can with the new Memory Chaser. So are you staying the night with us, Chase?"

"That would be great. Is that okay with you, Rachel?"

"Sure, we'd love to have you. I think Ben could really use your help and input."

"Oh, Ben, and I guess you too, Chase," I announce. "Mom and I have decided on a place, or should I say places, we think we should spread Sally's ashes. Maybe tomorrow after you finish the move?"

"Of course, Dad, where are you two thinking we should spread the ashes?"

"We're thinking we'd spread some up at the overlook here and the rest at Seidel's Suckhole."

"Oh, that's perfect," Chase offers. "That was her favorite rapid—mine too, come to think of it."

"Hey, Ben," I ask, "can I have a word with you in private?"

As we enter the yurt, Ben asks, "Sup, Dad? Is everything all right?"

"Yeah, everything's fine, well except Chase. What's up with you two? For that matter, what's going on with Chase being buddies with Mom? It's starting to rub me the wrong way."

"Oh, are you jealous?"

"No, of course not. I just find it weird how one minute you're punching the guy in the face, and the next, you're buddies. He just seems to be forcing his way into our family."

"Yeah, I know; it's just that, well, we had a great talk, and I realized he's a little off. He's so brilliant but can be socially awkward. I think he has a hard time judging boundaries. I think he might be on the spectrum. You know, I think he has Asperger's or something. I kinda feel sorry for him. I just figured we should give him some latitude."

"Really, I never thought of that. Perhaps you're right. It would explain a lot. One thing is still bothering me though. He hasn't said one thing about Mac. What do you make of that?"

"There's been a lot of shit going on, Dad. I hear you though; it's kinda strange. Let me handle it. I think he'll open up to me."

As late afternoon turns into evening, Rachel prepares us a beautifully simple dinner of corned beef hash and cowboy beans. While eating around the firepit, we just chitchat for once. Nothing existential or cosmic is brought up. Of course, it did eventually lead to telling fond stories of Sally. It's eye-opening and charming to hear Chase talk about Sally and her love of rafting and hiking in the valley. I had somehow forgotten how much she loved this place. I can tell Rachel is feeling the same thing as she scoots close to me and squeezes my hand tightly. As the sun begins to set, I'm overcome with exhaustion and can't stop yawning. It suddenly dawns on me that there's a not-so-minor sleeping arrangement to sort out. Before I can say a word, Rachel gets up while still holding my hand.

"Are you ready for bed, Sandman?" Rachel says coolly.

"Oooh, Sandman, I know you're ready for bed," Chase says clumsily.

Without a reply, Rachel and I slither into the cabin with a creak and slam of the screen door.

Ashes to Ashes

We spend the morning moving the new Memory Chaser to the studio and rigging it up. Ben and Chase never shut up. They're like children on Christmas morning. I think they covered every aspect of the Memory Chaser's functionality. Chase's excitement about version two is contagious. Apparently they stayed up late, and Ben let Chase run in a variety of events of Chase's choosing. They all included Sally. I'm genuinely happy for him. Perhaps this could be another application for the Memory Chaser. Maybe it can be used for grieving people following a death. The grieving could revisit their loved ones at a true time of need and longing.

With Chase's guidance, we climb on the roof of the studio and help him rewire the antenna. A number of the connections are fried and burned completely off. Chase climbs to the top of the antenna and inspects the magnetic receiver; all seems to be in order. It gives me the willies to see him dangling twenty-some feet in the air. I recall being fearless with heights. I guess, with age, dangling twenty feet off the ground becomes a memory I'd rather not repeat.

By midafternoon, we're wrapping things up. Everything seems to be in order and functioning as designed. In short time, Chase has his halite crystal and the light-freezing chamber wired up. There's no way to test it without the assistance of an ALPs event, however. Ben and Chase run version two through its paces as Rachel and I lie together on the tree hammock.

As we gently swing in the shade of the enormous ponderosa pines, Rachel describes a dream she had last night.

"It was really strange, Sandy. I don't remember it all, but I'll never forget how it ended. There was a lot of running. I was continuously trying to catch up to Sally. I don't know if we were running to or from something, but there was urgency. It was weird because we weren't really anywhere—there was no landscape. It was like we were running in the fog or something, but in the dream, it seemed totally normal. Suddenly, Sally stopped and started talking to people I couldn't see. As I caught up to her, she turned to me in midconversation. Her mouth wasn't moving, but she was talking; I could hear her but her lips were sealed. All of a sudden, she got very anxious and tensed up. She looked skyward and screamed, 'How could you do this to us; you have no right!' It scared the bejeebers out of me, and I immediately woke up. I tried to wake you up, but you were dead to the world."

"Now that's weird. Do you think she was telepathically speaking with the Gods?"

"Come on, Sandy. I'm totally serious; it was very disturbing."

"Welcome to my world, Rachel. Nothing is real; everything is permitted."

With that, Rachel smacks me on the chest and says, "I was thinking on the lines of *l'dor v'dor*, you smartass. I had a distinct feeling she was talking to our ancestors."

"Well, now you're part of our little club, Rach. Sounds more like a reverse *l'dor v'dor* to me though."

"What do you mean by that?"

"Well *l'dor v'dor* is the connection of generations, the passing down of traditions from one generation to the next. Sounds to me like Sally wasn't happy about how this went down."

"That's too deep for me, Sandy. Hey, don't you think we should get the show on the road and spread Sally's ashes?"

"Yeah, I think it's time. I'll round up the boys, and we'll head up the hill."

We clean up and get Sally's urn. Rachel comes out of the bedroom with four tallits and yarmulkes she had sewn for our makeshift service. I am so touched that she would think of this. She brings them over to me for closer examination. The yarmulkes are personalized with the Grateful Dead's Stealie logo centered on the top. It's a symbol Sally always had near her. Seeing this brings tears to my eyes. I have nothing to offer Sally but words. I'm so proud of Rachel. I hug her long and hard and whisper in her ear, "You are a true mensch, my dear."

I call the boys into the cabin so Rachel can present their garments. Ben is overwhelmed and reacts as I did.

Ben pulls Rachel in close and gives her a head-down hug and begins to weep. "Oh, Mom, I can't believe you did this; it's amazing—I *love* them."

Chase is touched as well and, in his somewhat robotic way, thanks her. "Rachel, I can't believe your thoughtfulness. I've never had my own yarmulke, let alone a tallit. I'm very grateful."

143

I'm impressed that Chase knows exactly what they are. I suppose I shouldn't be surprised, being raised around all the religions that are represented at Crestone.

We don our garments and head up the hill to the overlook. As we break through the large stand of ponderosa pines into the open sagebrush, the wind picks up in gusty fits. Our tallits are blowing sideways in the wind. Luckily our yarmulkes are pinned to our hair and stay in place, another detail attributed to Rachel's foresight and thoughtfulness. As we reach the overlook, we feel the enormity of the moment and fall completely silent. We each take a turn saying our last words to Sally, each other, and to the universe in general. The four of us simultaneously hold the urn, and we pour a portion of the ashes at the foot of the rock ledge. As the ashes slowly trickle out of the urn to the ground, we can hear the wind howling and swirling a short way off. Suddenly, the swirling wind bears down on us and blows the ashes upward and into every inch of our bodies and faces. We're stunned and don't know how to react. As I seal the urn and we stand erect, we turn and look at each other. We look like ghosts with the pale gray ashes dusting our faces.

"Holy Ghost," Chase exclaims. The four of us instantly break into belly laughs. We put our arms around each other as if in a football huddle, all the while laughing at our situation. Sally has the last laugh, and that's perfect. Our huddle begins to sway back and forth and our laughter begins to turn to tears. We pull our huddle into a group hug. "We love you, Sally," I proclaim. The four of us keep repeating these words together until it slowly trails off into silence.

Our final gesture is for each to take a turn adding a rock to a cairn on top of what is left of her ashes. This is a modified version of the Jewish tradition of leaving a pebble at a loved one's gravestone. This is done to show that the deceased is being looked after and had visitors who paid their respects.

We turn away from our makeshift memorial and head down the hill. The three of them are slightly ahead of me. I notice something strange on their backs. They each have a handprint made of ashes perfectly formed in the middle of their shoulders. I hope I have one too.

We make our way back to the cabin, and the four of us pile into my truck and head for Seidel's Suckhole to spread the last of Sally's ashes in her favorite rapid. The short ride there is solemn and quiet. As we make the turn for Hecla Junction, Rachel speaks up.

144

"Sandy, I'm so glad you thought of this. I think it's very fitting. I believe Sally would have wanted this."

"Of course, Rach. I think she would have liked this too."

We park the truck and head downriver on the well-worn path that follows the west side of the Arkansas River to Seidel's Suckhole. It's a gorgeous setting at the end of Browns Canyon. Here the canyon widens somewhat, and the river correspondingly spreads out into shallow riffles. The ancient bedrock is sparsely covered in a variety of conifers, and the river's edge is brimming with willows. Occasionally the river tightens up, and large pools eddy around enormous boulders that impede the water's flow. Ahead of us we can hear the roar of water coursing through the narrows at Seidel's Suckhole. We scramble up and over large boulders that guard the mighty rapid. The four of us scoot on our butts to the edge of Seidel's Suckhole, being careful not to slip into the raging water.

I suggest that we first spread the ashes together, and then we can have our final words. We roll on our bellies facing the torrent so we can each have a hand on the urn. I unscrew the urn's lid, and we pour all but a bit of the ashes into the rapid. As I'm putting the lid back on the urn, a huge gush of water-laden wind slaps our faces with a chilling mist. As we wipe the water off of our faces, something catches our eyes just upriver from the rapid. We can't believe what we're seeing. A turquoise white water raft is headed for Seidel's Suckhole. This would be a common sight—except there's no one in the raft. It's a ghost raft. We stare in disbelief as the raft gracefully guides its way unmanned through the mighty rapid and then just heads downriver.

Clinical Trial Preparation

Over the next few days, the three of us hang out and simply enjoy each other's company. It's nice to not be consumed by metaphysical madness. Spreading Sally's ashes really forces us to focus on what her life meant. This is something the three of us have not done together. I feel responsible for this not happening and am glad that it finally has. I guess these feelings are residual collateral damage from my drinking days. It's the drug that keeps on giving. I can't help but wonder if Rachel and Ben see it this way. If they did, they never expressed it. So it goes.

"Hey, Rach, come join me on the hammock," I holler.

Rachel immediately turns my way and dances a jig all the way to me. It warms my heart to see her so happy around me. As she attempts to climb aboard, the hammock swings erratically. I try to help her on and stabilize the wayward hammock. In a split second, we're unceremoniously dumped to the ground. As we lie there laughing hysterically, I roll over on top of her and pin her to the ground. While holding her there, I stare deep into her sparkling green eyes and ask her in a soft but serious voice, "Who's your buddy? Who's your buddy?" This makes her laugh even harder, and she's unable to reply. "Who's your buddy, Rachel? Who's your buddy?"

She struggles to get the words out and finally manages to squeal out, "You are; you're my buddy, Sandman; you are!" I roll off of her and put my arms around her as I pull her in tight. I give her a passionate kiss that neither of us will soon forget. While lying on the dusty, pine-needled ground with my face inches from hers, I get real serious and ask her, "Will you come and live with me here in the valley? I don't ever want you to leave me."

"Why, Sandman," Rachel responds with a Southern drawl, "are you being fresh?"

"As fresh as I can, Scarlett, as fresh as I can," I reply in my best Rhett Butler.

"I would love that, Sandy, but where are we going to live? I can't live in no ham shack—you know that."

"We can find a place. At worst, we can rent a place until then. What do you say?"

"Oh, Sandy, I do have a job, you know, and a house and life in San Fran."

"We can sort that stuff out. We can rent a place right up the road at Mount Princeton Hot Springs. They have really cool cabins."

"All right, you lovebirds," Ben interrupts. "Why don't you two get a room?"

"Now there's a capital idea, Ben! Why don't we get a room, Rach?"

"Hey, Dad, you got a couple packages from Denver. This could be the info you've been waiting on for the clinical trials."

"Oh really? I guess you missed your chance, Rach."

We drag ourselves up off the ground, and I wander over to Ben to have a look at the packages. Ben's correct; there are packages from both the Criminal Rehabilitation Center and the Denver Alzheimer's Association. I take the packages and head into the cabin to see what they sent.

The documents are exactly what I've been waiting for. They're legal contracts and authorization to proceed with the clinical trials. This is actually going to happen. Each packet is accompanied by a personal note from Dr. Souvenir and Dr. Charles. Beyond getting the official approval, the most fascinating thing they sent are the bios of the two participants that will take part in the study, Jane Doe and John Doe. Jane is a middle-aged woman suffering from early onset Alzheimer's. John is a young convict who pummeled his girlfriend and a Good Samaritan who tried to stop him. I leaf through the documents, and it becomes apparent they're going to take time to get through. There's a portion of each document that describes how to access the digital images and videos of Jane's and John's lives. What they provided is exactly what we discussed in our meetings and then some. There's even a portion where each doctor provided suggestions as to how the events should be produced. I forgot that this was something I had encouraged them to do. I'm very impressed. The seriousness of this project suddenly weighs heavily on my mind. We're going to be messing with people's minds, and that troubles me. I get up and go outside to let Rachel and Ben know it's time to get to work.

"Hey, you guys, we got the official go-ahead with the clinical trials! This is incredible. It's a bit overwhelming, but it's going happen!"

Rachel comes running over to me and gives me a huge hug. "Wow, that's amazing! Congratulations! I guess we should call you Dr. Stern now."

Ben gives me a big hug as well and congratulates me. Before he can say anything else, I interrupt him, "Ben, none of this would have happened without your genius. I thank you from the bottom of my heart."

"Thanks, Dad, but you know who we really have to thank for all this? It's really all about Sally; she started all of this."

"Of course, Ben, you're so right. It all started with Sally."

"That's for damn sure, you two," Rachel chimes in. "It looks like you guys are going to be busy for a while. I think I'm gonna head into town and do some shopping."

I usher Ben into the cabin and give him the portion of the documents that describes how to access the digital imagery. I explain to Ben how sensitive this information is and that he should treat it with the utmost respect. I tell him that he should download all the imagery and prep it for the construction of an event for both Jane and John. I explain that I need some time to read through the documents and that, after I'm done, we'd collaborate on how to produce each event. Ben eagerly takes the documents and scampers off to the ham shack.

I make myself comfortable on the living room couch and start reading through Jane Doe's biography and diagnosis. Jane was a child psychiatrist and until recently was a big runner. At some point she converted to Buddhism. Apparently Dr. Souvenir and her people were very discriminating on the selection of Jane. These three characteristics demonstrate we're on the same page regarding participant selection for the first trial run.

As I continue reading, I learn who Jane is. She's fifty-five years old and is in the midstage of early onset Alzheimer's. She is a resident at a memory-care facility outside of Denver. Jane entered the facility two years ago, and since that time, the disease has steadily progressed. She has more bad days than good ones. On bad days, her memory is so impaired she doesn't recognize her own family. On good days, her memory fades in and out. One minute she's fully aware of her surroundings and the next has no idea where she is. Like many Alzheimer's patients, her body is in perfect shape as compared to her mental state. Jane is still able to run on a treadmill in the facility's gym. It's one part of the day she somehow always remembers.

Dr. Souvenir's directives indicate that Jane loves the outdoors, and when she was healthy, she participated in mountain-cross running competitions. One of her pastimes was gardening. Jane had designed and created a xeriscape for her home. She used to spend hours perfecting her landscape. Apparently her xeriscape was so popular that it was a regular stop on an annual garden tour of Denver. I'm not surprised when I read that her family was the greatest love of her life.

John Doe is not going to be so easy. John is a convict who's serving time for violently assaulting a woman and a Good Samaritan who intervened in his assault. He's a native of Loveland, Colorado, and had what is described as a normal upbringing. John Doe's parents and siblings were completely shocked to learn that one of their own could possibly commit such a heinous crime.

Dr. Charles indicates in his notes that John Doe was selected for several key reasons. John went from being described as a perfectly normal young man to a violent criminal in a short period of time. From all indications, his change in behavior happened quickly. Dr. Charles felt that, because of this, he was a good candidate for rehabilitation since he wasn't a hardened criminal. As it turned out, the crime was partially captured on video. Prior to coming to the assistance of the female victim, the Good Samaritan captured video of the assault as it began. Other portions of the crime were captured on security cameras, and ultimately, police body cameras captured the scene up to and including John being apprehended.

Halfway through reading John Doe's history, I become overwhelmed with emotions. The whole story is sickening and disturbing. I begin to question what I'm doing. There's no way I'm qualified to address any of this. What was I thinking? Why do I want to help this man? He pummeled this poor woman and then turned on an innocent bystander that was just trying help. Jesus, what have I gotten myself into?

I compose myself and trudge on through the John Doe documents. As I continue reading, my mind keeps wandering back to the crime scene. I envision how an event can be constructed. I think about our original idea of forcing criminals to witness their crime. The most important part of our event has to be the crime scene, and we have multiple videos to accomplish this. This part seems to be mostly a technical one. What are we going to do to make it more than that?

As I sit on the couch contemplating how to best construct the events, I hear the screen door creak, and I see it's Ben. As the door slams behind him, he approaches, and I see in his face that something is wrong.

"What's going on, Ben?"

Ben lets out a guttural growl and says, "This is so wrong, Dad!"

"It's John Doe, isn't it?"

"What the fuck? What are we doing? You want to rehabilitate this punk? What are we doing here? I don't want any part of this, Jesus."

"I know. I had the same reaction, believe me. I can't imagine what the crime scene looks like. I guess it's pretty gruesome?"

"It's disgusting. This guy doesn't deserve a second chance."

"I get it. I suppose you could say he's getting a second chance if it works, but the idea is to correct his behavior, to cure him, if you will. That's what criminal rehabilitation is all about. Punitive measures don't work. In many cases sitting in jail just hardens their criminal mindset."

"I get all that. I just don't think I'm the one who should have to do it. I'm not cut out for this. It's too disturbing."

"I hear you loud and clear, bud. It's gruesome and disturbing, and I haven't even seen the footage yet. We need to follow through on this one; we've come too far. It's not something we're gonna make a career out of. The idea was to develop this tool and pass it on to Astral Computational to market it. If you don't want to participate with the next criminal participant, we can have Astral Computational do it. It's not a big deal, but we need to complete this one. Trust me—you're doing a good thing here. We'll work together from here on out."

"I don't know, Dad. I just don't know."

"Let's go out to the studio, and you can walk me through the imagery they sent. We can focus on Jane Doe. Maybe it'll energize us so we'll have the strength to work through John Doe's mess."

We head to the ham shack to review the images of Jane Doe. The images Dr. Souvenir sent are neatly organized by various time frames of Jane's life. Her organizational skills are impressive. There are pictures of Jane that start when she was a child to present day. We very quickly begin to feel we know her.

As we slog our way through the voluminous store of images and videos, we reach the latter part of her life. We notice there's a change in the expression on her face in nearly all the images. Something's missing; she's stone faced. It's the disease we're viewing. It was robbing her of her essence.

As we sit there staring at Jane Doe's reality, we become energized with the idea of possibly bringing some of Jane back. Ben and I begin to formulate what the event should entail. In the middle of all this, Ben suggests something brilliant.

"You know, Dad, this whole thing is all about sensory input, but there's one sense we've left out. What if we introduced a fragrance that ties into something specific in the event? What if, for instance, we introduce the scent of lavender or sage when we're projecting her xeriscape? Scent is strongly tied to memories. Maybe it'll give her an extra push to recall her memories?"

"That's an outstanding idea; that's genius, Broccoli!"

"Thanks, Dad, it seems like it could help put her in a specific place and time."

"I think we've got this designed as far as we can go for now. Why don't you construct the event, and we'll edit as we see fit after you get your first pass done."

We leave the chore of John Doe for the morning.

As we sit sipping our morning coffee, I tell Ben John Doe's history. I explain that I think our goal should be to bridge the gap between the good John Doe and the bad one. Ben seems to like this idea; I can see his gears turning.

As a child, John Doe seems normal enough. He wore his auburn hair in a long ponytail and was gangly and awkward. He has a somewhat crooked smile that's authentic and persistent.

If there was a point where his life turned, it seems to be in his early twenties when he dropped out of Metropolitan State University. Most notable is the change in his appearance. He cut his long hair off and sported a buzz-cut. His short-cropped hair gave him a menacing look. He barely resembles his younger self, and his crooked smile took on a devious flare.

I mention to Ben that, after he dropped out of school, he had a series of odd jobs, with his last job managing a place called The Escape Room. I suggest to Ben that maybe we can use this as a metaphor in the event. He was trying to escape something.

We work our way through the imagery with little fanfare until we get to the videos of his crime. I turn to Ben and ask if he's ready. He silently nods his head. There are three perspectives of the crime scene. The first is shot from the Good Samaritan's phone. The second is from a security camera on a fire station. The third is captured from police body cameras.

The violence is unbelievable. John Doe is so filled with rage he seems superhuman; his swinging arms are a blur. He fights with the female victim, the Good Samaritan, and the police before being subdued.

"Oh Jesus, Ben, I can't believe I had you watch this by yourself."

Ben turns toward me and is speechless.

It's obvious that we have our work cut out for us. We take a break and walk around the property to gain our composure. For the rest of the day, we hang out at the firepit and discuss how to tackle the event. By the end of the afternoon, we have a good handle on what we want to construct. Over the next few days, Ben pulls together a first run of the event. It would not be easy for him.

I wake to Rachel putzing around the cabin. As I sit up in bed, I see that her suitcase is packed and is positioned by the door. It becomes obvious that she's waiting for me to get up.

"What's going on, Rachel? Are you going somewhere?"

"Yes, I'm afraid so, Sandy. I think it's a good time for that."

"You're going back to San Francisco?"

"Yes, dear, I need some clean underwear."

"What? You know they have that in town?"

"Why don't you get up and have some coffee. Then we'll talk."

"Not the talk. Wait, which talk are we talkin' about?"

Slowly the fog of sleep begins to lift as Rachel dries the last of the dishes. I scoot over on the couch to make room for her. She sits down next to me and looks me in the eyes.

"Sandy, you and Ben have a lot of important work to finish. It's best if I get out of the way for a while. I've got a lot of things to take care of back home.

The sooner I get back there, the sooner I can move on. I got a flight back this afternoon. Are you going to be all right without me?"

"Move on? What do you mean move on? I thought everything was going so good. What happened?"

"Yes, move on, Sandy. If I'm going to move here, I've got a lot of things to do in San Francisco first."

My jaw drops as I compute fully what she just said to me. My eyes well up with tears of joy. "Move on? Like, move on to here? Is that what you're saying?"

"Yes, silly. What did you think I was talking about?"

"Oh, Rachel, you've made me the happiest man in the world!"

I lunge at Rachel and embrace her as I wriggle like a puppy. We hold each other for what seems like an eternity. As we lie there, crumpled on the undersized couch, the screen door creaking breaks the silence. It's Ben.

"Ben, guess who's coming to Chaffee County?"

"What're you talking about?"

"Mom's decided she's gonna move here! She's going to move here with us or me or whatever. She's back, baby! She's back!"

"Holy shit, Mom. You're really gonna move in with us?"

"Well, sort of. We haven't figured that part out, but I'm moving back in with your Dad."

Ben takes two huge steps and launches himself on top of us, giggling like a little girl. I'm stunned at his reaction. He's ecstatic. This is something I know he's been dreaming of since Rachel and I split up. He's in heaven.

"We should celebrate somehow," I suggest. "How about we head up to Mount Princeton Hot Springs and take a soak. We've got a few hours before Mom has to go."

"I'd love that, Sandy."

Sitting in the infinity pool that overlooks the Chalk Cliffs of Mount Princeton, everything seems perfect. Things are definitely going my way. I'm feeling strong and invigorated. We talk of old times and vacations we took when our family was young. We're all smiles and loaded with purpose and possibilities. Way too soon, it's time to head out. We dry off and head back to the cabin.

As Rachel drives off down the gravel driveway, I put my arm around Ben as her car becomes a dust cloud dispersing in the distance. I thank Ben profusely for doing his part in getting me and Rachel back together. We turn and head back to the cabin arm in arm. There's much work to do.

Astral Computational

"Good morning, gentleman, and welcome to Astral Computational," Dr. Petra announces. "It's so good to see you two again. Why don't you two come into our conference room, and I'll get us some coffee."

Well, gentlemen, how have you two been doing?" Dr. Petra asks as he takes a seat at the head of the conference table. "When did you get into town? Did you have any trouble finding the place?"

"We got in yesterday afternoon and spent the evening at my place in Denver. I haven't been to Louisville in a long time. It sure has grown."

"I saw on the news you had an earthquake up near your place in Chaffee County last night," Dr. Petra informs. "Quite rare I understand."

Ben and I look at each other, somewhat startled. Dr. Petra seems to pick up on this and offers comforting words.

"They said it was minor, and there was no damage. I'm sure everything's okay."

"We didn't hear that, but then again we haven't seen any news since we got into town. Earthquakes are quite rare up there, but they do happen from time to time."

"So you have a couple big days ahead of you. I want to assure you that everything is set up and ready to go. We have a private room dedicated for the Memory Chaser. All the computers and hardware that control the Memory Chaser are housed in a neighboring room with a one-way mirror, as you requested. We fully recognize that since this is a medical procedure of sorts, we will treat it with absolute confidentiality. You and your clients will control who is allowed access to the Memory Chaser room. We'll head over there shortly after we talk a little business."

"We definitely want to perform a complete run-through on both events," Ben requests. "Did your team run the events I uploaded?"

"Of course, Ben, we figured you'd want the day to test everything out. Our shop is very diligent in keeping the two Memory Chasers synchronized. Our staff will be in shortly; I believe you've met most of them. I wanted to talk a little bit about Astral Computational's business strategy.

"Yes, it's not really anything new; in fact, it's your idea. I'm talking about the recreational aspect of the Memory Chaser. We really think for us, as a business concept, the recreational aspect of the Memory Chaser is something we'd like to put the majority of our efforts into. This is not to say we aren't fully committed to what we already have on our plate. We're very excited to see how these clinical trials go. We're fully behind your efforts and goals for these two applications. We do think, however, that the real potential for growth with the Memory Chaser is in the recreational sector."

"I see," I say. "As we've said before, we fully expect Astral to develop whatever application you think has potential. We just want to make sure any new applications are something we can put our name on."

"Of course. We're a team here, and we expect your input. Our recreational idea is really nothing different than what you two conceived. We want to expand on the concept by making it interactive. By that I mean we envision two or more people at remote locations participating in events simultaneously. With ultrahigh internet speeds, we believe we have the computation power to integrate two or more people in the same event from anywhere around the globe. We have a functioning prototype we'd like to show you."

"Wow," Ben interjects. "That sounds crazy."

"Oh, it's very crazy indeed."

"So you're able to integrate two people in the same event?" I ask. "I assume both are projected in the virtual perspective? Do they see each other?"

"Yes, the observer sees the others from the virtual reality viewpoint. You don't, however, see them to your side, if that's what you're asking."

"Now that would be a challenge," Ben offers.

"We'll walk you through a demonstration later in the day if you have time."

"That would be great," I reply. "We really want to focus on the clinical trials, but sure, if there's time, we'd love to."

"Yes, of course. We certainly don't want to be a distraction. There's a specific business item we need to fill you in on."

"What would that be, Dr. Petra?"

"Since we have considerable capital invested in the Memory Chaser and we expect further investment, we want to make sure we control our destiny. The God Helmet is an integral component of the experience, and, well, we don't want to get tangled up with copyrights and patents. We have recently bought the parent company that owns the rights to the God Helmet. I think this was a prudent move that you two will benefit from."

"Wow, that's big news, congratulations."

"Yes, we think it's a big step as a company. Congratulations to you two as well. You're now partial owners of the God Helmet."

"That's outstanding," Ben says. "We own the God Helmet, wow!"

"I know you two have a lot to do, but before you get down to business, I'd like you to meet our Memory Chaser staff."

With that, Dr. Petra makes a call to his staff, and shortly, they march into the conference room in single file. They're not the older, stoic lab coat–wearing scientists I was expecting. They're all quite young and energetic.

Dr. Petra provides introductions for my benefit as Ben knows most of them. Ben zeroes in on Angelica and gives her a big hug. Angelica is one of the team members Ben met on previous trips and is his go-to for technical assistance. We spend the next couple hours discussing detailed aspects of the Memory Chaser. The group is excited to get face-to-face feedback, especially on the dyed-air component and the spatial-congruity suit. It's time to check out the Memory Chaser and run it through simulated tests on both events that we're to go live with tomorrow.

As Dr. Petra is leading us to the Memory Chaser room, my phone rings. It's Willy. I look at Dr. Petra and tell him I need to take the call. Dr. Petra assures me it's fine and points to a door down the hallway where they'll be.

"Hello, Willy. What's going on, my friend?"

"Holy Jesus, Sandy, you won't believe what's going on up here! Did you hear about the earthquake we had last night?"

"I just did, but I haven't seen the news or anything. What's going on? Are you all right?"

"Oh, I'm fine. There wasn't any damage. It's the ALPs, Sandy, the ALPs. It was unbelievable. People here are going crazy."

"What do you mean?" I question as the phone line begins to crackle. "There were lights along with the earthquake?"

"It was incredible. About an hour before the tremor hit, Crestone was lit up from Valley View Hot Springs clear down to the stupa you visited. I could see the lights dancing along the base of the mountain from my cabin and immediately headed up to town. By the time I got there, everyone in town had emptied into the streets and were bathed in the lights."

"Can you hear me, Willy? You're breaking up really bad."

"Sandy," Willy says in fractured urgency. "Can you hear me? It was so beautiful…"

"Willy, I can barely hear you. I'll call you this evening."

I lean against the wall, staring at my phone, and slide down to the floor. Why is all this happening at once? I take a couple deep breaths and compose myself. As I sit there, I search the news on my phone, and there it is: "Strange Lights Dazzle Chaffee and Saguache County Residents Prior to Earthquake." *The Denver Post* second-page headline seems to signify that the cat is out of the bag.

In my fog, I hear someone calling my name. I'm daydreaming until the voice becomes clear as a bell. It's Dr. Petra.

"Are you okay, Sandy? Is everything all right?"

I slowly stand up and try to focus on my surroundings. I must look like I've seen a ghost because Dr. Petra puts his arm around my shoulders.

"You don't look so good, Sandy. Did you get some bad news? Are you okay?"

"No, no, it's nothing like that. I was just talking to a good friend who witnessed the earthquake in Crestone. There are some very strange things going on up there. It's in all the news feeds. There was some type of bizarre light show that accompanied the tremor. It's a long story, but somehow the Memory Chaser is connected to it."

"What do you mean? How is it connected to the Memory Chaser?"

"Like I said, it's a long story. We got cut off, so I didn't get the details. I really don't want to get into it until I learn more, no offense."

"None taken. Please do tell when you know more. Shall we head to the Memory Chaser?"

As we walk into the Memory Chaser room, I'm startled by a dark figure that resembles Spider-Man, only the tight-fitting leotard is black as pitch. It's Ben, and he's wearing the spatial-congruity suit. Ben prances around, flailing his arms like a mock spirit while teasing Angelica. It's a sight to behold, as I'm not quite used to seeing the suit.

"You startled me, Ben. The suit's creepy. I will say you wear it well."

"I think we're about ready, Dad. Angelica's going to participate as an observer and assist with any technical issues for the trials. She's already viewed the events and has a pretty good idea how this thing is going to go down."

Dr. Petra shows me around the surprisingly comforting inner room. The four walls are murals of an aspen grove that extend from floor to ceiling. The narrow white-and-pale-green tree trunks disappear into a dazzling display of autumn leaves a foot from the ceiling. The aspen leaves are a variety of bright yellow, orange, and red and seem to light the room. Randomly spaced beams of sunlight break through the aspen grove and light the space. It looks strangely familiar.

"What do you think of the mural, Sandy?" asks Dr. Petra. "Do you recognize the scene?"

"I feel like I should. It looks like one of our events?"

"It is indeed; it's not a mural though—it's an image. The walls are extralarge LCD screens. We manipulated the leaves to provide an autumn scene. We thought it would be more relaxing. There are a variety of scenes to pick from."

"That is something. I love it."

"We're ready to fire this thing up, Dad. Come check out the control room."

The control room is lit with subdued blue light. The back wall is lined with computers that blink random signals from their tiny red indicator lights. It's quite ominous. The control desk looks out through a one-way mirror into the

Memory Chaser room. On either side of the mirror are two large LCD screens. Dr. Petra explains that the two screens are view ports that provide video from inside the Memory Chaser egg. One screen is a head-on view of the participant. The other is a feed from the Memory Chaser screen.

"This is really something, Dr. Petra. Is there anything you haven't thought of?"

"I hope not, Sandy. I think you'll find our team is quite thorough."

We spend the rest of the day running the Memory Chaser through its paces with the two trial events. Angelica gets Ben familiar with the controls as they are slightly different from ours. The two of them run through both events twice. The first round, Ben's the participant, and then he switches with Angelica. They're like two kids playing with their new favorite toy.

Dr. Petra and I take a seat in the control room and watch in amazement as Ben and Angelica rattle back and forth in a seemingly foreign language. Their combined knowledge of the Memory Chaser is impressive. They seem to know what the other is going to say as a fix is initiated before the other is finished describing the problem. We're in good hands.

My thoughts turn toward Willy and the latest phenomenon. To this point, Dr. Petra and his people know nothing of Sally's final run on the Memory Chaser or our experience with ALPs and all that Willy is uncovering. They have no idea there's a natural force that affects people in a way that's similar to the Memory Chaser. I figure there's no time like the present.

"So the call I took out in the hallway was my friend Willy. He's been doing research on a thing called Tectonic Strain Theory. It's an obscure theory that ties anomalous lights on Earth's surface to fault-related strain deep in the Earth. These lights are more than just lights. They affect people in strange ways."

"Wait a minute, Sandy. You're talking about Dr. Persinger, aren't you?" Dr. Petra asks.

"I am."

"Dr. Persinger is an amazing man, quite widely published. If there's one person that defines thinking out of the box, it's him. What did he call the lights?"

"He called them ALPs; it's an acronym for anomalous luminous phenomena. ALPs were seen yesterday prior to the earthquake in the mountains near our cabin. That's what my friend Willy was trying to tell me before the call was dropped."

"You don't say."

I tell Dr. Petra our story. I tell him about Sally and the funeral pyre. I tell him Chase had captured Sally's last moment in the light-freezing chamber, the crazy energy stream and beams of lights from her eyes. I explain how Willy got involved and visited the folks at Laurentian University. I tell him about Sid Thor and his experience. I relate to him Ben's and my recent experience where we witnessed someone else's memory. Dr. Petra could barely contain his excitement.

"While all this is pretty incredible stuff, the thing that has me scratching my head is the similarities between the Memory Chaser experience and the ALPs experience. They both involve an out-of-body experience, the recalling of vivid memories, an overwhelming feeling of empathy, and the presences of others. In some cases, people report that they become telepathic, not just with people close by but also with those far removed. It sounds like Willy may have just had his first ALPs experience," I say.

"That is very interesting. What do you think the relationship is?"

"I have no idea, but it looks like Willy is dragging us into Persinger's world."

"Listen, Sandy, this is the type of thing that Astral Computational has been waiting for. We love the Memory Chaser not because it's some kind of memory-recall device. It's the 'why' behind the Memory Chaser that we're after. It's definitely a link to explaining memory, identity, and possibly spirituality. If you and Ben or Willy ever need any technical support to uncover these mysteries, we're all in."

"Well that's quite compelling, Dr. Petra. We will discuss it. I'm not sure what we need help with, but I do know we're gonna need some."

Ben and Angelica come into the control room and announce that everything seems to be in working order. It's already four o'clock. How can this be? I didn't bother to question where the time went. It had become a common theme, to be lost in the moment. Ben and I gather our things and thank Dr. Petra and Angelica for the help and hospitality. We tell them we'll see them tomorrow morning, and we head for home.

Ben and I inhale our take-out Mexican food from one of our favorites, El Tajado, and take a seat in the living room. It's been a long time since Ben was in my Denver home. It was never really his home. When Ben left for college, we were still in Evergreen. Nonetheless, it still feels homey to him, as I have a lot of furniture and decorations from the Evergreen house. I suspect it feels strange but comforting.

"Hey, Ben, I talked with Willy today. He witnessed the earthquake."
"Jesus, is he all right?"

"He's just fine. There wasn't any damage or anything like that, but there's more to the story. There was a large ALPs event just prior to the tremor."

"No shit, what did he say?"

"It was a really bad connection, and the call was dropped before he could finish. Willy said that the lights were extensive. They went from north of Crestone all the way to the stupa we visited and lasted for nearly an hour. The people in Crestone came out en masse and were enveloped in the light. He said they were all going crazy. Just before the line went dead, I think he said, 'It's so beautiful.' "

"Now that's spooky. Seems to be a common reaction these days."

"I told him we'd call him tonight," I say, picking up my phone.

"Hello, Willy, it's Sandy. Ben's here, and we have you on speakerphone. How're you doing?"

"Sandy, Jesus, thank you for calling me back."

"What's going on up there? Is everything back to normal?"

"Well, it depends on what you mean by normal. Normal seems to have redefined itself."

"Well, all righty then, can you elaborate?"

"I don't have a lot of time. There's going to be a town meeting with the residents and all the spiritual folks up here shortly. This is the deal: an hour before the tremor hit, the base of the mountains lit up for some twenty miles. I was told it was the largest ALPs event they've ever seen up here. By the time I made my way up into town, the place was going crazy. It was like the whole town had taken too much LSD. They were dancing in the streets in some kind of oddly correlated twirling dance. Half of them were speaking in tongues, and they all had crazy, ecstatic, dazed looks on their faces. In the middle of the chaos, suddenly, they all stopped and appeared to be normal again. Within thirty seconds or so, they randomly picked a partner, and each pair put their arms on the other's shoulders. As they did this, they were staring directly into each other's eyes without speaking a word. Suddenly, the lights pulsed and rose up out of the ground, enveloping everyone. The pairs separated, and the mob started back in on the crazy twirl-dance thing."

"What about you, Willy? Did it affect you the same way?"

"Not at first—I kept my distance. After seeing the pattern repeat several times, I headed over to the stupa to see if I could find Sid. As I pulled up to the stupa, I could see there was a crowd of mostly Buddhist monks twirling around in a similar fashion. As I got out of my truck, Sid came running up the hill from the stupa to greet me. As he approached, the lights started pulsing out of the ground and rose thousands of feet in the air and back again. Each time it pulsed, it got into me."

"What do you mean, it got into you?"

"It's not easy to describe, as you know. It sounds exactly like what you and Ben experienced. My mind was suddenly going a thousand miles an hour, and I was feeling or seeing memories flash, strobe-like, at an extremely high rate of speed. It would then get kind of staticky, and when it cleared, I was witnessing what I can only describe as someone else's memories in the same rapid-fire delivery. I felt someone put their hands on my shoulders, and it snapped me out of it. When I focused, I realized it was Sid, and I had my hands on his shoulders as well. We were staring directly into each other's eyes, and I was communicating with him telepathically. He 'told' me what was going on with the monks telepathically. They were performing the whirling dervish dance like they do in Tibet. Within a few seconds, he downloaded to me his entire discussion he had just had with the spiritual leaders regarding what the ALPs meant. It was intense, Sandy, intense."

"Wow, I don't know what to say!"

"Yeah, I'm still in shock. I'm not sure how long this went on, but it kept repeating itself. Each time the light ascended, we were coated in a barely visible orange-and-blue light that swirled around us. Ultimately, we fell to the ground, and just before we passed out, I was looking up into the ALPs light as it retracted back into the ground. We came to a couple hours later."

"Are you sure you're all right?"

"No, I'm not all right! I've been woke, Sandy. Look, I gotta go; the meeting's about to start. We'll talk soon."

Ben and I sit there, once again at a loss for words. As I stir and stare at my coffee, something comes to me that now makes sense. It's the survey all the participants at the mall kiosk filled out. I look at Ben and tell him, "I've been meaning to tell you something. Remember the surveys from the mall participants? There's something that was nearly identical in each survey. In the comments, most of them said the same thing. 'It's so beautiful, so beautiful!' "

Clinical Trials

Sitting in the main conference room at Astral Computational, I can't stop drumming my fingers on the table. I'm as nervous as I can ever recall. I'm not sure if my voice can function without the telltale nervous warble that will belie my confidence. I get up and pace the room and stop behind Ben's chair. I put my arms on his shoulders and lower my head to his ear.

"We're gonna be all right, aren't we?"

"Come on, Dad, don't go soft on me now—let's do this thing!"

As I am about to reply, the door swings open and the office manager announces that our guests have arrived. I straighten up and approach our guests with an outstretched hand.

"Dr. Souvenir, it's so good to see you on this glorious morning. And, Ms. Pelbow, I remember you from our last meeting."

"Thank you, Mr. Stern," Dr. Souvenir replies. "This is Allie Calhoun. She is a patient of mine and will be your participant in today's trial. Allie, this Mr. Stern."

"Glad to meet you, Mr. Stern," Allie says, shaking my hand. "I can't wait to see your running machine. I'm a big runner, you know."

"My pleasure. I've heard that you're a big runner. Please call me Sandy. This is Ben Stern. He's not only a genius but he's my son. This is Dr. Lenard Petra and Angelica Sterling. Dr. Petra is the principal at Astral Computational, and Angelica is the head of the Memory Chaser project. Please have a seat."

As we sit around the long mahogany conference table exchanging glances, Dr. Petra provides the introduction. I can't help but observe Allie. Her eyes are darting everywhere but not directly at anyone. It's obvious she's at least nervous. I can't help but think she's only partially with us.

"Well that is the short version of our history here at Astral Computational," Dr. Petra concludes. "With that, I'll turn the table over to Mr. Stern."

"Thank you, Dr. Petra," I say, realizing I missed his whole introduction. "We're so pleased to be partnered with Astral Computational. Without them, what you will witness today wouldn't be possible. It's been a fabulous partnership, and we're excited to see how we can help people with our Memory Chaser.

"In a minute, we'll go to another room that holds the Memory Chaser. The first thing you'll notice is that it's housed in an elongated sphere we like to call the Egg. It may appear to be a bit claustrophobic, but we find once the participant is engaged, none of that will mater. We'll start off with a short run—"

"I'd like to go for my run now," Allie says excitedly. "Is it time to go to the treadmill?"

"Yes, Allie," Dr. Souvenir consoles. "You're gonna go for your run once Mr. Stern finishes."

The room gets quiet and motionless for a moment. I start back in on my discussion and realize that maybe I should cut it short, as Allie seems to be getting uncomfortable. I turn toward Allie and ask, "Allie, are you ready to go for your run? We have a special jogging suit we'd like you to try out." Allie doesn't answer as she fiddles with a coaster. Her face is stone-cold and lacks emotion.

Angelica pulls a small gym bag from under the table and reveals Allie's new jogging suit. "What do you think of this, Allie?" Angelica says as she unfurls the pitch-black spatial-congruity suit.

"Oh, I think I like it. It's very dark."

Angelica, Ms. Pelbow, and Allie then go to the changing room and fit Allie with the suit. The rest of us make our way to the Memory Chaser room. Once in the room, Dr. Souvenir takes me aside and fills me in on Allie's condition.

"Allie is not having such a good day. Change is a dementia sufferer's enemy. I've explained to her what today is about many times, but she doesn't seem to retain any of it. I really appreciate you cutting your presentation short. I think it's best if we just get on with it. I think she'll be fine once she starts running. We all love the event you constructed. It's very helpful that you sent it out ahead of time. We really feel like we know what to expect. Her family will be here soon. Angelica is going to bring them in here at the end, is that correct?"

"I could tell she was a bit antsy. Yes, the office manager will greet them and then coordinate with Angelica. It's all taken care of."

"Okay, stations, everybody," I announce. "It's gonna be me and Dr. Souvenir and Allie in the Memory Chaser room, and the rest of you will be in the control room. Ben, do you have the smudge sticks, holder, and a lighter at the ready?"

"Yes, they're on the corner table next to the couch."

"Great, will you cue me when we get close to those scenes?"

"Yes, of course. Let's do this thing!"

As Allie stands there in the spatial-congruity suit, I can't help but feel sorry for her. No one wants to be the only one with a costume on. She, of course, probably has much bigger fish to fry, considering the alien environment she's now in.

As Dr. Souvenir helps Allie on the treadmill, I explain what's going to happen. As the scene is cued up, Allie instinctively starts running with it. Slowly, the music rises in volume. We selected the Cowboy Junkies' "Misguided Angel" for the warm-up. It's haunting and slow with beckoning vocals reminiscent of Patsy Cline, only more lounge-like. She'll do a short warm-up run to Sally's original loop through the forest.

Allie is running at about half speed in time with music, viewing herself from behind and above. She's not labored and seems to be enjoying herself. From my perspective, I can't see that everything is in three dimensions, but for Allie it definitely is; the Egg is filled with dyed air. Ahead of her, beams of light shine down like pillars, illuminating some unknown treasure. The strobe light begins to modulate the pillars in sync with the music. Very slowly, the God Helmet induces a feeling of comfort and well-being. Allie brushes her shoulder against a tree branch, which causes the spatial-congruity suit to clinch her in precisely the same spot on her shoulder. Allie lets out a gasp of recognition. She's now entering the out-of-body experience. As she passes through the towering beams of sunlight, the suit heats and cools with precision.

"Allie," I question. "Are you doing all right? Are you comfortable?"

"Oh my, I feel funny. We're not at the gym, are we?"

"Well, you're not at your usual gym. Just try to relax and follow the music and scenery. You're going to see some images shortly; don't be startled; it's all part of your run."

"This music is slowing me down. Can we go faster?"

"Of course we can, but this is just your warm-up. There'll be plenty of time to go faster."

On cue, the aspen grove can be seen off in the distance. Its broken canopy lights vibrate to a subbeat in the music. The God Helmet switches to a feeling of longing and desire at maximum intensity. Allie brushes up against branches on either side of her body, and the corresponding sensation is activated in the suit. She lets out a loud, ecstatic moan, and it's clear she's in full out-of-body mode. As she enters the aspen grove, an image is faintly visible off in the distance. When the merged image gets closer and larger, she can see it's her husband when he was young, before they were married. Allie calls out his name multiple times. As the image gets closer, he begins to age to present time, and then he's gone.

Another image appears off in the distance. It's an image of their young family, with Allie and her husband on either side of their two young children. The God Helmet switches to the pure-love setting. They're dressed in their Sunday best and all look so incredibly happy. As the image gets closer, the children say something: "We love you, Mommy!" With that, the image disintegrates as Allie exits the aspen grove and starts the slow turn back to the beginning. As she exits the forest and enters the sunbaked sagebrush meadow, the suit heats up. I tell her she's just about at the end, and she should prepare to stop.

As Allie comes to a stop, she's not breathing hard. She's clearly still a high-caliber runner. I tell her to relax for a minute and have a drink of water. I explain that the fun part is about to begin and ask her if she's ready.

She responds, "Is my family going to be there?"

Dr. Souvenir steps up and talks to Allie in a soft voice. She encourages her and asks if she's ready for the next run. I can hear Allie ask where her husband is. Dr. Souvenir tells her that he's just around the next corner near the lavender patch.

The next part of Allie's event is derived from footage and photos from various competitive trail runs she participated in as recently as five years ago. She wore a head-mounted camera in one of these races, and it's the foundation of this event portion. The event is from Allie's perspective with the back of her body projected into the scene as usual. She's reliving the race from above and behind herself. I'm beginning to wonder if it will be too much for her.

Most of the trail run is in an old-growth blue spruce forest in the mountains surrounding Aspen. From the minute Allie starts, she knows what she's looking at. She talks frequently to herself. Her voice is joyous and positive; she's encouraging herself. She's in full out-of-body mode from brushing up against low-hanging branches. The God Helmet is tickling her adrenal glands and activating endorphins. The occasional light that breaks through is amplified and pulses to the slick guitar riffs and is perfectly in time with her footfalls. Allie's gait is beautifully long and graceful; it looks effortless. The shady, wooded scene is breathtaking.

An image emerges from the background; it's Allie's mother when she was in her twenties. The image of her face gradually fills the screen and slowly morphs through her years to her current age. The image dissolves, and Allie calls out her mother's name repeatedly. The scene repeats with her father aging before her eyes. Allie reaches out to grab her father, all the while calling his name. He fades away as she is passed by another runner. Allie picks up her pace in an effort to not fall too far back.

She's now viewing footage of her young family overlaid on the dimly lit, wooded scene. Her children are darting back and forth, giggling and screeching, looking for hidden eggs—it's Easter. Her husband's face appears from the side as he approaches the camera to kiss Allie. Allie puckers up and kisses him. Her children push their dad out of the way and proudly hold their Easter baskets up to show her their booty. Allie congratulates them just as she did so many years ago.

As Allie progresses, a series of images parade by of her relatives and close friends. Allie calls each and every one of their names out in a display of perfect recall. Dr. Souvenir is astounded, as Allie has a hard time recalling her immediate family's names. Allie's face is loosening up, and her facial expressions are animated. She's coming back.

She's now in the last mile of the trail run, and her pace increases to a full-on run. She's passing runner after runner. She knows exactly where she is in the run and is giving her all. There are spectators on both sides of the trail, all cheering the runners on. As she approaches the finish line, the viewpoint changes. Allie is now viewing herself head-on as she guts out the last fifty yards. Her loved ones can be heard screaming encouragement at the tops of their lungs. Allie crosses the finish line and is mobbed by her family. Her face is beet red, and her expression is pure joy. Her husband grabs her and lifts her in the air. They both fall to the ground. Her two young children are now squirming on the ground with them as laughter erupts. Her children can be heard calling out, "Who's a winner? Who's a winner? Mommy is; Mommy is!"

Allie comes to a full stop, and the event holds on the four of them squirming on the ground in silent slow motion. Allie drops to her knees and cries like a baby. She's trying to say something between her sobbing gasps for air. "I miss you all so much; you're so beautiful, so beautiful."

Dr. Souvenir enters the Memory Chaser and kneels with Allie. Allie is visibly shaken. "It's all right, Allie; it's going to be all right." We give her some time to regroup and offer her a cup of water. Dr. Souvenir tells her that she's almost done. "When you're ready, you can visit your home."

This perks Allie up and she asks, "Home? I'm going home? Oh, I so much want to go home."

"Yes, you are, but just for a visit."

"Can we go now?"

I get a cue from Ben that I need to prepare the smudge sticks. I pick them up and check on Allie. She's more than ready, so I nod to Ben to initiate the last part of the event. Very slowly, "Take Me Home, Country Roads" picks up in volume, and Allie is viewing her home from the front yard. She's running at a slow pace. She seems a bit confused as the scene is stationary. She quickly adjusts and continues running. We hear her muttering to herself.

Allie rounds her house to the backyard, revealing her precious garden. It's late June, and her beloved plants are in full bloom. The landscaping is an exceptional example of what a xeriscape garden can be. The low-lying ground near the house is carpeted in plush deep-green dog turf grass. The event scans the breadth of her xeriscape. In the background are tall green grasses and violet Russian sage. In front of that are strategically placed bright-yellow Spanish Gold Broom. The varieties of brightly colored plants are too numerous to name. They descend in height away from the back of the yard. The varied colors are perfectly positioned and resemble an impressionist painting.

Allie is now viewing herself kneeling down, weeding and pruning her prized plants; she's gently humming a tune. The event holds as she methodically works her way through her garden. Very slowly, an image is overlaid on the scene. As it comes into focus, she can see it's a bride and groom slow dancing at a wedding. The couple is facing away, gracefully moving across

170

the dance floor that's surrounded by wedding guests. As the couple turns toward Allie, she realizes it's her and her husband. Their faces slowly fill the screen. Pure love and joy are emanating from their glowing faces as they stare deeply into one another's eyes. She feels her husband through the suit as the God Helmet initiates love and desire. The focus now pans across the gathering, examining each attendee. Allie calls their names out as they pass by.

The view is now focused on a patch of lavender and sage. I light the smudge stick and hold it through the port in the Memory Chaser. As the scent wafts around Allie, she breaths deeply through her nose and exhales, proclaiming how beautiful they smell as she closes her eyes and hugs herself. When she opens her eyes, the scene has shifted. She's now viewing herself holding a beautiful arrangement of wildflowers, including sage and lavender. She's handing them to her husband. Allie mouths the words she uttered that day, when she was healthy and certain, "For you, my darling; don't they smell gorgeous?"

Allie hears her young children clambering to get out the back door. They burst out the door and run toward her and hug her legs. She suddenly stops running and falls to her knees. She's sobbing uncontrollably, all the while trying to get the words out: "Take me home; take me home." John Denver's final refrain echoes: "Take me home, country roads..."

Dr. Souvenir consoles Allie and helps her out of the Memory Chaser. I signal Ben to have Angelica bring her family into the Memory Chaser room. As Allie exits the Memory Chaser, she turns, and directly in front of her is her family. They are surely hoping that she knows who they are. Allie's face instantly transforms from tears of longing to ecstatic joy. Allie jumps into her husband's arms, calling his name over and over. Her grown children join in for an extended group hug. Allie cups her daughter's face in the palms of her hands and calls her by her full name. She does the same for her son. Allie's stone face is gone; she's beaming with joy. She looks like her healthy, normal self. I'm stunned at the transformation.

I'm alone in the Memory Chaser room, sprawled out on the couch. It's nearing the noon hour, and I'm exhausted, realizing I have to do this all over again with John Doe. Allie's experience was so impactful, I fear what John Doe's event will be like. I can't help but think what Allie is feeling. Did she really have a moment of clarity in her jumbled mind? I'd like to think so. I never thought it would be me needing couch solitude. The door to the control room slowly opens, and Ben peers in at me.

"Are you all right, Dad?"

He doesn't wait for my answer and wedges his way onto the couch.

"I'm whooped; that was intense!"

"I know. It was pretty intense watching the video feed. I could tell you were engaged. I'm proud of you, Dad. You followed through. I respect that."

"Thanks, Ben. You're no slouch yourself. Remember you wanted to bail on the whole thing? You're the one who followed through. I'm proud of you, and I thank you from the bottom of my heart. We're not done though; are you ready?"

"No way, but I'm carrying some serious energy. I was thinking that I should be with John Doe, and you run the knobs. I don't think you should be that close if it gets crazy."

"Are you serious? I'm not worried about that; besides, I don't have a clue how to run this thing like you two. I really appreciate the sentiment, but Dr. Charles is a large, imposing man. He'll have a deputy with him. I'll be fine."

"They're bringing cops with them? Jesus, Dad, now I'm really freaked."

"Well, yeah, he's a violent criminal, and it's not like we're set up for a mishap."

Dr. Petra enters from the main door and asks if we want some lunch. He tells us we should be ready in forty-five minutes; they're in transit.

While we sit around the conference table eating Goldie's Deli pastrami sandwiches, Dr. Petra tells us straight up, "I don't know how much thought you've given this, but you realize you're going to be working with a violent felon? I think it would be a good idea for me to be in the room with you, Sandy. I have a Taser just in case. It's not worth anybody getting hurt."

Angelica sets her sandwich down and takes a long, gulping drink from her soda.

"We were just talking about that. I appreciate your offer, but let's wait and see what Dr. Charles has to say. I don't know what kind of protocol they have. John Doe will be escorted by a deputy sheriff, and that's about all I know."

"Well, you just let me know, Sandy. I'd better go make sure there's someone at the front desk. I'll be right back."

"Are you okay, Angelica?" I inquire. "We'll have the door to the control room locked, and Ben will be with you."

"I'm fine. I'm just a bit out of my element is all."

We see Dr. Petra talking to a small group out front and scramble to clean up our mess. The show is on. My stomach tightens, and I struggle to shake it off.

Dr. Petra, Dr. Charles, and company enter the conference room, and an awkward silence ensues. Dr. Charles is accompanied by an assistant, a deputy, and John Doe. John is wearing an orange jumpsuit and is handcuffed. His shaved head hangs low, and he makes no eye contact. It's getting very real.

"Good to see you again, Sandy," Dr. Charles says sincerely. "I want you to know how appreciative we are for your efforts in criminal rehabilitation. We're excited to see how this goes. This is my assistant, Tyler Paige. This is Deputy Reggie Knox, and this is Drake Kovo."

"Dr. Charles," I begin. "You've met Dr. Petra; he's the principal here at Astral Computational. This is Angelica; she leads the Memory Chaser team at Astral, and this is Ben Stern; he's the brains of our side of the partnership with Astral. Yes, he's my son, but don't hold that against him."

We all take seats around the conference table, and Dr. Petra gives his spiel about Astral Computational and our partnership. It's my turn, and I begin to explain how the Memory Chaser works. I pause and ask Dr. Charles what Mr. Kovo knows about today's activities.

"My staff and I have viewed the video of the event you provided. It's quite compelling, and I thank you for sending that out ahead of time. Mr. Kovo has been told what today is about but not in any detail. He's been running in the gym as preparation, and that's about it. He's apprehensive but committed to following through."

I realize I should tell Mr. Kovo as little as possible. I look around the room and am met with waiting stares. I turn to Mr. Kovo and tell him, "Today may be difficult for you, but you need to know it can have a positive outcome, very positive. Our device is designed to help you recall memories you may have lost connection with. You'll be subject to a meditative state that will make the recall possible. There are no drugs involved. As you are aware, you will be jogging inside of what we call the Memory Chaser. It may feel a bit claustrophobic at first, but once you get going, it will be the last thing you'll be thinking about—trust me. Mr. Kovo, do you have any questions?"

"Yes, I do," Mr. Kovo says as his crooked grimace twitches. "Is this thing gonna fry my brain?"

"No, no, no. It does nothing of the sort. Your brain will be mildly stimulated to help with the meditative state, but that's the only invasive aspect. There is a special running suit you'll need to wear. Angelica, can you provide Deputy Knox with the TC suit, please?"

I shut my introduction down before I reveal any more details. We head to the Memory Chaser room as Dr. Charles and deputy Knox get Mr. Kovo suited up in the changing room. Entering the Memory Chaser room, I see they've changed the display on the LCD walls. It's no longer the fall-colored aspen grove; it's a familiar-looking room that appears to be staged. It dawns on me that it is one of the escape rooms where Drake Kovo worked. This must have been Ben's idea.

Dr. Charles, Deputy Knox, and Mr. Kovo enter the room. Mr. Kovo is struck with the scene laid out before him. It was the last place he worked and was subject to much scrutiny during his trial. "Oh Jesus!" he says. "I'm not sure I like this." I'm feeling anxious and explain to him that this is all part of the process. I assure him it's going to be all right.

Dr. Charles and I guide Mr. Kovo into the Memory Chaser as Deputy Knox paces back and forth. I signal to Ben and Angelica to start the event. I explain, "As you jog on the treadmill, try to keep pace with the music and always face forward. Some of the images will appear to be quite real; don't attempt to touch them. Whatever you do, don't turn around, keep your focus forward, and let your mind go where it wants to."

Slowly the music volume increases; it's Traffic's "Dear Mr. Fantasy." The song is dreamy and eerie and expresses a desire to be happy again, to be lifted out of gloom. Mr. Kovo starts out at a slow pace and holds it. He's viewing himself from the VR perspective as he's jogging down the dirt road that leads to his grandparents' house. The sides of the road are lined by tall cottonwood trees. Beyond the narrow line of cottonwoods are acres and acres of tall sunflowers struggling to face the sun.

The Egg is filled with electric-blue dyed air that provides the three-dimensional affect. From behind, he is bumped hard by a dog, and he misses a step. This sets off the tactile-congruity suit, and he is launched into out-of-body mode. The God Helmet warms his heart with longing. The dog is running beside him, bumping into his leg as the suit replicates it. We hear him call out, "Ringo, how's it goin', boy?" Ringo was his grandparents' dog. Ringo is entirely animated from still images.

Off in the distance, a small image appears. As it gets closer and fills the screen, he sees it's his grandparents, and they are saying something to him. They're calling for little Drake. They seem so happy and excited to be with their grandson. Grandma kneels down as little Drake runs into the scene and leaps into her open arms. She grabs him and tosses him into the air. Little Drake is giggling uncontrollably. Kovo is now looking at a close-up of the two of them. Grandma is smothering him with kisses as little Drake continues giggling. The God Helmet is bombarding him with a sense of belonging and acceptance. He's overcome with a feeling of self-empathy. The scene zooms out as Grandpa joins in the fray. They play on the grass in effortless summer freedom. Eventually, the scene fades, and he's alone, running on the tree-lined country road again.

Another image appears in the scene, off in the distance. As it draws closer and begins to fill the screen, he sees it's a lacrosse game from his high school years. It zooms in on his ponytailed younger self, sweaty and amped up as he retrieves a pass and is hit hard by a defender. The suit replicates the physical contact. The God Helmet summons adrenaline, and he's feeling the intensity of that moment. As he races down field toward the goal, he can hear his family screaming for him to *go*. His pace on the treadmill is now at a full-on run. He dodges defenders and feels the contact. Drake fires a shot on goal from twenty yards out and scores. A deafening roar erupts, and Drake jumps skyward screaming with joy as the God Helmet switches to the elation and joy setting. He runs toward the sidelines to celebrate with his family. He's ecstatic and beaming as he is mobbed by his parents and sister. He sees the pride on his family's faces as he is reliving a high point in his high school life. It's glorious.

Kovo is now running alone again down the dirt road. He's breathing heavily and slows his pace down. A dog is running toward him from far off in the distance. As it gets closer, he calls out the dog's name—it's Hunter, his family dog. Hunter knows exactly who it is and begins to wriggle as Kovo closes in at high speed. Kovo slows to a stop and drops to his knees to grab the leaping Hunter. He's filled with God Helmet love as he attempts to grab Hunter. The collision sets off the spatial congruity suit. Kovo is shocked that there's no dog to embrace and begins to sob.

Dr. Charles leans into the Memory Chaser and pats Kovo on the back, asking him if he's okay. He hands him bottled water and tells him to take a breather. There's more to come, he tells him. He pulls himself together and turns toward Dr. Charles. "I'm not feeling good about where this is going!"

Kovo is now viewing the escape room where he worked. The song "Swastika Eyes" by Primal Scream is at full volume. It's a very scary yet transcendental song that represents the best in industrial-acid house rock. Kovo is seeing a video of customers that are pretending to be panicked as if they can't get out of the escape room. They're running back and forth, bouncing off the walls. The impacts are replicated on the suit, and he's out of his body again. The God Helmet elicits fear and panic. Kovo see their faces, and it's him and Juliet, the girl he attacked. Their faces have been morphed onto the bodies of the random customers. It's completely believable. They're clamoring to open the door to the next escape room. He hears the sound of the electric dead bolt release, and they burst through the door. He's suddenly alone in a dark room.

A lone streetlight illuminates a late-model sedan and reflects off the wet pavement. There are two people arguing next to the sedan. He's viewing himself and Juliet from the Good Samaritan's perspective. Kovo is watching the back of his body approach the scuffle. Anger and frustration surge from the God Helmet. He hears the Good Samaritan screaming for him to leave her alone. Kovo tells the Good Samaritan to fuck off and begins to slap Juliet as he attempts to push her in the sedan. Kovo feels the sting of the slaps on his hand through the suit. He feels absolute rage. The viewpoint rapidly approaches Kovo as the camera is jostled about, breaking up the scene. The Good Samaritan is grabbing at Kovo as he tries to separate them. The camera phone falls to the ground, and the perspective changes to looking up at the violence from the ground. Kovo sees flashes of arms flailing and hears Juliet screaming for him to stop. Kovo is struck in the head and falls to the ground. The view is now straight up at the glaring streetlight. Kovo is screaming, "I'll get you, bitch." A car can be heard squealing its tires, and it goes completely dark.

Kovo is back in the dark escape room. He's breathing heavily, trying to get his bearings. With a flash, he's observing his sixteenth birthday. He's sitting behind a candlelit birthday cake. He hears his mother telling him, "Blow the candles out, dear." Kovo freaks out and runs directly through the scene to a door that leads to the next escape room. He slams into the door as the spatial congruity suit clamps down hard. He fumbles for the door; it is unlocked, and he escapes to the next room.

Kovo is back on a dimly lit street. "Swastika Eyes" fades away and Eminem's epic life struggle "Lose Yourself" fades in. He's viewing the Good Samaritan's car from the side of the road. The perspective is from a security camera on a fire station. A screeching car can be heard approaching. As the Good Samaritan and Juliet get out of the car, their car is struck from behind with tremendous force. It's Kovo. He jumps out of his car, and the view zooms in on his rage-filled face. The God Helmet pulses with anger and hatred. The music is pulsing with angst as the suit squeezes his entire body. Kovo is extremely anxious and is losing his mind. He watches himself close in on the frightened couple and begins to savagely beat them. He feels the pain from his own strikes as well as those from the Good Samaritan's and Juliet's through the suit. It is complete pandemonium.

Flashing blue-and-red lights illuminate the scene. A police siren chirps several times, and over the cruiser's loudspeaker, he hears the cops tell him to stand down immediately. Kovo watches in horror as he continues to flail away. The perspective changes again. The view is from the officers' body cameras. Kovo is now running toward himself as the officers pull their guns. It's an all-out brawl as the officers engage, screaming for Kovo to stand down or they'll shoot. Kovo feels every strike from the suit as the God Helmet switches to abject fear. The gun is now a yellow-handled Taser, and he's looking down on the fallen Kovo. The sound cuts out as the Taser lets loose its high-voltage wires directly into Kovo's heart. The spatial-congruity suit shocks Kovo, and panic fills his mind from the God Helmet. Kovo is convulsing on the wet pavement as foam gurgles from his crooked, stiffened mouth. The scene holds for an eternity. From the Memory Chaser, we hear Kovo screaming in horror, followed by complete silence, and a loud thump.

Crestone Lights Up

Ben and I robotically set out for Chaffee County early in the morning. Last week is an experience neither of us will ever forget. As we stare at nothing in particular in the passing scenery, our thoughts struggle to be free from the replaying scene. As we grind our way mile after mile, the mountainous beauty seems to wrap her arms around us and provides much-needed comfort. We've been silent for an hour and are about to crest Kenosha Pass. Before we know it, we're careening around the big turn that reveals South Park, and it's time to howl in recognition of its majesty. Simultaneously, we look at each other and let loose bloodcurdling coyote howls. We stop when we run out of breath. As we struggle to catch our breaths, we're overtaken with the giggles. We dare not look at each other, as that would surely make it worse. Two miles into the giggles, we land on the floor of South Park. The immense scale and beauty of the place slaps us back to reality. It feels like the truck has shrunk to the size of a toy car, and we're only traveling twenty miles per hour instead of the seventy miles per hour that the speedometer reads.

"I'm so glad the trials are behind us," I say. "I'm still in shock."

"I'm exhausted. I don't think I could take another day of that."

"Me too, Ben, me too."

"Do you think the experience will have a lasting effect on them?"

"That's the big question, isn't it? It's all I can think about, well, other than Mr. Kovo writhing on the ground, crying like a baby. I think it will. I think it will certainly affect Mr. Kovo for a long time to come. It's amazing how it affected him even though he didn't make it to the end of the event. Allie is a little different story. Her dementia is a well-defined medical condition. I will say that her face at the end looked twenty years younger. She was no longer stone faced and devoid of any emotions. She was full of color and had a spring in her step. The way she interacted with her family was so heartwarming. I want to cry just thinking about it. It was like she zapped back in time, like the disease never happened. I think it will help her. Maybe it's like exercising; you gotta keep doing it. What do you think?"

"Obviously time will tell. Having them repeat the event is a great idea that I think will help solidify the experience. I think it will make a lasting difference. I don't have much to base this on, but I believe that. Our exposure to the Memory Chaser sure changed how we communicate,

Broccoli. It did something to our brains that's unexplainable. Why can't it do something similar for them?"

"I like how you think, Ben."

As we sneak through the traffic light in Fairplay, I bring the truck back up to cruising speed, and we continue heading south to the cabin. My thoughts turn toward Willy and his well-being.

"So tomorrow I think I'll head down to Crestone and pay Willy a visit. I'm more than curious and a bit worried. Do you think the big ALPs event had anything to do with the impending polar reversal Willy was telling us about?"

"I have no idea. Something's going on, and while it's exciting, it's a bit scary. I can't wait to hear the rest of his story; we didn't get much detail from him. The whole thing is kinda freaking me out."

"No, we didn't. That's part of the reason I want to see him. Did I tell you he texted me to see if I wanted to join him on his mapping project? I guess he's about done, at least with the first phase. I'm gonna get my own rock hammer—that's exciting! Seriously though, it's all very freaky. I filled Dr. Petra in on our whole story. He told me wants in, whatever that means."

"What do you mean, he wants in, in on what? We don't even know what *it* is."

"I know, he certainly zeroed in on the crux of the matter. He told me the whole reason he's interested in the Memory Chaser is the 'why' of it all. As in, why memory, identity, and spirituality exist, I guess. He said that Astral Computational is at the ready to help out."

As we make our way down and through Trout Creek Canyon, we're ready for our next howl as Mount Princeton is about to be revealed. As we round the magical turn, all we can see is the base of the grand mountain—it's completely socked in with clouds.

"Well, I guess sometimes it needs to be obscured to make the clear days more special," I explain to Ben.

Pulling up to the cabin feels like home. The low-hanging clouds that shroud everything above nine thousand feet make the landscape seem alien yet comforting as the view scape is now at a manageable scale. The Collegiate Peaks are taking a rest from their dominance. We spend the rest of the day nesting our abode back to home. The day goes fast, and before we know it, it's time for bed. In the morning, I'll be headed to Crestone. I'll need my rest for what lies ahead.

"All right, Ben, are you sure you're going to be okay here all by your lonesome? I'll be back in a couple days. I'll be in touch. Keep in mind the phone service sucks down there. I may only be in range in the evenings."

"Sounds good, Dad. I'll be fine. I got some technical stuff to work on that Astral provided. It should be interesting and keep me busy. See you in a couple days."

I hug Ben and head south with a head full of questions.

As I pull up to the The Cloud Station in Crestone, I see Willy's truck parked out front. I make my way into the café. Before I make it to the door, I hear Willy call my name. I turn, and there he is, in all his glory, basking in the sun on the side patio with his feet up, sporting a straw cowboy hat. We hug long, and I take a seat next to him. He seems happy enough, but that's always the case with Willy. I keep trying to peer into his eyes—looking for what, I'm not sure. At least he isn't a zombie.

"So, how're you doing, Willy? You had quite the experience last week. Have things settled down much?"

"I'm just fine, Sandy. Yeah, it was life changing. I still can't believe what I witnessed. The town is still in shock. The spiritual leaders, especially the Buddhist monks, have done a great job calming everyone down."

"It was that impactful? What do people think is going on?"

"It depends on who you ask. Most of the townies think it's the fulfillment of a prophecy. The monks and natives think it's more than that. Of course no one can stop talking about Glen Anderson. It's hard to explain away his story."

"Who's Glen Anderson?"

"Do you know much about this place?"

"No, not really. I'd never heard of Crestone until Sally's passing. I guess I've come to know it as a hippie town that has some serious religious traditions. Faiths from all over the world are represented here, I understand.

Besides the monk who prepared Sally's funeral pyre, Sid was the first spiritualist I've met here."

"The history is a long story, but the beginnings are important, as that's where Glen Anderson comes in. In the seventies, a couple moved here from Canada, Maurice and Hanne Strong. He was a big muckety-muck who made gazillions in the Canadian oil business. Through a partnership, they owned two million acres of land in the southwest. Nearly 150,000 acres of that is right here on the east side of the San Luis Valley. Hanne is the real story; she's responsible for the unique fellowship of the couple dozen faiths calling this home. As Hanne tells the story, she fell in love with this place the minute she arrived. I guess it was a spiritual moment. She convinced her husband to divest of all the other property so they could focus on what she called the Baca.

"Hanne claims that a few months after moving here, a stranger appeared at her door; it was Glen Anderson. Glen was a drifter, mystic, prophet. As the two sat for tea, Glen told Hanne that 'he was waiting for her to arrive.' Glen ends up staying for four days and loads Hanne's head full of predictions and spiritual enlightenment. He tells her that her land was to become the home for all the spiritual traditions of the world. Spiritual leaders from around the globe would come for enlightenment and enhanced awareness. This community would create a new civilization that would be in balance with nature and each other. It was to be a utopian society that shed the old and boldly bore the new. Glen said that thousands of young people would seek refuge in the Baca and that she needed to be ready for them. He told her that 'this is what you've come to Crestone to do.' This is the best part, Sandy: Glen Anderson said that the spiritual vibrations would intensify so much that those that had not embraced spirituality would not be able to handle the vibrations and would have to leave."

"What do you mean, vibrations? That sounds very new age."

"I don't know. I sure was vibrated to the core last week, believe me. The important part is that most of what Glen Anderson prophesized has come true. Granted, a lot of it is because Glen told Hanne what she should do. This place has world-famous religious leaders who spend a great deal of time here. Hell, the Dalai Lama has been here. Native Americans are represented here in abundance. You don't hear about it because, besides the Carmelites, Western religions aren't represented here. Hanne has granted thousands of acres to the various religious groups that live here. She put this thing together, and now it's happening. The town's going crazy over the Glen Anderson connection and what they've experienced here. The ALPs lights are nothing new in Crestone. Last week was the granddaddy of them all,

181

however. Everyone thinks its end of days up here—only not the Christian version."

"Well that's crazy. Glen Anderson? It's a rather unassuming name; who knew? Is Glen still with us?"

"No, Glen died sometime in the early eighties. No one really knows what happened to him. They say he just wandered off one day up into the Sangre de Cristo Mountains."

"What do the religious leaders have to say about last week's ALPs experience? Do they have an explanation?"

"They don't need explanations, Sandy; they just believe. They have been participating in ALPs events for some time now. What I've learned I learned from Sid when we were communicating telepathically. I can't begin to explain what happened, but I will say I experienced a lifetime of knowledge in a matter of seconds. The Buddhist monks believe that ALPs are a connection to a higher state of consciousness where knowledge of all human existence resides. Laypeople who experience this connection describe it as completely overwhelming. For most, it's very uncomfortable and frightening. The stream of information completely overwhelms the brain. The Buddhists have figured out how to channel this information stream. They're able to focus on specific elements within the stream. They describe it as the voices of all living beings, as well as those no longer with us. They're able to zero in on specific voices. They claim the voices are memory streams. They say they're being guided by an entity they call Sarah. Sarah is teaching them how to navigate the memory streams. Pretty crazy, huh?"

"Jesus, Willy, I don't know what to say. Do you think this has anything to do with the polar reversal you told us was about to happen?"

"It's funny you ask. I don't know, but just the other day, I set up a magnetic field monitor. This device records the strength and direction of Earth's magnetic field. I'm now tracking Earth's magnetic field and recording it. I'll know if it changes or fluctuates. I even have an alarm set up on my phone if the device detects significant changes in the magnetic field. We'd better finish up here. We've got a lot of fieldwork I'd like to get done. Are you ready to don your rock hammer?"

We finish our breakfast and head out in Willy's truck. We're headed south of the stupa to do a second pass over Willy's mapping area. As we approach the stupa, Willy slows way down in respect for its holiness. The stupa is no more than thirty yards down a small embankment. A couple dozen ropes radiating out from its golden crown dangle Tibetan prayer flags. The colorful flags snap rhythmically in the wind. I can see there's quite the crowd gathered around its western side, which overlooks the San Luis Valley. There's a group of Tibetan monks clad in saffron robes and a variety of Native Americans elaborately dressed in their ceremonial tribal garb. The tribal members are dancing and chanting in their native tongue. The rhythmic chanting is accented by bass-heavy, guttural throat singing from the Tibetan monks. It's ominous, to say the least.

The farther south we go, the more treacherous the road gets. To our right, down valley, the mountainside steeply falls away from the road. I avoid looking down as it sends my mind imagining a gruesome end. Willy stops the truck to point something out ahead of us.

"This steep side of the mountain in front of us is a fault escarpment. You're looking at the Sangre de Cristo Fault. That's what I'm mapping. I've avoided mapping the really steep stuff; it's too dangerous. I don't really need to map it anyway; you can see the fault right there, so I know where it is. The escarpment in front of you was one of the strongest emissions of ALPs energy last week. You could see it glowing above all the other light. I'm sure there's some excellent ALPs mineral precipitates there. We'll park just above the steeps and be on foot from there."

A chill runs through my body. The landscape, though gorgeous, takes on an ominous feel. I distinctly feel an energy to the place, and at the same time, I can sense its history. My anxiousness quickly turns to awe. Willy drives us the last quarter mile up the hill and parks.

"Let me show you what I've been working on, Sandy. I got some great maps that'll help you visualize what we'll be doing."

"Excellent, I love maps. They tell a story beyond words."

"They sure do. My life has been defined by maps. So this is a USGS 7.5-minute geologic quadrangle map. It's the most detailed their work gets for published maps. On my first pass at mapping, I followed the trace of the fault you see here," he says, pointing at the map. "Once I was sure I was on or near the fault, I recorded multiple transects that intersect the main fault perpendicularly. I was recording the magnetic intensity of specific minerals precipitated by the ALPs energy. Since you only see the fault on exposed bedrock, the magnetic response will help me pinpoint where the fault is when it's covered up. From that, I can locate where to sample the rocks that are in close proximity to the fault. I've done all the transects and have mapped their intensity; the rainbow colors overlain on the fault are the magnetic data. See how it doesn't always follow the USGS interpreted fault lines? I have the same map in my computer. We'll be using the computer to guide us, as well as inputting our sample locations as we go. Are you ready, pardner?"

"As ready as I'll ever be, Willy."

We head south on foot around the steep fault scarp. When we get to the other side, Willy begins to intensely study his map. He gets out a traditional palm-sized compass and uses it to orient us to the fault trace. He says that sometimes you gotta go old school to keep things honest. I take his word for it.

Willy zeros in on the first sampling point and measures its magnetic intensity and correlates it to his map. He surveys the immediate area around the sampling point to verify he's in the highest magnetic spot. Once he's confident he's in the correct location, he calls me over and shows me how to take a sample.

"So this is how it's going to work. We want samples every five hundred feet or so along the fault, as identified by the highest magnetic intensity. We'll want additional samples on the extremely high magnetic locations as well. I'll identify the sample locations, and you'll collect the sample as I head to the next location."

Willy then gets on his knees and begins digging down into the ground cover with his rock hammer. He keeps digging until he encounters bedrock. Once he uncovers the bedrock, he whacks a piece of it off and shows me what we're looking for.

"This piece of bedrock is what we hope to find. Do you see the tiny crystals coating the outer surface of the rock? If you hold it in the sunlight, you can see them sparkle. Watch what happens when I hold this compass right next to it—it deflects the needle away from north. If I move the sample around, the needle attempts to follow the sample."

"That's very clever; it seems simple enough."

"That was a good example. It's not always going to be that easy. Sometimes you won't find any bedrock, and you'll just have to get a grab sample of the largest pieces of rock you can find. Check the samples with the compass to see if they're magnetic. They may not always deflect the needle, and that's okay. I'd try several samples to see if you can find one that's magnetic, and of course, always be looking for the tiny crystals gleaming in the sun. We've got a lot of ground to cover; do you understand your mission?"

"I think I got it. I'll do my best."

With that we start methodically marching southward along the fault. Willy takes the lead, zigzagging back and forth across the fault line, taking measurements as he goes. He marks the sampling points with small yellow flags as he trudges along. I follow him, digging in his marked locations for bedrock. If I find bedrock, I crack a piece of it off with my rock hammer and run the compass test. Often I can't find any bedrock, so I collect the largest pieces of rock I can find. I'm feeling like a real prospector. The farther we go, the heavier my pack gets with the growing number of samples. We continue methodically for several hours until Willy announces it's time for lunch.

As we sit on a rock outcrop eating our lunch, staring off into the grand expanse of the San Luis Valley, I quiz him on the geology and sampling techniques. Willy points out the fault trace in both directions, and I'm able to see what he's describing. He explains how the San Luis Valley is the result of movement on the massive Sangre de Cristo Fault system. The mountains moved up, and the valley dropped down. Over thirty million years, as the valley dropped, it filled with sediment being shed from the Sangre de Cristo Mountains. He pulls out his compass to show me how to take a bearing measurement of the fault we're sitting on.

"Well, that's weird; my compass won't sit still; it's wandering all over the place. Look at this."

I lean over and see that the compass needle is swinging back a forth on either side of north. Every so often, it stops swinging and zeroes in on north. After a short period, it starts swinging again.

"What's that all about? Shouldn't it just point at north?"

"I have no idea; it could be we're sitting on a highly magnetic area, but that's not what I have mapped."

As Willy reaches in his backpack, the shrill of an alarm breaks our solitude. Willy pulls his cell phone out of his backpack; the alarm is coming from his phone. He fumbles with it for a minute, then turns toward me.

"It's happening, Sandy. It's happening right now!"

"What's happening?"

"It's the polar reversal. That's the alarm for my magnetic field–detection device I was telling you about. It's detected a complete shutdown of Earth's magnetic field!"

"What's going to happen? Are we going to be all right?"

Something catches my eye off in the distance behind Willy to the south. It's a series of bright lights sparkling just above the ground along the fault line. I grab Willy's arm and point behind him.

"Over there, what's that?"

"Holy shit, it's an ALPs event!"

As we sit in motionless awe, the light begins to change form. It shifts from a diffuse, sparkling cloudlike haze to a distinct, discontinuous plane of light that's razor thin. The fragmented plane of azure light throbs from the ground to several thousand feet in the air and back. It reminds me of the aurora borealis, only it's a very distinct plane coming from the ground, not from the sky. We hear a static crackling off in the distance. As the light surges up to the sky and back, its azure color begins to display streaks of orange. In an instant, the light plane leaps toward us along the fault line, stopping a few hundred feet away in the bottom of a gully, then jumps skyward and horizontally toward us. The crackling is now very clear, and it feels like we're about to be electrocuted. Suddenly, the entire lightshow retracts into the earth and falls ominously silent.

Willy's alarm sounds again. He looks at his phone and reports that the magnetic field is back at full strength. Willy looks toward me, his face ashen. I don't know what to say, and I'm beginning to feel very anxious.

"Are you okay, man? You don't look so good."

Before he can answer, his alarm goes off for a third time. Somehow I know this isn't going to be good. Just like before, a diffuse cloud of sparkling light appears in the same place, off in the distance to the south. Within ten seconds, the pattern repeats as before. The light turns into a pulsing, razor thin plane of azure-and-orange light that reaches to the sky and back. Ten seconds later, the crackling light surges horizontally, directly toward us. This time it doesn't stop in the gully; it comes racing directly at us and continues northward as far as we can see, directly on the fault line we just traversed. We are now bathed in an ethereal glow of azure-and-orange light coming out of the fault plane we're sitting on. As we look northward, the slim wall of light flickers on and off. One second, it's an immense, imperceptibly narrow light plane reaching from the ground skyward, pulsing vertically in intensity. The next second, it's completely gone, as if it never happened. It's like Earth is short-circuiting.

The short-circuiting suddenly stops as the wall of pulsing light remains in place without flickering on and off. We can smell sulfur as the static crackling softens. We stand up to get a better view. We can see the translucent plane of light extending along the fault line as far as we can see north and south. I turn and look at Willy and can tell he understands what I'm thinking. We simultaneously sit down on the outcrop; we're beginning to feel unsteady.

Our minds suddenly become overwhelmed with activity. It feels like a super-high-paced nightmare of scattered, disjointed thoughts. Waves of unfamiliar voices mumble in undercurrents that are broken by very clear, vaguely familiar voices. We can't control our thoughts, and we feel like panic is about to overtake us. Our brain activity seems to pulse with the surging light plane. I reach for Willy's hand as he's doing the same. We grip each other's hands tightly in search of stability. In an instant, the confusing maelstrom of voices and strange memories falls away, and we're observing a common memory together—that fateful day years ago in college when we met. Our viewpoint is from above and slightly removed from the scene. We can clearly see Willy in his Grateful Dead Stealie shirt. Behind my ponytailed younger self is my car; I'm pointing at the parked vehicle I'd just hit. We focus back on Willy and his red-Solo-cup friends. We then hear young Willy say to me, "I've been waiting for you to arrive!"

Our minds then race through hundreds of scenes of us together, from college to the present. It's like a high-speed slideshow periodically interrupted with normal-speed video of us doing nothing in particular.

We feel the pulsing of the light wall increase in intensity, and we're once again overcome with a flood of random visualizations that is a mix of our memories and people we don't know. I'm beginning to feel nauseated—I think I'm going to puke. I squeeze Willy's hand hard and hold on. Very slowly our perspective switches, and we're hovering over and looking down on ourselves. Our viewpoint gradually begins to move skyward. Staring in disbelief at our distancing bodies below, we're overcome with a feeling of empathy for ourselves. We look so tiny and helpless in the vast landscape engulfing us as our viewpoint ascends farther skyward. How insignificant we seem, splayed on the ground below as an incomprehensible wall of light streams right through us. How can we comprehend what's happening? How can we know anything? We're so tiny, inconsequential. We feel sorry for ourselves, humbled.

Willy's hand slips away, and I feel panicked; my thoughts become singular. By letting go of one another, we're launched into our own separate trips. I'm now witnessing Sally's funeral pyre in rapid-fire still-and-motion images. I see people talk but can't understand what they're saying. When I try to zero in on any one person, I'm shocked to realize that I'm feeling their emotions. I can feel their emotions but not necessarily what they're thinking. I focus on Rachel, and experiencing her emotions from that day is like a gut punch. Her mind is so troubled, scared, and helpless.

I feel a strong static fuzz begin to crackle, and my vision completely blurs, like I'm going to pass out. I feel nauseous waves slosh back and forth in my brain. My mind is switching channels, and I move forward in time, now witnessing Ben and me in the studio, exploring the Memory Chaser. It's part removed and movie-like, but at the same time, I'm interacting with the memory. My mind rapidly moves through each and every event since then and suddenly stops at the time Chase showed us the frozen-light hologram of Sally. It isn't my actual memory; in this version, I kneel down and put my hand in the opaque light beams emanating from Sally's eyes. The tiny squiggling characters of code tickle the palm of my hand as the patterns morph into an undecipherable language. I feel the overwhelming presence of Sally. I distinctly sense she's trying to communicate with me through the transforming character patterns. I strain to concentrate on what she's trying to tell me. I feel that she's reaching out to me, telling me that she's okay. Overcome with emotion, I sob uncontrollably. I pull my hand away from the light beams and instantly lose the entire scene. I'm lying on the ground, staring skyward at the wall of light again. I'm back at the outcrop. As I turn toward Willy, I hear a rolling boom wash over us—then the shaking begins. I'm now very scared as the earth beneath us shakes uncontrollably. As I pray, looking to the sky, I see the wall of light instantaneously retract into the ground, and the earth stops shaking. Completely exhausted, I pass out.

As I struggled to regain consciousness, I realize I'm in a deep subconscious state. I'm on a primal, subhuman plane. It's very dark and completely silent. I'm not panicked; I'm calm, even though the situation seems dire. I have a feeling that I'm not alone; something's stirring nearby. Instinctively, I begin communicating with whatever it is. I begin encouraging the other being to wake up. The other one's presence gradually increases as I continue to encourage it. It's then I recognize who the other one is—it's me, my conscious self awakening from what seems like the dead. My consciousness is rebooting as my subconscious self stands guard. I'm witnessing the two parts of my brain, the subconscious and the conscious selves, communicate with each other. As my conscious self regains more and more functionality, my subconscious self slowly drifts off into the darkness, handing over control to my conscious self.

I'm now staring up at the beginnings of twilight. I turn to the east, and to my wonderment, I'm looking at the Sangre de Cristo Mountains silhouetted against a cloudless deep-blue sky. What is left of the snow high on the mountain range is glowing bloodred. It's Sangre de Cristo, the blood of Christ. For a moment, I think I'm back at Sally's funeral pyre. I roll over toward Willy and see that he's awake, staring at the same thing.

Willy and I make our way back to the truck just before it gets too dark to see. It's a long, silent hike. There's much to ponder on our own, and words seem a lame tool for describing our experience. We hop in the truck and slowly make our way north, back to Crestone. As we pass the stupa, we can see a large gathering of folks sitting in concentric semicircles around the front of the stupa. It's completely silent. I can't imagine what's going on, but I'm certain it's important.

The silence is suddenly broken by the ringing of my phone—it's Ben. I'm so overcome by our experience that it never occurred to me to check in with him. I'm struck by the thought that he may have had a similar experience, and I was negligent in not calling him.

"Ben, is everything okay?"

"Not really, Dad. I had an encounter with Sally. I'm freaking out."

"Oh shit, Ben, did you have an ALPs event there as well? Are you all right? What happened?"

"Oh yeah, we did, but we're okay, just shook up I guess. You had an event too?"

"Yes, we did; we certainly did. We're heading back into town from our fieldwork. Is someone with you?"

"Yes, Chase is here; he witnessed the whole thing with me."

"Listen, we'll be in town in fifteen minutes or so, and it'll take me an hour from there to get to the cabin. Let's just wait until I get there to sort this out. I'm glad you're okay. Is Chase gonna stay with you?"

"Yeah, he's staying the night. I'll see you in a bit. I love you, Dad."

"I love you too, son. See you in an hour or so."

It's now pitch black, and as we make our way back on the unlit gravel road, we encounter numerous people walking zombielike toward town. We stop and ask if they need any help or a ride into town. No one responds until we get to the leader of the staggered group. He turns and, without any prompt, says, "It's so beautiful, friend, so beautiful."

"Jesus, Sandy, where have we heard that before?"

I don't know what to say. I don't have the strength to explain my history with that phrase. It seems like Willy knows what the connection is, and that's enough for me. I reach over and grab Willy's arm.

"Listen, Willy, we don't have to talk about all this right now, but I want you to know that we are in this thing together; you're not alone. I gotta get back to the cabin. Ben needs me right now. Will you be all right?"

"I'll be fine. I appreciate your sentiments. I really do. I can't help but think back on how important we thought we were back then. I know you'll be there for me. You gotta be with Ben; don't be stupid."

"Thanks for understanding. You've always been my soul brother."

"Oh, there's one other thing—that car you bumped into on our first night? That was my car, Sandy."

As I pull away from Crestone, I'm deeply conflicted. I know I need to be with Ben, but leaving Willy is brutal. The streets of Crestone are filled with half zombies milling about in silence. It's quite scary, even though we know they're harmless. Willy's the kind of guy that's probably hanging out just to check and make sure the townies are all right. I assure myself that this is the case and accelerate into the darkness.

Sally, Can You Hear Me?

As I pull up to the cabin, I see there's a fire burning out back. I hop out of my truck and head to the firepit. As it comes into view, I see Ben and Chase with beers in hand, talking a mile a minute. As Ben sees me coming, he jumps up, tosses his beer into the firepit, races toward me, and jumps into my arms.

"Oh my God, Dad." Ben weeps. "Sally, I was with Sally, Dad; it was so intense."

"It's all right, Ben; it's all going to be okay. This is our new reality, and we're going to embrace it."

As Ben lets loose of his bear hug and stands back, I realize Chase is right there. He looks directly at the side of my head and says, "I missed you, Pops!"

I pull him in for a hug and whisper in his ear, "I wish you wouldn't call me that." We take a seat at the firepit as we all exhale. I'm still battling a road buzz from my existential ride back from Crestone. I take a couple deep breaths and, for the first time in forever, wish I had a drink. A deep chill races through my body, and instinctively I shake to warm myself and brush off the thought. How to even begin this conversation? Apparently, I don't have to.

"Jesus, Dad, I don't even know where to start. It was unbelievable!"

"Just start at the beginning."

"Well, Chase just happened to call me this morning. He'd spent the night at the hot springs. He showed up late in the afternoon. I was working on some of the enhancements Astral uploaded. He wanted to revisit some of the events that he and Sally had constructed. While he was running in an event, a bright-blue light began shining down through the skylight. He didn't notice at first, so I halted the event so we could go outside and see what was going on. As we exited the ham shack, we couldn't believe what we were seeing. All along the mountain front, a broken plane of deep-blue-and-orange light was rising up out of the ground. It was surging and dancing up and down from its source in the ground to near the height of Mount Princeton. We could hear crackling and a hum off in the distance. The plane of light was extremely narrow, and you could see through it. As we stared in disbelief, the light retracted into the ground momentarily. It soon came raging back, only this time there was a similar wall of light perpendicular to the original.

It was coming from the hot springs and ran directly through the ham shack and continued halfway into the valley."

"Holy crap, Ben, it went right through the ham shack?"

"Yes, and the antenna was crackling and buzzing as the blue-and-orange light swirled and pulsed up and down its length. It was overwhelming.

"We took a seat at the firepit, and then it got really strange. As I was gazing bewildered at the light show, I began revisiting memories in excruciating detail. The memories were disjointed and jumped back and forth through time. Without warning I was revisiting the 'Home' event. As I became absorbed in the memory, running on my own through the pine forest just before the lake, I felt it. Sally was running with me. I could hear her breath huff, but I couldn't see her. I distinctly felt her presence, and she was encouraging me onward, like there was something ahead I needed to see. As I started down the decline to the lake, I could see the crowd of people near the Keys on the Green. I felt Sally tell me that it's Mom—go to Mom. I ran straight toward Mom as she was cheering me on. I gave her a huge hug, only this time it wasn't an illusion. I was hugging a real person; it was Mom, or so I thought."

"What do you mean, or so you thought?"

"As I pulled away, I couldn't believe my eyes. It wasn't Mom at all; it was Sally, and she said something really weird. She said, 'This is why you're here.' What the hell, Dad? I was with her, and then she lays some riddle on me? What's that all about? I didn't know what to say, so I asked her what she meant. She didn't respond, so I asked her if she could hear me, but she just smiled and blew me a kiss. I screamed at her, '*Sally, can you hear me?*' I know it was Sally for sure, but what am I here for?"

"Something's going on, and Sally seems to be part of it. So tell me, was it scary, or was it comforting?"

"I was never scared. I guess I felt comforted, but really it was more of a warmth, like being in the assuring arms of Mom when I was a kid or something. It seemed totally normal until I saw her face right in front of me, and then I was spooked more than anything. It was so unexpected."

"That's quite the encounter. Willy and I had a bizarre experience as well. I felt Sally's presence; she was trying to communicate something. I revisited the frozen-light hologram that Chase showed us. I was staring at Sally's hologram in bewilderment, and I put my hand in the beams of light coming from her eyes. The squiggles were tickling my palm, but it was more than that. I had the distinct feeling the squiggles of code were language that was telling me something I couldn't understand. The one thing I heard loud and clear was Sally's thoughts. She was telling me that she was okay. I think I understand the meaning of her riddle."

"Wow, I'm glad we aren't the only ones. She was with you too?"

"She certainly was."

"What's the answer to the riddle?"

"It's a long story. I want to hear the rest first, and I'll fill you in."

"The lights were still going crazy," Ben explains. "It felt like we were on another planet or something. We made our way up to the overlook and sat down on the outcrop where we placed Sally's ashes. The plane of blue-and-orange light was directly behind us and caused our hair to stand on end. We were tingling with goose bumps, and very gradually, we were both encased in a faint torrent of blue-and-orange light. We lay down and stared up at the immense wall of translucent light behind us. We could see Mount Princeton through the light.

"As we lay there, we grabbed each other's hands, and we began to share our thoughts and memories. It was more of a feeling of emotion, each other's emotions, but they were accompanied by visions of the other's memories. I could see snapshots of Chase's memories, and they were being narrated not by words but by what he was feeling at that time. I could feel Chase's love for Sally, and I was overcome with a feeling of empathy and understanding."

"I had a similar experience," Chase adds. "I was flooded with rapid-fire images of Ben from when he was a small boy to the present. It was mostly Ben with you and your family. It was all coming at me so fast, I had to just let it roll over me. There was no time to contemplate any of it. Every so often, it would slow down and be more movie-like. I saw Ben in a synagogue, standing behind the bema, dressed in a suit, wearing a tallit and yarmulke. It was his bar mitzvah, and he was reading from the Torah. Then the rapid-fire images restarted. It seemed to slow down for important events in his life. I was overcome with empathy for Ben and understood him in a way that people only understand themselves. It culminated with an image of a beautiful girl who I'd never met. She seemed like an angel or something. She had a smile that oozed affection. The affection somehow switched and was originating from Ben. I was so happy for Ben, so tickled because I knew the feeling—it was pure love. As I stared into the eyes of this angel, I understood—she wasn't an angel. It was her name, Angelica."

"Well, now that's interesting," I say, staring directly at Ben. "Angelica, I thought I saw something in your eyes last week."

News Flash

As I sit on the couch in the cabin sipping my morning espresso, trying to make sense of the previous day, my thoughts turn toward Rachel. Sally's somehow revealing herself, and it's obvious that Rachel needs to be here. Once again, I feel like I missed an obligation. Why didn't I call Rachel immediately last night? What's wrong with me? I feel so selfish and stupid. I grab my phone to check the time; it's just after eight o'clock, too soon to call. As I'm setting the phone down, it rings.

"Sandy? Are you all right?" Rachel says in a shaky voice.

"Oh my God, I was just going to call you, but I thought it was too early. I'm fine, I guess. The shit's hitting the fan. You gotta get out here."

"Thank God. I'm scared, Sandy. What's going on? It's all over the news; it's all they're talking about. It's happening all around the globe. They had to shut down all the airports yesterday."

"Holy shit, Rachel, we haven't watched any news. What are they saying?"

"The lights, Sandy, the lights! The world is in a panic right now; people are going crazy! The Earth is coming apart. I'm scared, Sandy, I wish I were there with you."

"Listen, I'm fine; you're going to be okay. We're going to get you out here as soon as possible. Are you going to be all right until then? I had no idea. I assumed it was just happening here. Listen, the world isn't coming apart. There are some very weird things happening. Somehow it involves Sally. Ben and I both communicated with her yesterday. She's all right, Rachel; somehow she's all right!"

"What do you mean, you communicated with Sally? How is that possible?"

"I don't know how to explain it, but the lights are loaded with memories. Somehow it enables people to relive memories and communicate telepathically. It's not harming anyone, that I'm aware of. Sally is trying to communicate with us. She told Ben and me that she's okay and that soon we'd be able to talk to her. Listen, I gotta check the news, and I'll call you right back."

"I don't understand any of what you just said. What are you talking about?"

"I know it all sounds crazy. It is crazy, but you gotta just believe me; it's going to be okay."

"Call me right back, Sandy. I love you so much!"

"I love you too, dear. I'll call you right back. I promise."

The headline of *The New York Times* reads "Earth's Magnetic Field Vanishes." *The Washington Post*'s reads "Millions Worldwide Have Visions as Magnetic Field Collapses." From the London and Indian *Times* to the *China Daily*, around the globe, the headlines are the same. They all report similar accounts that are exactly the same as what we experienced the day before. We're not alone. It's happening, and the weight of this sends shivers up and down my spine. I had seen enough for now and head to the yurt to wake Ben up.

I gently shake Ben awake. At first he doesn't move; he only groans as if faking he's in pain. He very quickly goes silent and sits up sharply. As he rubs his mangled curls into an exotic parade of confusion, he looks at me with certainty.

"What did Mom say?"

"Wait, what? How did you know Mom called?"

"Don't be an idiot, Broccoli. We're in the new world; of course I knew."

"Jesus, Ben, Mom's pretty shook up. I need to call her back, but I did a quick review of the news, and you won't believe what's going on. You gotta get up and check it out. There have been ALPs events around the globe, and people are going crazy from the effects. I'm going to call Mom back, and we can watch the news together. I'll make some coffee."

"No shit, the lights aren't just here? Well, that would make sense, but how are people reacting?"

"Not good, Ben, not good at all. People are going crazy. The magnetic field went completely dead globally for several hours. The media's not helping by warning of all kinds of horrific consequences. Nothing of the sort has happened yet, but that hasn't stopped them from throwing gas on the fire. Airports worldwide shut down yesterday due to navigational concerns. The president is scheduled to speak later today. I'm gonna go call Rachel back; come on down to the cabin, and we'll have some breakfast and coffee. Will you go rouse Chase? It's all hands on deck."

"Rachel, I just scanned the news reports; it's truly crazy. You need to get here as soon as possible. What's going on with your move? How soon can you head this way?"

"Um, I'm actually pretty close to being able to shut my place down and ship my stuff your way. I was going to call you today and sort out some of the details—and then this. Do you have a place for us?"

"I don't, but Chase has a lead on a place at Mount Princeton. He was just up there and happened to stay in a place that's coming open for a long-term rental this month. I think I'll head up there today and secure it. I'll take care of it and get back to you ASAP."

"Sandy, what did Sally say to you?"

"She said she was okay and not to worry about what's happening. She said we'd communicate soon. It was more than that though. It was the feeling. I felt her presence, and it was undeniable. It was her. I believe this with all my heart. She's out there somewhere, and I think she's trying to help us understand what's going on."

"How's Ben doing? Is he all right?"

"Ben's fine. He's shook up like the rest of us, but he seems eager to dive into whatever it is that's happening. He saw Sally too and is as convinced as I am that this thing is real."

"What did she say to him?"

I don't know how to explain Sally's riddle to Rachel. It seems like too much and involves a long and detailed story. I pause for too long, and Rachel asks if I'm still there. I know I have to get it out. I assure Rachel I'm still here and begin my story. I tell her all I know about Crestone and Glen Anderson. I tell her how his prophecy is coming true. I tell her about the Buddhists, the Native Americans, and the other religious sects and how they have been interacting with ALPs events for some time. I back even further up and tell her about Dr. Strange at Laurentian University and the evidence of an impending polar reversal. I tell her about Dr. Persinger and his theories that are related to all of this. I tell her that she needs to trust me, that no matter how strange this all sounds, she has to have faith that this is leading to some place good and important. I tell her not to worry and pack her car up and head this way as soon as we arrange for shipment of her stuff. I tell her that

197

our daughter needs us, and we're going to need her to guide us through these incredible times.

"Sally told Ben, 'This is why you're here.' "

"I see."

Ben, Chase, and I spend the morning in the ham shack huddled around the computer screens, reviewing various news reports. It's clear that the scientific responses, regardless of vagueness, all agree that the magnetic field completely collapsed for several hours. None of them have an explanation other than pointing to the past as examples of polar reversals. We were overdue by several hundred thousand years. None of the science folks wanted to speculate about what the future held. It was an ominous nonresponse.

The reporting from the broader news streams and social media is spectacular. There are endless clips of people scrambling manically around the planar lights that originated from fault zones. The most amazing are clips of motionless people cocooned in swirling blue-and-orange light. It reminds me of Vietnamese monks who set themselves on fire in protest to the Vietnam War. It was called self-immolation. The difference, of course, is that it isn't suicide by flames; it's brain invasion of concepts no one is ready for. It drove people mad, they said. Not everyone was driven mad, however. There are random interviews with people whose accounts were quite different and compelling. These people spoke quite calmly and frankly of their experience with the lights. They described in wonderment how they revisited memories they had long forgotten. Commonly, these memories included loved ones that were no longer with them. Others described being in the presence of loved ones who were nowhere near them. Their convincing accounts and precise recall of details gave an air of credibility to their stories. When pressed on what they thought the meaning of it was, they all were at a loss for words. They'd stumble in their explanation and pause while looking directly in the camera, saying, "It was so beautiful."

The reports from US-based news centers all started their story with the event that occurred a week earlier at Crestone and Mount Princeton. It was the event Willy experienced that, up until now, only the Denver news had covered. They were all making a story of Crestone and its heavy religious leanings as somehow having a relationship to the existential experience that affected so many people around the world. Little do they know how right they are.

After hearing storyline after storyline intro with Crestone and Mount Princeton, we know what's to come: the mad rush of religious fanatics looking for salvation, or at least the next sign, in our backyard. Deep inside, the three of us fear being discovered and driven way off course.

I stand up and back away from the computer screens as if they're causing harm and announce, "That's enough already. We have to be prepared and plan for the next event. We know that the polar reversal is coming back, and when it does, it could be here for a very long time. What does this mean to you two? Sally is directly in the middle of this. I have no idea of what that means, but I mean it—she's in the middle of all this. Are you with me? Do you hear me? Sally, do you hear me?"

"Are you all right, Dad?" Ben questions. "I get what you're saying, but you're starting to freak me out."

"I'm not all right. I just wish I knew what to do. We gotta do something, right?"

"What about Astral Computational, Dad? They said they wanted in on it. Maybe they have some ideas?"

"Sandy," Chase follows, "Ben filled me in on all that Astral has done for you guys. They seem to be superbrilliant and multifaceted. What if we get them to take a look at the frozen-light capture of Sally? Maybe they could analyze the light energy from the halite cube? That was Sally's and my plan to begin with. There has to be something to be gleaned from it; it's so unique."

"Yeah, Dad," Ben chimes in. "What about the light beams? You said you thought it was trying to communicate with you. I think we'd all agree that the squiggles sure look like some type of hieroglyphic code. Maybe they could decode it. It's got to mean something, right? It seems like an obvious place to start unraveling this."

"God damn it! You two are brilliant. I'm sorry I was losing it there for a minute. This whole thing is overwhelming. I think I'm a bit in shock. It's all just too much."

"I know, Dad; we're right there with you. I know I haven't begun to digest what we went through. I'm worried about Mom. Do you think she's gonna be okay?"

"Your mom is one tough cookie. She's gonna be fine, but we need to get her out here. That reminds me—I need to go up to the hot springs and check on Chase's cabin."

"Oh shit," Chase blurts out. "I gotta call my dad. I'm such an idiot. I can't imagine what's going on there. I'm gonna head to the yurt."

"I'm glad I'm not the only one. I guess we all have a bit on our minds," I offer. "So, Ben, we need to talk about what Sally said."

"Yeah, are you going to tell me what I'm here for?"

"Well, I don't know about that, but let me tell you what I know. Crestone's recent past is a peculiar one. Did you ever wonder why there are so many religious groups from around the globe there?"

I tell Ben about the origins of current-day Crestone. I relate to him all of what Willy told me. How Hanne Strong stumbled upon Crestone and fell in love with the place. "Hanne Strong being sucked into Crestone wasn't the beginning. The real mystery started with a man named Glen Anderson. The townsfolk in Crestone believe he predicted all of this."

"Glen Anderson?" Ben questions. "Sounds pedestrian enough. What did he predict?"

I relate to Ben all that I had learned from Willy about Glen. I tell him about Glen's predictions and specifically about what Glen told Hanne, that she was here to initiate the prophecy. "Ben, he told Hanne, 'This is why you are here'!"

"Wow, but I'm not Hanne. Why do you think Sally repeated those words to me?"

"Well, Sally isn't Glen Anderson either. Sally is in the energy that has been revealing itself in increasing frequency. I think that somehow she's connected to the same prophecy that Glen Anderson was. I think she's reaching out to prepare us for the age of awakening. We're part of this whether we like it or not. I think we need to embrace it. I think that's what she was telling you, that you need to accept it and embrace it. I think you, or we, need to wake up to the coming reality and share it with others."

"I don't know what to say. I need some time to sort this out, Dad."

200

"We all do, Ben, but we may not have that luxury. I think you and Chase need to take the light-freezing chamber down to Astral Computational and see if they can decipher the code and characterize the light energy. I don't know what else we can do at this point."

"I totally agree. I'll talk to Chase and see what his schedule looks like."

Becky, The Jilted 'Stang

The next morning, as Ben and Chase are preparing the light-freezing chamber for transport to Denver, I head to Poncha Springs to have breakfast with Willy. Willy is headed to Laurentian University to have a sit-down with Dr. Strange. I'm still feeling guilty leaving him the other night in Crestone and am glad to have an opportunity to meet with him. As I head down the dirt road to Highway 285, I'm perplexed by a row of cars parked on the side of the road. No one ever comes up this road, as it dead ends just past the cabin. There are several clusters of young adults mingling by their cars. They have binoculars and at least one telescope and appear to be looking at Mount Princeton. Others are examining maps and seem to be having a lively conversation. I slow down but do not stop. Several of them stare me down as I pass. I can't help but wonder if they are friend or foe.

As I pull up to Highway 285, I am astonished at the traffic. It is a weekday morning, a time when hardly anyone is on the road. Where is everyone going? I eventually catch a break in the traffic and head south to Poncha Springs.

As I pull up to the Poncha Pub, I see their inflatable pickle is flying, indicating they are open. I realize there is no parking, so I head around to the back parking lot. As I am getting out of my truck, something extremely bright is reflecting in my eyes. I cover my eyes and walk toward the glimmering light source. I can't tell what it is so I walk behind it in the shade of the pub. It is a statue of a galloping stallion made from old chrome car bumpers. I stand there examining its intricately welded chrome bumper parts, and I flash back in time. I am pulling up to Denver's airport, staring at Blucifer, the glowing-red-eyed blue mustang. I recall Luis Jimenez, the artist who died creating Blucifer. I remember that his family took up his mantel and finished his work on the beast. As a rushing chill races up my spine, I recall that Ben and I are similarly finishing Sally's work. I feel strangely embarrassed that I hadn't thought of this again until now.

I walk into to the pub, and every seat in the house is taken, and there is a line going out the door. I have never seen so many people in the Poncha Pub. It must be finally taking off. I see Willy seated with several ranchers in the corner having a spirited conversation. I walk up to Willy and pat him on the back. Willy turns and jumps up when he realizes it is me.

"Oh, Sandy, my Sandy, so good to see you my friend; you look no worse for the wear!"

Before I can answer, one of the ranchers directs a question at me.

"So what do you think the earthquake lights are all about?" asks the rancher. "Do you think it's the second coming like your friend here?"

I am completely taken off guard and at a loss for words. Lord knows what Willy has gotten himself into, spirited conversation indeed.

"Well I don't have a clue. I will say this though, it certainly has my feathers ruffled!"

"Good answer, son," the rancher retorts. "Good answer."

"It was certainly pleasant to meet you, Willy," says the second rancher. "Try not to get fried by the next light show, or you'll never finish your mapping project. We'll see you next time."

"Oh I'll be more than careful," Willy replies. "I'll let you know what the continuum is up to next time I visit it."

Willy shakes his head while removing his cowboy hat and combs back his hair with his fingers.

"That was interesting. Have a seat, Sandy, please."

"What was that all about?"

"Oh you know, word travels fast in the ranching community. They knew all about Crestone and Mount Princeton. They're just a little concerned people are making this into some liberal new age thing. They're ready to move on and don't want a lot of outsiders coming here."

"From the look of things, we are past that point. Where are all these cars going? I've never seen more than a handful of people in this place. What's going on?"

"Well, Sandy, I think we owe this one to Glen Anderson. They are all headed to Crestone. They've already got roadblocks up to keep people out. It took me an hour to get to the Crestone turnoff from my place. It's out of control and completely mad there. I had to get away until things cool off a bit."

"Holy shit, it's happening, isn't it? Holy shit! There's a row of cars parked down the road from the cabin. It never occurred to me that's what's going on. Why do you think they're at the cabin?"

"Probably because they can't get into Crestone. You know Mount Princeton is second on the list for maximum ALPs energy locally. I'm sure it's all over social media. News travels faster on social media than in ranching circles. You know the UFO Watch Tower south of Crestone in Hooper? They have put some two thousand kids in that place. I tell you it's just crazy. I don't know what they are going to do. Glen should have given us a heads up on how many kids he was talking about!"

"That is out of control. Well that doesn't surprise me about Mount Princeton; Ben said it was spectacular. He and Chase had their own trip there. It sounded a lot like ours. We're still trying to sort it all out."

We order our food and settle in chitchatting. We share how our friends and family are doing. I tell him Rachel is moving here shortly and I had secured a place in Mount Princeton for us. Willy is glad Chase was in good hands during the event. Sid told him Chase had the mother of all bonding experiences with Ben. I was not surprised.

"So, Sandy, I keep thinking about our trip back to college. Apparently human contact takes you to a different place in the ALPs. I know that you know we were there together. I keep thinking and looking at things totally different the last couple days. I can only say I feel like I'm looking at the world the way I did way back then. I'm all bright eyed and eager to take on the world, and I'm full of energy. We felt so important back then…"

"Now how would I tell the difference? You're the same bright-eyed and eager person now as you were back then. I do get what you're saying, Willy; I do. I'm feeling pretty important right now too."

"This isn't over, Sandy; we are only getting started."

"I hear that. Do you have any idea when the next one is coming?"

"I haven't a clue. That's one of the reasons I'm going to Laurentian to see Dr. Strange. I'm taking all our samples up there with me. They are dying to analyze them. He told me his entire department is 100% focused on studying the polar reversal and ALPs activity. I'm concerned that science is no match for whatever it is we are facing. It's kinda weird; he called me out of the blue. I guess I made an impression."

"That doesn't surprise me. You always impress people. I can't wait to hear what you find out on your visit. We're getting our science on as well. Remember I told you about the light-freezing chamber Chase has. Ben and

Chase are taking it down to Astral Computational for them to analyze. We're hoping to learn something about the light energy and the strange beams of light that were coming out of Sally's eyes; it seems important."

"I still can't believe that kid knows anything, let alone particle physics. He's kinda goofy, but I love him to death. That's a capital idea. Do you think Astral would share their findings with Dr. Strange and the folks at Laurentian?"

"I don't see why not. I'll talk to Dr. Petra."

We continue discussing our ALPs experience and postulate what it all means as we finish our breakfast. Talking with Willy gets me fired up and a little anxious. The future seems uncertain yet so urgent. As we head to our cars, we agree to meet up once he gets back to town. I point out the silver mustang and ask if he knows what it's all about.

"Oh that's Becky, the jilted 'stang. Some local artist made it. Apparently she made it for her boyfriend, but then she got dumped. You know you can't hide anything in a small town like this. She didn't want it anymore, so here it sits. I think her name was Mac."

The shock of that name sends my head spinning. I flash back to my mini-ALPs experience with Ben at the funeral pyre. Crazy Wisdom echoes in my mind. Maybe Becky doesn't mean anything, but I doubt that.

"Sandy, are you with us, Sandy?" Willy asks.

"Oh, sorry, I was thinking about something related to Becky here. Have you ever seen the giant red-eyed mustang at Denver's airport?"

"Of course, Blucifer, that thing gives me the willies."

"When Ben first came out here, I picked him up at the airport. As I was pulling into the airport, I was mesmerized by Blucifer. Out of nowhere, I recalled the story behind the beast. The artist died creating it. It fell over on him and crushed him. The important part is that his family finished his creation. I can't help but think we're on the same mission, with Sally and all."

"Oh I love that. I believe you are."

We say our goodbyes, and off we go on our separate ways.

As I head back to the cabin, I realize that I never heard back from Dr. Petra at Astral. Ben and Chase can't just show up with a light-freezing chamber.

"Hello, Dr. Petra, it's Sandy Stern. How are you today?"

"I'm okay, considering. What about you?"

"Oh it's always something, but it's interesting, that's for sure."

I've been thinking about you; sorry I haven't called you back. I understand you had quite the lightshow up there. Is everything all right? We're all anxiously awaiting any news about this historic event."

"I'm all right. It was some experience, that's for sure. Listen, I can't get into that right now. I'll fill you in later. I've got something to ask you; we need some help."

"Of course, Sandy, what can I do you for?"

"It's the light-freezing chamber I told you about. Remember, it's the device that captured Sally's image?"

"Oh I certainly do. I've been wishing I could get a look at that superb piece of work. What about it?"

"Well, we're hoping you could take a look at it and analyze the light energy it captured. We believe the light energy is an ALPs event. We think it's a perfect piece of evidence to help characterize ALPs."

"I see what you're saying. That's an excellent idea, Sandy. We'd love to have a look and see what we can learn. I told you I wanted in on this."

"There's one other thing. As you'll recall, there was a very strange phenomenon going on with Sally's eyes. The cube captured these otherworldly beams of light coming out of her eyes. Inside the beams are strange characters that look like some type of code. We're thinking you might be able to decipher the code for us."

"Yes, how could I forget? Your description of that is still with me. Listen, whatever it is, we are here for you. I have a wide range of scientific talent I can call on. If we don't have who or what it takes to get the job done, it's a phone call away."

"That's great; actually Ben is ready to head out today. I hope that's not rushing it. He's bringing Chase with him; he's the brains behind the device. He will get you familiar with the light-freezing chamber. I'm sure he'll be a big help."

"No, that's fine. We will certainly need Chase; what he has is extremely cutting-edge stuff. I doubt we'd get very far without him. Oh, and I got one for you, Sandy."

"What's that?

"We are accelerating the rollout of the recreational Memory Chaser. We're going to start with kiosks in public places. I was wondering if we could take over the kiosk at the mall. I believe you said you were done with it."

"Go right ahead, my work is done there. Man, you're moving quickly. I hope it takes off. Hey, listen, there is something happening on the road ahead. I need to get off the phone. Let's talk after you get the goods."

Just ahead, a line of cars a mile long is backed up on the highway, no one is moving. It looks like the front of the line is at the Mount Princeton turnoff. The cabin turnoff is a quarter mile past the road to Mount Princeton so I carefully pull onto the shoulder to evade the mess. A county sheriff stops me at the Mount Princeton turnoff. As he approaches my window, I realize it's Sheriff Broadless. I ask him what is going on, and he informs me that it's the Light Seekers, kids and young adults trying to get to the earthquake light source. Wow, they already have a name for them. He tells me they're only letting cars in to replace cars that are leaving.

As I head up the incline to the cabin I can see there are even more cars than there were a couple hours ago. This is getting out of hand. As I pull up to the cabin, there are a half dozen strangers talking to Ben and Chase. I hop out of my truck and join the fray.

"Ben, what's going on? Is there a problem?"

"No, there's not a problem yet. These folks are looking for the ALPs light source. They call themselves the Light Seekers, and they want to hike over to Mount Princeton from here. I told them this is private property, and they'd have to leave. There are just too many of them."

"I see. Look, you guys, Ben is right; we can't have all you people parking your cars for who knows how long and use our property to get to Mount Princeton. You realize it's five miles as the crow flies. I don't think that's a good idea. Why don't you try to get there from the north? There's a road from Buena Vista directly to the hot springs."

The group groans in disapproval as one of them responds, "We tried that road, and they have it blocked off. We gotta get there!"

The group huddles for a minute and then turns and heads for their cars. Ben, Chase, and I head to the firepit for a quick discussion before they head to Denver.

"How's Willy doing?" Ben inquires. "Did he survive Crestone after you abandoned him?"

"Very funny, Ben. He's fine, he's still dealing with the fallout just like us, but he's okay. He's headed to Laurentian University to meet with Persinger's colleagues and discuss polar reversals and the major ALPs event."

"All hands on deck," Chase chimes in.

"So I spoke with Dr. Petra, and he's expecting you. Are you guys okay with being there a couple days to make sure they can access the light-freezing chamber properly?"

"Of course," they say in unison.

"I contacted Dr. How at MIT just in case we need some specialized equipment to access the frozen light," Chase explains. "I'm fairly certain I have what we need, but you never know."

With that Ben and Chase toss their bags in Chase's truck, and off they go. I am looking forward to some peace and quiet for once. I am in dire need of recharging my spent mind. Hopefully the gathering hoards won't interfere.

Calm Before the Storm

It's been six months since the big event. The magnetic field has been completely stable, and there has not been a single ALPs event since. Though it's still in the news, it seems more of an obligation to cover it than the bestselling apocalyptic end it was originally reported to be. Oddly, much of the public seems to be okay with this. It's like they want to bury their heads in the sand and forget about it. The news coverage is focused on describing how people are putting it behind them rather than seeking answers to what happened. Every few days, there are interviews with psychologists who describe it as motivated forgetting. They say this is either suppression, which is the conscious form of intentionally forgetting, or repression, which is the subconscious form. They say motivated forgetting is a reaction to severe stress caused by a traumatic event. I find it ironic that our involvement all started with bringing forgotten memories back, while half the world is actively trying to forget.

There are, however, plenty of people who will never forget. These folks come from all walks of life. If they have anything in common, it's that they have some type of religious or spiritual leanings. In many cases, some of these people managed the maelstrom of memories, alien thoughts, telepathic communication, and disembodiment brought on by the ALPs activity. The experience was very spiritual and life changing for this group. A subset of the ones who will never forget are those that did not experience ALPs activity but wish they had. The Light Seekers are in this group. These folks felt there was something missing and hollow in their existence. To them, this is it. They believe the secrets of life will be revealed to them by interacting with an ALPs event. They are all frustrated with the government for not having answers. Some believe the government wants it to go away and is actively attempting to change the narrative. There has been a nearly continuous protest outside the White House since the big event. They all want answers and assurance that, if it happens again, they won't be completely on their own. Many of the protesters believe it was the first contact with aliens. They see it as an information-gathering visit, and the next visit will have consequences.

There are good sources of information if you know where to look. The scientific journals are loaded with reports on what happened. No one has had enough time to fully study it, but there are plenty of smart people hypothesizing. None of the reports are from governmental research organizations. The USGS and NASA are completely silent on the subject. This has given credence to the government-conspiracy theories. As it turns out, most of the ALPs events occurred along older, dormant fault zones. Large, active fault zones, like the San Andreas or, on a larger scale, the highly active Pacific Ring of Fire, had little, if any, ALPs activity. I read somewhere that 2 percent of the world's population interacted with an ALPs event that day. This would mean 150 million people directly experienced an ALPs event. Many of the reports are focused on a potential polar reversal that some say is imminent. There are plenty of reasons to be concerned if the magnetic field ceased to exist, no matter how long. Interestingly, historic polar reversals have never been linked to any type of mass-extinction event.

These reports point to the geologic record as evidence. Starting in the late sixties, the Glomar Challenger, a government-sponsored research vessel, spent fifteen years drilling core holes of the ocean bottom across the Atlantic Ocean. Their research proved the theory of plate tectonics by identifying seafloor spreading at the mid-Atlantic ridge. The cores they drilled held the evidence of polar reversals. Frozen in solidified lava are metallic minerals that aligned themselves to the magnetic field at the time. Every two hundred thousand years or so, the poles reverse, and it's reflected in the orientation of these minerals. There are a few cores where these same minerals are aligned randomly. This represents a time of zero magnetic field. During a polar reversal, there is evidence that the magnetic field vanishes completely. They say this is what we experienced, a time of zero magnetic field before total polar reversal.

Reports on what ALPs are about are few and far between. Even harder to find are reports on the effect of ALPs on living creatures. No one has ever measured or tried to quantify ALPs energy. It's so rare—and typically identified as a UFO event—that science either has no way to time one or shrugs it off due to its relationship to UFOs. A few have postulated that strong magnetic energy could disrupt brain function in mammals, and that's about it.

To me, the most compelling lead to the truth emanated from Crestone. Willy and I have met with Sid a couple of times since the big event, and his insight was revealing. The Buddhists and others have been able to channel the incoming visions and voices, as they call it. They've been able to reach a conscious state that enables them to focus on single visions or voices, as well as shut it down completely. They claim a spirit they call Sarah has been guiding them. As Sid describes it, ALPs consciousness is like having every radio station in the world playing in your mind at the same time. Via extreme concentration and focus, the monks and others are able to filter out all but the one radio station they want to listen to. They claim they're experiencing other people's memories, both the living and the dead. They are reaching out and teaching others their techniques. Every day they have sessions in town and at the UFO Watchtower encampment. It's not something people learn overnight. The Buddhists get people started, then it's up to them to practice the technique in order to master it. Apparently, a big part of their technique's success is believing that there's more to our world than we can possibly comprehend and accepting this. They say they will make themselves available to the public and help people navigate the mental onslaught if another big ALPs event occurs.

Rachel and I have been living in a funky cabin near the Mount Princeton Hot Springs Resort. It sits on the south side of Chalk Creek in a steep and narrow valley and has an unobstructed view of the Chalk Cliffs. We have a room for Ben, but he spends most of his time at Sally's cabin. We are enjoying our solitude and have settled into a routine of reading in the morning, hiking in the afternoons, and attending to our hobbies. Rachel has taken over the loft for her sewing, and I have a nook where I do my fly tying. For now, it seems perfect, and we're very happy just being.

"Hello, is this Sandy? It's Dr. Petra."

"Yes, it is. How are things, Dr. Petra?"

"Quite well. We haven't talked recently, and I wanted to update you on our research into the light-freezing chamber. Do you have a minute?"

"Yes, of course, I'm all ears."

"First of all, as I've told you before, the chamber is an amazing piece of work. I've read about light freezing but had no idea someone had constructed a portable one. Chase is a brilliant young man. I met his mentor, Dr. How, some time ago; she's on a whole other level. This has been quite the puzzle. It's taken us a while, but since the last time we spoke, we've made a huge discovery."

"Is that so? Please, do tell."

"As you'll recall, there are two energy sources you suggested we analyze. You guys were right on with that call; they have completely different characteristics. They're both highly complex magnetic energies. We've never seen anything like it. We've nicknamed it 'neutral plasma,' in that it has many characteristics of plasma energy, only it's neither extremely hot nor cold. The structure of the magnetic energy emanating from Sally's helmet is infinitely less complex than the ALPs-sourced magnetic energy. It has a distinct pattern to it. The ALPs-sourced magnetic energy is extremely complex. We were struggling to find any structure to it at all. As it turns out, Sally's magnetic energy is the key to decoding the more-complex ALPs magnetic energy."

"That's curious. You're already way above my pay grade, so I'll take your word for it."

"Yes, I know this is complicated. I'll put this as simply as possible. We believe the magnetic energy from Sally's helmet is a small snippet of her memory. We also believe the ALPs magnetic energy contains memories, but it's a cacophony of thousands, if not millions, of memories from God knows how many different people. We've figured a couple of very important things out. We believe we can block all incoming ALPs-memory chatter. We also believe we can isolate Sally's memories from the rest of the ALPs memories. By using Sally's memory snippet as a filter on the ALPs magnetic energy, we were able to identify hundreds of Sally's memories in the ALPs cloud. This is a really big deal, Sandy. Do you understand what this means?"

"I have no idea."

"It means that during an ALPs event, we can block out the myriad of random-memory noise, preventing the sensory overload that plagued so many people in the recent ALPs event. This is huge, Sandy. We also believe we can filter all memory streams but Sally's. We are trying figure out how to filter out specific people's memories but haven't gotten there yet. Get this— with some modifications, the memory filtering is accomplished with the God Helmet. I'd say this is a strange coincidence, but I'm not sure I believe in coincidences anymore."

"I don't know what to say. I do understand what you're saying. Our experience with the ALPs energy alternated from singular, discrete memories to total chaos of overlapping memories, with no focus whatsoever. It was quite frightening and overwhelming."

"I have a request for you; it's going to sound strange. The code in the light beams emanating from Sally's eyes has a remarkable resemblance to the structure found in DNA. We'd like to get a sample of your DNA. Actually we need Sally's DNA, but since that's not possible, I think we can make yours work. We'd like to compare the structure or code of her DNA to the light-beam patterns."

"Now that's spooky. You know, we have some of Sally's ashes. Can you get DNA from cremation ashes?"

"You do? I mean, of course you do. Yes, DNA can be extracted from human ashes. This is a weird thing to ask for—so if you'd pardon me because this is going to sound gruesome—but if there are any bone fragments, I think we'd have a better chance of recovering DNA."

"We spread most of the ashes, but I'll send you a sample of what's left. I see the bigger picture here, so don't worry about offending me. I'll put something together and get is out ASAP. I'll throw in some of Rachel's and my hair as a backup. How does that sound? Oh, and I was wondering, how's the rollout of the recreational Memory Chaser going?"

"That's great, Sandy. I appreciate your candor. The rollout is seeing some serious traction. The kiosk at the mall is booked out several weeks. The timing is really quite astonishing, you know with the ALPs coverage and memory visitations and all. People's interest in anything memory related is seriously piqued. We're going to be installing the Memory Chaser in big cities like New York, San Francisco, LA, London, and Beijing. We're going big time with this, Sandy."

"Wow, that's exciting! Sally wouldn't believe it. Thanks, Dr. Petra, for all you've done for us. When do you think we can see the modified God Helmet? How's that going to work?"

"Well for now, this is all theoretical. It needs to be tested in an actual ALPs event. I want to send someone up to Chaffee County with several of the modified God Helmets to be ready for the next ALPs event. It's the only way to determine if it works. Would you be available to test it out should we have another ALPs event? I was thinking we'd be ready in a week or two to send someone your way. Angelica seems to be the obvious choice. She's developed quite the rapport with Ben. I didn't think we were going to get her back from her recent trip up there; she loves those mountains."

"That would be great. I'd love to be a guinea pig for your ALPs-blocking device."

Which Way Is North

Angelica has been in the county for a couple weeks now. Apparently, there's way more going on between Angelica and Ben than anyone knew. Ben is very private that way; I don't know why. He's like his sister, and I guess I shouldn't be surprised. She's staying at the cabin with Ben. They seem so happy together. She's such a warm and grateful human. Their relationship seems so organic and easy. Rachel and I are very happy for the two of them. Ben seems to be on cloud nine. They've been up to our place at Mount Princeton several times for a soak in the hot springs and dinner. They spend much of their days experimenting with the Memory Chaser, designing new routines for the recreational application.

On a quiet evening, sitting on our cabin's front porch overlooking Chalk Creek as the last rays of the sun light up the Chalk Cliffs across the valley, I recall a memory. It's getting close to spring, and this time of year always reminds me of a college tradition Willy and I and others used to practice: the spring equinox party. While mostly it was an excuse to have a party, deep down we hoped the pagan ritual would provide much-needed connection or, at least, a proper salute to our mother Earth's position in the solar system and beyond. As I resurface from deep recollection, I turn to Rachel.

"Rach, do you remember me telling you about our equinox parties?"

"Of course I do. When you first told me about your equinox party, I thought it was such a cool thing. Part hippie and part pagan, very exotic yet rooted."

"That's very accurate. I think we should restart the tradition. I was thinking we'd invite a quorum of folks over here for it. You know it's next week? It doesn't have to be a rager or anything, just a get-together. It would be nice to be looking forward to something we know is going to happen."

"Make it so, number one," Rachel says with a chuckle.

"It'll be fun. We need to have some fun; it's been too serious lately."

"I know. It's been way too serious. Sandy, have I told you how happy I am here with you? I'm so glad to be back together, and this place is just so special. I love you."

"Ah, Rach, I couldn't be happier. I love you more!"

That night, from a deep sleep, I sit straight up, trying to catch my breath. I'm having a vivid dream where I'm sitting on a huge boulder overlooking

Seidel's Suckhole. I'm witnessing total carnage of rafters who'd just flipped in the mighty rapid; all were tossed randomly in its churning current. I'm frozen with dread watching them flounder. I hear Sally screaming from downstream. She's standing on the ghost raft, slowly drifting downstream. She's screaming at the top of her lungs, but it isn't directed at the swimmers—it's directed at me. *"Swim, Dad, swim!"*

The equinox is finally upon us. It's a small gathering. Our guests—Ben, Angelica, Chase, Sid, and Willy—are all here. I can't help but think that seven is a good biblical number and a strong quorum. In Hebrew, the word *seven* is spelled with seven consonants and means fullness or completeness. Not so oddly, the exact time of this year's equinox is 7:07 p.m. As we gather on the front porch, the talk among the group verifies we've summoned the right folks. Hearing Sid and Angelica discuss ALPs filtering is straight out of an Arthur C. Clarke science fiction novel. Sid's background avails him to the nuances of Angelica's scientific jargon, and apparently Angelica is versed well enough in Buddhism to follow Sid. It's crazy yet grounding to hear them banter their diametrically opposed views to our existential crisis. One, a science-based solution leaning on technology, and the other purely spiritual that requires a ton of faith. I feel at home yet strangely alone.

Chase is standing way too close to Rachel, nearly backing her off the porch, while spilling his heart out about Sally. Rachel, God bless her true soul, never takes her eyes off the poor lad as she tries to interject. Chase can be a handful, but he's seriously committed. Willy and I bore Ben to death with stories of our college equinox parties. I can tell he relishes the intel he's gathering about his younger dad. It seems important for him to know me when I was young.

It is nearing five o'clock, and the plan is to be in the infinity pool for the arrival of the equinox. Angelica huddles the group for a meeting. She tells us that we need to familiarize ourselves with the modified God Helmet should an ALPs occur. She explains our escape plan as an elephant line dance, only the lead elephant talks a lot. She then pulls out a God Helmet for each of us and has everyone download the app that controls it. Once everyone has the app, she guides us through its functionality—most importantly, the panic button. She explains the God Helmet is programmed to block all the ALPs-memory noise. She tells us that we will start with this setting. If it works, we'll switch to the Sally-memory-filter setting. The hope is to experience Sally's memories exclusively. She can't testify what this might entail other than one invading voice, especially a familiar one, will be way more manageable than all of humanity's. As she finishes her drill, she turns toward Sid and asks, "Do you have anything to add, Sid?"

"Thank you, Angelica. As everyone here knows, my associates at Crestone and I have been studying this ALPs thing for quite some time now. We have developed meditative techniques to help us deal with this strange new reality. It is something I can teach you but not now; it takes time. We believe ALPs contain the truth, and the truth should not be taken lightly. We humans are not currently capable of understanding what it's telling us because, at times, the volume of information is way more than we can decipher. Our techniques take time to master, but for now I will say this: ALPs are not evil; it's just alien, albeit, at times, very disturbing. ALPs should be accepted with an open heart. Do not panic, accept that it's much bigger than us, and listen, just listen. It's trying to teach us."

With that we all head to the hot springs for a soak and cheer on the arrival of spring. The infinity pool at Mount Princeton Hot Springs is an exceptional example of what an infinity pool should be. The infinity portion of the pool overlooks Chalk Creek Canyon to the west. In the foreground, rising up out of the canyon floor, are the towering Chalk Cliffs, which is a perfectly vertical light-gray wall, two thousand feet tall. Above the Chalk Cliffs, the peak of Mount Princeton can be seen, keeping an eye on us. Surrounding the canyon and beyond are other massive fourteen-thousand-foot-tall snowcapped peaks of the Sawatch Range. It's a spectacular setting, especially from the vantage of the reflective surface of water that seems to end in the middle of it all.

Willy is assigned clock-watching duty to ensure we don't miss the exact time we enter spring. As we huddle in a group, leaning against infinity's edge, staring off in the distant mountainous glory, the conversation is sparse. After an hour, we're approaching spring's arrival. As I'm about to ask Willy how close we are, his alarm sounds. Our quorum erupts in hoots and howls of acknowledgment, only Willy is silent. I turn toward him and ask what's up. His face is solemn and ashen.

"That was not the equinox alarm. Oh my God. That alarm is a notification from my magnetic field sensor. It's happening again. Earth's magnetic field has vanished!"

"How much time do we have until spring?" Chase asks.

"What are you talking about, Willy?" inquires Angelica. "What sensor?"

Before Willy can answer, the canyon starts to crackle with thousands of ground-level points of light. The points rapidly coalesce into a swirling iridescent-pink cloud that's hanging in the valley like an early morning fog.

"Everyone out of the pool," Angelica shouts. "This is not a drill; the ALPs is forming! Out of the pool and get in the evacuation line!"

As we scramble out of the pool, we smell sulfur as a great rushing sound passes through us and dissipates skyward. We see off in the valley that the iridescent cloud is rapidly transforming into an immense, translucent planar wall of light. As we form our elephant escape line, the wall of light expands up and down the valley and passes directly through the infinity pool and coats each of us in a swirling cocoon of orange-and-blue light. We all freeze in place as our minds flood with torrents of alien thought.

"Hold on to your partners," Angelica calls out. "We're all right; it's the ALPs; we're going to be all right. It's just chatter; it'll subside."

Our grips on each other's hands tighten as we brace for the worst. Angelica attempts to narrate our experience, but it cannot be described. We are tuned in to a myriad of radio stations all yapping at once. Angelica then does something that's pure genius. She starts singing Bob Marley's song "One Love":

One love, one heart
Let's get together and feel all right
As it was in the beginning (one love)
So shall it be in the end (one heart)
All right! Give thanks and praise to the Lord and I will feel all right

We all immediately join in, repeating this one verse as we snake our way out of the pool area toward the cabin. One love, one heart. Our minds are being bombarded with rapidly changing random voices and alien scenes. We have no control of what's running through our minds. Singing the verse from "One Love" is a meditative salve that distracts us enough to not engage in the alien onslaught of memory noise. It doesn't stop any of it but prevents us from focusing on it and possibly losing control. The lyrics take on a whole new and powerful meaning. I, for one, have never felt more spiritual.

As we're midway across the small pedestrian bridge that crosses over Chalk Creek, we're once again in the middle of the towering planar light wall. We all pause to stare at the wall of translucent-blue light ascending to the heavens while singing "One Love." As we're gazing, the light instantaneously retracts into the ground, pulling our cocoon light with it. The invading mind noise lets up a bit, and we can sense what each of us is thinking and feeling. Within each of our minds is the presence of the other

217

six. We immediately feel comfort and warmth from the others' presence. No one needs to say anything, as it's evident to all that our minds are in direct contact.

Angelica then commands we all continue—but not with words. She thinks to us that we need to continue. We all stop singing "One Love," though the song is still rattling in our minds. Angelica starts to narrate the rest of our trek, not with words but thoughts. She addresses what each of us is feeling while interjecting thoughts of encouragement. She provides a mantra to each of us to counteract negative thoughts. As we march up the incline to our cabin, she encourages us to hang on since we're almost there. As we enter the cabin, she thinks to us to lie in the middle of the living room floor with our heads in the center of a radiating circle and to keep holding hands.

Angelica retrieves and hands out the God Helmets to each of us while we lie in the circle. As we don our God Helmets, the invasive thoughts and images begin to short-circuit, cutting in and out like a bad phone connection. Slowly, one by one, the multitude of memory noise goes completely silent. A communal sigh of relief is shared by all. The silence is welcome, but we're all waiting for what is to follow. We're praying the God Helmet continues to block all the random memory noise.

Angelica provides further instructions in a soft, reassuring voice. "This is good; this is very good. The God Helmet is working. We are going to lie here for a bit, and I want everyone to take this time to try to relax. Think of a calming place, a favorite place, that gives you solace. In ten minutes, I'm going to turn the God Helmets off for a short period and then back on to verify they're working. Don't be scared; there's no reason to panic; we're going to be hearing and seeing memories from others, nothing more. Let it wash over you like a warm rain. Don't engage; just watch and listen."

As she turns the God Helmets off, a raging torrent of images and voices immediately fill our minds. It's a huge, chattering rush of not only images and voices but also rapidly changing emotions. We sense each other's reactions, and not all of us are handling it. Angelica must've felt this—she announces she's switching the God Helmets back on. With that, the invading memories go completely silent. A sigh of relief spins around our circle.

"All right, folks," Angelica announces. "I guess it works. Let's all try to calm down; it's going to be okay. Willy, do you have your phone with you? Can you check your magnetic field sensor and tell us the status of the magnetic field please?"

"I do; hang on," Willy answers. "It's reading a near-zero magnetic field."

218

"Okay, roger that," Angelica replies. "Let's all just get our bearings. We're going to lie here for a bit, and then I want to test the Sally filter. If at any point, it gets too weird for you, switch your God Helmet back to full ALPs-blocking mode with the panic button."

The ensuing wait seem like an eternity. Rachel now has my hand in a death grip. I feel high anxiety from the rest of the group. It's very intense. Angelica announces she's switching to the Sally-filter mode. Several minutes pass and nothing happens. It's totally silent, and the anticipation is overwhelming. Where is she?

We can feel something faint, way off in the distance of our minds. It's the feeling you get when someone is sneaking up on you, and though nothing directly tells you it's happening, your sixth sense alerts you to danger. The feeling takes the form of a soft, childlike voice; it's barely audible. As it gets closer, it's apparent that it *is* a child, and she's talking in a reassuring tone. It reminds me of hearing one of my young kids playing by themselves in a neighboring room, talking quietly in a make-believe world. Suddenly, we're momentarily blinded by a flash of light. As our eyes adjust, we're staring at a child swaddling an infant baby doll. She's whispering sweet reassurances to the helpless doll. As she tucks the last piece of fabric in, we can hear her say, "Oh, poor baby, that doesn't look comfy." Rachel starts bawling, and in that instant, we know who the child is—Sally!

I squeeze Rachel's hand tightly to comfort her, and this small action sends a wave of reassurance and love whipping around the circle that comes back to me, only it has personal touches from each it passed through. It makes me shudder. The scene morphs to later in Sally's life, when she was in elementary school. It is an average day, and we're seeing Sally, Ben, and one of Sally's friends playing in our backyard at our Evergreen home. The perspective is through a window in our family room. We can hear but not understand what they're saying. The three of them begin to chase each other in tight, looping circles. Little Ben can't keep up and trips, falling to the ground in a heap. He's crying facedown. Sally runs over and sits with Ben and pulls him in for an extended hug while offering soft words of comfort and encouragement. Sally stands Ben upright, and things seem to be okay. Ben wipes his remaining tears away with a filthy shirtsleeve. Ben then reaches out, as if Sally is the family dog, and pets her long hair several times. We can feel the tears well up in each of us.

The scene fades out and resumes with rapid-fire images through Sally's adolescence. We are all seeing our family together at various vacations we took. Every scene shares a common theme: carefree enjoyment of each other.

219

Bodysurfing together in the ocean, camping in the Rocky Mountains, skiing at Arapahoe Basin, and so much more, it's a beautiful encapsulation of some of our favorite times together. The blast of images suddenly stops, and now we're viewing Rachel, Ben, and myself on our front porch in Evergreen, waving goodbye. The perspective is from Sally's eyes, from inside her beat-up Jeep. We're seeing and feeling what Sally experienced that day so long ago. It's the day she left home for Chaffee County to be a raft guide. She's waving goodbye and trying to tell us she loves us, but her tears halt her words. We all feel the conflicted pain and elation she feels—she's off on a grand adventure, leaving her family for who knows how long. We all feel her deep pain while cheering her strength to seek her own path. It's extremely powerful. The memory stream fades as her Jeep backs out of the driveway.

We're all lying motionless, staring at the ceiling, trying to compose our emotionally rattled selves. The ceiling suddenly turns black as coal, and the room darkens. Gradually, points of light pepper the ceiling. We're staring into the brilliantly infinite, starlit night sky. The emotion Sally just shared with us comes racing back and fills each of us with a feeling of loss and sorrow that's intermixed with exhilaration and possibility. Directly in the middle of the cosmos, a single star begins to glow ever brighter until it washes out all the other stars. The room slowly fills with a faint blue light. The singular star now engulfs the center of the ceiling and is pulsing streams of highly energetic light directly at us. In the center of the brilliant light emerges a perfectly formed clear crystal cube. From the center of the cube, tiny indigo electrical charges, like miniature lightning bolts, begin to rotate and extend outward beyond the cube. The group is now enveloped in a glowing halo of orange-and-azure-light energy. The crystal cube's lightning bolts are spinning at an extremely high speed and begin to arc directly at each of us. Our glowing halos begin to reach skyward and mix with the cube's energy. The two energy sources are now intermingled as they pulse to and from the cube. We feel Sally's sorrow and loss fade away, and we're left with an immersive feeling of exhilaration and wonderment. We're living Sally's last moments from her perspective.

As in Sally's last moments, all the light energy is sucked up into the crystal cube. The room becomes dark again, with the only light coming from the brilliant, star-filled sky. The room is deadly still, and we can hear each other breathing in anxious gasps. Until…

"Hello, Momma," Sally greets affectionately. "You have no idea how much I miss you! You have given and taught me so much—I don't have a clue where to begin. I'm okay, Momma, I'm okay!"

220

As Rachel starts breaking down, I interrupt the ring of hands and roll over and embrace her. Surprisingly, the breaking of the ring doesn't change anything, and everyone starts squirming separately on the floor.

"Why don't you all make yourselves comfortable," Sally informs. "You should keep your silly bathing caps on though. I'm not sure who's controlling what at this point, but just in case, I'd keep them on. Go ahead and grab a seat; we need to talk. I don't have much time."

Stunned, we all collect ourselves and take seats in the living room. All the while, Sally hums "One Love."

"Sally, is it really you?" I stammer. "I love you so much. What's happening? Where are you?"

"Oh, Dada," Sally replies. "I love you so very much. I'm very impressed with what you and Ben have accomplished. You knew you'd find me, so here I am. Give yourself some credit. It's not really where I am but who I am now, isn't it? Like the song says, 'In the beginning so shall it be in the end.' "

Sally continues, "Oh, Ben my sweet, sweet Ben, without you none of this would have happened. You had the drive to go to my cabin and seek the truth. You made Dad go with you and follow the trail. I so love you, dear brother. The world will one day thank you."

"I'm still mad at you, Sally," Ben struggles to say through his emerging tears. "I needed you here. Why did you do this?"

"I know, Ben. I'm so sorry," Sally answers. "It wasn't what I wanted either, but I guess, I guess I needed more. I had no idea it would lead to here, but that doesn't matter now. The world is about to be turned upside down. It was going to happen eventually. I'm over that now; you will be too, soon enough."

"Sally, can you hear me, Sally?" Chase jumps in. "Is it really you? I'm so sorry!"

"Ahh, Chase, my dear Chase. You don't have to apologize; if anyone does, it's me. I got too impatient, and I took it out on you. I'm sorry we got in a big fight over it. What's important now is that the light-freezing chamber worked. It enabled you guys to create a tool that helped make this communication possible. You should be proud of what you've done. I know I am. We'll be together soon. I love you, Chase."

"Wait a minute," Sid interjects. "Can we back up a second please? What do you mean, 'the world is going to be turned upside down'? What's going to happen, and why is it inevitable?"

"Dear, dear Sid," Sally says earnestly. "I so wish I could've met you. Chase talked about you endlessly. You, of all people, should have been expecting this. You and your compatriots at Crestone have so accurately defined what this is all about. I do love the modified God Helmet, but your approach to the memory cloud is what's going to get the majority through this. The truth is being revealed to all of humanity. It's going to take some time, but eventually, everyone will be able to navigate the memory cloud. Please stay true to your mission; it will help so many.

"Listen to me clearly. My time is running out for now. What you have surmised is mostly correct. There's a place where all human thought lives. It's where I exist now. The magnetosphere contains all living experiences. It's not limited to humans. The connection to the memory cloud has been blocked for hundreds of thousands of years by Earth's strong magnetic field. It's only accessible when Earth's magnetic field is very weak. Willy, you and your colleagues at Laurentian are spot on; we've entered the beginning of a polar reversal. The poles may take thousands of years to flip. During the in-between time, there will be no magnetic field. The lack of magnetic interference will make the connection to the memory cloud possible. Over time, humans will learn to navigate the memory cloud. It won't be easy, but it will happen. Sid and his people can make this transition easier; listen to them if you want this transition to be as painless as possible.

"You will all be able to experience things you could never imagine," Sally continues. "You will learn that all things are connected; we are all truly one. You will see how truly beautiful life is. We will meet like this again, but I must be careful. For now, learn how to engage with your new reality. If you fight it, you will never be at peace."

Which Way Is South

I take stock of my surroundings while struggling to clear my mind. The others are beginning to stir, and I ask if everyone is okay, but no one responds; they're still recovering. I try to get up but am overcome with vertigo, my head pounding. I sit back down and begin to piece together what just happened. It's three in the morning, and I'm still wearing my God Helmet. I wonder if the memory cloud is still trying to penetrate my thoughts. I dare not touch any of the God Helmet controls. I look around and realize that Sid isn't in his chair. Where's Sid? I scan the room; he's sitting in the lotus pose, meditating in the corner of the room. He's not wearing his God Helmet. I slither to the floor and crawl over to him. I prop myself up against the wall and wait for him to notice me. His eyes are closed; he's draped in a blanket, listening to music via headphones, and has a small bowl with incense burning in it. The smell of sage and lavender sends a wave of relaxation through my body, and my head begins to clear.

"Sandy, how are you feeling?" Sid asks in a soft but confident voice.

"I'm okay, but I don't think I can stand up yet."

"It will clear soon enough. Relax and let you mind wander; don't focus on anything."

"I'm trying to relax but—"

"I didn't say try. Trying is a conscious function; just do it; don't engage."

Sid then puts his arm around me and pulls me close while maintaining his forward gaze. He hands me the incense. His touch passes a calming energy that creeps through my body. I can barely make out the music he's listening to, but then I hear "It Is You" leaking out of his headphones. He's listening to Toots and the Maytals' "Pressure Drop," my mantra song from my satori.

"Did you meet yourself when you were coming to?"

"I did."

"Do you know what it means?"

I immediately have a flashback to Jack Trimpey's book, *Rational Recovery*. I recall the two parts of the brain he leans on for explaining addiction. The midbrain controls involuntary functions and is the primal part of the brain. The neocortex, or new brain, controls sensory perception, motor commands, and reasoning. That's what I just experienced, the two parts of the brain communicating.

"I think it's the two parts of my brain communicating."

"Very good, Sandy. Our technique for combating the memory cloud is centered on bringing the midbrain to the forefront while quieting the neocortex. It's simpler than you might think. Our senses are part of the neocortex. If we provide stimulus to each of our five senses, the neocortex has something to be occupied with. My blanket provides tactile stimulation, the incense provides olfactory stimulation, hard candy provides stimulation for my taste buds, and music provides auditory stimulation. By closing my eyes and visualizing my involuntary functions, such as breathing, my heart beating, and my blood coursing through my veins, I summon my midbrain. It's truly an elegant solution to combat the magnetic energy that contains the memory cloud that's trying to overload my brain via its magnetoreceptors. Did you know we have a sixth sense?"

"I did not. I assume it's magnetic sensing?"

"Yes, we can detect magnetism. Did you know most species have this ability? One of the most primitive life-forms has this ability. Bacteria are able to navigate by sensing magnetic field lines. It's dormant in many terrestrial creatures, but aquatic animals commonly use magnetism to not only navigate but also to communicate. Most plants can sense magnetism."

"Who knew?"

"Precisely, Sandy. I believe that's all about to change! Like Sally told us, all of life's experience throughout time is contained in the magnetosphere. We just have to reactivate our magnetoreceptors and learn how to navigate the memory cloud."

"How are we going to do that? It sounds like a biological function to me."

"Biology is overrated. Our minds control our biology; biology is just a tool the brain designed; it's a construct of the brain. It is known that the brain can rewire itself when part of it is damaged. It can reassign functions within itself. We jokingly call the brain a meat computer. I believe our brains can awaken their magnetoreceptors so we'll be able to effortlessly navigate the memory cloud. It's going to take some time though."

"Wow, you've really been studying this stuff, haven't you? Everything you're saying makes total sense to me. I just don't know if I'm ready for all this. I'm trying my hardest to not be scared."

"I don't blame you for being scared. This is some scary shit. Our world is truly about to be turned on its head. I have something I need to tell you. Remember I told you how my brothers and sisters and I have been guided by a spirit named Sarah? I had my suspicions, but now I'm certain. Sarah is actually Sally! The way that Sally spoke or thought to us is very similar to Sarah's delivery. I'm sure you're aware that Sarah, the wife of Abraham, was one of the four matriarchs; she was a prophet. The name Sally is a derivative of Sarah."

"I don't know what to say. That sends a chill up my spine. Sally is a modern-day prophet, I guess? We'd better heed her words."

We hear the rest of the group stirring. I crawl over to Rachel and pull myself up on the couch and give her a long hug. She's totally silent as she stares off into space. Sid visits with each of the others and offers his sage advice. I ask how everyone is and receive only groans and sighs. Suddenly, Rachel speaks up and asks if Ben is okay; he nods and mumbles something unintelligible.

Eventually everyone is alert, and we begin to discuss our experiences. The first thing out of everyone's mouths is how odd Sally's reaction was. While she did express her love and longing, she was so matter-of-fact about the whole situation. Of course, she's on a different plane, one that we can't begin to fathom. Rachel then advises us that perhaps we forgot what Sally was like. "She was always blunt and to the point; she was never touchy feely," Rachel explains. Her joke about our silly bathing caps was perhaps an attempt to lighten the situation. Ultimately, the conversation turns toward her comments about running out of time. What was her urgency? We all agree that it seemed like something was going on with her. That she said she had to be careful really makes us suspicious. Be careful of what? If the magnetosphere is such a beautiful place, why is there a need to be careful? Something doesn't seem right.

Sid then takes the floor to express a concern. "I have to tell you, Angelica, Astral's modifications to the God Helmet are an incredible piece of technology. I'd say it worked in spades, but there's one problem. While it does seem to block out the magnetic-memory cloud, it only treats the symptoms—it does not address the real issue. Sally said that we will eventually be able to manage the memory cloud on our own. If we block it out completely we will never learn how to deal with it, to navigate it, engage it. We all heard what she said; our meditative techniques are what will allow us to advance to the next level. Perhaps the God Helmet should be viewed as a stepping stone. I'm assuming that most of the world's population is struggling mightily right now. The masses are going to need assistance. It makes sense to me that first responders could use the God Helmet to keep them sane while they help those crippled by the bombardment of alien visions and voices."

A deafening silence fell over the room as we all realize what the rest of the world must be going through. Willy then offers his two cents: "Earth's magnetic field is still absent. The ALPs event we witnessed last night was gone before we even reached the cabin. I think we're dealing with something quite different now. I'm assuming that the lack of a magnetic field is acting like an ALPs event, only it's not restricted to fault zones. The memory cloud is most likely present everywhere, leaving no one unaffected. Isn't that what Sally said to us?"

"Why isn't anyone talking about the experience we had visiting Sally's memories?" Rachel says, with a quivering lower lip. "It was an incredible experience. I was there like I was dragged back in time. Each event we witnessed was accompanied with the exact emotions I had on those days. It was so powerful. I want to go there; I want to be with her and be part of this new reality. It was so beautiful, so beautiful."

Rachel begins to sob. Her sobbing alternates between sorrow and tears of exultation in the possibilities. She's right, of course. While humanity has an unimaginable task at hand, there's a whole new world waiting for us. We need to keep our eye on the prize.

Our eyes are suddenly diverted from the prize to a loud thump. To our horror, Angelica is lying on the floor convulsing and seems to be speaking in tongues. We huddle around her as Ben lies down with her in a full-body embrace. It's not helping; she keeps twitching while mumbling in an unknown language.

"Check her God Helmet," Chase bellows.

Ben fiddles with her God Helmet controls, but it's not responding. He determines it's out of batteries. How could such a sophisticated piece of technology be betrayed by something as simple as a battery? Sid grabs his God Helmet and hands it to Ben. Ben puts it on Angelica and makes sure it's on the memory-cloud-blocking setting. Immediately, she stops convulsing and babbling but is not conscious. The group turns toward Sid in astonishment, having just realized he hasn't been wearing his God Helmet.

As Sid rubs his forehead, as if to wipe away the horror, he says, "This is precisely why you all need to learn our meditative techniques."

"How long have you not been wearing your helmet?" Willy inquires.

"For a couple hours now," Sid replies. "I'm not immune though. Our technique lasts for a period of time after a meditative session. I will soon lose my immunity and possibly end up like Angelica if I don't recharge."

"Oh this is bad; this is real bad," Willy says shakily. "We need to see what's going on out there. Can we get a computer or turn the TV on. I can't imagine."

Chase turns the TV on, and channel after channel is sounding an alarm and displaying a static billboard from the Emergency Alert System. It reads:

Emergency Alert System
We are currently under a state of emergency.
This is not a drill.
All residents must seek immediate shelter.
Do not leave your home under any circumstance.
The president will address the nation soon.

Instinctively, everyone pulls out their phones, and somehow they're all working. We all received the same message from the EAS. Its time signature corresponded to the time we were unconscious. Frantically, the group fiddles with their phones to see what's out there. Social media is loaded with accounts of the onslaught, which lasted just a few minutes, at best, before the originators were overcome by the memory cloud. Some of us have unfinished texts and phone calls that were terminated abruptly. I have a text from Dr. Petra that reads: "Complete collapse of the magnetic field. The memory cloud is everywhere. God Helmet is working perfectly. We need to talk." I read the text aloud to the group. We all take a seat as cold fear fills the silent room.

The Global Memory Cloud

It's been nearly three months since Earth's magnetic field vanished. There's been no sign of it returning. The world's infrastructure is apparently fully intact. It's the people who are unable to function and keep things going. All levels of government have been focused on helping those who are struggling to function under the relentless memory-cloud onslaught. The federal government has enacted its emergency protocol it secretly established shortly after the big ALPs event last summer. That we have a functioning government at all is a big surprise. Apparently the federal government took the big ALPs event very seriously and, through a variety of brain trusts, devised an emergency-response plan should a similar event occur again. In an amazingly short period of time, they had at least some of the pieces in place in time for the polar reversal.

The daily Emergency Alert System announcements and presidential addresses have been extremely frank and forthright. It's clear that they don't want the public to panic any more than they already are and figure honesty will be the best remedy. The president described how they are protecting vital government personnel from this unknown magnetic energy and have constructed specialized "bomb shelters" that shield against the magnetic energy. These magnetic shelters are composed of specialized alloys made from nickel, cobalt, and steel, or something they call MuMetal. They built numerous large magnetic shelters in Washington, DC, and strategically placed these magnetic shelters in major cities across the country. They informed people how to make their own makeshift magnetic shields or deflectors, as they are more properly called. Apparently, nothing can shield magnetism, but it can be redirected.

The government had been stockpiling drugs, mostly sedatives and tranquilizers, to have on hand for the most severely affected. They have been distributing them at a crazed pace. They had also been stockpiling MREs, which are prepackaged military food rations. The MRE kits had been strategically stockpiled all across the country as well. All branches of the military have been engaged in the distribution of medicine and food. This humanitarian effort is unprecedented in human history. While all this is somewhat reassuring, most people who need help are still waiting for it.

Somehow Dr. Petra contacted the feds immediately after the collapse of Earth's magnetic field and offered the God Helmet to frontline workers to shield them from the madness. Our factory that manufactures them has been upscaled to attempt to handle the demand. They're manufacturing them around the clock, but it's just a drop in the bucket for what's actually needed.

Sid and his people in Crestone have also reached out to the government to offer assistance with their meditative techniques. Apparently, Sid and the Buddhist community in Crestone had been coordinating with major Buddhist temples around the world for some time, teaching them their techniques. With the assistance of governments, they are fanning out and teaching their methodology far and wide. They have numerous dedicated social media sites as well as broadcast and cable channels that teach their technique. The masses that include the Light Seekers, who have been camped at the UFO observation center outside of Crestone since the big ALPs event, never stopped growing in numbers. The estimated thirty thousand of them have established other camps on private ranches and have even taken over Sand Dunes National Park. Most of these folks have been trained directly or indirectly by the Buddhists of Crestone and have been recruited to train others across the country on how to achieve the protective meditative state. Despite all this, reaching everyone in need is falling woefully short.

There are a few news stations that are somehow functioning and are covering the event, and what they reveal is astonishing. The reporters and broadcasters all wear a variety of motorcycle helmets and the like. Their helmets are shrouded in thin metallic layers that appear to be hammered into shape. The reporters travel around in armored vehicles, mostly Hummers that have been modified with additional metallic shielding that covers the passenger portion of the vehicle. Every city reported on has a similar scenario playing out. There are thousands and thousands of people who resemble the homeless, with their ragged and filthy clothing, wandering the streets in small groups, walking arm in arm, singing softly in unison. They don't engage with reporters but do accept their offerings of food and water. The singing and embracing, as we discovered, minimizes the onslaught of alien thoughts and visions.

Buildings that are constructed of steel, especially those that have metal siding and metallic roofs, are overrun with people seeking reprieve from the visions and voices. These overcrowded structures have runners who venture out in homemade armored vehicles in search of food and supplies. There are rumors that in the beginning of the polar reversal, bridges across the nation were barricaded to prevent jumpers. The government has no idea how many people have taken their lives to escape the madness that overtook them. It's believed that it's far less than initially thought. Thankfully, there's been no outbreak of violence. Looting has been minimized by the fact that grocery stores and shop owners have left their doors open. Those in need take what's necessary. There's been very little hoarding.

The biggest problem has been the lack of medical care and food. The very sick, confined to beds in hospitals and care facilities, were initially abandoned. While there are skeleton shifts that are now caring for these people, the situation worldwide is dire. With so many people in need of help, advanced triage has been the call of the day. The sickest, who require the most resources to care for, are often left to their own demise. There simply aren't enough caregivers, and the resources that are available have been directed to less-acute patients.

Social media is too painful to watch. There are endless accounts of people huddled in their homes, paralyzed by fear, staring off into space, muttering to themselves. One thing that strikes me is that, in these homes, there always seems to be one person who appears to be somewhat less affected by the memory cloud and is caring for the others. The same is true for the wandering groups on the streets. There's always one of them that seems to be somewhat in charge and is vaguely guiding them. Apparently not everyone is affected to the same degree.

Rachel, Ben, Angelica, Willy, and I have spent a great deal of time doing outreach in Chaffee County. We have focused primarily on the first responders and military personnel, who are worn down to a nub. We make sure they have what they need and ask them where we can be of most benefit. There's never enough time in the day. But we always find time at the end of each day to pick random houses to visit and check on the occupants. One of these random houses happens to be Sheriff Broadless's home. This giant of a man can barely finish a sentence and definitely isn't able to get around. It crushes me; he was always a pillar in this community. We do what we can for him and tell him we'll be back soon. As we're leaving, he motions for me to come to him. As I kneel down, he puts his arms on my shoulders, with a tear running down his cheek, and struggles to say something. When he finally gets it out, it's one word: *Sally*. I don't have a clue what to say.

The five of us were trained by Sid in his meditative technique. Before too long, we were adept at it and use meditation as much as we can in lieu of the God Helmet. Regardless, we never go anywhere without fully charged God Helmets.

With so many people worldwide affected by the memory cloud and so few to help them, it's difficult to see any way out of this. We pray nightly that all this suffering will lead the world to a better place. Whatever faith we have is being severely tested.

The Great Awakening

As I sit on our front porch having my morning coffee and gazing at the early morning sun that's shining brilliantly on the Chalk Cliffs, strange feelings come over me: positivity and hope. I have no reason to feel anything but dread, yet it's undeniable. It's the way you feel when you wake up completely refreshed from a perfect night's sleep. I feel like I can tackle anything, and the outlook for the day includes all possibilities. Realizing I haven't felt this way in a long time, it brings tears to my eyes. *It is you!*

I begin to randomly recall memories and find myself fully engaged in each memory. At first, the memories are short and bounce about through time. They're very vivid and realistic, like a Memory Chaser event. The more I concentrate, the more detailed the memories get. In a short period of time, I'm able hold a memory in place without bouncing randomly to the next memory. I'm able to recall and hear every word in discussions with others from events that happened years ago. I start to play with it and focus on an event I want to recall, and—*boom*—I'm there, reliving my desired memory in exquisite detail. The memories are not removed and distant video clips; I'm experiencing them seemingly in real time. I can look around 360 degrees and see everything clearly. I'm feeling the emotions I felt at that time. I can hear my thoughts I was thinking at the time, but I'm completely aware that I'm sitting on my porch. It's very trippy but not scary, as it's familiar and welcoming.

I experiment and focus on Sally's bat mitzvah, a deeply meaningful event. The memory starts with Sally standing at the bema reading from the Torah; her Hebrew is perfect. I'm able to rewind the memory and see Rachel, Ben, and I helping set up the noshes in the back room just prior to the service. I fast-forward and observe the four of us at the bema reciting our Torah portions. Every word, every expression, every cough from the congregants is intact. I can feel the overwhelming love we shared that day. I can even feel my nerves as I recite my Torah portion. I fast-forward to my speech I offer to Sally. The theme of my speech is *l'dor v'dor*. This is the concept of generational continuity in the Jewish faith. It's the passing on of spiritual knowledge and customs from generation to generation for the purpose of sustaining heritage and the collective memory of our people. I had chosen this topic for my speech because none of Sally's grandparents were there. All four died a few years before, within one year of each other. I had to acknowledge them; we were still raw from the experience. As I'm telling the story of generational ties, the room takes on a feeling, a feeling of pure crystalline love. The temple is rapidly filled with sunlight filtered through multicolored stained glass windows as a cloud moves on. A warm shiver races from my feet to the top of my skull. I pause my speech momentarily and look to see if anyone else feels it. Rabbi Mink is grinning ear to ear, and I know it's real. It's the spirits of our parents, and it's undeniable. Tears of joy run down the contours of my massive grin, and I taste their saltiness. Immediately after the service, Rabbi Mink comes up to me, still grinning away, and asks me if I felt it, if I felt our parents' presences. Another rush of love and possibilities courses through my body; it's just as strong as that proud day years ago.

Rustling from inside the cabin rips me away from my memory chasing. I'm excited to share this with Rachel. I sense her closing in, and I call out in an exulted voice, "Oh what a day for a daydream; what a day for a daydreaming boy!"

"Yes, it sure is, Dada," Sally thinks to me.

For some reason, I'm not freaked; it seems normal somehow. Without taking my adoring gaze off of the Chalk Cliffs, I answer back frankly, "Sally? I thought you were Mom. What brings you here on this glorious morning?"

"I'm really sorry it's been so hard these last few months. This transition is new ground, but the planet has shown amazing resiliency. You should be proud of yourselves as a people in the way you've looked out for each other. Humanity is showing its true colors. Today is a new day."

"What do you mean?" I ask. "Do you know something I don't?"

"Now, that's a silly thing to ask, Dada. You know I'm aware of everything. I'm not bragging; it's just the way it is out here. Do you remember the poem you discovered in the ham shack, in my filing cabinet? The one that fell on the floor?"

Sally begins to recite the poem, and out of nowhere, remembering every last word, I join in.

it's time to get down to business
this business of writing
to spill the beans
get it out for all to see
it's time to stop tying knots
to stop folding coconuts
let's point at the man
let's run him into a corner

Aand film it for his TV
I'm sick of this hideous guilt
I've done nothing but to bare
all this mental strife
I want to be rid of this righteous guilt
this hopeless despair
it's time to get out of Dodge
to cleanse this yellow panic
from our tense selves
no more wandering in anxiety
I won't let them take
this dove to the streets
I'll flush the land first
I'll damn the man
and his righteous propaganda
I'm sick of your opinions
I can't digest another bite
your botched civilization
won't suck me under
I'll never fold my coconut
I need these thoughts

I'm no monkey man
I'm no hollow man
you've been sneaking
up on us now for too long
I don't need big brother
I will not be fooled
by this forced guilt
by this mind fuck of yours
my God dances
he is not grace
my God rolls in laughter
and pisses in the river
I'm no monkey man
I'm no stuffed man

you're not accusing me
not this time
I don't need protection

I've turned in my paranoias
I will not be fooled
by this circular reasoning
by this political blackmail
my God walks with me
he is not selfish
my God wears no clothes
he barks at the moon
I'm no monkey man
I'm no bald head.

"This poem is what's known as a shared memory or experience. It's an example of what can happen in the memory cloud. If you recall when you wrote this, it wasn't a conscious process; as you said, it just came to you. At that moment in time you were in direct contact with the memory cloud. This poem has been written many times in various forms throughout history. It's exactly what happened to me when I wrote it. You and I, along with countless others, have shared this thought in its entirety. Of course, this is just the tip of the iceberg, but I think you get my point."

"Is something happening, Sally? Are things getting better?"

"Go see for yourself, Dada. You're happy for a reason."

And with that, she was gone. Her visit was nothing like previous experiences. I was not overcome and exhausted. I didn't pass out from the sensory overload. It was like having a short chat with a neighbor passing by on a morning walk and relating some good news. It was magnificent. I jump up and race into the cabin to wake Rachel up and nearly knock her down not realizing she was nearing the front door.

"We have to head into town! We gotta go now; something's happening! Call Ben and Angelica. I'll wake Willy."

As the five of us head into town, I tell them of my experience with the memory cloud and how Sally visited. I tell them that I think we're going to be pleasantly surprised with what we see in town. I tell them I'm happy for a reason. Something's odd; there're others on the road, and it's not the military—it's regular people. As we pass the Poncha Pub, we see they're flying their inflatable pickle—they're open. Driving down Old Poncha Road, we pass a couple riding bikes. Near Salida, we see there are a few people actually golfing. As we head for the military-staging grounds across the F

Street Bridge, we pass numerous people strolling downtown as if it were just a normal day. It's an awakening; we struggle to believe what we're seeing.

As we pull in, we see Sergeant Carter talking to his troops; he's animated, and his troops seem eager. We all run over to get an update. He sees us coming and signals us to wait a minute.

"Sandy?" Rachel asks. "Did Sally tell you that it's over? That everyone is going to be okay?"

"Not in so many words. She just said we had to go see for ourselves."

"Can you believe it, guys?" Sergeant Carter asks.

"No we can't, but you gotta get us caught up," I say. "We see that people are out and about but have no idea what's going on."

"Oh shit, Sandy," Carter says excitedly. "The siege is lifting; it's a goddamned miracle. We can't believe it. A large portion of the population woke up this morning, and their heads were completely clear of the memory cloud. No more constant visions and voices and all that madness. I talked to central command earlier, and the word is that it's happening globally. No one knows why, but at this point, no one cares. Only a couple of my men are still feeling the effects of the cloud. There's something very strange going on, however. I'm experiencing it myself. My mind is as clear as a bell, and my memory is different. I can recall any point in my life and experience it if I let my mind wander. All my troops are reporting the same phenomenon, as is every last townie I've spoken to. It's really weird, but I feel grateful and close to everyone I run into."

"That's truly amazing. I can't believe it. I experienced the same thing when I woke this morning. I had quite the trip down memory lane. What can we do to help out?"

"If you guys could do some spot checks on homes around town and let me know what you find, that would be awesome. I'm sure our mission is going to shift gears in the next few days. Thanks, you guys, you've been a huge help."

"Of course. You and your troops have been a godsend; thanks so much for your service."

We decide to do a loop downtown and have a look around. As we pass over the F Street Bridge, we stop and look down at the river. As we're mesmerized by the flowing water, a blue white water raft approaches. As it closes in on the bridge, we see it's guided by a solo oarsman. It's a young woman with rainbow-colored dreadlocks wearing a tie-dyed Stealie shirt. We all hoot and holler, encouraging her on her journey. She looks up at us as she disappears under the bridge and pronounces, "It's so beautiful, so beautiful."

We stroll through downtown. After a couple blocks, we turn the corner to loop back. As we round the corner, there he is, bigger than life itself—Sheriff Broadless—and he's having an animated discussion with someone. I can't believe my eyes. The last time we saw him, he was nearly catatonic. I take two quick steps toward him and give him a huge hug.

"Oh, Sandy, am I glad to see you," Broadless says. "Thank for checking up on me; you gave me hope when I had none. I had a dream Sally came to you. Did you see her?"

"Yes, Sheriff, I certainly did. I'm so glad to see you're back. You had me really worried."

On our way back to our truck, more and more people are filtering downtown. They all have glowing faces that emanate joy. Most are walking arm in arm and stop frequently to greet strangers they pass. For a small town like Salida, this isn't unusual, but *this* is different. The sincerity and joy they greet each other with is very moving. A Dead lyric surfaces in my mind: "strangers stoppin' strangers, just to shake their hand." It makes us want to dance and sing. Ben puts his arm over my shoulder and the other over Angelica's as Rachel and Willy join in. Ben then shouts, "Hit it, Ang." Angelica breaks into "Three Little Birds."

Don't worry, about a thing
'Cause every little thing, gonna be all right
Singin', don't worry about a thing
'Cause every little thing, gonna be all right

Rise up this morning
Smile with the risin' sun
Three little birds
Pitched by my doorstep
Singin' sweet songs
Of melodies pure and true
Sayin', "This is my message to you, whoo-hoo"

236

We sing and dance our way back to the river. We pause again on the F Street Bridge to take it all in. As we stand there gazing at the perfect beauty that surrounds us, my mind wanders, and I begin to relive my first Hooligan Race. The Hooligan Race is the preeminent event at Salida's annual FIBArk river celebration. It's a short, drunken race down the river in homemade rafts decorated in themes. The approaching raft below is tropically themed, with three large pink flamingos riding on the bow. I look over to see what the others think of the three little birds. I see four glazed looks with orgasmic grins. They're clearly having their own little trip down memory lane.

I let them be for a few minutes and then rapidly clap my hands twice as if to turn off a light Clapper-style. The four of them turn toward me and utter in unison, "Whoaaaa, where did I go?"

"Welcome back, memory chasers! Now you know what I'm talking about. What do you say we go check on our people?"

Miss Franny is a tough old bird. She lives by herself in a small brick house a few blocks from downtown Salida. She was once the town's baker. When she doesn't answer the door, we call out; the silence is ominous. As we strain to hear anything, a faint mumbling breaks the quiet. We head straight in and find her alone in the parlor, swaying in a rail-back rocking chair with her feet facing the unlit fireplace. "Hello, boys and girls," Franny says. "I was just visiting with my grandchildren. Come have a seat."

Each house we visit is similar; at least one of the occupants is tripping out on a memory chase. When we approach and engage, every last one immediately snaps out of it and is completely lucid. No one mentions the last few months' torture, and we don't bring it up. One house is the home of three young adults. As we approach, Sheila shakes her head violently to clear her memory trip away and looks us in the eyes. "This is why we're here. Glen was right!"

As I point the truck north, back to Mount Princeton, I cue up "Who Are You," and we zone out to the impossibly majestic Sawatch Range as who-are-we-really thoughts saturate our minds. Willy breaks the silence: "Glen fucking Anderson, where has he been the last few months? Jesus Christ, I don't get this! All these shiny, happy people but not everyone made it. We were just wiping some of these people's asses."

"Oh, Willy, I believe we all feel the pain. Trust me—we do," Rachel responds. "But we better make sure our ship is seaworthy first and foremost.

We can't be certain how this is going to end. My trip on the bridge was convincing enough; there was nothing normal about it. What if we get another curveball? We'd better be ready."

"I feel horrible for those that didn't make it, Willy. I don't know what to make of Glen Anderson," I say. "Glen was a potential prophet, not a savior. I do believe that Sally wouldn't lead us astray. Though she's been quite cryptic, she hasn't been wrong. I'm anxious to find out what's going on out there."

"Social media is blowing up, you guys," Ben says urgently. "It's truly an awakening. People are swarming churches, temples, and mosques in celebration and remembrance. The Shambhala Mountain Center in Crestone is inviting any and all that want to share in what they are calling 'The Great Awakening.' This is crazy; what do think it all means?"

As we prepare dinner at our cabin, we surf as many different news outlets as we can find. Around the globe, it's happening; the relentless alien-thought cloud is lifting. It isn't happening all at once, but throughout the day, more and more people are emerging from the crippling effects of the magnetic-memory cloud. The near-instantaneous turn of events is overwhelming and has left many unanswered questions. For now, we are humbled and grateful.

Many accounts of The Great Awakening report on what they're calling side effects of the vanishing invasive-memory stream. All around the globe, people are struggling to explain a dramatic change in their memories. As people's minds are cleared of the invasive thoughts and alien memories, their thinking becomes exceptionally clear and pristine. They claim they're recalling memories that have been inaccessible for years. They're experiencing exactly what we did earlier in the day. The looks on the faces of those interviewed are unmistakable; it is pure joy and exultation. Many people break down in tears describing their experiences.

While the turn of events is spectacularly good news, we are worn out emotionally. We turn the TV off and gaze silently into space. Rachel gets up and announces that she needs some fresh air. She wanders down to the edge of Chalk Creek and takes a seat on one of the Adirondack chairs that surround the firepit and drifts off to the sound of the babbling brook.

As the hour draws late, I walk out onto the porch to take in the golden-hour light. The setting is gorgeous, and I feel a connection to this place. For the moment, I want only to bask in my gratitude. I look skyward and thank God the worst is over. My solitude is broken by a panicked scream from Rachel.

She is yelling out Sally's name repeatedly. I leap past the porch steps and race down to her side.

"Rachel, are you okay?" At first she doesn't acknowledge me; she appears to be in a trance. "Rachel, what's going on? Are you with Sally?"

"Oh my, Sandy, oh my," Rachel utters. "It's Sally."

I pull a chair up to her so that we are face-to-face, and I rub her thighs, assuring her it is okay. I give her time to compose herself.

"Oh my God, that was too much. It was so real. No, it *was* real. I was there, then Sally appeared and then, then she was gone. Why does she keep doing that?"

"It's okay, Rach; it's just like this morning at the bridge. Tell me what you visited; it will help to share it."

"I was at my sweet-sixteen celebration. Mom and Dad took me to the side of the banquet hall. They wanted to tell me something. It was so real. I could smell Mom's perfume, and I recognized every detail of her outfit. It was so precise. I could see every wrinkle in Dad's face, and I could smell cigar smoke on his breath. The DJ was playing my songs, and I could identify my friends by their voices. I was there Sandy. I was there…"

She trails off, and I tell her softly to continue.

"They were telling me how much they loved me and were proud of me. It's weird because it's not like I forgot that day, but the detail was precise. They told me never to forget where I came from, that I should always have those that came before me in my heart. They handed me a small, wrapped gift. It was my locket I wear to this day. As I'm hugging them, I came to like nothing happened.

"The next thing I know Sally is thinking to me as if she just witnessed the same thing. She told me how beautiful my memory was. I asked her if she sent me there, and she said no, that I can go anywhere I've been, that this was how it was meant to be. Why does she always talk in riddles?

"She said we'd be together soon, but first there are some things I had to figure out. Before she vanished, she said I was very close, that I would soon discover who I am. What did she mean?"

Magnetic Memories

In the six months since the complete collapse of Earth's magnetic field, the world has gone from total chaos to what can only be described as global enlightenment. No one can explain the first three months of madness brought on by the invasive-alien thought, or as it's being called, the memory cloud. There was no way to study it, as it was utterly debilitating. The day of The Great Awakening came just as suddenly, but unlike the memory cloud, it is benevolent. As the memory cloud lifted, it somehow changed the way our minds work. Humanity now has complete access to all of their life's experiences by virtue of having total recall of every last memory. This is astonishing, as up until now, it was believed that humans forget up to 90 percent of their experiences. While this is an incredible phenomenon, it's not the whole story. The enlightenment brought on by complete self-awareness is truly a miracle.

From the first day of The Great Awakening, people the world over slowly began to have access to more and more of their lost memories and experiences. Nearly everyone has had similar experiences. For me, it started with revisiting Sally's bat mitzvah. While I never forgot the overall experience of her bat mitzvah, the details were long gone. The visitation of Rachel's and my parents at the ceremony was something that I knew I would never forget. The reality is that I had lost the emotional intensity of the indescribable experience of suddenly knowing the dead were still out there—a life-changing moment that, over time, dissolved into something less impactful. That I would ever lose any of that now seems as impossible as having it all back.

The world's smartest scientists and theologians are singularly focused on explaining what's happening. In the center of all of this brainpower is Dr. Strange and his fellows at Laurentian University. The late Dr. Persinger's research on Tectonic Strain Theory and ALPs, as well as his theories on telepathic communication via Earth's magnetic field, appears to be spot on. Most relevant is his hypothesis that Earth's magnetic field is related to memory and potentially contains humanity's communal brain. Persinger's claim that these phenomena are only possible when Earth's magnetic field is very weak is holding true.

The folks at Laurentian have conclusive evidence that Earth's magnetic field isn't completely gone. There still remains a very weak magnetic field that's extremely constant in its intensity. They have conducted numerous experiments on a wide variety of people since The Great Awakening. They have measured brain activity in participants while they're recalling restored memories and have demonstrated that their brains are behaving normally.

Their breakthrough study involves investigating the sleeping brain. Something very strange is happening in these same participants when they're sleeping. Their brains are running in hyperdrive when they sleep. Their research demonstrates that this hyperactive sleeping-brain state coincides with a barely detectable magnetic field. The flow lines of the sleeping brain's magnetic field extend outward and connect with what remains of Earth's magnetic field. While sleeping, the brain is in communication with Earth's magnetic field. They believe that, while sleeping, the brain is downloading memories from Earth's magnetic field. They call the restored memories magnetic memories. Each and every night while sleeping, the brain is filled with more and more lost memories.

It appears that Sid and his compatriots at Crestone came to this conclusion without the aid of science before any of this happened. We have regained our sixth sense, the ability to connect to the mysterious and invisible magnetic world. That there is a scientific explanation is comforting to many, but to me, knowing that there are two diametrically opposed methodologies that reached the same conclusion is fascinating. I doubt that science will be able to explain the enlightenment that people are experiencing as a result of being reconnected to everything that makes us who we are. For this, I will be paying close attention to Buddhists and other theologians.

What Rachel, Ben, Willy, Chase, Sid, Angelica, and I are experiencing is identical to what the rest of the world is experiencing. We set aside an hour or more a day to experience our magnetic memories. As the last three months unfolded, we have had access to more and more magnetic memories. It's believed that our minds are close to having a complete download of all of our experiences. Having access to life's experiences in their entirety, especially in excruciating detail, changes a person dramatically. It has been compared to the phenomena of having one's life flash before them during a near-death experience. Magnetic memories are not a static video that one watches from a removed standpoint. It's more like transporting back in time. All the senses are active, in that touch, smell, taste, sound, and, of course, sight are part of it. Feelings and emotions are huge factors as well. Nothing is ever out of context. When recalling a particularly cringeworthy memory, the sensation of that embarrassing event has embedded with it the feeling and emotions associated with that memory. The memory is not altered by looking back from a more mature time frame. Pleasant or disturbing memories are equally accepted as we view them from the context of the time they occurred.

The immersion in one's total self provides explanation and understanding of who we are. There is no hiding—nor need to hide. The result is acceptance of self, and out of this comes total and absolute love for one's self. This love for one's self doesn't end there. As they say, you have to love yourself before you can love someone else. The Great Awakening is not just self-awakening; it's the awakening to others as well—it is global empathy. We are all finally able to accept everyone for who they are, no exceptions. This is exactly what's happening to all eight billion of us.

Magnetic-memory visitation is completely controllable. It's not like the memory cloud that could overtake all thought patterns. Learning to attend to one's responsibilities can be problematic, as magnetic-memory tripping can be very pleasant, even entertaining. Millions of people have gone AWOL from their jobs as they explore themselves. One side effect is the uncertainty of a linear time frame. As Ben and I experienced with the Memory Chaser, past events get juggled in time. A twenty-year-old revisited magnetic memory can give the sensation that it just happened. It's castings doubt that time is linear.

Ben recently showed me a mind-bending social media site that compares people's favorite magnetic memories they most frequently visit. Based on millions of user responses, their statistics indicate that we all have common memories or experiences. The details aren't identical, but the story line embedded in the magnetic memory is. This has led to the speculation that we are a simulation. I think it says we are connected in ways no one can begin to explain.

There's little discussion of full-blown telepathic communication. Though some have communicated telepathically, what most have experienced is more akin to what Ben and I experienced with the Memory Chaser. Knowing what someone is going to say before they say it and starting and finishing other's sentences are extremely common.

We have not heard from Sally since the beginning of The Great Awakening. I recently received a cryptic message from Sid. As I read between the lines, it indicated he and other Buddhist monks have made contact with her. The only thing I could think of was that it must be important.

We Come In Peace

"Hello, Sid, it's Sandy; how are you today?"

"I'm doing well. Thanks so much for calling me back."

"Of course, what's up?"

"I'm guessing you're calling about my message. I apologize for being so vague. There have been some rather critical goings-on here. I'm not really supposed to be talking about it, but given that it involves Sally, I felt compelled."

"I take it you've been in contact with her. What's going on? We haven't heard a peep from her."

"Yes, we have. As you can imagine, we've been quite busy here trying to understand what the meaning is behind The Great Awakening. Sally has been leaking us tidbits and clues to keep us on the right path. She continues to be very cryptic, and to be honest, we all believe there is something even bigger going on that she won't, or can't, tell us. I know that sounds impossible given what The Great Awakening has blessed us with. I realize this is short notice, but Sally has asked us to gather at the stupa tomorrow night, and she wants you, Rachel, Ben, and Angelica to be there as well. You know tomorrow night is the summer solstice? I'm sure this is no coincidence."

"What do you think's going on? This sounds ominous."

"I think it's best if you just show up. I'll send Willy down to get you through the barricade at the turnoff to Crestone. If you could be there at six, Willy will escort you to the stupa."

"We'll be there at six sharp."

I hang up my phone and slump into the overstuffed chair in our living room. What could possibly be coming next? I fight off a wave of anxiety and deeply exhale, trying to calm myself. I wish I could go there now and get it over with. Tomorrow seems like an eternity away. What will I do with myself until then? The anticipation is palpable. I'm tense and nervous and can't relax. I get up and wander outside to discuss it with Rachel.

Rachel is sitting by the creek in one of the Adirondack chairs. As I approach, it's obvious that she's tripping on magnetic memories, so I quietly take a seat next to her and let her finish. I can barely sit still and squirm in my seat, trying to find a comfortable position. I close my eyes and attempt to meditate on the present, but my mind is racing. I concentrate on the gurgling creek and the gentle pine-scented breeze that's moving down the valley. I feel Rachel's hand softly stroke my arm.

"What's the matter, dear? You seem agitated."

"Oh, Rach, something really big is about to go down. I just got off the phone with Sid, and we've been summoned to Crestone for a meeting at the stupa."

"What do you mean? What could be bigger than where we are now? What's Sid going to tell us?"

"It's not Sid. It's Sally. Sally summoned us and the folks at Crestone. He won't say what's going on. He just said we needed to be there."

"I see. Well, we better be there then."

"What magnetic memory were you visiting?"

"Oh, I was just experiencing the day we first met. Do you remember how we both immediately knew we were going to be spending the rest of our lives together? How do you think that was possible? How's it possible that something so important and complex could be instantly understood? We didn't even know each other."

Today is the longest day of the year—the summer solstice, a celestial day that now looms with unknown cosmic importance. As Rachel, Ben, Angelica, and I head up Poncha Pass, the truck is ominously silent. I cue up some classic dub to help us relax with transcendental rhythmic minimalism. I realize that it's silent because the three of them are visiting magnetic memories, not because of the existential dread I'm experiencing. I'm not disturbed by this as everyone uses the shortest downtime to visit with magnetic memories. As we crest Poncha Pass, the vast expanse of the San Luis Valley spreads across my entire field of vision. To the east, the valley's creator, the Sangre de Cristo Mountains, rises majestically out of the valley floor, standing unchanging and permanent. There's a thin layer of smoke hovering a thousand feet off of the valley floor. Far off in the distance are hundreds of narrow, vertical plumes of smoke that are feeding the smoke layer from the ground. It dawns on me that these are the campfires of thirty thousand Light Seekers who have been camped out in the valley since the first big ALPs event. A chill runs through my body. This is epic.

I turn the music way up and rouse my passengers to the scene before us. "Do you see that? You're looking at the original believers camped out, waiting for Glen's prophecy. How can thirty thousand people be wrong?"

"Is that what this is about, Dad?" Ben inquires. "I thought it was going to be another esoteric two-minute riddle by Sally. Are you not telling us something?"

"Sid won't tell me what's going on. The Crestonians suspect there is more going on than Sally has been revealing. Whatever it is, it appears to be very important."

As we make the turn at Villa Grove, we see the first of the encampments. They have taken over Joyful Journey Hot Springs. There are thousands of Light Seekers milling about; their brightly colored tents fill the parched sagebrush field behind the hot springs and trail off into the distance. As we pass by, their hoots and hollers can be heard over the music.

We're approaching the turnoff for Crestone, and on both sides of the highway, the ranchlands are filled with Light Seeker camps. We approach the barricade, and a smiling crowd immediately surrounds our truck. We creep up to the barricade, and a highway patrolman approaches. I show him my license and explain that Sid has arranged for Willy to escort us to the stupa. The trooper returns to his cruiser and radios the command center in town. I hear someone calling my name, and I peer through the gathering for Willy. I can see him standing on the cab of his truck above the crowd, waving both arms. The trooper signals us to pull up to the gate. The crowd immediately grows restless and surges toward the gate. A half-dozen troopers appear out of nowhere and herd the crowd out of the way. As we pull through the gate, the crowd erupts in jeers and boos as it is evident they aren't going anywhere.

Willy runs up to our truck, and I jump out for a full-on Willy hug. "Can you believe this?" Willy exclaims. "The natives sure are restless! It's so good to see you! Let's get out of here before something happens."

As we head up the gentle incline to Crestone, we see that the barbed wire fences on both sides of the road are draped in Tibetan prayer flags as far as we can see. The place seems to be alive with energy; I can feel my hair stand on end. Angelica blurts out, "Can you feel that?" It's getting intense, and we aren't even to Crestone.

Passing through town, we're amazed at how vibrant it is. There are people lining the streets. They're wearing every kind of native and hippie garb imaginable. There are many Buddhists in robes of varying colors representing their origin. There are a variety of Native Americans in their colorful, ceremonial tribal attire. The hippies and Light Seekers outnumber them all. It looks like a mix of Deadheads and EDM fanatics. Every last one of them is smiling and engaged or gently dancing. I don't see a single law enforcement officer; perhaps they're indistinguishable in the menagerie.

As we near the stupa, there are cars everywhere, but Willy keeps going. He pulls all the way up, adjacent to the stupa, and there are two spots for us. I ask Willy if we are VIP or something. He looks at me and grins. "You have no idea, Sandy." I feel very awkward. What does he mean by that? We huddle up; Willy has something to say.

"Look, you guys, I don't know much more than you do about tonight, but I feel I've got to tell you this. Sid has related your experience, especially the Sally connection, to everyone up here. As you know, they've been in contact with Sarah, or Sally, for some time now. They believe she is some type of high spirit. They also believe you all are deeply connected with what's going on. Don't be freaked out if their respect seems a bit over the top. I guarantee they are sincere."

"Thanks for filling us in, Willy. I was wondering what you were talking about. Are you guys ready for this? We should be prepared for anything. Angelica brought God Helmets for all of us just in case. We need to be together at all times when things get going. Is everybody good?" They confirm, and we all group hug as I tell them, "This is for Sally; let's see this through!"

Dropping down the steep steps to the stupa, we can see Sid waving at us. He's wearing a saffron robe and is beaming. He is standing in the middle of a large crowd of Buddhists, Native Americans, and a variety of internationals. We exchange warm greetings, and he introduces us to several of the sitting monks at the Shambhala Center. They know exactly who we are and praise us. It's very surreal. We realize just saying thank you is enough. We meet several tribal elders, and they are equally gushing to meet us. It is starting to feel very spiritual, and I am struck with humility and a case of the weak legs, so I take a seat. This is very, very heavy. The magnitude of the event is crashing down on me. Rachel asks if I'm okay, and I tell I just need a minute.

As the evening progresses, we feel more and more comfortable; everyone is warm and welcoming. Rachel and I are standing by the stupa gazing at the golden Buddha inside; a young woman is sitting lotus-style, praying to the

Buddha. We are approached from behind and are embraced by welcoming arms.

"I couldn't wait to see you two; it's been a while," Chase greets us.

"Oh, dear Chase," Rachel gushes. "How've you been?"

As I'm about to say something, the young woman who was just praying walks up to us and stops several feet away. I'm startled when I realize who it is—Mac. Before the awkward silence goes on too long, Chase interjects, "You remember Mac of course?"

Rachel and I are conflicted, as Mac's departure was not a pleasant one. Our wokeness overrides these memories, and we're filled with joy and love for this sweet child. We now understand completely what happened and are thrilled to see her. We exchange pleasantries and are about to engage when there's an announcement. They're asking if everybody is in, as the ceremony is about to begin. As we move in closer, they ask if the Stern party would join them at the front. The gathering claps and hoots in appreciation.

Standing in front of this eclectic gathering, I'm taken aback and pull Rachel in for a warm hug. I look at our group and nod at them in approval and gratitude. We're standing with our backs to the grand expanse of the San Luis Valley. In front of us is the gathering, the stupa behind them, and far off in the background are the Sangre de Cristo Mountains. Sid takes the lead, and as he starts the ceremony, the light slowly shifts to golden-hour brilliance. The Sangre de Cristo's are beginning to glow bloodred. I'm not hearing a thing as I'm in total rapture. Sid stops addressing the crowd as I snap out of it. A gamelan band starts playing in its unique half-note-out-of-tune harmony. The gathering is completely silent, taking it all in, when we hear a woman's voice singing unintelligible words over the top of the music.

The attendees are scanning the sky and softly confirming with each other that it's Sarah. The singing slowly trails off. From the hills behind the stupa, a warm breeze wafts through the gathering. The breeze conveys strong emotions to the crowd. It feels like the rush of a psychoactive drug taking hold. As the rush passes, we're all left with the undeniable warmth of love. As we stand there, mouths agape, staring skyward, Sally begins to think to us.

"Good evening, congregants, I so greatly appreciate you meeting me here. You all have been through a lot. I'm proud of how you have looked out for your fellow man. My condolences to those who are grieving for the ones who did not make it. These are unprecedented times. The Great Awakening is now in full force. You should know that this is the way it was meant to be. In the beginning, man's mind worked like this, but it was lost. While I'm sure what you are now experiencing is glorious, it is not the end. There's much more to come. It will require faith that what you will soon learn is the truth. Trust that it leads to a much better place. I am not alone out here—"

Sally is interrupted by an extremely brilliant point of white light centered a thousand feet directly above us. The crowd reacts in astonishment. The point of light explodes and expands outward in all directions. Within seconds, the light expands across the San Luis Valley, illuminating the entire valley. As it expands, the light changes from a brilliant white to a soft, intermixed swirl of azure and orange and then slowly dissipates. Static crackling can be heard from all directions and slowly becomes quiet. There is a faint smell of sulfur wafting through the air. It's completely silent and still. Far off in the distance, there's a muffled rumble. We can't make out what it is. The rumble slowly sharpens, and we recognize that it's the sound of tens of thousands of people cheering and screaming in unison. It's the roar of excitement from the encampments.

Out of the sky, a very stern and confident voice booms: *"We come in peace!"* It is not Sally. This is followed by complete silence. Rachel grabs me, trembling in fear. I hold tight and tell her I'm right here with her.

"Oh, I hope we didn't startle you," the voice says. "I've wanted to say that for a very long time. Let me correct myself, we didn't come here—we have always been here. We are benevolent. We represent the ultimate state of consciousness on this planet. We are part of all living things; in fact, we are an outgrowth of all living things since the beginning."

The voice then goes silent for way too long, and the crowd becomes restless. Sid walks to a platform that overlooks the great valley and climbs on top of it. As he stretches his arms skyward, Moses-style, he starts to call out but is interrupted.

"Sid, Sid R. Thor, now that's a curious name. You were going to say?"

"Are you God? Why are you here? What's going to happen? How many of you are there?"

"Oh, Sid," the voice answers. "Don't be silly, we are not God, but I appreciate the compliment. We are here for the same reason you are, to experience and flourish. We would like you to join us. If you give me minute, I'll explain. Oh yes, your last question, there is only one of us.

248

"As you might have gathered, we are not of physical form; we never were. We are a construct that exists in Earth's magnetic field. We came into existence when the most primal life started here. All life here has a magnetic potential. This potential coexists in the magnetic field that encompasses the planet. As life branched out into more and more diverse forms, so did the coexisting magnetic potential. We are the sum all life-forms' magnetic potential. We are the culmination of all life through time, only we have identities—we are sentient. Our evolution does not fit in your definition of the word; it is too confining. You are to us as an amoeba is to you. That we are communicating is a miracle, believe me.

"Our structure is far removed from yours. While you have the ability to act as a whole, you seldom do. I will say I was impressed with how you handled the memory cloud. That was a good one. We most closely resemble organisms that exist as a colony. We live compartmentalized as individuals but function as one cohesive being. This will be evident should you decide to join us.

"It gets better though," the voice continues. "The magnetic potential is persistent, even after an organism dies. It is kind of like your heaven. As you are experiencing all your lost memories in The Great Awakening, out here we can access any life-form's memory, alive or dead. The loss of Earth's magnetic field made it possible for you to access your coexisting magnetic potential. Of course, you only have access to your personal memories. Access to other life-forms is an upgrade. Oh, that's a good one, 'upgrade.' "

The voice again goes silent. The attendees are in an agitated form of shock. Rachel turns my way with an empty look and asks, "What's going on? I don't like this." Chatter starts to spread, and several people are crying. I'm beginning to be troubled by the crowd's growing anxiety. I motion to Ben, Angelica, and Willy to huddle up. As I'm about to speak, Sid, Chase, and Mac snuggle in too. I tell the group, "Is everybody okay? Are you okay, Ben, the rest of you? We have to keep our composure and give him a chance. I know this is hard to take in, but we have to try. Sid, do you have any ideas?"

"I'm with you, Sandy. Let me talk to the group; we've got to get them calmed down.

"Listen up, everyone. We all need to take a deep breath and focus. I know this is difficult, but we need to hear him out. We need to learn as much as possible. There's nothing to fear. We just need to let him talk. This is our first encounter; it's going to take a while to feel comfortable with them. This is all good; this is positive."

"I'm sorry," the voice restarts. "I'm getting a lot of questions out here. What was I saying? Oh yes, The Great Awakening is the reconnecting to your coexistent magnetic potential. This is the way it once was. The time has come, for those of you who are willing, to cross over and join us. Out here you will experience what we experience, all of life's existence in a very personal way. Your available experiences out here are literally endless as you will have access to every living thing's memories. You will persist as long as Earth does. Given your life span, this would be an eternity. I know this is a huge and mysterious step for you. No one will be forced to join us; it is a personal decision that only you can make. As I speak, all of humanity is hearing me; this is a global message.

"There are caveats that we need to be clear about. If you cross over, there is no going back; it is final. There is a time frame to cross over. Once Earth's polar reversal is complete and Earth's magnetic field is back to full strength, that will be it; crossing over will not be an option. No one knows for sure when the polar reversal will be complete. We do know that your numbers are way off; polar reversals can take from a couple years to a few hundred years to complete.

"We anticipate a substantial percentage of you will elect to cross over to our world. These people will be able to communicate with the remaining humans. They will be able relate back to the leftovers what it is like out here. We are certain their experience will be compelling. This, of course, will only be possible while there is no magnetic field.

"Those that choose to cross over will not regret it; I assure you. We look forward to reuniting with all of you. That will be all for now; may there be peace on Earth, sleep tight, and don't let the bed bugs bite!"

The Decision

"Hello, Sandy, it's Dr. Petra. It's been a while. How are you?"

"I'm fine, considering. I'm still in shock after the encounter the other night."

"Yes, you're not alone. These are incredible times. Listen, before we get into that, I have something to tell you."

"What's that?"

"As you can imagine, the memory cloud shut our research down. We were solely focused on manufacturing God Helmets at breakneck speed. The Great Awakening put an end to all that. Thank God. Listen, we had Sally's DNA sequenced from her ashes. We have also successfully decoded the light-beam energy emanating from Sally's eyes in the light-freezing chamber. As we suspected, the beams of light contain Sally's DNA, the two codes match exactly. Her entire DNA genome sequence is in the light beams. We're not sure what this means. Given that she ended up in the memory cloud, I'd say, to get there, she needed her DNA."

"That's interesting. So you're saying that her DNA code is in the memory cloud?"

"Well, to be honest, we have no idea what's going on, other than the beams of light contain her DNA sequence. Given recent events, I believe that's what's happening. If her essence is represented as memories in the memory cloud, how could she be distinguishable from the millions of other memories that are out there? We think that her DNA could be her identification that separates her from all the other memories out there."

"I'm following you. It's like a tag or index that precedes her memories; it makes her unique in the maelstrom of memories. It makes her searchable."

"Exactly. You know this is all superfluous at this point. It worked for Sally. I presume whoever decides to cross over will experience the same thing. It's part and parcel with the process."

"Yes, that's true, but I still appreciate you letting me know. So, are you going to cross over?"

"I have no idea yet. Obviously, we're all going to need some time to sort this out. It's so very compelling. I've spent my life pursuing science, and I feel like I'm ready for something new. I'd like to learn more about the why of existence, as I think I understand the how. I put my time in, so to speak, and I don't have a lot of attachments here family-wise. I don't know, Sandy; right now I'd say I'm a cross-over candidate. What about you? You're kind of in a special category."

"Yes, yes I am. I'd go in a heartbeat, but it's not up to just me. We'll discuss it as a family and go from there I guess. I wish you comfort in your decision, Dr. Petra. Thanks again for all you've done for us. We greatly appreciate it."

"You're most welcome. I thank you for letting me participate. You're one of a kind, Sandy!"

Sitting in the silence from a phone conversation just ended, I'm not sure what to do. Where was I? For that matter, who am I? I just had a conversation about leaving my body for good, like it was no big deal. I struggle to hear Toots tell me "It is you, (oh yeah)," but it does not come. Confidence is such a fickle thing. I focus hard on that fateful day in college so long ago when I was tripping to Toots, and suddenly I'm gone. I'm standing in front of my bathroom mirror, forty some years ago, confirming what Toots has to say, "It is you, (oh yeah)." The rush of that realization, that satori, fills me with self-confidence and understanding. It's up to me to establish my attitude, my outlook. Don't let the world tell you how to see things. I step away from the mirror and am instantly back in the present.

We're literally at a junction in humanity. Crossing over means leaving our lives as we know them forever. It also means we'll receive total consciousness, which is nice, but the experiences that will be available—it is too inviting. The decision that must be confronted is more than humans should be asked to make. We only know what we know, and for most, straying far off that course is very scary. I, for one, am too far down the path to turn back now. Rachel has indicated she's all in, but we'll see.

We are enjoying a beautiful evening at Sally's cabin with Ben and Angelica. It's been a long time since we've hung out at the cabin. The ham shack seems to be calling, but I ignore it. It feels strange, given our experiences here, and now those experiences are juxtaposed to the Decision; it seems surreal to say the least. We're here together to discuss what our choice shall be. It's surprisingly relaxed and enjoyable. We auger into camping chairs around the firepit and begin to banter the pros and cons. Rachel has no qualms whatsoever; she wants to go. Given what she has intimated in the past, I'm not surprised. I've never asked her why and realize I should. Her answer is somewhat surprising. She says she's bored and misses her daughter.

Ben and Angelica explain that they are all in, less one thing, one very important thing. They want to have a family. I'm shocked that this never occurred to me. That's clearly one thing that will only happen here on Earth, as a human. I don't know how to react. My voice is locked. I turn toward Rachel, the mother, and with my eyes, ask for an assist. As she's about to provide her insight, Sally is suddenly present.

"Hello, family, I see you are taking on the Decision."

"Oh, Sally," Rachel reacts. "I was hoping you'd come help us. Are you with the aliens? Is what they say true? Why do they behave so flippantly? It's not helping."

"I'm in the same space as them, but I'm not with them; at least I don't think I am. What they say is all true. I have experienced so many things; the possibilities are truly endless. I have witnessed the most primal human form. I have communicated with everything from plants and microbes to fish and mammals. I've actually spent time with our family dog, Louie; he's so funny—you won't believe it. Millions of people have already crossed over and are communicating to their loved ones what it's like out here. The first to cross over were the disabled. As you can imagine, being freed from their disability made their Decision an attractive one. The next wave was the disenfranchised poor and destitute from around the globe. For them, it wasn't a difficult choice. There are a lot of religious folks crossing over from all faiths. Buddhists, Hindus, Confucians, and Taoists are crossing over in droves. Native Americans are crossing over en masse too. It's truly amazing.

"My behavior toward you all has been intentional, and I apologize. I have been hiding from the aliens or, as they are now calling themselves, MagMem. I know the name is confusing, but whatever; they can be awkward. I have no idea if they know I'm here. It could be an elaborate ruse; I just don't know. I fear they aren't telling the whole story, and it troubles me."

"What do you mean by that?" Ben questions. "This changes everything. What aren't they telling us?"

"I'm not entirely sure this is the case; maybe they are going to reveal to everyone our truth and just haven't gotten around to it. It has to do with how we evolved; they interfered with it. My plan is to continue to hide and find a way to expose them should it come to that."

"How can you be hiding from them?" I ask. "Aren't they aware of everything?"

"That's why I think it might be a ruse. Maybe I'm part of their plan. Either way, I'm gonna see this thing out."

"What should we do about our Decision now?" Rachel asks. "I don't like this at all."

"Don't panic, Mom. It's going to be all right. This step was supposed to happen at some point. Earth's strong magnetic field put it off until now. It's part of our evolution as a species. This is where we all belong, I assure you. I gotta go; something is happening."

"Holy crap," Angelica cries out. "What's going on? Is Sally dodging MagMem? Is that what's happening? I sure hope she knows what she's doing."

Another conversation cut short with Sally. At least we know what's going on in her world. The thought that MagMem is hiding something is not reassuring at all. We have to hope that Sally can solve this one. What could have happened in our evolution? Are we not men? For now, our Decision has been put on hold until we learn more.

Around the globe, we're learning more and more about crossing over. The stories are unbelievable. It's being described as our second wokeness; not only do cross-overs attain full consciousness but they also gain complete understanding of others by living their memories. There are reports that cross-overs are not freely surfing MagMem; it's not automatic—apparently it takes time to learn how to navigate it. Despite this, all of human history is slowly being relived. Those that have a penchant for history are having a field day. Biologists are communicating with animals and learning their true nature, botanists are communing with plants, and so on. The most immediate realization is the knowing of others. Cross-overs can freely explore other's memories. By learning every detail about someone else's life, cross-overs are bonding with each other in ways humans could never achieve. This bonding is generating a common spirit among the cross-overs. Love, pure, unadulterated love, is what we keep hearing.

There's grassroots opposition, however. There are many people who are staunchly against the idea of crossing over; they want to remain on Earth. They believe it goes against God's plan. I can understand this; it's a massive leap of faith to cross over. No one knows what these folks will do. MagMem have said they can stay human, and maybe that's what they will do. To me it seems like reverse faith. To each their own is most people's answer to this paradox.

Neanderthal's Fate

It has been several days since Sally revealed that MagMem interfered with our evolution. We have been very anxious waiting to learn more. The weight of this knowledge is agonizing. We have not shared this outside our small circle.

Then it came; MagMem alerts humans and cross-overs that there will be an announcement in one hour. Though there have been plenty of announcements, this one rings with urgency. MagMem suggests we gather with friends and family for this announcement.

"Humans and cross-overs alike, we need to inform you of an important fact about our shared past. This is something that should have been revealed to you early on. We have interacted with humans before. Roughly 780,000 years ago, we became very interested in your species. Your will for life was impressive, and you demonstrated potential beyond any beings we had encountered. We wanted a closer relationship with your kind.

"This interaction occurred during the last polar reversal, when the Earth's magnetic field was very weak, as it is now. MagMem coexisted in the human mind during this period. More precisely we coexisted in what you call Neanderthal. This continued until the poles were about to switch and the Earth's magnetic field returned to full strength. At that point MagMem disengaged with Neanderthals and returned to the magnetosphere.

"This coexistence resulted in two unintended consequences. MagMem's coexistence with Neanderthal brains initiated the development of a new part of their brains, what you refer to as the neocortex. Up until this point, humans only had their midbrain for involuntary, voluntary, and cognitive functions. Humans now had a whole new part of their brain dedicated to cognitive function. As your neocortex developed, this resulted in an exponential leap in your cognitive ability. Since that time so long ago, your neocortex has grown to account for 76 percent of your total brain mass. This is not what we intended.

"The other consequence of our coexistence was the human brain lost its ability to communicate with MagMem once the magnetic field returned to its normal strength. Humans retained the ability to upload all of their memories/experiences to MagMem, but it became a one-way street. Humans could no longer access MagMem for species-specific memories/experiences, that is until now.

"We have been accused of violating the Prime Directive, that we favored one subspecies over another. You claim we favored Homo sapiens over Homo neanderthalensis—by altering Homo sapiens' brain. At least one cross-over has visited human memories from this time frame and witnessed the change in Homo sapiens and the disappearance of Neanderthal. I assure you this is not the case; MagMem did not create an imbalance between these two subspecies. Your insistence on subdividing everything you encounter is an overuse of classifying life. There is no difference between Homo sapiens and Neanderthals, other than your implied bias based on extremely limited evidence. Homo sapiens are merely the outcome of this unnatural selection. As MagMem has stated, we coexisted in Neanderthals. Homo sapiens are the outcome of our unintended modifications to Neanderthals. Your paleontology and anthropologic conclusions are incorrect. You were fooled by your sample size, among other things.

"To say we interfered with human development, that we violated the Prime Directive is an odd concept to MagMem. Life on this planet is not insular. Species constantly interact with each other and affect each other's development. Humans are certainly guilty of this. The domestication of wild animals has dramatically changed the balance of life on Earth. You have over populated to the detriment of all species, including yourselves. You've made a mess of the planet. The examples are endless. All of this will become blindingly evident should you choose to cross over.

"We deeply regret not disclosing this sooner and apologize profusely. We figured you'd find out on your own once you spent some time out here. We greatly underestimated your curiosity and tenacity. For this we are humbled and ashamed. Please accept our apology."

Oddly, the majority of humans are not overly concerned with this revelation. There are bigger fish to fry, namely the Decision. Most seem to not care about something that happened three-quarters of a million years ago. Humanity is ecstatic with the never-ending extremely positive reports from cross-overs. The Decision is becoming less controversial as more and more cross over. The fact that MagMem altered human evolution is more of an existential curiosity than a game-changing revelation to most.

There are some who want nothing to do with crossing over after hearing the announcement. Most of these people were already skeptical. It now seems there will be humans occupying Earth for some time to come. In addition to this population, an extremist group sprouted up after MagMem's confession. This group advocates returning to Neanderthal form. They're furious that MagMem interfered with human evolution and want to set the clock back

780,000 years. It's unclear how they are going to eliminate 76 percent of their brains.

For now, only Ben, Angelica, Rachel and I know the truth about MagMem's coerced confession. We are certain Sally was behind it. While we will always carry a certain level of suspicion, there's no doubt the four of us were swooned by MagMem's handling of the controversy. Confessing their shortcomings immediately, in such a public fashion, was admirable. This is something humans are not accustomed to from their own leaders—it was refreshing. There's no doubt our wokeness and enhanced empathy played a role in this immediate forgiveness. Whether this was an elaborate plan to enhance MagMem's appeal to humans, we may never know. If it was, it was truly diabolical and several moves ahead of anything we're capable of anticipating.

To Infinity and Beyond

Now that the controversy has been resolved, the four of us, Rachel, Ben, Angelica, and I, meet at Sally's cabin again to act on our Decision. We are all in agreement that it's time—we are ready to cross over. Sid, Chase, and Willy have resolved to stay human for the foreseeable future. They want to help those still struggling with their Decision. Once they've done all they can, their Decision is to cross over. Hopefully the completing of the polar reversal will hold off that long. The four of us can't help but feel selfish thinking only about ourselves in our Decision. We are not alone shouldering this feeling.

Sitting at the firepit, we all confirm that each of us is confident that the Decision is fully accepted, that it is a personal choice, and is not the result of coercion. Ben and Angelica have come to terms with not having a human family. In the MagMem, they will be able to fully experience the love of child-rearing through countless others. We all agree that we will initiate the cross over in the ham shack. We figure it will be a wonderful acknowledgment to Sally, the first to cross over. We stand up and huddle in a group hug. The anticipation is beyond overwhelming. I remind the three of them that this isn't the end to anything but rather the beginning of endless possibilities.

We're sitting on the floor of the ham shack in a circle, holding hands, as we summon MagMem. The room immediately fills with an ethereal presence. A calming relaxation causes our anxieties to lift. We feel comforted and loved. We have a strange sensation that something is leafing through our memories, as we are viewing thoughts we didn't conjure on our own. The memories all concern our contemplations of crossing over. MagMem is verifying our commitment. The room gradually illuminates with a faint-blue light from above. The light source is entering through the skylight. As the light intensifies, we feel a vibration from within—it's happening. As I gaze at the others, something strange is going on with their eyes. They're glowing from within. I feel a tingling sensation in my eyes as the vibration's frequency increases. I'm very lightheaded and feel like I'm going to pass out. Just before I black out, I see beams of light streaming out of everyone's eyes. I squeeze Rachel's and Ben's hands as I lose consciousness.

"Welcome, Sandy," MagMem announces. "You have crossed over; congratulations on your graduation. I trust your trip was a pleasant one. You will need some quiet time while you acclimate to MagMem. Once you are rested, you will be provided with an orientation along with the others."

The welcome is foggy and distant. There's something strangely familiar. I'm groggy and fade off.

"Sandy, is that you?" Rachel questions from a considerable distance. "Are you with us? They're ready to start."

I struggle to shake my body awake, but it's no use—I have no body. I concentrate in the direction of Rachel and feel her presence. I get the sensation she's rubbing my back to bring me out of my stupor. In a flash of recognition, I snap into the present. Rachel, Ben, and Angelica are all next to me. There is nothing to see but plenty to sense and feel.

"Glad you could join us, Sandy," MagMem quips. "Are you feeling okay? It's time for your orientation."

"I'm not sure. Are you guys okay?"

I sense them grinning and softly giggling. I better get on board this trip.

"There is no way to explain your new existence," MagMem begins. "It's something you will learn in time. It will be blindingly obvious when you truly conceive it—I promise you. We like to start new cross-overs with a little education on the world you just left. We will reveal to you many of your misconceptions about life on Earth. By revealing some of your misconceptions, you will become open to the possibilities that exist here.

"As you've been informed, all life has a magnetic potential. This magnetic potential coexists in MagMem. We are the summation of all magnetic potential from all living things that ever existed. All living organisms have the ability to communicate, to varying degree, with MagMem. Not all life-forms take advantage of this. Your species is an example of the latter, albeit by no fault of your own.

"Let's start with a rather obvious misconception. Modern humans are compulsive in your need to have an explanation for everything. Instead of recognizing that some things are simply beyond your comprehension, you explain them away. Instinct is a perfect example of this. With one word, you've neatly explained away one of the most obvious connections to MagMem. You claim creatures of all kinds come into existence with everything they need to survive; it is their instinct, you've concluded. These creatures are not born with everything they need to survive. This is, of course, a biological impossibility. Knowledge is not contained in the genome. These creatures are in constant contact with MagMem and have access to all that is known as a species. No living thing is born with knowledge. What they need to know for survival is acquired from MagMem. They do learn from each other and adapt, but their basic survival skills come from MagMem.

"Migratory animals are an obvious example of this. There are a plethora of migratory animals, both terrestrial and marine, that travel enormous distances to specific locations without ever having learned how to do this. They acquire this knowledge from MagMem.

"Spiders construct perfect webs, from their very first to their last. This knowledge is not learned; it is available to them via MagMem.

"One of my favorites is the Jewel Wasp. This lowly insect knows precisely how much venom to inject into a cockroach to subdue it. Too little venom would be ineffective, and too much would kill the cockroach. The wasp needs the captive cockroach alive, as it will be the home for her eggs she lays inside the poor zombie cockroach. This is such complex behavior that it should be obvious that it could not be learned. It is hard to imagine how this wasp knows how to do this without an assist, an assist from MagMem.

"All living things on Earth have access to MagMem. Not only do they use MagMem to access their species-specific traits but they use it to communicate. This ability to communicate ranges from the most rudimentary form in single-celled organisms to highly complex forms of communication in higher-level organisms. While similar to language, it is not the same. It is far more sophisticated than conveying thoughts, ideas, or feelings with language. MagMem communication conveys thoughts, ideas, and feelings directly, without the need to translate it into words. We find it curious that you struggle with the concept of whether lower species can communicate. Not only do all living things communicate on some level but there is limited communication between species.

"Symbiotic relationships between species are an ingenious development and an excellent example of interspecies communication. There are many examples of symbiotic relationships. The relationship of the pistol shrimp and the gobie fish is another one of my favorites. This nearly blind shrimp digs a burrow for itself and the gobie fish to shelter safely in. The gobie uses its sight to detect prey for both. The fish lets the shrimp know where its food is. You claim this communication is via fin taps and chemical secretions. While this does happen, the real story lies in MagMem. The two communicate through MagMem. Furthermore, this behavior is not learned; it is conveyed to them through MagMem."

MagMem continues with many examples of how life on Earth accesses MagMem. With each one, we are viewing memories of it playing out as if it were a presentation. We are humbled with the acknowledgment of our misconception of life on Earth. MagMem finishes his presentation with an example of one of the most primitive, least understood, and potentially dangerous life-forms, the virus. MagMem explains that their ability to mutate is an intentional effort to change what doesn't work by accessing what has worked for them in their species' past. Their past is available to them through MagMem; they spontaneously mutate to mimic previous forms to achieve a successful configuration. This life-form has no brain but is capable beyond its individual essence.

"All these examples share a common thread. We've described how all this works, but there is one thing we cannot explain. What is the driving force at work in all living things? The persistence to live, to keep going no matter how hard the fight, is a mystery to us. We ask you, what is 'will,' the will to live? Humans are the only creature that will occasionally quit, will take their own life because it becomes too difficult to persist. In an otherwise healthy individual, reason takes over this will to live. This will is a lifelong drive, yet at times, it can be instantaneous. On the deathbed, the dying often come face-to-face with the question 'Is it your time?' Life or death, at that point, is a concrete option that is chosen and is actualized. Here the will of life is boiled down to a single question. How is this possible? We don't have an answer for this, but we suspect you might. As I turn you loose in MagMem, I ask you to keep this thought in mind. We'd love to know the answer.

"Your initial time in MagMem will be unfettered by our presence. MagMem contains the memories of all things, from the primal bacteria to the most highly developed of all creatures, the octopus. Every human that ever was exists out here. You don't need to be taught how to navigate MagMem, as you would say—it is innate. Navigating it will become natural in a short period of time. You will be able to congregate with other cross-overs as you would on Earth and behave as you are accustomed to. You will only be able to do this with cross-overs. You will spend a great deal of time exploring the wonders of Earth's creatures' thoughts throughout time, especially your loved ones. At some point you will come face-to-face with the truth. It will not need to be explained—you will know. I wish you good fortune, until we meet again, my friends."

The next thing we know, we're seated on a park bench next to a large, grassy field. We see on the opposite side of the field a woman running at full speed toward us. It all looks so familiar, and then I realize it's Virginia Kendal Park, my favorite park where I grew up in Akron, Ohio. The woman is halfway across the field running directly at us as Rachel clutches my thigh tightly. I squint to make out who the woman is. It's Sally. The four of us jump to our feet and run toward her. We collide full speed and crumple to the grass, laughing hysterically. We roll on the ground like puppies playing, squirming over top of each other, nuzzling, and embracing.

I'm not sure if I'm actually participating or if it is some elaborate illusion, a simulation. It's so completely real I can't help but go with it—it's so incredibly beautiful. I want to believe it; do I have a choice? Like a phantom limb to an amputee, the physical feelings are undeniable, but my reasoning reminds me I am without a body. We are humming and nearly glowing with love. We had finally found Sally. My brain is struggling with the completeness of the circle.

We prop ourselves up, sitting in a tight circle, arm in arm, rocking side to side. Sally begins to sing, and we join in.

Don't worry, about a thing
'Cause every little thing, gonna be all right
Singin', don't worry about a thing
'Cause every little thing, gonna be all right

Rise up this morning
Smile with the risin' sun
Three little birds
Pitched by my doorstep
Singin' sweet songs
Of melodies pure and true
Sayin', "This is my message to you, whoo-hoo"

"Holy Jesus, you guys, can you believe this?" Sally exults. "It actually happened; you are here! I'm sitting with you; it's a goddamned miracle. Are you guys okay? How was your orientation? They can be a complicated lot; they mean well; you'll see. I understand Chase, Sid, and Willy are remaining behind for now to help with the Decision. I told them they better not take too long as they could get left behind. You won't believe what awaits you."

We share our gratitude and love for one another. Rachel is beside herself. Finally being with her daughter again is overwhelming. We can feel the love pulsing between the two of them; it's glorious.

"Hey, I want you to say hello to someone. Clear you mind of all thought and concentrate on what I'm thinking. This is what we call sharing a common thought. Check it out—it's Louie!"

Rachel, Ben, and I completely lose it at the sudden apparition of our family dog. He appears out of nowhere and bounds out of Sally's lap, wriggling his entire body in joy while darting back and forth between us. We can feel Louie's thoughts. They are crude and fleeting, but we feel his unadulterated doggy love for each of us. He knows exactly who we are; he knows our names but prefers his own nicknames for us. Apparently he calls me Tatter. I turn toward Angelica, and she is softly quivering with tears of joy at the sight of the reunion. What a sly thing to introduce Louie as a salve to our challenged minds.

"So Louie is not really here as we are," Sally explains. "The four of us are probably not seeing him exactly the same. We're seeing him how each of us remembers him. Angelica sees him but only through our common memory lens. To her, Louie is a composite since she's accessing our memories and merging them. We can visit him whenever we like, at least his memories."

We spend considerable time walking around the park talking. We are reacquainting ourselves; it's been a long time. Like any reunion, there's much to get caught up on. Sally doesn't mention the fact that she's aware of every minor detail of our lives. She's kept a close eye on us, as well as explored everything we have ever done or thought. Ben, in short time, is back to teasing her; we can feel how they sorely miss each other—she even misses his teasing. Sally takes us to a beautiful overlook on an outcrop that provides a gorgeous view of the Cuyahoga River valley. We have a seat on the rocks, and I realize I'm at one of my favorite spots in Virginia Kendal Park. I spent many a lazy summer day at this very spot when I was young, whiling away the time.

"So this place is going to take time to get used to. Our meeting today is set up to help you transition. Out here, context and connection are everything. I am controlling what you see to an extent. The five of us are not viewing the same geographic place. Each of us is seeing their own favorite natural overlook. We are not all in Virginia Kendal Park like Dad is. In your transition, this will be common. Time is different here. You will slowly learn that the passage of time is irrelevant. Time only had context when we were in human form. We still like to use temporal terminology though. Once you transition, there will be no need for sleep. Again this is only needed by physical beings. For the time being, you will need to recharge by shutting down. We can call this sleep if you like. I think we have covered enough for now. You guys need to get recharged; tomorrow's going to be a big day. If the four of you would lie back, relax, and think of the place you'd like to be sleeping, MagMem will take over from there."

I suggest to Rachel we sleep in our Evergreen home. Ben and Angelica want to spend the night at Sally's cabin. We're instantly transported there and just as quickly shut down.

The Last Step

We awake but are not in bed. We're on the front porch of our Evergreen home. It's another beautiful bluebird day, and the cool Colorado morning air is crisp and refreshing. Ben and Angelica are with us. No one is speaking. We have coffee, bagels, and lox before us. We are wide awake and alert. Apparently shutting down is not accompanied with the slow wake up from sleep. I wonder if eating and drinking is a thing out here, or is it just an elaborate hallucination? I take a sip from my coffee, and it's quite real and delicious.

"Hey, Dad," Ben inquires. "Do you know what day it is?"

"Are there days out here?"

"Don't overthink it, Dad. It's the Fourth of July. I'm guessing we're gonna go for a run. Mom, you can't fake an injury this time—it's on."

"I wasn't faking anything, Ben," Rachel snaps. "I'm gonna take you down."

"I think you're right, Ben," I explain. "This is very familiar. If you're right, Mossy should be coming down the street announcing the countdown for the race."

We're distracted by the sound of trash cans banging. From around the corner of the house, we hear Sally cursing. She rounds the corner of the house and begins doing tight mock laps before us in the front yard. She has her running gear on, including a racing bib, and is wearing a plastic batter's helmet with a small camera mounted on the front. She stops in front of the porch below us and starts taunting us.

"I'm the Wiz," Sally proclaims. "No one beats the Wiz! No one beats the Wiz!"

We're stunned when we realize it's adolescent Sally. Rather than being freaked out, we all burst out laughing hysterically. I doubt any of us remembered Sally liked to pretend she was a wizard until now. As our laughter calms, we see Sally is pretending to be upset, glaring at us with hands on her cocked hips and head tilted. The scene is interrupted by a call from the street. "Twenty minutes until start time!"

"Mossy, oh, Mossy," Sally calls out as she runs to him and gives him a big hug. "No one beats the Wiz; isn't that right, Mossy? Are you guys ready?"

Time suddenly moves forward, and there's a stream of runners making their way down our street. Sally comes bursting out the front door and commands us to try to catch her. We all jump up and run to catch up with her. It has started; we are reliving the "Home" event. A few houses down, there's a group of people cheering us on; we know most of them. They call our names and slap us on the butts as we pass. Feeling their encouraging slaps, we're conflicted with actual memory and the Memory Chaser reenactment. We catch up with Sally as we pass through the pine-forest trail that leads to the downhill stretch toward the golf course.

"Remember this one, Dad?" Sally asks. "It's one of my favorite Memory Chaser events."

I turn toward Sally and see it's adult Sally. It's very trippy, but I'm not alarmed; it seems normal enough somehow. Topping the hill, Ben and Angelica take off, leaving us in the dust. This irritates the Wiz, and she puts it into high gear and quickly makes up the lost ground, passing them with ease.

I'm now running with Rachel as we head out of the trees down the hill toward the golf course. I grab her hand and squeeze it and ask her if she's ready. We both know what's coming as we've run this event many times in the Memory Chaser. As we run along the golf course path, Evergreen Lake comes into view; it's so beautiful, perfectly nestled in pine-covered hills. As we cross over the Bear Creek foot bridge, we can hear her cheering us on: it's Rachel. As we approach her, Rachel speeds up and gives herself a huge hug. This time the hug is real. Rachel turns toward me, and I see she's visibly upset. I comfort her and tell her it's going to be all right.

It all vanishes, and Rachel and I are sitting on our front porch again. Sally, Ben, and Angelica are marching up the front yard, arguing over who won the race. They take a seat, and Sally begins to laugh.

"Oh that was fun, you guys. I can't tell you how happy I am being back together again. I hope that wasn't too much. I figured we'd start with something familiar. In case you haven't figured it out, I'm your tour guide to help you get acquainted to MagMem. Your experience with the Memory Chaser should make your transition easier; there are so many similarities. I've been meaning to tell you how impressed I was with version two of the Memory Chaser. You really took it to the next level. You know the Memory Chaser didn't really cause you to relive your past. It essentially prepared your mind to accept MagMem. It dislodged your consciousness and opened your mind to be able to be in contact with MagMem. Isn't that crazy? It goes to show that things aren't always what they seem.

"We're going to continue on our tour of MagMem today. I want to visit some memories, starting with our extended family. We won't spend much time in any one memory; there will be plenty of time for that later, an eternity to be exact. Angelica, I realize these won't be your memories or even people you know, but I think it will familiarize you with MagMem."

In a flash, we're witnessing the memories of a particularly poignant Passover Seder. Sally and Ben are very young, and all four of their grandparents are present. This was the last Passover we'd spend with our parents; within a year they'd no longer be with us. There are a number of other relatives and close friends seated around the long table, anxiously awaiting the first prayer and a sip of wine. The large Seder plate is the centerpiece of the elaborately adorned table. Rachel's father offers the opening Kadeish, or prayer, and we drink from the first of four cups of wine. We each take turns reading from the Haggadah, telling the Passover story. We're witnessing the thoughts and feelings of each reader as the Seder progresses. There's a remarkable similarity in what the participants are feeling.

Memories in MagMem are not just the recording of events from a singular viewpoint. They contain the thoughts, feelings, and emotions associated with the memories. It's quite a moving experience, as the memories have context. We can feel the children trying their hardest to believe in the ceremony. We can feel the adults embracing the Passover story, contemplating the current-day parallels to the fate of their ancestors. The grandparents are fully engaged, and we feel their connection to their ancestors' hardships, enduring plagues and ultimately fleeing Egypt in search of their promised land. We feel them reaching out and connecting to their collective past.

We sense the similarity in how the relatives perceive life, how they feel; they all think alike. Their commonality is undeniable, as observed in how they confront their existence. The friends have a commonality in their thinking, only it's not as intertwined. We feel the connection in the gathering, and it's more than we ever imagined. This connection is way more than any language could convey.

The end of the ceremony concludes with the reading of the Hallel, the final redemption, and the pouring of Elijah's cup of wine. The front door is left open to allow Elijah to join in and take his seat, which has been left unoccupied during the Seder. To our amazement, we can feel his presence as he enters through the front door and takes his honored seat. His presence is felt by everyone, especially the elders. We can't help but feel that the second redemption is crossing over to MagMem.

267

The memory slowly dissolves, and we see the outline of a tall, slender bearded man pacing in front of a window. As the image sharpens, we see it is none other than Abraham Lincoln. His mind is troubled and is replaying a conversation he just had with a regiment of Ohio soldiers who had just taken part in one of the bloodiest battles in the Civil War. "Remember that our nation remains an inestimable jewel well worth fighting for, not just for your generation but to guarantee equal privileges for our children's children as well."

Lincoln's mind is racing and desperate for answers. We traverse his memories and all the associated emotions and feelings. He is interconnected with all his people, beyond any normal human connection. He feels the communal pain of the enslaved. He feels the fear that the free people experience from the uncertain future that the end of slavery holds.

Lincoln is connected with humanity on an unprecedented level, and he knows he cannot betray this connection. His empathy and compassion are unparalleled. We sense his acknowledgment that his duty is profound and is accepted. His mind functions on a plane well above his contemporaries; he is connected to MagMem.

Sally suggests we visit memories that are a little less weighty. She describes how music has more meaning than any of us can imagine. From the mystical creation of a song to the impact a musical performance can impart, music is part of the fabric of MagMem. MagMem adores music, created by humans and animals alike. Sally asks us what concert we wish we could have attended. She tells us to meditate on whatever show that is, and we'd be there.

I focus on the Grateful Dead, a band I had only seen a couple times. They were notorious from the beginning, with their heavy use of LSD and the mystical trips their live shows induced. I want to drop in on one of Ken Kesey's Acid Tests, where the Dead was the house band.

I'm bouncing around the hall, jumping from memory to memory, and land in a very intoxicated woman's tripping mind. I'm seeing her hallucinations and feeling the music just as she is, in extremely heightened LSD awareness. I'm feeling orgasmic waves of love ripple through my body. It's being propagated by the band. I'm communicating with the band, and they're answering back with notes and rhythm. It's not translatable, but it's fully understood. I realize the rest of the hall is doing the same thing. Fans are communicating telepathically. I feel a complete oneness with everything around me. I make my way inside Jerry Garcia's young head. Jerry is flying so high that his thoughts are notes, not language. He's not alone; the other band members are somehow in Jerry's head as well. Their essence is actualized as music in Jerry's mind. The band is interacting telepathically with the audience, and it influences what they are playing. I can't believe what I'm witnessing; it's like the audience is one singular, multiheaded creature, all interconnected. I look out in the audience and see Sally dancing madly in the front row. She tells me it's time to go, and the whole thing dissolves.

We're back on our porch in Evergreen. Everyone has eyes as big as saucers. Sally asks us if we felt it. She explains that a live musical performance can be transformative. "Music has feeling that, when in the groove, can be very emotional; it's a form of communication between performer and audience. The performer integrates feelings from the audience, and it becomes a living feedback loop. This is more akin to how MagMem communicates. Dad, your experience is an extreme example of this, good choice."

We spend the rest of our time visiting a variety of influential people through time. Sally shows us that many religious prophets lived near known ALPs sites. She tells us that it has been suggested that these prophets may have been influenced by ALPs visions. Jesus's mysterious forty days in the desert was very near the Dead Sea Fault. Siddhartha, the Buddha, sat under the Bodhi Tree for forty-nine days at the base of the Himalayas near the Patna Fault. These and other religious locations had very active ALPs activity during the memory-cloud onslaught. She cautions us that this does not take away any religious significance. MagMem is agnostic.

Face-to-Face

Rachel and I wake to the sound of someone singing softly from no particular direction. It's curious, as it sounds like me. I ask Rachel if she recognizes the voice. She says don't be silly—it's her voice. A chill runs through my mind, and for a moment, I'm frightened. I call out and ask who it is.

"We are MagMem; have you been entertained?"

"Beyond entertained," I respond. "We have so much to learn. What's your name?"

"We are MagMem; we have one name only; we are one. Are you ready?"

I turn toward Rachel, and I see she is interacting with MagMem, only it's a different one. I'm very confused. MagMem senses this and explains, "Rachel is having an identical conversation with MagMem; she is fine. Your orientation and tour of MagMem is complete. We would like some alone time with you. Are you ready?"

This didn't really make me feel any more comfortable, but there's something about them, like a foreigner who butchers the language yet still makes perfect sense. Language is not how they communicate. I gather my wits and ask them, "Ready for what?"

"You people ask many questions. We'd like you to know more about us. We exist in a way that is incomprehensible to humans. This is why we provide orientations and tours, to ease you into your new reality. You will soon have a grasp of what is out here. You and Rachel will take this next step with us on your own; this is how it is done.

"The duality of life is a common theme that is undervalued by humans. We've pointed out to you the special relationship in symbiotic pairs. This is something whose origin is a mystery yet is responsible for the most essential development of life on Earth. Life loves pairs, as you demonstrate in your lifelong-partner bonding. Life on this planet only began to flourish beyond microscopic single-celled organisms when mitochondria were absorbed into a larger bacteria cell. This represents the first symbiotic relationship on our younger planet. The mitochondria became the engine, the energy provider for these primitive bacteria. The bacteria fed the mitochondria in exchange for vital energy that would enable the bacteria to grow exponentially. This symbiotic-fueled growth eventually led to all higher life-forms. Did you know the mitochondria carry their own genome, separate from the cell and organism they are part of? It reminds me of something humans acknowledge but give little credit to: the two sides of the brain. I believe you refer to it as the midbrain and the neocortex. Humans have numerous names for this paradox, including the conscious and the subconscious, the id and the ego, the voluntary and involuntary, the heart and the soul. This duality originated with the original symbiotic relationship, when bacteria absorbed the first mitochondria."

I'm suddenly elsewhere, viewing the night sky, only instead of stars, I'm viewing an immensely complex random pattern of infinitesimally thin, multicolored streams of light arcing from horizon to horizon. The light streams weave in and out of each other in balled-up bunches and then spread out in bowing arcs before entangling in the next bunch. It reminds me of illustrations I've seen of nerve cell synapsis in the brain.

"Before you is a realization of what MagMem structure looks like at a random point in time. Our structure is built on magnetic energy. This energy supports our essence. Think of the most complex computer ever built, only it is not constructed of solid mater. We are a constantly changing structure and morph to meet our needs. This is a limited simulation meant to provide you with a visualization of MagMem.

"In Earthly terms, we are like a coral, in that the coral is comprised of thousands of tiny polyps. Each polyp is a singular animal that participates in the communal being that is the coral. The polyp colony thinks and exists as one singular being, the coral. MagMem is similar. MagMem is comprised of thousands of polyps that together, as one, are MagMem. Individuality is inconceivable to MagMem.

"The coral analog can be further visualized as it relates to life on Earth. As each new species came into existence on Earth, it was replicated in MagMem as a magnetic potential. Species in MagMem are organized in discrete coral family groups or reefs. Each species has their own coral reef. Every human that ever existed has a permanent home in the human coral reef.

"I am telling you all of this because I want you to see where your magnetic potential resides. Are you ready?"

I can barely conceive of what MagMem is telling me, let alone acknowledge I'm ready for anything. I shrug and with zero confidence nod in approval.

I'm watching a point of light travel along a single light stream back and forth across the sky, dodging between tangles of light wires above me. The point of light zigs and zags in and out of the twisted bunches of light streams and eventually comes to rest on the edge of a tangled light-stream bunching.

The perspective now zooms in on this location at incredible speed. Light streams are zipping past me as I draw in ever closer. Like a mathematical fractal, the detail multiplies exponentially as I get closer and closer. I come to rest, hovering above a shallow sea glimmering with azure radiance. I concentrate on what is below the refracted surface. It is a massive coral colony just below the water.

"Is this an analogy? An aid in my conceptualization of MagMem or is this real?"

"Oh it's real; look closer and listen."

I drop from my hovering position into the tropical bathwater with an awkward splash. I swim underwater toward what sounds like my name being called out. There's a twinkling from a singular spot on the lower edge of the coral reef. I swim toward it. As I get closer, I hear it clearly call my name. I'm floating directly in front of the twinkling light that's calling me. I instantly grasp what it is. *It is you, (oh yeah)!*

"Welcome home, Sandy. It has been a very long time. You see, you were MagMem all along. There was never any difference between you and MagMem. You are MagMem and we are you. It is so beautiful!"

www.ingramcontent.com/pod-product-compliance
Lightning Source LLC
Chambersburg PA
CBHW051539260626
47170CB00003B/1008